The Giant Book of Bedtime Stories
Classic Nursery Rhymes, Bible Stories, Fables, Proverbs, and Stories

Edited By William Roetzheim

Level 4 Press, Inc.

THE GIANT BOOK OF BEDTIME STORIES

Dedication

To my wife, Marianne for giving me three wonderful children leading, with some luck, to grandchildren so that I can read these stories to a whole new generation.

THE GIANT BOOK OF BEDTIME STORIES

This is a work of fiction. All of the characters and events portrayed in this novel are either fictitious or used fictitiously.

Copyright © 2007 by Level 4 Press, Inc.

All rights reserved, including the right to reproduce this book, or portions thereof, in any form.

Illustrations by Blanche Fisher Wright, M.T. Ross, DJ Munro, Arthur Rackham, Jennie Harbour, John Gruelle, R. Emmett Owen, Peter Newell, and Gustave Dore. Text by Edith Brown Kirkwood, Watty Piper, Charles Perrault, Flora Annie Steel, Edric Vredenburg, Jacob Grimm, Wilhelm Grimm, Aesop, V.S. Vernon Jones, and Guy Wetmore Carryl.

This book is printed on acid-free paper.
Published by
Level 4 Press, Inc.
13518 Jamul Drive
Jamul, CA 91935
www.level4press.com

BISAC Subject Heading JUV012000   JUVENILE FICTION / Fairy Tales & Folklore / Anthologies
Library of Congress Control Number: 2006937613

ISBN: 978-1-933769-20-2

Printed in China

The Giant Book of Bedtime Stories

Table of Contents

Nursery Rhymes 1
  The Real Mother Goose 1
    LITTLE BO-PEEP 1
    THE CLOCK 2
    LITTLE BOY BLUE 3
    RAIN 3
    WINTER 3
    FINGERS AND TOES 3
    A SEASONABLE SONG 4
    DAME TROT AND HER CAT 4
    THE OLD WOMAN UNDER A HILL 4
    THREE CHILDREN ON THE ICE 5
    TWEEDLE-DUM AND TWEEDLE-DEE 5
    CROSS PATCH 5
    OH, DEAR! 6
    PAT-A-CAKE 6
    OLD MOTHER GOOSE 6
    LITTLE JUMPING JOAN 7
    ROBIN REDBREAST 7
    MONEY AND THE MARE 7
    A MELANCHOLY SONG 8
    JACK 8
    GOING TO ST. IVES 8
    BEES 9
    THIRTY DAYS HATH SEPTEMBER 9
    BABY DOLLY 9
    COME OUT TO PLAY 10
    IF WISHES WERE HORSES 10
    OLD CHAIRS TO MEND 10
    TO MARKET 11
    ROBIN AND RICHARD 12
    A MAN AND A MAID 12
    THE CLEVER HEN 13
    HERE GOES MY LORD 13
    LUCY LOCKET 14
    TWO BIRDS 14
    WHEN JENNY WREN WAS YOUNG 15
    LEG OVER LEG 15
    BARBER 16
    THE FLYING PIG 16
    SOLOMON GRUNDY 16
    THREE WISE MEN OF GOTHAM 17

THE GIANT BOOK OF BEDTIME STORIES

HUSH-A-BYE 17
THE HUNTER OF REIGATE 17
BURNIE BEE.. 18
LITTLE POLLY FLINDERS... 18
PUSSY-CAT AND QUEEN 18
LITTLE POLLY FLINDERS... 19
RIDE AWAY, RIDE AWAY... 19
PIPPEN HILL 19
THE WINDS 20
CLAP HANDIES 20
JUST LIKE ME 20
HEIGH-HO, THE CARRION CROW......................... 21
PLAY DAYS 22
CHRISTMAS 22
ELIZABETH.. 22
BANBURY CROSS 22
ABC 23
THE MAN IN OUR TOWN 23
A NEEDLE AND THREAD 23
FOR EVERY EVIL 24
CUSHY COW 24
GEORGY PORGY 24
SEE-SAW 25
WEE WILLIE WINKIE... 25
ROBIN-A-BOBBIN 25
JOHN SMITH 25
ABOUT THE BUSH 26
FIVE TOES 26
SIMPLE SIMON 26
THREE BLIND MICE 27
A LITTLE MAN.. 28
DOCTOR FOSTER 28
DIDDLE DIDDLE DUMPLING 29
JERRY HALL 29
LENGTHENING DAYS... 29
THE BLACK HEN 29
THE MIST 30
MISS MUFFET 30
CURLY-LOCKS 30
A CANDLE.. 31
HUMPTY DUMPTY... 31
PINS... 32
ONE, TWO, THREE 32
THE DOVE AND THE WREN.................................. 32
MASTER I HAVE 33
SHALL WE GO A-SHEARING? 33

GOOSEY, GOOSEY, GANDER	33
OLD MOTHER HUBBARD	34
THE COCK AND THE HEN	36
BLUE BELL BOY	36
WHY MAY NOT I LOVE JOHNNY?	37
JACK JELF	38
JACK SPRAT	38
DAFFODILS	39
HUSH-A-BYE	39
HUSH-A-BYE	40
THE GIRL IN THE LANE	40
NANCY DAWSON	40
HANDY PANDY	41
JACK AND JILL	41
THE ALPHABET	41
DANCE TO YOUR DADDIE	42
RAIN	42
TEETH AND GUMS	42
ROBIN HOOD AND LITTLE JOHN	42
ONE MISTY MOISTY MORNING	44
THE OLD WOMAN FROM FRANCE	44
THE ROBINS	45
PANCAKE DAY	45
THE OLD MAN	45
A PLUM PUDDING	45
MY KITTEN	46
T'OTHER LITTLE TUNE	46
IF ALL THE SEAS WERE ONE SEA	46
FOREHEAD, EYES, CHEEKS, NOSE, MOUTH, AND CHIN	47
A SURE TEST	48
THE LION AND THE UNICORN	48
THE MERCHANTS OF LONDON	48
LOCK AND KEY	49
I'LL TELL YOU A STORY	49
I HAD A LITTLE HUSBAND	49
TO BABYLON	50
A STRANGE OLD WOMAN	50
SLEEP, BABY, SLEEP	50
BAA, BAA, BLACK SHEEP	51
LITTLE FRED	52
DOCTOR FELL	52
CRY, BABY	52
THE CAT AND THE FIDDLE	52
A COUNTING-OUT RHYME	53
BUTTONS	53

HOT BOILED BEANS	54
ONE, HE LOVES	54
JACK AND HIS FIDDLE	54
LITTLE PUSSY	55
SING A SONG OF SIXPENCE	56
TOMMY TITTLEMOUSE	57
THE DERBY RAM	57
THE MULBERRY BUSH	58
THE HOBBY-HORSE	59
YOUNG LAMBS TO SELL	59
OLD WOMAN, OLD WOMAN	60
BOY AND THE SPARROW	60
TWO PIGEONS	61
THE HOUSE THAT JACK BUILT	61
THE FIRST OF MAY	63

The fair maid who, the first of May, Goes to the fields at break of day, And washes in dew from the hawthorn-tree, Will ever after handsome be.

SULKY SUE	63
SATURDAY, SUNDAY	64
THE OLD WOMAN AND THE PEDLAR	64
LITTLE JENNY WREN	65
BOBBY SNOOKS	66
THE LITTLE MOPPET	66
THE MAN IN THE MOON	67
I SAW A SHIP A-SAILING	67
A WALNUT	68
BAT, BAT	68
MY LOVE	68
HARK! HARK!	69
THE MAN OF BOMBAY	69
THE HART	69
A DIFFICULT RHYME	70
A SIEVE	70
POOR OLD ROBINSON CRUSOE!	70
GOOD ADVICE	71
MY MAID MARY	71
PRETTY JOHN WATTS	71
BYE, BABY BUNTING	72
TOM, TOM, THE PIPER'S SON	72
I LOVE SIXPENCE	72
COMICAL FOLK	73
COCK-CROW	73
THE THREE SONS	74
TOMMY SNOOKS	74
THE BLACKSMITH	74
ONE, TWO, BUCKLE MY SHOE	75

TWO GRAY KITS	75
COCK-A-DOODLE-DO!	76
PAIRS OR PEARS	76
BELLEISLE	76
OLD KING COLE	76
PUSSY-CAT MEW	77
COFFEE AND TEA	77
DAPPLE-GRAY	78
FOR BABY	78
A COCK AND BULL STORY	78
DREAMS	79
MYSELF	79
THE LITTLE GIRL WITH A CURL	79
FEARS AND TEARS	80
THE KILKENNY CATS	80
OVER THE WATER	80
CANDLE-SAVING	81
A WEEK OF BIRTHDAYS	81
A CHIMNEY	81
LADYBIRD	82
INTERY, MINTERY	82
OLD GRIMES	83
THE MAN WHO HAD NAUGHT	83
THE TAILORS AND THE SNAIL	84
CAESAR'S SONG	84
AROUND THE GREEN GRAVEL	84
AS I WAS GOING ALONG	85
ROCK-A-BYE, BABY	85
BILLY, BILLY	85
HECTOR PROTECTOR	86
THE BIRD SCARER	86
THE MAN IN THE WILDERNESS	86
MARY, MARY, QUITE CONTRARY	87
LITTLE JACK HORNER	87
BESSY BELL AND MARY GRAY	87
DANCE, THUMBKIN DANCE	88
PUSSY-CAT AND THE DUMPLINGS	89
BIRDS OF A FEATHER	89
NEEDLES AND PINS	89
AN ICICLE	90
TONGS	90
THE LITTLE BIRD	90
A STAR	90
MARY'S CANARY	91
A SHIP'S NAIL	91
THE GREEDY MAN	91

THE DUSTY MILLER 92
THE TEN O'CLOCK SCHOLAR 92
WILLY, WILLY 92
COCK-A-DOODLE-DO 93
THE BOY IN THE BARN 93
THE OLD WOMAN OF LEEDS 94
SUNSHINE 94
MY LITTLE MAID 94
THE QUARREL 95
JACK JINGLE 95
SHOEING 96
FOR WANT OF A NAIL 96
THE PUMPKIN-EATER 96
THAT'S ALL 97
DANCE, LITTLE BABY 97
BETTY BLUE 98
BEDTIME 98
THE CROOKED SIXPENCE 99
PEASE PORRIDGE 99
RING A RING O' ROSES 100
THIS IS THE WAY 100
THE DONKEY 100
IF 101
DUCKS AND DRAKES 101
LITTLE GIRL AND QUEEN 102
THE BELLS 102
THE KING OF FRANCE 103
PETER PIPER 103
THE TARTS 103
ONE TO TEN 104
AN EQUAL 104
WHAT ARE LITTLE BOYS MADE OF? 104
COME, LET'S TO BED 104
JENNY WREN 105
LITTLE MAID 105
THE GIRL AND THE BIRDS 106
BANDY LEGS 106
A PIG 107
LITTLE TOM TUCKER 107
WHERE ARE YOU GOING, MY PRETTY MAID 107
MULTIPLICATION IS VEXATION 108
A THORN 108
LITTLE KING BOGGEN 108
THE OLD WOMAN OF GLOUCESTER 109
BELL HORSES 109
WHISTLE 109

TAFFY	110
THE ROBIN	110
YOUNG ROGER AND DOLLY	111
THERE WAS AN OLD WOMAN	111
THE OLD WOMAN OF HARROW	112
THE PIPER AND HIS COW	112
THE COACHMAN	113
THE MAN OF DERBY	113
THE LITTLE MOUSE	113
THE LOST SHOE	114
THE OLD WOMAN OF SURREY	114
LONDON BRIDGE	115
BOY AND GIRL	116
MARCH WINDS	117
DING, DONG, BELL	117
WHEN	117
SING, SING	118
A CHERRY	118
HOT-CROSS BUNS	119
THREE STRAWS	119
HOT CODLINS	119
THE BALLOON	120
SWAN	120
THE MAN OF TOBAGO	120
A SUNSHINY SHOWER	121
THE FARMER AND THE RAVEN	121
CHRISTMAS	122
THE DEATH AND BURIAL OF POOR COCK ROBIN	122
WILLY BOY	124
POLLY AND SUKEY	125
PUSSY-CAT BY THE FIRE	125
THE MOUSE AND THE CLOCK	125
BOBBY SHAFTOE	126
THE BUNCH OF BLUE RIBBONS	126
THE WOMAN OF EXETER	127
SNEEZING	127
WHEN THE SNOW IS ON THE GROUND	127
Animal Children	128
Stories	215
LITTLE RED RIDING HOOD	215
THE GOOSE-GIRL	221
THE SLEEPING BEAUTY	229
SNOWDROP AND SEVEN LITTLE DWARFS	233
CINDERELLA, OR THE LITTLE GLASS SLIPPER	239
BLUE BEARD	251
THE STORY OF THE THREE BEARS	259

TATTERCOATS 265
JACK THE GIANT-KILLER 271
JACK AND THE BEANSTALK 294
THE THREE LITTLE PIGS 309
HANSEL AND GRETHEL 315
SNOW-WHITE AND ROSE-RED 326
RUMPELSTILTSKIN 338
BEAUTY AND THE BEAST 342
THE VALIANT LITTLE TAILOR 350
RAPUNZEL 362
THE FROG PRINCE 368
THE TRAVELS OF TOM THUMB 373
THE BOGEY-BEAST 380
Fables 384
THE FOX AND THE GRAPES 384
THE GOOSE THAT LAID THE GOLDEN EGGS 385
THE CAT AND THE MICE 385
THE MISCHIEVOUS DOG 386
THE CHARCOAL-BURNER AND THE FULLER 386
THE MICE IN COUNCIL 387
THE BAT AND THE WEASELS 387
THE DOG AND THE SOW 388
THE FOX AND THE CROW 388
THE HORSE AND THE GROOM 389
THE WOLF AND THE LAMB 389
THE PEACOCK AND THE CRANE 390
THE CAT AND THE BIRDS 390
THE SPENDTHRIFT AND THE SWALLOW 391
THE OLD WOMAN AND THE DOCTOR 391
THE MOON AND HER MOTHER 392
MERCURY AND THE WOODMAN 392
THE ASS, THE FOX, AND THE LION 394
THE LION AND THE MOUSE 394
THE CROW AND THE PITCHER 395
THE BOYS AND THE FROGS 395
THE NORTH WIND AND THE SUN 396
THE MISTRESS AND HER SERVANTS 397
THE GOODS AND THE ILLS 397
THE HARES AND THE FROGS 398
THE FOX AND THE STORK 399
THE WOLF IN SHEEP'S CLOTHING 400
THE STAG IN THE OX-STALL 400
THE MILKMAID AND HER PAIL 401
THE DOLPHINS, THE WHALES, AND THE SPRAT 402
THE FOX AND THE MONKEY 402
THE ASS AND THE LAP-DOG 403

THE FIR-TREE AND THE BRAMBLE	403
THE FROGS' COMPLAINT AGAINST THE SUN	405
THE DOG, THE COCK, AND THE FOX	405
THE GNAT AND THE BULL	406
THE BEAR AND THE TRAVELLERS	406
THE SLAVE AND THE LION	407
THE FLEA AND THE MAN	408
THE BEE AND JUPITER	409
THE OAK AND THE REEDS	410
THE BLIND MAN AND THE CUB	410
THE BOY AND THE SNAILS	411
THE APES AND THE TWO TRAVELLERS	411
THE ASS AND HIS BURDENS	412
THE SHEPHERD'S BOY AND THE WOLF	413
THE FOX AND THE GOAT	413
THE FISHERMAN AND THE SPRAT	414
THE BOASTING TRAVELLER	414
THE CRAB AND HIS MOTHER	415
THE ASS AND HIS SHADOW	416
THE FARMER AND HIS SONS	416
THE DOG AND THE COOK	417
THE MONKEY AS KING	417
THE THIEVES AND THE COCK	418
THE FARMER AND FORTUNE	419
JUPITER AND THE MONKEY	419
FATHER AND SONS	420
THE LAMP	420
THE OWL AND THE BIRDS	420
THE ASS IN THE LION'S SKIN	421
THE SHE-GOATS AND THEIR BEARDS	422
THE OLD LION	422
THE BOY BATHING	423
THE QUACK FROG	424
THE SWOLLEN FOX	424
THE SWOLLEN FOX	425
THE MOUSE, THE FROG, AND THE HAWK	425
THE BOY AND THE NETTLES	426
THE PEASANT AND THE APPLE-TREE	426
THE JACKDAW AND THE PIGEONS	427
JUPITER AND THE TORTOISE	427
THE DOG IN THE MANGER	428
THE TWO BAGS	428
THE OXEN AND THE AXLETREES	428
THE BOY AND THE FILBERTS	429
THE FROGS ASKING FOR A KING	429
THE OLIVE-TREE AND THE FIG-TREE	430

THE LION AND THE BOAR	431
THE WALNUT-TREE	431
THE MAN AND THE LION	431
THE TORTOISE AND THE EAGLE	432
THE KID ON THE HOUSETOP	432
THE FOX WITHOUT A TAIL	433
THE VAIN JACKDAW	433
THE TRAVELLER AND HIS DOG	434
THE SHIPWRECKED MAN AND THE SEA	434
THE WILD BOAR AND THE FOX	435
MERCURY AND THE SCULPTOR	436
THE FAWN AND HIS MOTHER	436
THE FOX AND THE LION	437
THE EAGLE AND HIS CAPTOR	437
THE BLACKSMITH AND HIS DOG	438
THE STAG AT THE POOL	438
THE DOG AND THE SHADOW	439
MERCURY AND THE TRADESMEN	439
THE MICE AND THE WEASELS	440
THE PEACOCK AND JUNO	440
THE BEAR AND THE FOX	441
THE ASS AND THE OLD PEASANT	442
THE OX AND THE FROG	442
THE MAN AND THE IMAGE	443
HERCULES AND THE WAGGONER	443
THE POMEGRANATE, THE APPLE-TREE, AND THE BRAMBLE	444
THE LION, THE BEAR, AND THE FOX	444
THE TWO SOLDIERS AND THE ROBBER	444
THE LION AND THE WILD ASS	445
THE MAN AND THE SATYR	446
THE IMAGE-SELLER	447
THE EAGLE AND THE ARROW	447
THE RICH MAN AND THE TANNER	447
THE WOLF, THE MOTHER, AND HER CHILD	448
THE OLD WOMAN AND THE WINE-JAR	448
THE LIONESS AND THE VIXEN	449
THE VIPER AND THE FILE	449
THE CAT AND THE COCK	449
THE HARE AND THE TORTOISE	450
THE SOLDIER AND HIS HORSE	451
THE OXEN AND THE BUTCHERS	452
THE WOLF AND THE LION	453
THE SHEEP, THE WOLF, AND THE STAG	453
THE LION AND THE THREE BULLS	454
THE HORSE AND HIS RIDER	455

THE GOAT AND THE VINE	455
THE TWO POTS	456
THE OLD HOUND	457
THE CLOWN AND THE COUNTRYMAN	458
THE LARK AND THE FARMER	459
THE LION AND THE ASS	460
THE PROPHET	460
THE HOUND AND THE HARE	461
THE LION, THE MOUSE, AND THE FOX	461
THE TRUMPETER TAKEN PRISONER	461
THE WOLF AND THE CRANE	462
THE EAGLE, THE CAT, AND THE WILD SOW	463
THE WOLF AND THE SHEEP	464
THE TUNNY-FISH AND THE DOLPHIN	464
THE THREE TRADESMEN	464
THE MOUSE AND THE BULL	465
THE HARE AND THE HOUND	465
THE TOWN MOUSE AND THE COUNTRY MOUSE	466
THE LION AND THE BULL	467
THE WOLF, THE FOX, AND THE APE	467
THE EAGLE AND THE COCKS	468
THE ESCAPED JACKDAW	469
THE FARMER AND THE FOX	469
VENUS AND THE CAT	469
THE CROW AND THE SWAN	471
THE STAG WITH ONE EYE	471
THE FLY AND THE DRAUGHT-MULE	472
THE COCK AND THE JEWEL	472
THE WOLF AND THE SHEPHERD	473
THE FARMER AND THE STORK	473
THE CHARGER AND THE MILLER	474
THE GRASSHOPPER AND THE OWL	474
THE GRASSHOPPER AND THE ANTS	475
THE FARMER AND THE VIPER	475
THE TWO FROGS	476
THE COBBLER TURNED DOCTOR	476
THE ASS, THE COCK, AND THE LION	477
THE BELLY AND THE MEMBERS	478
THE BALD MAN AND THE FLY	478
THE ASS AND THE WOLF	479
THE MONKEY AND THE CAMEL	480
THE SICK MAN AND THE DOCTOR	480
THE TRAVELLERS AND THE PLANE-TREE	481
THE FLEA AND THE OX	482
THE BIRDS, THE BEASTS, AND THE BAT	483
THE MAN AND HIS TWO SWEETHEARTS	483

THE EAGLE, THE JACKDAW, AND THE SHEPHERD . 484
THE WOLF AND THE BOY 484
THE MILLER, HIS SON, AND THEIR ASS 485
THE STAG AND THE VINE 487
THE LAMB CHASED BY A WOLF 488
THE ARCHER AND THE LION 488
THE WOLF AND THE GOAT 489
THE SICK STAG 489
THE ASS AND THE MULE 490
BROTHER AND SISTER 490
THE HEIFER AND THE OX 491
THE KINGDOM OF THE LION 491
THE ASS AND HIS DRIVER 492
THE LION AND THE HARE 492
THE WOLVES AND THE DOGS 493
THE BULL AND THE CALF 493
THE TREES AND THE AXE 494
THE ASTRONOMER 495
THE LABOURER AND THE SNAKE 495
THE CAGE-BIRD AND THE BAT 496
THE ASS AND HIS PURCHASER 496
THE KID AND THE WOLF 497
THE DEBTOR AND HIS SOW 498
THE BALD HUNTSMAN 498
THE HERDSMAN AND THE LOST BULL 499
THE MULE 499
THE HOUND AND THE FOX 500
THE FATHER AND HIS DAUGHTERS 500
THE THIEF AND THE INNKEEPER 501
THE PACK-ASS AND THE WILD ASS 502
THE ASS AND HIS MASTERS 502
THE PACK-ASS, THE WILD ASS, AND THE LION 503
THE ANT 504
THE FROGS AND THE WELL 505
THE CRAB AND THE FOX 505
THE FOX AND THE GRASSHOPPER 505
THE FARMER, HIS BOY, AND THE ROOKS 506
THE ASS AND THE DOG 507
THE ASS CARRYING THE IMAGE 507
THE ATHENIAN AND THE THEBAN 508
THE GOATHERD AND THE GOAT 508
THE SHEEP AND THE DOG 509
THE SHEPHERD AND THE WOLF 510
THE LION, JUPITER, AND THE ELEPHANT 510
THE PIG AND THE SHEEP 512
THE GARDENER AND HIS DOG 512

THE RIVERS AND THE SEA	513
THE LION IN LOVE	513
THE BEE-KEEPER	513
THE WOLF AND THE HORSE	514
THE BAT, THE BRAMBLE, AND THE SEAGULL	515
THE DOG AND THE WOLF	515
THE WASP AND THE SNAKE	516
THE EAGLE AND THE BEETLE	516
THE FOWLER AND THE LARK	517
THE FISHERMAN PIPING	518
THE WEASEL AND THE MAN	519
THE PLOUGHMAN, THE ASS, AND THE OX	519
DEMADES AND HIS FABLE	519
THE MONKEY AND THE DOLPHIN	520
THE CROW AND THE SNAKE	521
THE DOGS AND THE FOX	521
THE NIGHTINGALE AND THE HAWK	521
THE ROSE AND THE AMARANTH	522
THE MAN, THE HORSE, THE OX, AND THE DOG	522
THE WOLVES, THE SHEEP, AND THE RAM	523
THE SWAN	523
THE SNAKE AND JUPITER	524
THE WOLF AND HIS SHADOW	524
THE PLOUGHMAN AND THE WOLF	525
MERCURY AND THE MAN BITTEN BY AN ANT	525
THE WILY LION	526
THE PARROT AND THE CAT	526
THE STAG AND THE LION	527
THE IMPOSTOR	527
THE DOGS AND THE HIDES	528
THE LION, THE FOX, AND THE ASS	528
THE FOWLER, THE PARTRIDGE, AND THE COCK	529
THE GNAT AND THE LION	530
THE FARMER AND HIS DOGS	531
THE EAGLE AND THE FOX	532
THE BUTCHER AND HIS CUSTOMERS	533
HERCULES AND MINERVA	533
THE FOX WHO SERVED A LION	534
THE QUACK DOCTOR	534
THE LION, THE WOLF, AND THE FOX	535
HERCULES AND PLUTUS	536
THE FOX AND THE LEOPARD	536
THE FOX AND THE HEDGEHOG	537
THE CROW AND THE RAVEN	537
THE WITCH	538
THE OLD MAN AND DEATH	538

- THE MISER 539
- THE FOXES AND THE RIVER 540
- THE HORSE AND THE STAG 540
- THE FOX AND THE BRAMBLE 541
- THE FOX AND THE SNAKE 541
- THE LION, THE FOX, AND THE STAG 541
- THE MAN WHO LOST HIS SPADE 543
- THE PARTRIDGE AND THE FOWLER 543
- THE RUNAWAY SLAVE.. 544
- THE HUNTER AND THE WOODMAN 544
- THE SERPENT AND THE EAGLE 545
- THE ROGUE AND THE ORACLE 545
- THE HORSE AND THE ASS 546
- THE DOG CHASING A WOLF................................... 547
- GRIEF AND HIS DUE 547
- THE HAWK, THE KITE, AND THE PIGEONS 547
- THE WOMAN AND THE FARMER 548
- PROMETHEUS AND THE MAKING OF MAN............ 549
- THE SWALLOW AND THE CROW 549
- THE HUNTER AND THE HORSEMAN 549
- THE GOATHERD AND THE WILD GOATS................ 550
- THE NIGHTINGALE AND THE SWALLOW 551
- THE TRAVELLER AND FORTUNE............................ 551
- THE AMBITIOUS FOX AND THE UNAPPROACHABLE GRAPES.. 551
- THE ARROGANT FROG AND THE SUPERIOR BULL... 554
- THE PAMPERED LAPDOG AND THE MISGUIDED ASS 557
- THE SYCOPHANTIC FOX AND THE GULLIBLE RAVEN 559
- THE CONFIDING PEASANT AND THE MALADROIT BEAR 561

Some Selected Proverbs.. 564
- Afghan 564
- Chinese.. 564
- English 565
- German... 569
- Italian 571
- Kurdish... 572
- Nigerian 574
- Russian 577

Bible Stories... 579
- The Story of Adam and Eve..................................... 579
- The Story of Noah and the Ark................................ 583
- The Tower Of Babel 590
- The Story of Hagar and Ishmael.............................. 593
- The Story of Abraham and Isaac 599
- The Story of Jacob 603

The Story of the Ladder That Reached To Heaven 610
The Story of Joseph and His Coat of Many Colors 614
The Dreams of a King 619
The Story of the Money in the Sacks 627
The Mystery of the Lost Brother 632
The Story Of Moses, The Child Who Was Found In The River 639
The Story of Gideon and His Three Hundred Soldiers . 644
The Story of Samson, the Strong Man 652
The Story of Ruth, the Gleaner 664
The Story of David, the Shepherd Boy 670
The Story of the Fight with the Giant 676
The Story of Solomon and His Temple 681
The Story of Elijah, the Prophet 685
The Story of the Fiery Furnace 688
The Story of Daniel in the Lions' Den 694
The Story Of Jonah And The Whale 698
The Story Of Jesus, The Babe Of Bethlehem 703
The Story of the Star and the Wise Men 706
The Story of the Child in the Temple 712
The Story of the Stranger at the Well........................ 716
The Story of the Fishermen 721
Feeding the Multitudes 725
Jesus Calms the Tempest 729
The Story of the Sermon on the Mount 731
The Story of the Miracle Worker 736
The Good Shepherd and the Good Samaritan 743
The Story of the Palm Branches 748
The Story of the Betrayal 752
The Story of the Empty Tomb 757
The Story of Stephen, the First Martyr 769
The Apostle Paul 773

THE GIANT BOOK OF BEDTIME STORIES

THE GIANT BOOK OF BEDTIME STORIES
Preface

Perhaps the most important gift that a parent can give to their children is time spent reading to them in the evening before bed. This tradition involves quality one-on-one time spent between parent and child, builds language skills in the children at a critical time in their development, and is the single greatest factor determining children's attitude toward books and reading as they mature. There are many books to pick from for this purpose, but perhaps the most important are those that have been with us for hundreds of years. These stories have stood the test of time and, perhaps more important, carry cultural allusions and significance that will help your children gain a deeper appreciation for other literature. *The Giant Book of Bedtime Stories* collects together the most important of these classic works into a single, lavishly illustrated volume.

    I have made a potentially controversial decision to include Bible stories as part of this volume. In doing this my intention is not to make a statement that the Bible stories are myths, but rather to emphasize that reading Bible stories to children is integral to their education as well. I believe that this is true whether or not you are religious, because even taken as stories without religious significance the Bible stories are historically interesting and rich in culturally significant allusion.

William Roetzheim
Editor

The Giant Book of Bedtime Stories
Nursery Rhymes

The Real Mother Goose

LITTLE BO-PEEP

Little Bo-Peep has lost her sheep,
And can't tell where to find them;
Leave them alone, and they'll come home,
And bring their tails behind them.

Little Bo-Peep fell fast asleep,
And dreamt she heard them bleating;
But when she awoke, she found it a joke,
For still they all were fleeting.

Then up she took her little crook,
Determined for to find them;
She found them indeed, but it made her heart bleed,
For they'd left all their tails behind 'em!

It happened one day, as Bo-peep did stray
Unto a meadow hard by--

There she espied their tails, side by side,
All hung on a tree to dry.

She heaved a sigh and wiped her eye,
And over the hillocks she raced;
And tried what she could, as a shepherdess should,
That each tail should be properly placed.

THE CLOCK

There's a neat little clock,--
In the schoolroom it stands,--
And it points to the time
With its two little hands.

And may we, like the clock,
Keep a face clean and bright,
With hands ever ready
To do what is right.

LITTLE BOY BLUE

Little Boy Blue, come, blow your horn!
The sheep's in the meadow, the cow's in the corn.
Where's the little boy that looks after the sheep?
Under the haystack, fast asleep!

RAIN

Rain, rain, go away,
Come again another day;
Little Johnny wants to play.

WINTER

Cold and raw the north wind doth blow,
Bleak in the morning early;
All the hills are covered with snow,
And winter's now come fairly.

FINGERS AND TOES

Every lady in this land
Has twenty nails, upon each hand
Five, and twenty on hands and feet:
All this is true, without deceit.

Nursery Rhymes

A SEASONABLE SONG

Piping hot, smoking hot.
What I've got
You have not.
Hot gray pease, hot, hot, hot;
Hot gray pease, hot.

DAME TROT AND HER CAT

Dame Trot and her cat
Led a peaceable life,
When they were not troubled
With other folks' strife.

When Dame had her dinner
Pussy would wait,
And was sure to receive
A nice piece from her plate.

THE OLD WOMAN UNDER A HILL

There was an old woman
Lived under a hill;
And if she's not gone,
She lives there still.

THREE CHILDREN ON THE ICE

Three children sliding on the ice
Upon a summer's day,
As it fell out, they all fell in,
The rest they ran away.

Oh, had these children been at school,
Or sliding on dry ground,
Ten thousand pounds to one penny
They had not then been drowned.

Ye parents who have children dear,
And ye, too, who have none,
If you would keep them safe abroad
Pray keep them safe at home.

TWEEDLE-DUM AND TWEEDLE-DEE

Tweedle-dum and Tweedle-dee
Resolved to have a battle,
For Tweedle-dum said Tweedle-dee
Had spoiled his nice new rattle.

Just then flew by a monstrous crow,
As big as a tar barrel,
Which frightened both the heroes so,
They quite forgot their quarrel.

CROSS PATCH

Cross patch, draw the latch,
Sit by the fire and spin;
Take a cup and drink it up,
Then call your neighbors in.

Nursery Rhymes

OH, DEAR!

Dear, dear! what can
the matter be?
Two old women got up
in an apple-tree;
One came down, and
the other stayed till
Saturday.

PAT-A-CAKE

Pat-a-cake, pat-a-cake,
Baker's man!
So I do, master,
As fast as I can.

Pat it, and prick it,
And mark it with T,
Put it in the oven
For Tommy and me.

OLD MOTHER GOOSE

Old Mother Goose, when
She wanted to wander,
Would ride through the air
On a very fine gander.

LITTLE JUMPING JOAN

Here am I, little jumping Joan,
When nobody's with me
I'm always alone.

ROBIN REDBREAST

Little Robin Redbreast sat upon a tree,
Up went Pussy-Cat, down went he,
Down came Pussy-Cat, away Robin ran,
Says little Robin Redbreast:
"Catch me if you can!"

Little Robin Redbreast jumped upon a spade,
Pussy-Cat jumped after him,
and then he was afraid.
Little Robin chirped and sang, and what did
Pussy say?
Pussy-Cat said: "Mew, mew, mew,"
and Robin flew away.

MONEY AND THE MARE

"Lend me thy mare to ride a mile."
"She is lamed, leaping over a stile."

"Alack! and I must keep the fair!
I'll give thee money for thy mare."

"Oh, oh! say you so?
Money will make the mare to go!"

Nursery Rhymes
A MELANCHOLY SONG

Trip upon trenchers,
And dance upon dishes,
My mother sent me for some barm, some barm;
She bid me go lightly,
And come again quickly,
For fear the young men should do me some harm.
Yet didn't you see, yet didn't you see,
What naughty tricks they put upon me?
They broke my pitcher
And spilt the water,
And huffed my mother,
And chid her daughter,
And kissed my sister instead of me.

JACK

Jack be nimble, Jack be quick,
Jack jump over the candlestick.

GOING TO ST. IVES

As I was going to St. Ives
I met a man with seven wives.
Every wife had seven sacks,
Every sack had seven cats,
Every cat had seven kits.
Kits, cats, sacks, and wives,
How many were going to St. Ives?

BEES

A swarm of bees in May
Is worth a load of hay;
A swarm of bees in June
Is worth a silver spoon;
A swarm of bees in July
Is not worth a fly.

THIRTY DAYS HATH SEPTEMBER

Thirty days hath September,
April, June, and November;
February has twenty-eight alone,
All the rest have thirty-one,
Excepting leap-year, that's the time
When February's days are twenty-nine.

BABY DOLLY

Hush, baby, my dolly, I pray you don't cry,
And I'll give you some bread, and some milk by-and-by;
Or perhaps you like custard, or, maybe, a tart,
Then to either you're welcome, with all my heart.

Nursery Rhymes
COME OUT TO PLAY

Girls and boys, come out to play,
The moon doth shine as bright as day;
Leave your supper, and leave your sleep,
And come with your playfellows into the street.
Come with a whoop, come with a call,
Come with a good will or not at all.
Up the ladder and down the wall,
A half-penny roll will serve us all.
You find milk, and I'll find flour,
And we'll have a pudding in half an hour.

IF WISHES WERE HORSES

If wishes were horses, beggars would ride.
If turnips were watches, I would wear one by my side.
And if "ifs" and "ands"
Were pots and pans,
There'd be no work for tinkers!

OLD CHAIRS TO MEND

If I'd as much money as I could spend,
I never would cry old chairs to mend;

Old chairs to mend, old chairs to mend;
I never would cry old chairs to mend.

If I'd as much money as I could tell,
I never would cry old clothes to sell;
Old clothes to sell, old clothes to sell;
I never would cry old clothes to sell.

TO MARKET

To market, to market, to
 buy a fat pig.
Home again, home again,
 jiggety jig.
To market, to market, to
 buy a fat hog,
Home again, home again,
 jiggety jog.
To market, to market, to
 buy a plum bun,
Home again, home again,
 market is done.

TO MARKET, TO MARKET, TO BUY A FAT PIG

Nursery Rhymes

ROBIN AND RICHARD

Robin and Richard were two pretty men,
They lay in bed till the clock struck ten;
Then up starts Robin and looks at the sky,
"Oh, brother Richard, the sun's very high!
You go before, with the bottle and bag,
And I will come after on little Jack Nag."

A MAN AND A MAID

There was a little man,
Who wooed a little maid,
And he said, "Little maid, will you wed, wed, wed?
I have little more to say,
So will you, yea or nay,
For least said is soonest mended-ded, ded, ded."

The little maid replied,
"Should I be your little bride,
Pray what must we have for to eat, eat, eat?
Will the flame that you're so rich in

Light a fire in the kitchen?
Or the little god of love turn the
spit, spit, spit?"

THE CLEVER HEN

I had a little hen, the prettiest ever seen,
She washed me the dishes and kept the house clean;
She went to the mill to fetch me some flour,
She brought it home in less than an hour;
She baked me my bread, she brewed me my ale,
She sat by the fire and told many a fine tale.

HERE GOES MY LORD

Here goes my lord
A trot, a trot, a trot, a trot,
Here goes my lady
A canter, a canter, a canter, a canter!

Here goes my young master
Jockey-hitch, jockey-hitch, jockey-hitch, jockey-hitch!
Here goes my young miss

Nursery Rhymes

An amble, an amble, an amble, an amble!

The footman lags behind to tipple ale and wine,
And goes gallop, a gallop, a gallop, to make up his time.

LUCY LOCKET

LUCY LOCKET

Lucy Locket lost her pocket,
Kitty Fisher found it;
Nothing in it, nothing in it,
But the binding round it.

TWO BIRDS

There were two birds sat on a stone,
Fa, la, la, la, lal, de;
One flew away, and then there was one,
Fa, la, la, la, lal, de;
The other bird flew after,
And then there was none,
Fa, la, la, la, lal, de;
And so the stone
Was left alone,
Fa, la, la, la, lal, de.

WHEN JENNY WREN WAS YOUNG

'Twas once upon a time,
when Jenny Wren was young,
So daintily she danced
and so prettily she sung,
Robin Redbreast lost his heart,
for he was a gallant bird.
So he doffed his hat to Jenny Wren,
requesting to be heard.

"Oh, dearest Jenny Wren,
if you will but be mine,
You shall feed on cherry pie
and drink new currant wine,
I'll dress you like a goldfinch
or any peacock gay,
So, dearest Jen, if you'll be mine,
let us appoint the day."

Jenny blushed behind her fan
and thus declared her mind:
"Since, dearest Bob, I love you well,
I'll take your offer kind.
Cherry pie is very nice
and so is currant wine,
But I must wear my plain brown gown
and never go too fine."

LEG OVER LEG

Leg over leg,
As the dog went to Dover;
When he came to a stile,
Jump, he went over.

BARBER

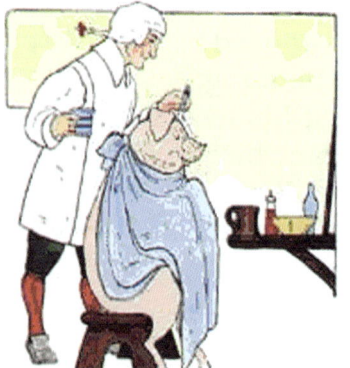

Barber, barber, shave a pig.
How many hairs will make a wig?
Four and twenty; that's enough.
Give the barber a pinch of snuff.

THE FLYING PIG

Dickory, dickory, dare,
The pig flew up in the air;
The man in brown soon brought
him down,
Dickory, dickory, dare.

SOLOMON GRUNDY

Solomon Grundy,
Born on a Monday,
Christened on Tuesday,
Married on Wednesday,
Took ill on Thursday,
Worse on Friday,

Died on Saturday,
Buried on Sunday.
This is the end
Of Solomon Grundy.

THREE WISE MEN OF GOTHAM

Three wise men of
Gotham
Went to sea in a
bowl;
If the bowl had been
stronger
My song had been
longer.

HUSH-A-BYE

Hush-a-bye, baby, on the
tree top!
When the wind blows the
cradle will rock;
When the bough breaks
the cradle will fall;
Down will come baby,
bough, cradle and all.

THE HUNTER OF REIGATE

A man went a-hunting at Reigate,
And wished to leap over a high gate.
Says the owner, "Go round,
With your gun and your hound,
For you never shall leap over my gate."

Nursery Rhymes

BURNIE BEE

Burnie bee, burnie bee,
Tell me when your wedding be?
If it be to-morrow day,
Take your wings and fly away.

LITTLE POLLY FLINDERS

Little Polly Flinders
Sat among the cinders
Warming her pretty little toes;
Her mother came and caught her,
Whipped her little daughter
For spoiling her nice new clothes.

PUSSY-CAT AND QUEEN

PUSSY-CAT AND QUEEN

"Pussy-cat, pussy-cat,
Where have you been?"
"I've been to London
To look at the Queen."

"Pussy-cat, pussy-cat,
What did you there?"
"I frightened a little
mouse
Under the chair."

LITTLE POLLY FLINDERS

Little Polly Flinders
Sat among the cinders
Warming her pretty little toes;
Her mother came and caught her,
Whipped her little daughter
For spoiling her nice new clothes.

RIDE AWAY, RIDE AWAY

Ride away, ride away,
Johnny shall ride,
And he shall have pussy-cat
Tied to one side;
And he shall have little dog
Tied to the other,
And Johnny shall ride
To see his grandmother.

PIPPEN HILL

As I was going up Pippen Hill,
Pippen Hill was dirty;
There I met a pretty Miss,
And she dropped me a curtsy.

Little Miss, pretty Miss,
Blessings light upon you;
If I had half-a-crown a day,
I'd spend it all upon you.

Nursery Rhymes
THE WINDS

Mister East gave a feast;
Mister North laid the cloth;
Mister West did his best;
Mister South burnt his mouth
Eating cold potato.

CLAP HANDIES

Clap, clap handies,
Mammie's wee, wee ain;
Clap, clap handies,
Daddie's comin' hame,
Hame till his bonny wee
bit laddie;
Clap, clap handies,
My wee, wee ain.

JUST LIKE ME

"I went up one pair of stairs."
"Just like me."
"I went up two pairs of stairs."
"Just like me."

"I went into a room."
"Just like me."

"I looked out of a window."
"Just like me."

"And there I saw a monkey."
"Just like me."

HEIGH-HO, THE CARRION CROW

A carrion crow sat on an oak,
Fol de riddle, lol de riddle, hi ding do,
Watching a tailor shape his cloak;
Sing heigh-ho, the carrion crow,
Fol de riddle, lol de riddle, hi ding do!

Wife, bring me my old bent bow,
Fol de riddle, lol de riddle, hi ding do,
That I may shoot yon carrion crow;
Sing heigh-ho, the carrion crow,
Fol de riddle, loi de riddle, hi ding do!

The tailor he shot, and missed his mark,
Fol de riddle, lol de riddle, hi ding do!
And shot his own sow quite through the heart;
Sing heigh-ho, the carrion crow,
Fol de riddle, lol de riddle, hi ding do!

Wife! bring brandy in a spoon,
Fol de riddle, lol de riddle, hi ding do!
For our old sow is in a swoon;
Sing heigh-ho, the carrion crow,
Fol de riddle, lol de riddle, hi ding do!

Nursery Rhymes

PLAY DAYS

How many days has my baby to play?
Saturday, Sunday, Monday,
Tuesday, Wednesday, Thursday, Friday,
Saturday, Sunday, Monday.

CHRISTMAS

Christmas comes but once a year,
And when it comes it brings good cheer.

ELIZABETH

Elizabeth, Elspeth, Betsy, and Bess,
They all went together to seek a bird's nest;
They found a bird's nest with five eggs in,
They all took one, and left four in.

BANBURY CROSS

Ride a cock-horse to Banbury Cross,
To see an old lady upon a white horse.
Rings on her fingers, and bells on her toes,
She shall have music wherever she goes.

RIDE A COCK-HORSE TO BANBURY CROSS

ABC

Great A, little a,
Bouncing B!
The cat's in the cupboard,
And can't see me.

THE MAN IN OUR TOWN

There was a man in our town,
And he was wondrous wise,
He jumped into a bramble bush,

And scratched out both his eyes;
But when he saw his eyes were out,
With all his might and main,
He jumped into another bush,
And scratched 'em in again.

A NEEDLE AND THREAD

Old Mother Twitchett had but one eye,
And a long tail which she let fly;

And every time she went through a gap,
A bit of her tail she left in a trap.

FOR EVERY EVIL

For every evil under the sun
There is a remedy or there is none.
If there be one, seek till you find it;
If there be none, never mind it.

CUSHY COW

Cushy cow, bonny, let down thy milk,
And I will give thee a gown of silk;
A gown of silk and a silver tee,
If thou wilt let down thy milk to me.

GEORGY PORGY

Georgy Porgy, pudding and pie,
Kissed the girls and made them cry.
When the boys came out to play,
Georgy Porgy ran away.

SEE-SAW

See-saw, Margery Daw,
Sold her bed and lay upon straw.

WEE WILLIE WINKIE

Wee Willie Winkie runs through the town,
Upstairs and downstairs, in his nightgown;
Rapping at the window, crying through the lock,
"Are the children in their beds? Now it's eight o'clock."

ROBIN-A-BOBBIN

Robin-a-Bobbin
Bent his bow,
Shot at a pigeon,
And killed a crow.

JOHN SMITH

Is John Smith within?
Yes, that he is.
Can he set a shoe?
Ay, marry, two.
Here a nail, there a nail,
Tick, tack, too.

Nursery Rhymes

ABOUT THE BUSH

About the bush, Willie,
About the beehive,
About the bush, Willie,
I'll meet thee alive.

FIVE TOES

This little pig went to market;
This little pig stayed at home;
This little pig had roast beef;
This little pig had none;
This little pig said, "Wee, wee!
I can't find my way home."

SIMPLE SIMON

Simple Simon met a pieman,
Going to the fair;
Says Simple Simon to the pieman,
"Let me taste your ware."

Says the pieman to Simple Simon,
"Show me first your penny,"
Says Simple Simon to the pieman,
"Indeed, I have not any."

Simple Simon went a-fishing
  For to catch a whale;
All the water he could find
  Was in his mother's pail!

Simple Simon went to look
  If plums grew on a thistle;
He pricked his fingers very much,
  Which made poor Simon whistle.

He went to catch a dicky bird,
  And thought he could not fail,
Because he had a little salt,
  To put upon its tail.

He went for water with a sieve,
  But soon it ran all through;
And now poor Simple Simon
  Bids you all adieu.

THREE BLIND MICE

Three blind mice! See
how they run!
They all ran after the
farmer's wife,
Who cut off their tails
with a carving knife.
Did you ever see such a
thing in your life
As three blind mice?

THREE BLIND MICE

Nursery Rhymes
A LITTLE MAN

There was a little man, and he had a little gun,
And his bullets were made of lead, lead, lead;
He went to the brook, and saw a little duck,
And shot it right through the head, head, head.

He carried it home to his old wife Joan,
And bade her a fire to make, make, make.
To roast the little duck he had shot in the brook,
And he'd go and fetch the drake, drake, drake.

The drake was a-
swimming with his
curly tail;
The little man made
it his mark, mark,
mark.
He let off his gun,
but he fired too
soon,
And the drake flew
away with a quack,
quack, quack.

DOCTOR FOSTER

Doctor Foster went to
Glo'ster,
In a shower of rain;
He stepped in a puddle,
up to his middle,
And never went there
again.

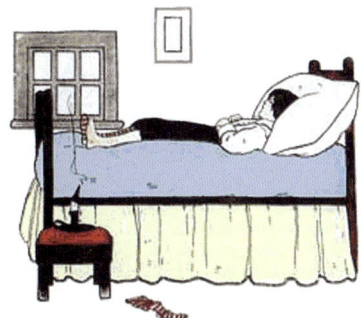

DIDDLE DIDDLE DUMPLING

Diddle diddle dumpling, my son John
Went to bed with his breeches on,
One stocking off, and one stocking on;
Diddle diddle dumpling, my son John.

JERRY HALL

Jerry Hall, he was so small,
A rat could eat him, hat and all.

LENGTHENING DAYS

As the days grow longer
The storms grow stronger.

THE BLACK HEN

Hickety, pickety, my black hen,
She lays eggs for gentlemen;
Gentlemen come every day
To see what my black hen doth lay.

Nursery Rhymes
THE MIST

A hill full, a hole full,
Yet you cannot catch a bowl full.

MISS MUFFET

Little Miss Muffet
Sat on a tuffet,
Eating of curds and whey;
There came a big spider,
And sat down beside her,
And frightened Miss Muffet away.

CURLY-LOCKS

Curly-locks, Curly-locks, wilt thou be mine?
Thou shalt not wash the dishes, nor yet feed the swine;
But sit on a cushion, and sew a fine seam
And feed upon strawberries, sugar, and cream.

CURLY-LOCKS, CURLY-LOCKS, WILT THOU BE MINE?

A CANDLE

Little Nanny Etticoat
In a white petticoat,
And a red nose;
The longer she stands
The shorter she grows.

HUMPTY DUMPTY

Humpty Dumpty sat on
a wall,
Humpty Dumpty had a
great fall;
All the King's horses, and all the King's men
Cannot put Humpty Dumpty together again.

Nursery Rhymes

PINS

See a pin and pick it up,
All the day you'll have good luck.
See a pin and let it lay,
Bad luck you'll have all the day.

ONE, TWO, THREE

One, two, three, four, five,
Once I caught a fish alive.
Six, seven, eight, nine, ten,
But I let it go again.
Why did you let it go?
Because it bit my finger so.
Which finger did it bite?
The little one upon the right.

THE DOVE AND THE WREN

The dove says coo, coo, what shall I do?
I can scarce maintain two.
Pooh, pooh! says the wren, I've got ten,
And keep them all like gentlemen.

MASTER I HAVE

Master I have, and I am his man,
Gallop a dreary dun;
Master I have, and I am his man,
And I'll get a wife as fast as I can;
With a heighty gaily gamberally,
Higgledy piggledy, niggledy, niggledy,
Gallop a dreary dun.

SHALL WE GO A-SHEARING?

"Old woman, old woman, shall we go a-shearing?"
"Speak a little louder, sir, I am very thick of hearing."
"Old woman, old woman, shall I kiss you dearly?"
"Thank you, kind sir, I hear you very clearly."

GOOSEY, GOOSEY, GANDER

Goosey, goosey, gander,
Whither dost thou wander?
Upstairs and downstairs
And in my lady's chamber.

There I met an old man
Who wouldn't say his prayers;
I took him by the left leg,
And threw him down the stairs.

Nursery Rhymes
OLD MOTHER HUBBARD

Old Mother Hubbard
Went to the cupboard,
To give her poor dog a bone;
But when she got there
The cupboard was bare,
And so the poor dog had none.

She went to the baker's
To buy him some bread;
When she came back
The dog was dead.

She went to the undertaker's
To buy him a coffin;
When she got back
The dog was laughing.

She took a clean dish
To get him some tripe;
When she came back
He was smoking a pipe.

She went to the alehouse
To get him some beer;
When she came back
The dog sat in a chair.

She went to the tavern
For white wine and red;
When she came back
The dog stood on his head.

She went to the hatter's
To buy him a hat;

When she came back
He was feeding the cat.

She went to the barber's
To buy him a wig;
When she came back
He was dancing a jig.

She went to the fruiterer's
To buy him some fruit;
When she came back
He was playing the flute.

She went to the tailor's
To buy him a coat;
When she came back
He was riding a goat.

She went to the cobbler's
To buy him some shoes;
When she came back
He was reading the news.

She went to the sempster's
To buy him some linen;
When she came back
The dog was a-spinning.

She went to the hosier's
To buy him some hose;
When she came back
He was dressed in his clothes.

The dame made a curtsy,
The dog made a bow;

The dame said, "Your servant,"
The dog said, "Bow-wow."

THE COCK AND THE HEN

"Cock, cock, cock, cock,
I've laid an egg,
Am I to gang ba--are-foot?"

"Hen, hen, hen, hen,
I've been up and down
To every shop in town,
And cannot find a shoe
To fit your foot,
If I'd crow my hea--art out."

BLUE BELL BOY

I had a little boy,
And called him Blue
Bell;
Gave him a little work,--
He did it very well.

I bade him go upstairs
To bring me a gold pin;
In coal scuttle fell he,
Up to his little chin.

He went to the garden
To pick a little sage;
He tumbled on his nose,
And fell into a rage.

He went to the cellar
To draw a little beer;

And quickly did return
To say there was none there.

WHY MAY NOT I LOVE JOHNNY?

Johnny shall have a
   new bonnet,
And Johnny shall go to
   the fair,
And Johnny shall have
   a blue ribbon
To tie up his bonny
   brown hair.

And why may not I love
   Johnny?
And why may not
   Johnny love me?
And why may not I love
   Johnny
As well as another
   body?

And here's a leg for a stocking,
And here's a foot for a shoe,
And he has a kiss for his daddy,
And two for his mammy, I trow.

And why may not I love Johnny?
And why may not Johnny love me?
And why may not I love Johnny
   As well as another body?

Nursery Rhymes

JACK JELF

Little Jack Jelf
Was put on the shelf
Because he could not spell "pie";
When his aunt, Mrs. Grace,
Saw his sorrowful face,
She could not help saying, "Oh, fie!"

And since Master Jelf
Was put on the shelf
Because he could not spell "pie,"
Let him stand there so grim,
And no more about him,
For I wish him a very good-bye!

JACK SPRAT

Jack Sprat
Could eat no fat,
His wife could eat no lean;
And so,
Betwixt them both,
They licked the platter clean.

JACK SPRAT

DAFFODILS

    Daffy-down-dilly has come to town
In a yellow petticoat and a green gown.

HUSH-A-BYE

Hush-a-bye, baby, lie still with thy daddy,
Thy mammy has gone to the mill,
To get some meal to bake a cake,
So pray, my dear baby, lie still.

HUSH-A-BYE

Hush-a-bye, baby,
Daddy is near;
Mamma is a lady,
And that's very clear.

THE GIRL IN THE LANE

The girl in the lane, that
couldn't speak plain,
Cried, "Gobble, gobble, gobble":
The man on the hill that
couldn't stand still,
Went hobble hobble,
hobble.

NANCY DAWSON

Nancy Dawson was so fine
She wouldn't get up to
serve the swine;
She lies in bed till eight or
nine,
So it's Oh, poor Nancy

Dawson.

And do ye ken Nancy Dawson,
honey?
The wife who sells the barley,
honey?
She won't get up to feed her
swine,
And do ye ken Nancy Dawson,
honey?

HANDY PANDY

Handy Pandy, Jack-a-dandy,
Loves plum cake and sugar candy.
He bought some at a grocer's shop,
And out he came, hop, hop, hop!

JACK AND JILL

Jack and Jill went up the hill,
To fetch a pail of water;
Jack fell down, and broke his crown,
And Jill came tumbling after.

Then up Jack got and off did trot,
As fast as he could caper,
To old Dame Dob, who patched his nob
With vinegar and brown paper

THE ALPHABET

A, B, C, and D,
Pray, playmates, agree.
E, F, and G,
Well, so it shall be.
J, K, and L,
In peace we will dwell.
M, N, and O,
To play let us go.
P, Q, R, and S,

Nursery Rhymes

Love may we possess.
W, X, and Y,
Will not quarrel or die.
Z, and ampersand,
Go to school at command.

DANCE TO YOUR DADDIE

Dance to your daddie,
My bonnie laddie;
Dance to your daddie,
my bonnie lamb;
You shall get a fishy,
On a little dishy;
You shall get a fishy,
when the boat comes home.

RAIN

Rain, rain, go to Spain,
And never come back again.

TEETH AND GUMS

Thirty white horses upon a red hill,
Now they tramp, now they champ, now they stand still.

ROBIN HOOD AND LITTLE JOHN

Robin Hood, Robin Hood,
Is in the mickle wood!
Little John, Little John,
He to the town is gone.

Robin Hood, Robin Hood,
Telling his beads,
All in the greenwood
Among the green weeds.

Little John, Little John,
If he comes no more,
Robin Hood, Robin Hood,
We shall fret full sore!

ROBIN HOOD

Nursery Rhymes
ONE MISTY MOISTY MORNING

One misty moisty morning,
When cloudy was the weather,
I chanced to meet an old man,
Clothed all in leather.
He began to compliment
And I began to grin.
How do you do? And how do you do?
And how do you do again?

THE OLD WOMAN FROM FRANCE

There came an old woman from France
Who taught grown-up children to dance;
But they were so stiff,
She sent them home in a sniff,
This sprightly old woman from France.

THE ROBINS

A robin and a robin's son
Once went to town to buy a bun.
They couldn't decide on plum or plain,
And so they went back home again.

PANCAKE DAY

Great A, little a,
This is pancake day;
Toss the ball high,
Throw the ball low,
Those that come after
May sing heigh-ho!

THE OLD MAN

There was an old man
In a velvet coat,
He kissed a maid
And gave her a groat.
The groat it was crack'd
And would not go,--
Ah, old man, do you serve me so?

A PLUM PUDDING

Flour of England, fruit of Spain,
Met together in a shower of rain;
Put in a bag tied round with a string;
If you'll tell me this riddle,
I'll give you a ring.

MY KITTEN

Hey, my kitten, my kitten,
And hey, my kitten, my deary!
Such a sweet pet as this
Was neither far nor neary.

T'OTHER LITTLE TUNE

I won't be my father's Jack,
I won't be my father's Jill;
I will be the fiddler's wife,
And have music when I will.
T'other little tune,
T'other little tune,
Prithee, Love, play me
T'other little tune.

IF ALL THE SEAS WERE ONE SEA

If all the seas were one sea,
What a *great* sea that would be!
And if all the trees were one tree,
What a *great* tree that would be!
And if all the axes were one axe,
What a *great* axe that would be!

And if all the men were one man,
What a *great* man he would be!
And if the *great* man took the *great* axe,
And cut down the *great* tree,
And let it fall into the *great* sea,
What a splish splash *that* would be!

FOREHEAD, EYES, CHEEKS, NOSE, MOUTH, AND CHIN

Here sits the Lord Mayor,
Here sit his two men,
Here sits the cock,
Here sits the hen,
Here sit the little chickens,
Here they run in.
Chin-chopper, chin-chopper, chin chopper, chin!

Nursery Rhymes

A SURE TEST

If you are to be a gentleman,
As I suppose you'll be,
You'll neither laugh nor smile,
For a tickling of the knee.

THE LION AND THE UNICORN

The Lion and the Unicorn were fighting for the crown,
The Lion beat the Unicorn all around the town.
Some gave them white bread, and some gave them brown,
Some gave them plum-cake, and sent them out of town.

THE MERCHANTS OF LONDON

Hey diddle dinkety poppety pet,
The merchants of London they wear scarlet,
Silk in the collar and gold in the hem,
So merrily march the merchant men.

LOCK AND KEY

"I am a gold lock."
"I am a gold key."
"I am a silver lock."
"I am a silver key."
"I am a brass lock."
"I am a brass key."
"I am a lead lock."
"I am a lead key."
"I am a don lock."
"I am a don key!"

I'LL TELL YOU A STORY

I'll tell you a story
About Jack-a-Nory:
And now my story's begun.
I'll tell you another
About his brother:
And now my story is done.

I HAD A LITTLE HUSBAND

I had a little husband no bigger than my thumb,
I put him in a pint pot, and there I bid him drum,
I bought a little handkerchief to wipe his little nose,
And a pair of little garters to tie his little hose.

Nursery Rhymes

TO BABYLON

How many miles is it to
Babylon?--
Threescore miles and
ten.
Can I get there by
candle-light?--
Yes, and back again.
If your heels are nimble
and light,
You may get there by candle-light.

A STRANGE OLD WOMAN

There was an old woman, and what do you
think?
She lived upon nothing but victuals and drink;
Victuals and drink were the chief of her diet,
And yet this old woman could never be quiet.

SLEEP, BABY, SLEEP

Sleep, baby, sleep,
Our cottage vale is deep:
The little lamb is on the
green,
With woolly fleece so soft
and clean--
Sleep, baby, sleep.
Sleep, baby, sleep,
Down where the woodbines

creep;
Be always like the lamb so mild,
A kind, and sweet, and gentle child.
Sleep, baby, sleep.

BAA, BAA, BLACK SHEEP

BAA, BAA, BLACK SHEEP

Baa, baa, black sheep,
Have you any wool?
Yes, marry, have I,
Three bags full;

One for my master,
One for my dame,
But none for the little boy
Who cries in the lane.

Nursery Rhymes
LITTLE FRED

When little Fred went to bed, He always said his prayers; He kissed mamma, and then papa, And straightway went upstairs.

DOCTOR FELL

I do not like thee, Doctor Fell;
The reason why I cannot tell;
But this I know, and know full well,
I do not like thee, Doctor Fell!

CRY, BABY

Cry, baby, cry,
Put your finger in your eye,
And tell your mother it wasn't I.

THE CAT AND THE FIDDLE

Hey, diddle, diddle!
The cat and the fiddle,
The cow jumped over the moon;

The little dog laughed
To see such sport,
And the dish ran away with the spoon.

A COUNTING-OUT RHYME

Hickery, dickery, 6 and 7,
Alabone, Crackabone, 10 and 11,
Spin, spun, muskidun,
Twiddle 'em, twaddle 'em, 21.

BUTTONS

Buttons, a farthing a pair!
Come, who will buy them of me?
They're round and sound and pretty,
And fit for girls of the city.
Come, who will buy them of me?
Buttons, a farthing a pair!

Nursery Rhymes
HOT BOILED BEANS

Ladies and gentlemen come to supper--
Hot boiled beans and very good butter.

ONE, HE LOVES

One, he loves; two, he loves;
Three, he loves, they say;
Four, he loves with all his heart;
Five, he casts away.
Six, he loves; seven, she loves;
Eight, they both love.
Nine, he comes; ten, he tarries;
Eleven, he courts; twelve, he marries.

JACK AND HIS FIDDLE

"Jacky, come and give me thy
fiddle,
If ever thou mean to thrive."
"Nay, I'll not give my fiddle
To any man alive.

"If I should give my fiddle,
They'll think that I've gone
mad;
For many a joyous day
My fiddle and I have had."

LITTLE PUSSY

I like little Pussy,
Her coat is so warm,

And if I don't hurt her
She'll do me no harm;

So I'll not pull her tail,
Nor drive her away,

But Pussy and I
Very gently will play.

SING A SONG OF SIXPENCE

Nursery Rhymes
SING A SONG OF SIXPENCE

Sing a song of sixpence,
A pocket full of rye;
Four-and-twenty blackbirds
Baked in a pie!

When the pie was opened
The birds began to sing;
Was not that a dainty dish
To set before the king?

The king was in his counting-house,
Counting out his money;
The queen was in the parlor,
Eating bread and honey.

The maid was in the garden,
Hanging out the clothes;
When down came a blackbird
And snapped off her nose.

TOMMY TIT-TLEMOUSE

Little Tommy
Tittlemouse
Lived in a little
house;
He caught fishes
In other men's
ditches.

THE DERBY RAM

As I was going to Derby all on a market-day,
I met the finest ram, sir, that ever was fed upon hay;
Upon hay, upon hay, upon hay;
I met the finest ram, sir, that ever was fed upon hay.
This ram was fat behind, sir; this ram was fat before;

This ram was ten yards round, sir; indeed, he was no more;
No more, no more, no more;
This ram was ten yards round, sir; indeed, he was no more.
The horns that grew on his head, sir, they were so wondrous high,
As I've been plainly told, sir, they reached up to the sky.

The sky, the sky, the sky;
As I've been plainly told, sir, they reached up to
the sky.
The tail that grew from his back, sir, was six
yards and an ell;
And it was sent to Derby to toll the market bell;
The bell, the bell, the bell;
And it was sent to Derby to toll the market bell.

THE MULBERRY BUSH

Here we go round the mulberry bush,
The mulberry bush, the mulberry bush,
Here we go round the mulberry bush.
On a cold and frosty morning.

This is the way we wash our hands,
Wash our hands, wash our hands,
This is the way we wash our hands,
On a cold and frosty morning.

This is the way we wash our clothes.
Wash our clothes, wash our clothes,
This is the way we wash our clothes,
On a cold and frosty morning.

This is the way we go to school,
Go to school, go to school,
This is the way we go to school,
On a cold and frosty morning.

This is the way we come out of school,
Come out of school, come out of school,
This is the way we come out of school,
On a cold and frosty morning.

THE HOBBY-HORSE

I had a little hobby-horse,
And it was dapple gray;
Its head was made of pea-straw,
Its tail was made of hay.

I sold it to an old woman
For a copper groat;
And I'll not sing my song again
Without another coat.

YOUNG LAMBS TO SELL

If I'd as much money
as I could tell,
I never would cry
young lambs to sell;
Young lambs to sell,
young lambs to sell;
I never would cry
young lambs to sell.

Nursery Rhymes
OLD WOMAN, OLD WOMAN

There was an old woman tossed in a basket,
Seventeen times as high as the moon;
But where she was going no mortal could tell,
For under her arm she carried a broom.

"Old woman, old woman, old woman,"said I,
"Whither, oh whither, oh whither so high?"
"To sweep the cobwebs from the sky;
And I'll be with you by-and-by."

THE OLD WOMAN TOSSED IN A BASKET

BOY AND THE SPARROW

A little cock-sparrow sat on a green tree,
And he chirruped, he chirruped, so merry was he;
A naughty boy came with his wee bow and arrow,

Determined to shoot this little cock-sparrow.

"This little cock-sparrow shall make me a stew,
And his giblets shall make me a little pie, too."
"Oh, no," says the sparrow "I won't make a stew."
So he flapped his wings and away he flew.

TWO PIGEONS

I had two pigeons bright and gay,
They flew from me the other day.
What was the reason they did go?
I cannot tell, for I do not know.

THE HOUSE THAT JACK BUILT

This is the house that Jack built.
This is the malt
That lay in the house that Jack built.

This is the rat,
That ate the malt
That lay in the house that Jack built.

This is the cat,
That killed the rat,
That ate the malt
That lay in the house that Jack built.

Nursery Rhymes

This is the dog,
That worried the cat,
That killed the rat,
That ate the malt
That lay in the house that Jack built.

This is the cow with the crumpled horn,
That tossed the dog,
That worried the cat,
That killed the rat,
That ate the malt
That lay in the house that Jack built.

This is the maiden all forlorn,
That milked the cow with the crumpled horn,
That tossed the dog,
That worried the cat,
That killed the rat,
That ate the malt
That lay in the house that Jack built

This is the man all tattered and torn,
That kissed the maiden all forlorn,
That milked the cow with the crumpled horn,
That tossed the dog,
That worried the cat,
That killed the rat,
That ate the malt
That lay in the house that Jack built.

This is the priest all shaven and shorn,
That married the man all tattered and torn,
That kissed the maiden all forlorn,
That milked the cow with the crumpled horn,
That tossed the dog,
That worried the cat,

That killed the rat,
That ate the malt
That lay in the house that Jack built.

This is the cock that crowed in the morn,
That waked the priest all shaven and shorn,
That married the man all tattered and torn,
That kissed the maiden all forlorn,
That milked the cow with the crumpled horn,
That tossed the dog,
That worried the cat,
That killed the rat,
That ate the malt
That lay in the house that Jack built.

This is the farmer sowing the corn,
That kept the cock that crowed in the morn,
That waked the priest all shaven and shorn,
That married the man all tattered and torn,
That kissed the maiden all forlorn,
That milked the cow with the crumpled horn,
That tossed the dog,
That worried the cat,
That killed the rat,
That ate the malt
That lay in the house that Jack built.

THE FIRST OF MAY

The fair maid who, the first of May,
Goes to the fields at break of day,
And washes in dew from the hawthorn-tree,
Will ever after handsome be.

Nursery Rhymes
SULKY SUE

Here's Sulky Sue,
What shall we do?
Turn her face to the wall
Till she comes to.

SATURDAY, SUNDAY

On Saturday night
Shall be all my care
To powder my locks
And curl my hair.

On Sunday morning
My love will come in.
When he will marry me
With a gold ring.

THE OLD WOMAN AND THE PEDLAR

There was an old woman, as I've heard tell,
She went to market her eggs for to sell;
She went to market all on a market-day,
And she fell asleep on the King's highway.

There came by a peddler whose name was Stout,
He cut her petticoats all round about;
He cut her petticoats up to the knees,
Which made the old woman to shiver and freeze.

When the little old woman first did wake,
She began to shiver and she began to shake;
She began to wonder and she began to cry,
"Lauk a mercy on me, this can't be I!

"But if it be I, as I hope it be,
I've a little dog at home, and he'll know me;
If it be I, he'll wag his little tail,
And if it be not I, he'll loudly bark and wail."

Home went the little woman all in the dark;
Up got the little dog, and he began to bark;
He began to bark, so she began to cry,
"Lauk a mercy on me, this is none of I!"

LITTLE JENNY WREN

Little Jenny Wren fell sick,
Upon a time;
In came Robin Redbreast
And brought her cake and wine.

"Eat well of my cake, Jenny,
Drink well of my wine."
"Thank you, Robin, kindly,

You shall be mine."

Jenny she got well,
And stood upon her feet,
And told Robin plainly
She loved him not a bit.

Robin being angry,
Hopped upon a twig,
Saying, "Out upon you! Fie upon you!
Bold-faced jig!"

BOBBY SNOOKS

Little Bobby Snooks was
fond of his books,
And loved by his usher
and master;
But naughty Jack Spry,
he got a black eye,
And carries his nose in
a plaster.

THE LITTLE MOPPET

I had a little moppet,
I put it in my pocket,
And fed it with corn and hay.
There came a proud beggar.
And swore he should have her;
And stole my little moppet away.

THE MAN IN THE MOON

The Man in the
Moon came
tumbling down,
And asked the
way to Norwich;
He went by the
south, and burnt
his mouth
With eating cold
pease porridge.

I SAW A SHIP A-SAILING

I saw a ship a-sailing,
A-sailing on the sea;
And, oh! it was all laden
With pretty things for thee!

There were comfits in the cabin,
And apples in the hold;
The sails were made of silk,
And the masts were made of gold.

The four-and-twenty sailors
That stood between the decks,
Were four-and-twenty white mice
With chains about their necks.

The captain was a duck,
With a packet on his back;
And when the ship began to move,
The captain said, "Quack! Quack!"

Nursery Rhymes
A WALNUT

As soft as silk, as white as milk,
As bitter as gall, a strong wall,
And a green coat covers me all.

BAT, BAT

Bat, bat,
Come under my hat,
And I'll give you a slice of bacon;
And when I bake
I'll give you a cake
If I am not mistaken.

MY LOVE

Saw ye aught of my love a-coming from the market?
A peck of meal upon her back,
A babby in her basket;
Saw ye aught of my love a-coming from the market?

HARK! HARK!

Hark, hark! the dogs do bark!
Beggars are coming to town:
Some in jags, and some in rags,
And some in velvet gown.

HARK! HARK! THE DOGS DO BARK!

THE MAN OF BOMBAY

There was a fat man of Bombay,
Who was smoking one sunshiny day;
When a bird called a snipe
Flew away with his pipe,
Which vexed the fat man of Bombay

THE HART

The hart he loves the high wood,
The hare she loves the hill;
The Knight he loves his bright sword,
The Lady--loves her will.

Nursery Rhymes
A DIFFICULT RHYME

What is the rhyme for porringer?
The king he had a daughter fair,
And gave the Prince of Orange her.

A SIEVE

A riddle, a riddle, as I suppose,
A hundred eyes and never a nose!

POOR OLD ROBINSON CRUSOE!

Poor old Robinson Crusoe!
Poor old Robinson Crusoe!
They made him a coat
Of an old Nanny goat.
I wonder why they should do so!
With a ring-a-ting-tang,
And a ring-a-ting-tang,
Poor old Robinson Crusoe!

GOOD ADVICE

Come when you're called,
Do what you're bid,
Shut the door after you,
And never be chid.

MY MAID MARY

My maid Mary she minds the dairy,
While I go a-hoeing and mowing each morn;
Gaily run the reel and the little spinning wheel,
While I am singing and mowing my corn.

PRETTY JOHN WATTS

Pretty John Watts,
We are troubled with rats.
Will you drive them out of the house?
We have mice, too, in plenty,
That feast in the pantry,
But let them stay
And nibble away,
What harm in a little brown mouse?

Nursery Rhymes
BYE, BABY BUNTING

Bye, baby bunting,
Father's gone a-hunting,
Mother's gone a-milking,
Sister's gone a-silking,
And brother's gone to buy a skin
To wrap the baby bunting in.

TOM, TOM, THE PIPER'S SON

Tom, Tom, the piper's son,
Stole a pig, and away he run,
The pig was eat,
And Tom was beat,
And Tom ran crying down the street.

I LOVE SIXPENCE

I love sixpence, a jolly, jolly sixpence,
I love sixpence as my life;
I spent a penny of it, I spent a penny of it,
I took a penny home to my wife.

Oh, my little fourpence, a jolly, jolly fourpence,
I love fourpence as my life;
I spent twopence of it, I spent twopence of it,
And I took twopence home to my wife.

COMICAL FOLK

In a cottage in Fife
Lived a man and
his wife
Who, believe me, were
comical folk;
For, to people's
surprise,
They both saw with
their eyes,
And their tongues
moved whenever they
spoke!

When they were asleep,
I'm told, that to keep
Their eyes open they could not contrive;
They both walked on their feet,
And 'twas thought what they eat
Helped, with drinking, to keep them alive!

COCK-CROW

Cocks crow in the morn
To tell us to rise,
And he who lies late
Will never be wise;

For early to bed
And early to rise,
Is the way to be healthy
And wealthy and
wise.

Nursery Rhymes
THE THREE SONS

There was an old woman had three sons,
Jerry and James and John,
Jerry was hanged, James was drowned,
John was lost and never was found;
And there was an end of her three sons,
Jerry and James and John!

TOMMY SNOOKS

As Tommy Snooks and
Bessy Brooks
Were walking out one
Sunday,
Says Tommy Snooks to
Bessy Brooks,
"Wilt marry me on
Monday?"

THE BLACKSMITH

"Robert Barnes, my fellow
fine,
Can you shoe this horse
of mine?"
"Yes, good sir, that I can,
As well as any other man;
There's a nail, and there's
a prod,
Now, good sir, your horse
is shod."

ONE, TWO, BUCKLE MY SHOE

One, two,
Buckle my shoe;
Three, four,
Knock at the door;
Five, six,
Pick up sticks;
Seven, eight,
Lay them straight;
Nine, ten,
A good, fat hen;
Eleven, twelve,
Dig and delve;
Thirteen, fourteen,
Maids a-courting;
Fifteen, sixteen,
Maids in the kitchen;
Seventeen, eighteen,
Maids a-waiting;
Nineteen, twenty,
My plate's empty.

TWO GRAY KITS

The two gray kits,
And the gray kits' mother,
All went over
The bridge together.

The bridge broke down,
They all fell in;
"May the rats go with you,"
Says Tom Bolin.

Nursery Rhymes
COCK-A-DOODLE-DO!

Cock-a-doodle-do!
My dame has lost her shoe,
My master's lost his fiddle-stick
And knows not what to do.

Cock-a-doodle-do!
What is my dame to do?
Till master finds his fiddle-stick,
She'll dance without her shoe.

PAIRS OR PEARS

Twelve pairs hanging high,
Twelve knights riding by,
Each knight took a pear,
And yet left a dozen there.

BELLEISLE

At the siege of Belleisle
I was there all the while,
All the while, all the while,
At the siege of Belleisle.

OLD KING COLE

Old King Cole
Was a merry old soul,
And a merry old soul was he;
He called for his pipe,
And he called for his bowl,

And he called for his fiddlers three!
And every fiddler, he had a fine fiddle,
And a very fine fiddle had he.
"Twee tweedle dee, tweedle dee," went the fiddlers.
Oh, there's none so rare
As can compare
With King Cole and his fiddlers three.

PUSSY-CAT MEW

Pussy-cat Mew jumped over a coal,
And in her best petticoat burnt a great hole.
Poor Pussy's weeping, she'll have no more milk
Until her best petticoat's mended with silk.

COFFEE AND TEA

Molly, my sister and I fell out,
And what do you think it was all about?
She loved coffee and I loved tea,
And that was the reason we couldn't agree.

Nursery Rhymes
DAPPLE-GRAY

I had a little pony,
His name was Dapple-Gray,
I lent him to a lady,
To ride a mile away.
She whipped him, she slashed him,
She rode him through the mire;
I would not lend my pony now
For all the lady's hire.

DAPPLE-GRAY

FOR BABY

You shall have an apple,
YOU shall have a plum,
You shall have a rattle,
When papa comes home.

A COCK AND BULL STORY

The cock's on the housetop blowing his horn;
The bull's in the barn a-threshing of corn;
The maids in the meadows are making of hay;
The ducks in the river are swimming away.

DREAMS

Friday night's dream, on Saturday told,
Is sure to come true, be it never so old.

MYSELF

As I walked by myself,
And talked to myself,
Myself said unto me:
"Look to thyself,
Take care of thyself,
For nobody cares for thee."

I answered myself,
And said to myself
In the selfsame repartee:
"Look to thyself,
Or not look to thyself,
The selfsame thing will be."

THE LITTLE GIRL WITH A CURL

There was a little girl who had a little curl
Right in the middle of her forehead;
When she was good, she was very, very good,
And when she was bad she was horrid.

FEARS AND TEARS

Tommy's tears and Mary's fears
Will make them old before their years.

THE KILKENNY CATS

There were once two cats of Kilkenny.
Each thought there was one cat too many;
So they fought and they fit,
And they scratched and they bit,
Till, excepting their nails,
And the tips of their tails,
Instead of two cats, there weren't any.

OVER THE WATER

Over the water, and over the sea,
And over the water to Charley,
I'll have none of your nasty beef,
Nor I'll have none of your barley;
But I'll have some of your very best flour
To make a white cake for my Charley.

CANDLE-SAVING

To make your
candles last for aye,
You wives and maids
give ear-O!
To put them out's
the only way,
Says honest John
Boldero.

A WEEK OF BIRTHDAYS

Monday's child is fair of face,
Tuesday's child is full of grace,
Wednesday's child is full of woe,
Thursday's child has far to go,
Friday's child is loving and giving,
Saturday's child works hard for its living,
But the child that's born on the Sabbath day
Is bonny and blithe, and good and gay.

A CHIMNEY

Black within and red without;
Four corners round about.

Nursery Rhymes

LADYBIRD

Ladybird, ladybird, fly away home!
Your house is on fire, your children all gone,
All but one, and her name is Ann,
And she crept under the pudding pan.

LADYBIRD

INTERY, MINTERY

Intery, mintery, cutery corn,
Apple seed and apple thorn;
Wire, brier, limber-lock,
Five geese in a flock,
Sit and sing by a spring,
O-u-t, and in again.

OLD GRIMES

    Old Grimes is dead, that good old man,
        We ne'er shall see him more;
    He used to wear a long brown coat
        All buttoned down before.

THE MAN WHO HAD NAUGHT

    There was a man and he had naught,
        And robbers came to rob him;
    He crept up to the chimney pot,
    And then they thought they had him.

    But he got down on t'other side,
        And then they could not find him;
    He ran fourteen miles in fifteen days,
        And never looked behind him.

THE TAILORS AND THE SNAIL

>Four and Twenty tailors
>Went to kill a snail;
>The best man among them
>Durst not touch her tail;
>She put out her horns
>Like a little Kyloe cow.
>Run, tailors, run, or
>She'll kill you all e'en now.

CAESAR'S SONG

>Bow-wow-wow!
>Whose dog art thou?
>Little Tom Tinker's dog,
>Bow-wow-wow!

AROUND THE GREEN GRAVEL

Around the green gravel the grass grows green,
And all the pretty maids are plain to be seen;
Wash them with milk, and clothe them with silk,
And write their names with a pen and ink.

AS I WAS GOING ALONG

As I was going along, along,
A-singing a comical song, song, song,
The lane that I went was so long, long, long,
And the song that I sang was so long, long, long,
And so I went singing along.

ROCK-A-BYE, BABY

Rock-a-bye, baby, thy cradle is green;
Father's a nobleman, mother's a queen;
And Betty's a lady, and wears a gold ring;
And Johnny's a drummer, and drums for the king.

BILLY, BILLY

"Billy, Billy, come and play,
While the sun shines bright as day."

"Yes, my Polly, so I will,
For I love to please you still."

"Billy, Billy, have you seen
Sam and Betsy on the green?"

"Yes, my Poll, I saw them pass,
Skipping o'er the new-mown grass."

"Billy, Billy, come along,
And I will sing a pretty song."

HECTOR PROTECTOR

Hector Protector was dressed all in green;
Hector Protector was sent to the Queen.
The Queen did not like him,
No more did the King;
So Hector Protector was sent back again.

THE BIRD SCARER

Away, birds, away!
Take a little and leave a little,
And do not come again;
For if you do,
I will shoot you through,
And there will be an end of you.

THE MAN IN THE WILDERNESS

The man in the wilderness
Asked me
How many strawberries
Grew in the sea.
I answered him
As I thought good,
As many as red herrings
Grew in the wood.

MARY, MARY, QUITE CONTRARY

Mary, Mary, quite contrary,
How does your garden grow?
Silver bells and cockle-shells,
And pretty maids all of a row.

LITTLE JACK HORNER

Little Jack Horner
Sat in the corner,
Eating of Christmas pie:
He put in his thumb,
And pulled out a plum,
And said, "What a good boy am I!"

BESSY BELL AND MARY GRAY

Bessy Bell and Mary Gray,
They were two bonny lasses;
They built their house upon the lea,
And covered it with rushes.

Bessy kept the garden gate,
And Mary kept the pantry;
Bessy always had to wait,
While Mary lived in plenty.

Nursery Rhymes
DANCE, THUMBKIN DANCE

Dance, Thumbkin, dance;
(keep the thumb in motion
Dance, ye merrymen, everyone.
(all the fingers in motion
For Thumbkin, he can dance alone,
(the thumb alone moving

Thumbkin, he can dance alone.
(the thumb alone moving
Dance, Foreman, dance,
(the first finger moving
Dance, ye merrymen, everyone.
(all moving
But Foreman, he can dance alone,
(the first finger moving
Foreman, he can dance alone.
(the first finger moving
Dance, Longman, dance,
(the second finger moving
Dance, ye merrymen, everyone.
(all moving
For Longman, he can dance alone,
(the second finger moving
Longman, he can dance alone.
(the second finger moving
Dance, Ringman, dance,
(the third finger moving
Dance, ye merrymen, dance.
(all moving

But Ringman cannot dance alone,
(the third finger moving
Ringman, he cannot dance alone.
(the third finger moving
Dance, Littleman, dance,
(the fourth finger moving
Dance, ye merrymen, dance.
(all moving
But Littleman, he can dance alone,
(the fourth finger moving
Littleman, he can dance alone.
(the fourth finger moving

PUSSY-CAT AND THE DUMPLINGS

Pussy-cat ate the dumplings, the dumplings,
Pussy-cat ate the dumplings.
Mamma stood by, and cried, "Oh, fie!
Why did you eat the dumplings?"

BIRDS OF A FEATHER

Birds of a feather flock together,
And so will pigs and swine;
Rats and mice will have their choice,
And so will I have mine.

NEEDLES AND PINS

Needles and pins, needles and pins,
When a man marries his trouble begins.

Nursery Rhymes
AN ICICLE

Lives in winter,
Dies in summer,
And grows with its roots upward!

TONGS

Long legs, crooked thighs,
Little head, and no eyes.

THE LITTLE BIRD

Once I saw a little bird
Come hop, hop, hop;
So I cried, "Little bird,
Will you stop, stop, stop?"

And was going to the window
To say, "How do you do?"
But he shook his little tail,
And far away he flew.

A STAR

Higher than a house,
higher than a tree.
Oh! whatever can that be?

MARY'S CANARY

Mary had a pretty bird,
Feathers bright and yellow,
Slender legs--upon my word
He was a pretty fellow!

The sweetest note he always sung,
Which much delighted Mary.
She often, where the cage was hung,
Sat hearing her canary.

A SHIP'S NAIL

Over the water,
And under the water,
And always with its head down.

THE GREEDY MAN

The greedy man is he who sits
And bites bits out of plates,
Or else takes up an almanac
And gobbles all the dates.

Nursery Rhymes
THE DUSTY MILLER

Margaret wrote a letter,
Sealed it with her finger,
Threw it in the dam
For the dusty miller.
Dusty was his coat,
Dusty was the siller,
Dusty was the kiss
I'd from the dusty miller.
If I had my pockets
Full of gold and siller,
I would give it all
To my dusty miller.

THE TEN O'CLOCK SCHOLAR

A diller, a dollar, a ten o'clock scholar!
What makes you come so soon?
You used to come at ten o'clock,
But now you come at noon.

WILLY, WILLY

Willy, Willy Wilkin
Kissed the maids a-milking,
Fa, la, la!
And with his merry daffing
He set them all a-laughing,
Ha, ha, ha!

THE TEN O'CLOCK SCHOLAR

COCK-A-DOODLE-DO

Oh, my pretty cock, oh,
my handsome cock,
I pray you, do not crow
before day,
And your comb shall be
made of the very beaten
gold,
And your wings of the
silver so gray.

THE BOY IN THE BARN

A little boy went into
a barn,
And lay down on
some hay.
An owl came out,
and flew about,
And the little boy
ran away.

Nursery Rhymes

THE OLD WOMAN OF LEEDS

There was an old woman of Leeds,
Who spent all her time in good deeds;
She worked for the poor
Till her fingers were sore,
This pious old woman of Leeds!

SUNSHINE

Hick-a-more, Hack-a-more,
On the King's kitchen door,
All the King's horses,
And all the King's men,
Couldn't drive Hick-a-more, Hack-a-more,
Off the King's kitchen door.

MY LITTLE MAID

High diddle doubt, my candle's out
My little maid is not at home;
Saddle my hog and bridle my dog,
And fetch my little maid home.

THE QUARREL

My little old man
and I fell out;
I'll tell you what
'twas all about,--
I had money and he
had none,
And that's the way
the noise begun.

JACK JINGLE

Little Jack Jingle, He
used to live single;
But when he got tired of this kind of life,
He left off being single and lived with his wife.
Now what do you think of little Jack Jingle?
Before he was married he used to live single.

Nursery Rhymes

SHOEING

Shoe the colt,
Shoe the colt,
Shoe the wild mare;
Here a nail,
There a nail,
Yet she goes bare.

FOR WANT OF A NAIL

For want of a nail, the shoe was lost;
For want of the shoe, the horse was lost;
For want of the horse, the rider was lost;
For want of the rider, the battle was lost;
For want of the battle, the kingdom was lost,
And all for the want of a horseshoe nail.

THE PUMPKIN-EATER

PETER, PETER, PUMPKIN-EATER

Peter, Peter, pumpkin-eater,
Had a wife and couldn't keep her;
He put her in a pumpkin shell,
And there he kept her very well.

THAT'S ALL

There was an old woman sat spinning,
And that's the first beginning;

She had a calf,
And that's half;

She took it by the tail,
And threw it over the wall,
And that's all!

DANCE, LITTLE BABY

Dance, little Baby, dance up high!
Never mind, Baby, Mother is by.
Crow and caper, caper and crow,
There, little Baby, there you go!
Up to the ceiling, down to the ground,
Backwards and forwards, round and round;
Dance, little Baby and Mother will sing,
With the merry coral, ding, ding, ding!

Nursery Rhymes

BETTY BLUE

> Little Betty Blue
> Lost her holiday shoe;
> What shall little Betty do?
> Give her another
> To match the other
> And then she'll walk upon two.

BEDTIME

> The Man in the Moon
> looked out of the moon,
> Looked out of the
> moon and said,
> "'Tis time for all
> children, on the earth
> To think about getting
> to bed!"

THE CROOKED SIXPENCE

There was a crooked man, and he went a crooked mile,
He found a crooked sixpence beside a crooked stile;
He bought a crooked cat, which caught a crooked mouse,
And they all lived together in a little crooked house.

PEASE PORRIDGE

Pease porridge hot,
Pease porridge cold,
Pease porridge in the pot,
Nine days old.
Some like it hot,
Some like it cold,
Some like it in the pot,
Nine days old.

Nursery Rhymes

RING A RING O' ROSES

> Ring a ring o' roses,
> A pocketful of posies.
> Tisha! Tisha!
> We all fall down.

THIS IS THE WAY

> This is the way the ladies ride,
> Tri, tre, tre, tree,
> Tri, tre, tre, tree!
> This is the way the ladies ride,
> Tri, tre, tre, tre, tri-tre-tre-tree!
>
> This is the way the gentlemen ride,
> Gallop-a-trot,
> Gallop-a-trot!
> This is the way the gentlemen ride,
> Gallop-a-gallop-a-trot!
>
> This is the way the farmers ride,
> Hobbledy-hoy,
> Hobbledy-hoy!
> This is the way the farmers ride,
> Hobbledy-hobbledy-hoy!

THE DONKEY

> Donkey, donkey, old and gray,
> Ope your mouth and gently bray;
> Lift your ears and blow your horn,
> To wake the world this sleepy morn.

IF

If all the world were apple pie,
And all the sea were ink,
And all the trees were bread and cheese,
What should we have for drink?

DUCKS AND DRAKES

A duck and a drake,
And a halfpenny cake,
With a penny to pay the old baker.
A hop and a scotch
Is another notch,
Slitherum, slatherum, take her.

Nursery Rhymes
LITTLE GIRL AND QUEEN

"Little girl, little girl, where have you been?"
"Gathering roses to give to the Queen."
"Little girl, little girl, what gave she you?"
"She gave me a diamond as big as my shoe."

THE BELLS

"You owe me five shillings,"
Say the bells of St. Helen's.
"When will you pay me?"
Say the bells of Old Bailey.
"When I grow rich,"
Say the bells of Shoreditch.
"When will that be?"
Say the bells of Stepney.
"I do not know,"
Says the great Bell of Bow.
"Two sticks in an apple,"
Ring the bells of Whitechapel.
"Halfpence and farthings,"
Say the bells of St. Martin's.
"Kettles and pans,"
Say the bells of St. Ann's.
"Brickbats and tiles,"
Say the bells of St. Giles.
"Old shoes and slippers,"
Say the bells of St. Peter's.
"Pokers and tongs,"
Say the bells of St. John's.

THE KING OF FRANCE

The King of France went up the hill,
With twenty thousand men;
The King of France came down the hill,
And ne'er went up again.

PETER PIPER

Peter Piper picked a peck of pickled peppers;
A peck of pickled peppers Peter Piper picked.
If Peter Piper picked a peck of pickled peppers,
Where's the peck of pickled peppers Peter Piper picked?

THE TARTS

The Queen of Hearts,
She made some tarts,
All on a summer's day;
The Knave of Hearts,
He stole the tarts,
And took them clean away.

The King of Hearts
Called for the tarts,
And beat the Knave full sore;
The Knave of Hearts
Brought back the tarts,
And vowed he'd steal no more.

THE TARTS

Nursery Rhymes

ONE TO TEN

1, 2, 3, 4, 5!
I caught a hare alive;
6, 7, 8, 9, 10!
I let her go again.

AN EQUAL

Read my riddle, I pray.
What God never sees,
What the king seldom sees,
What we see every day.

WHAT ARE LITTLE BOYS MADE OF?

What are little boys made of, made of?
What are little boys made of?
"Snaps and snails, and puppy-dogs' tails;
And that's what little boys are made of."

What are little girls made of, made of?
What are little girls made of?
"Sugar and spice, and all that's nice;
And that's what little girls are made of."

COME, LET'S TO BED

"To bed! To bed!"
Says Sleepy-head;
"Tarry awhile," says Slow;
"Put on the pan,"
Says Greedy Nan;
"We'll sup before we go."

JENNY WREN

As little Jenny Wren
Was sitting by her shed.
She waggled with her tail,
And nodded with her head.
She waggled with her tail,
And nodded with her head,
As little Jenny Wren
Was sitting by the shed.

LITTLE MAID

"Little maid, pretty maid, whither goest thou?"
"Down in the forest to milk my cow."
"Shall I go with thee?" "No, not now;
When I send for thee, then come thou."

THE GIRL AND THE BIRDS

When I was a little girl, about seven years old,
I hadn't got a petticoat, to cover me from the cold.
So I went into Darlington, that pretty little town,
And there I bought a petticoat, a cloak, and a gown.
I went into the woods and built me a kirk,
And all the birds of the air, they helped me to work.
The hawk with his long claws pulled down the stone,
The dove with her rough bill brought me them home.
The parrot was the clergyman, the peacock was the clerk,
The bullfinch played the organ,--we made merry work.

BANDY LEGS

As I was going to sell my eggs
I met a man with bandy legs,
Bandy legs and crooked toes;
I tripped up his heels, and he fell on his nose.

A PIG

As I went to Bonner,
I met a pig
Without a wig
Upon my word and honor.

LITTLE TOM TUCKER

Little Tom Tucker
Sings for his supper.
What shall he eat?
White bread and butter.
How will he cut it
Without e'er a knife?
How will he be married
Without e'er a wife?

WHERE ARE YOU GOING, MY PRETTY MAID

"Where are you going, my pretty maid?"
"I'm going a-milking, sir," she said.
"May I go with you, my pretty maid?"
"You're kindly welcome, sir," she said.
"What is your father, my pretty maid?"
"My father's a farmer, sir," she said.
"What is your fortune, my pretty maid?"
"My face is my fortune, sir," she said.
"Then I can't marry you, my pretty maid."
"Nobody asked you, sir," she said.

MULTIPLICATION IS VEXATION

Multiplication is vexation,
Division is as bad;
The Rule of Three doth puzzle me,
And Practice drives me mad.

A THORN

I went to the wood and got it;
I sat me down to look for it
And brought it home because I couldn't find it.

LITTLE KING BOGGEN

Little King Boggen, he built a fine hall,
Pie-crust and pastry-crust, that was the wall;
The windows were made of black puddings and white,
And slated with pan-cakes,--you ne'er saw the like!

THE OLD WOMAN OF GLOUCESTER

There was an old woman of Gloucester,
Whose parrot two guineas it cost her,
But its tongue never ceasing,
Was vastly displeasing
To the talkative woman of Gloucester.

BELL HORSES

Bell horses, bell horses, what time of day?
One o'clock, two o'clock, three and away.

WHISTLE

"Whistle, daughter, whistle;
Whistle, daughter dear."
"I cannot whistle, mammy,
I cannot whistle clear."
"Whistle, daughter, whistle;
Whistle for a pound."
"I cannot whistle, mammy,
I cannot make a sound."

Nursery Rhymes
TAFFY

Taffy was a Welshman, Taffy was a thief,
Taffy came to my house and stole a piece of beef;
I went to Taffy's house, Taffy was not home;
Taffy came to my house and stole a marrow-bone.

I went to Taffy's house, Taffy was not in;
Taffy came to my house and stole a silver pin;
I went to Taffy's house, Taffy was in bed,
I took up the marrow-bone and flung it at his head.

THE ROBIN

The north wind doth blow,
And we shall have snow,
And what will poor robin do then,
Poor thing?

He'll sit in a barn,
And keep himself warm,
And hide his head under his wing,
Poor thing!

YOUNG ROGER AND DOLLY

Young Roger came tapping at Dolly's window,
Thumpaty, thumpaty, thump!

He asked for admittance; she answered him "No!"
Frumpaty, frumpaty, frump!

"No, no, Roger, no! as you came you may go!"
Stumpaty, stumpaty, stump!

YOUNG ROGER AND DOLLY

THERE WAS AN OLD WOMAN

There was an old woman who lived in a shoe.
She had so many children she didn't know what to do.
She gave them some broth without any bread.
She whipped them all soundly and put them to bed.

Nursery Rhymes
THE OLD WOMAN OF HARROW

There was an old woman of Harrow,
Who visited in a wheelbarrow;
And her servant before,
Knocked loud at each door,
To announce the old woman of Harrow.

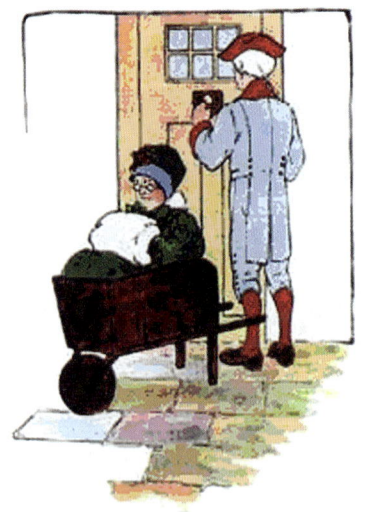

THE PIPER AND HIS COW

There was a piper had a cow,
And he had naught to give her;
He pulled out his pipes and played her a tune,
And bade the cow consider.

The cow considered very well,
And gave the piper a penny,
And bade him play the other tune,
"Corn rigs are bonny."

THE COACHMAN

Up at Piccadilly, oh!
The coachman takes his stand,
And when he meets a pretty girl
He takes her by the hand;
Whip away forever, oh!
Drive away so clever, oh!
All the way to Bristol, oh!
He drives her four-in-hand.

THE MAN OF DERBY

A little old man of Derby,
How do you think he served me?
He took away my bread and cheese,
And that is how he served me.

THE LITTLE MOUSE

I have seen you, little mouse,
Running all about the

house,
Through the hole your little eye
In the wainscot peeping sly,
Hoping soon some crumbs to steal,
To make quite a hearty meal.
Look before you venture out,
See if pussy is about.
If she's gone, you'll quickly run
To the larder for some fun;
Round about the dishes creep,
Taking into each a peep,
To choose the daintiest that's there,
Spoiling things you do not care.

THE LOST SHOE

Doodle doodle doo,
The Princess lost her shoe:
Her Highness hopped,--
The fiddler stopped,
Not knowing what to do.

THE OLD WOMAN OF SURREY

There was an old woman in Surrey,
Who was morn, noon, and night in a hurry;
Called her husband a fool,
Drove the children to school,
The worrying old woman of Surrey.

LONDON BRIDGE

London Bridge is broken down,
Dance over my Lady Lee;
London Bridge is broken down,
With a gay lady.

How shall we build it up again?
Dance over my Lady Lee;
How shall we build it up again?
With a gay lady.

Build it up with silver and gold,
Dance over my Lady Lee;
Build it up with silver and gold,
With a gay lady.

Silver and gold will be stole away,
Dance over my Lady Lee;
Silver and gold will be stole away,
With a gay lady.

Build it up with iron and steel,
Dance over my Lady Lee;
Build it up with iron and steel,
With a gay lady.

Iron and steel will bend and bow,
Dance over my Lady Lee;
Iron and steel will bend and bow,
With a gay lady.

Build it up with wood and clay,
Dance over my Lady Lee;
Build it up with wood and clay,
With a gay lady.

Wood and clay will wash away,
Dance over my Lady Lee;
Wood and clay will wash away,
With a gay lady.

Build it up with stone so strong,
Dance over my Lady Lee;
Huzza! 'twill last for ages long,
With a gay lady.

BOY AND GIRL

There was a little boy and a little girl
Lived in an alley;
Says the little boy to the little girl,
"Shall I, oh, shall I?"
Says the little girl to the little boy,
"What shall we do?"
Says the little boy to the little girl,
"I will kiss you."

MARCH WINDS

March winds and April showers
Bring forth May flowers.

DING, DONG, BELL

Ding, dong, bell,
Pussy's in the well!
Who put her in?
Little Tommy Lin.

Who pulled her out?
Little Johnny Stout.
What a naughty boy
was that,
To try to drown poor
pussy-cat.
Who never did him
any harm,
But killed the mice in his father's barn!

WHEN

When I was a bachelor
I lived by myself;
And all the bread and cheese I got
I laid up on the shelf.

The rats and the mice
They made such a strife,
I was forced to go to London
To buy me a wife.

Nursery Rhymes

The streets were so bad,
And the lanes were so narrow,
I was forced to bring my wife home
In a wheelbarrow.

The wheelbarrow broke,
And my wife had a fall;
Down came wheelbarrow,
Little wife and all.

SING, SING

Sing, sing, what shall I sing?
Cat's run away with the pudding-string!
Do, do, what shall I do?
The cat has bitten it quite in two.

A CHERRY

As I went through the garden gap,
Who should I meet but Dick Red-cap!
A stick in his hand, a stone in his throat,--
If you'll tell me this riddle, I'll give you a groat.

HOT-CROSS BUNS

Hot-cross Buns!
Hot-cross Buns!
One a penny, two a penny,
Hot-cross Buns!

Hot-cross Buns!
Hot-cross Buns!
If ye have no daughters,
Give them to your sons.

THREE STRAWS

Three straws on a staff
Would make a baby cry and laugh.

HOT CODLINS

There was a little woman,
as I've been told,
Who was not very young,
nor yet very old;
Now this little woman her
living got
By selling codlins, hot,
hot, hot!

THE BALLOON

"What is the news of the day,
Good neighbor, I pray?"
"They say the balloon
Is gone up to the moon!"

SWAN

Swan, swan, over the sea;
Swim, swan, swim!
Swan, swan, back again;
Well swum, swan!

THE MAN OF TOBAGO

There was an old man of Tobago
Who lived on rice, gruel, and sago,
Till much to his bliss,
His physician said this:
"To a leg, sir, of mutton, you may go."

A SUNSHINY SHOWER

A sunshiny shower
Won't last half an hour.

THE FARMER AND THE RAVEN

A farmer went trotting upon his gray mare,
Bumpety, bumpety, bump!
With his daughter behind him so rosy and fair,
Lumpety, lumpety, lump!

A raven cried croak! and they all tumbled down,
Bumpety, bumpety, bump!
The mare broke her knees, and the farmer his crown,
Lumpety, lumpety, lump!

The mischievous raven flew laughing away,
Bumpety, bumpety, bump!
And vowed he would serve them the same the next day,
Lumpety, lumpety lump!

Nursery Rhymes

CHRISTMAS

Christmas is coming, the geese are getting fat,
Please to put a penny in an old man's hat;
If you haven't got a penny a ha'penny will do,
If you haven't got a ha'penny, God bless you.

THE DEATH AND BURIAL OF POOR COCK ROBIN

Who killed Cock Robin?
"I," said the sparrow,
"With my little bow and arrow,
I killed Cock Robin."

Who saw him die?
"I," said the fly,
"With my little eye,
I saw him die."

Who caught his blood?

"I," said the fish,
"With my little dish,
I caught his blood."

Who'll make his shroud?
"I," said the beetle,
"With my thread and needle.
I'll make his shroud."

Who'll carry the torch?
"I," said the linnet,
"I'll come in a minute,
I'll carry the torch."

Who'll be the clerk?
"I," said the lark,
"If it's not in the dark,
I'll be the clerk."

Who'll dig his grave?
"I," said the owl,
"With my spade and trowel
I'll dig his grave."

Who'll be the parson?
"I," said the rook,
"With my little book,
I'll be the parson."

Who'll be chief mourner?
"I," said the dove,
"I mourn for my love,
I'll be chief mourner."

Who'll sing a psalm?
"I," said the thrush,

Nursery Rhymes

"As I sit in a bush.
I'll sing a psalm."

Who'll carry the coffin?
"I," said the kite,
"If it's not in the night,
I'll carry the coffin."

Who'll toll the bell?
"I," said the bull,
"Because I can pull,
I'll toll the bell."

All the birds of the air
Fell sighing and sobbing,
When they heard the bell toll
For poor Cock Robin.

WILLY BOY

"Willy boy, Willy boy,
where are you going?
I will go with you, if that I
may."
"I'm going to the meadow
to see them a-mowing,
I'm going to help them to
make the hay."

POLLY AND SUKEY

Polly, put the kettle on,
Polly, put the kettle on,
Polly, put the kettle on,
And let's drink tea.

Sukey, take it off again,
Sukey, take it off again,
Sukey, take it off again,
They're all gone away.

PUSSY-CAT BY THE FIRE

Pussy-cat sits by the fire;
How can she be fair?
In walks the little dog;
Says: "Pussy, are you there?
How do you do, Mistress Pussy?
Mistress Pussy, how d'ye do?"
"I thank you kindly, little dog,
I fare as well as you!"

THE MOUSE AND THE CLOCK

Hickory, dickory, dock!
The mouse ran up the clock;
The clock struck one,
And down he run,
Hickory, dickory, dock!

BOBBY SHAFTOE

Bobby Shaftoe's gone to sea,
With silver buckles on his knee:
He'll come back and marry me,
Pretty Bobby Shaftoe!
Bobby Shaftoe's fat and fair,
Combing down his yellow hair;
He's my love for evermore,
Pretty Bobby Shaftoe.

THE BUNCH OF BLUE RIBBONS

Oh, dear, what can the matter be?
Oh, dear, what can the matter be?
Oh, dear, what can the matter be?
Johnny's so long at the fair.

He promised he'd buy me a bunch of blue ribbons,
He promised he'd buy me a bunch of blue rib-

bons,
He promised he'd buy me a bunch of blue ribbons,
To tie up my bonny brown hair.

THE WOMAN OF EXETER

There dwelt an old woman at Exeter;
When visitors came it sore vexed her,
So for fear they should eat,
She locked up all her meat,
This stingy old woman of Exeter.

SNEEZING

If you sneeze on Monday, you sneeze for danger;
Sneeze on a Tuesday, kiss a stranger;
Sneeze on a Wednesday, sneeze for a letter;
Sneeze on a Thursday, something better.
Sneeze on a Friday, sneeze for sorrow;
Sneeze on a Saturday, joy to-morrow.

WHEN THE SNOW IS ON THE GROUND

The little robin grieves
When the snow is on the ground,

Nursery Rhymes

    For the trees have no leaves,
    And no berries can be found.

The air is cold, the worms are hid;
    For robin here what can be done?
Let's strow around some crumbs of bread,
    And then he'll live till snow is gone.

Animal Children

Sometimes I am so sorry
that my papa is a king,
It's really most annoying
and hurts like everything
To have the little girls and boys
all want to run away,
For if I am a Lion prince,
I'm a baby, anyway!

Nursery Rhymes

Some jungle boys,
by mischief made quite bold,
Once took the baby Tiger, so we're told,
And in broad stripes
they smeared his coat so fine,
And 'round his neck
they hung a "Fresh Paint" sign.

This monkey thought the Leopard's spots
Were pasted on for polka-dots,
He asked her how much it would cost
New ones to buy if those were lost.

Nursery Rhymes

In her red and white gown
Miss Weasel's so pert
We are very afraid she's a gay little flirt;
She is fearful of no one—beast, reptile or man,
Just winks and cries gaily:
"Catch me, if you can."

This dapper young chappy is Dude Ocelot,
With coat trimmed in many a dash and a spot;
He's graceful and elegant, sly, too, as well,
Just what he'll do next no one ever can tell.

Nursery Rhymes

The chetah is a great big cat
But very quick, for all of that,
She's cunning but she's gentle, too,
And if you're good she's good to you.

The little Bobcat and Canadian Lynx
Just must be related (so everyone thinks).
Except for their ears they're alike as two pins,
And look every whit as if they were twins.

Nursery Rhymes

A dainty, fastidious man is Lord Otter
Who can live just as well on land as in water,
He'll eat but the flakiest part of a fish,
And this he considers his favorite dish.

"It really is a bother to be sought by everyone"
The vain young Ermine boasted.
"Why, it keeps me on the run
To get away from kings and queens
and peers and ladies great—
It truly gets me all fussed up
and in a dreadful state."

Nursery Rhymes

Young ferret, detective, said:
"I'll show you where
To track the bold rabbit right into his lair."
Then he never saw bunny right under his eyes,
But went swaggering off
looking wondrously wise.

"Now, Johnnie, my child,"
said wise Mamma Sable,
"When you see a trap run as fast as you're able,
Or else, ere you know it, your skin will be gone
   As a beautiful fur for some lady to don."

Nursery Rhymes

Mother opossum says she'd like to ask
Just why other mothers should find it a task
To care for one baby. Why, here she has four,
And there's plenty of room
on her tail for some more!

Mr. and Mrs. Mongoose are popular as can be,
The reason being very plain,
as you will all agree,
They are cunning and affectionate
and clean and very nice,
They kill all snakes and insects
and naughty rats and mice.

Nursery Rhymes

It must be very easy
for the busy Beaver mother
To feed the Beaver sister
and her little Beaver brother,
For when they beg: "We're hungry, give us something to eat, please!"
She sends them off to nibble
at the bark of the big trees.

The puma is a bandit
who'll not meet you face to face
But waits to spring upon you
from some well-hidden place.
He'll strike you when your back is turned,
but away he's sure to fly
If you should turn to look him
right squarely in the eye.

Nursery Rhymes

Lemur stays in bed all day
And waits until the night to play;
That's why his soft feet make no sound
And why his eyes are big and round.

The bowery boy of the woods is young Mink,
His coat is so lovely one never would think
That'd he do naughty things,
but we've often been told
He is tricky and wicked and saucy and bold.

Nursery Rhymes

"I'm not so very big around
and not great as to length,
But one thing Peccaries have learned—
in numbers there is strength.
Now, if you do not bother me
I will not bother you,
But all my friends and family
will help me if you do."

who is this boy in clothes so neat?
Young Spring-bok, Africa's athlete.
He lives up in the mountains tall,
And as a jumper beats them all.

Nursery Rhymes

The Long-Eared Bat and the Flying Fox
and the Flying Squirrel, too,
Decided to give an aero-meet
just to show what they could do.
So they formed a club and went around
and invited everyone,
Then up they flew and did their stunts,
and had a lot of fun.

She is dainty as snowdrops
that fall from the skies,
Is this dear little Kitten with bright, shiny eyes
And velvety ears and pretty pink nose
And lovely white suit of soft, furry clothes.

Nursery Rhymes

Baby raccoon takes all his food
and goes straight to the pool,
He eats not one small bite of it
until it's wet and cool.
Now, although you may think this strange
and stop to wonder why,
He, no doubt, thinks it just as queer
for you to like yours dry.

The greatest of travelers that one can meet
Is the little Deer-mouse
with the pretty white feet;
North, south, east or west
she will go at her will,
And never, no never, is known to keep still.

Nursery Rhymes

The baby zebra ne'er should roam
So very far away from home,
Lest someone, thinking her striped gown
Was candy-stick, might eat her down.

The Giant Book of Bedtime Stories

"I'm stopping for a moment
just to say 'How-do-you-do?'
I've just been decorated
with this ribbon of deep blue
Because of all the gracefulness
with which I trot and prance—
No wonder that you give Sir Horse
your most admiring glance!"

Nursery Rhymes

This tale is not so very new,
And, no doubt, has been told to you,
But Donkey went to school to play,
And now he sits dressed up this way.

Here is the only baby
who never makes a noise
(Which must be very puzzling
to little girls and boys).
Yet the Giraffe is happy
'though he cannot shout or sing,
For with that great long neck of his
he can reach anything.

Nursery Rhymes

The tapir feeds on leaves and fruit
He's very, very hard to suit,
For boys who don't like bread and meat
Have to find other things to eat.

The Giant Book of Bedtime Stories

He has climbed to the top of a rocky throne
To look down on a land
once so proudly his own,
His people are scattered, he has no place to go,
He is weary and sad, poor King Buffalo.

Nursery Rhymes

"Lemonade, lemonade," the bold monkey cried,
"It's only five cents, and it's cooling beside."
Miss Camel just sniffed
and tossed high her head,—
"I drink only every nine days, sir," she said.

The Giant Book of Bedtime Stories

Milk or meat or leather for shoes,—
Almost anything that we choose,—
We'll find the good Cow gives with joy
To every nice little girl and boy.

Nursery Rhymes

I wonder where the names come from
(I'm sure that you do, too).
For instance, there's the animal
that has been called the Gnu.
His race is just as strange, too,
for no one seems to know
Just what he is—an antelope,
horse, bull or buffalo.

Big moose came boldly from behind
the tall trees,
And said in loud voice: "Who called,
if you please?
I'm ready to meet any one
who says 'Fight,'
But we'll come in the open
and do the thing right."

Nursery Rhymes

I am not sure I'd care to meet
This Big Horn Goat upon the street.
Not when his eyes and smile and air
Just seem to shout: "Come, if you dare!'

Brave soldier ibex stalks before
the mountain fortress high,
And watches eagerly to note
a stranger passing by.
"Who's there?" he calls, and to his friends
he whistles the alarm,
And off they go to mountain tops
where they are safe from harm.

Nursery Rhymes

The chamois lives in the mountains high,
He's ever and ever and ever so spry;
He leaps and he plays with never a fall—
I'm sure that you never could do that at all.

Billy Goat and Nanny Goat
went out one day to tea.
They promised Mother Goat they'd be
good as they could be,
But on the way they passed some goats
who cried: "Oh, see the dude!"
And then they had to go back home
for Billy got real rude.

Nursery Rhymes

Her coat is soft as velvet,
of a lovely yellow-brown,
With a bit of fawn for trimming
and a lining white as down.
Her eyes are large and kindly,
she is gentle, too, as well,
You would love a little playmate
as sweet as Miss Gazelle.

A sturdy young American
is Rocky Mountain Goat
With big, strong horns upon his head,
and shaggy, furry coat;
He loves to scramble over rocks
or leap a mountain brook,
And should you chase him he will fly
into his hidden nook.

Nursery Rhymes

"We reindeer come straight from your own Santa Claus,
In our gallop of joy we never will pause;
We eat from the mountain-tops,
drink from the dells,
And use for our skipping-ropes
merry sleigh-bells."

A large and handsome personage
is the Most Noble Yak,
His mantle is a fringe of hair
that drapes his sides and back;
He's very, very grand, indeed,
when he stands up, you see—
In fact, he's just as noble as
a noble ought to be.

Nursery Rhymes

When young Mrs. Kangaroo goes for a hop,
To call or to market or, perhaps, out to shop,
She has no nice carriage where baby can ride,
So he creeps in a pocket that hangs at her side.

He does not care when the sleet comes down, or
the chilly wind blows strong,
For he wears a hat that is made of horn
and a fur coat, warm and long.
He never gets frostbitten toes
'though in snow and ice he plays;
Now being a Muskox can't be bad
in the long, cold winter days!

Nursery Rhymes

"The very best I have, sir, fine
and a whole yard wide,
It wears, and has no bother
of a right and wrong side;
I'm sure she'd like a dress of it—
it will not spot or pull."
Then Miss Alpaca added:
"I know—it's my own wool."

This dear little Sheep has lost Bo-Peep,
She wandered away as he lay asleep,
He has found her bonnet and shepherd's crook,
But for little Bo-Peep in vain does he look.

Nursery Rhymes

Young Miss Rhinoceros gave a beach party;
She greeted her friends
with a welcome most hearty.
They laughed and they joked
and they swam in the sea,
And the party was gay, as a party should be.

She comes from Spain,
this proud, proud Dame,
Mistress Merino is her name.
Her wool weaves into dress goods rare,
Her skin makes gloves the ladies wear.

Nursery Rhymes

Merry guinea pigs one day
Went out in the fields to play.
Daisy smiled and wished that they
Would never, never go away.

The Giant Book of Bedtime Stories

Here is a Sister Piggy and a Brother Piggy, too,
The story they are telling here
would not apply to you,
For selfish little sisters
who make their brothers cry
Do not belong in houses but
with piggies in the sty.

Nursery Rhymes

Now here's a little lady
who seems a wee bit shy,
Or is it that a teardrop
is trembling in her eye?
Well, I am sure that you or I
would make an awful fuss
If we should have to have her name—
"Miss Hippopotamus."

In animal land, as everywhere,
there lives a Mr. Boar
Who never is contented
unless he holds the floor;
His fellows all may frown at him
but he cannot refrain
From pushing into everything—
he's so selfish and so vain.

Nursery Rhymes

Mother and father and little Miss Bear
Went out for a walk and a bit of fresh air,
Not through the dark woods
(the old tale to repeat)
But in their best clothes,
right down the front street.

When little Miss Polar Bear goes out to skate,
She never is bothered by having to wait
Until mother wraps her all snugly in fur,
For those are the clothes
that she carries with her!

Nursery Rhymes

Just look about and see if you
Can find a friend who's quite as true
As this old Doggie that you see
A-smiling here at you and me.

The Giant Book of Bedtime Stories

I'm just a little Puppy and good as good can be,
And why they call me naughty,
I'm sure I cannot see,
I've only carried off one shoe and torn
the baby's hat
And chased the ducks and spilled the milk—
there's nothing bad in that!

Nursery Rhymes

The mandrill looks so very queer
I'm glad he lives way off from here;
He's purple, blue, red, black and brown,
I'm sure he is the jungle clown.

The baby gorilla, of the family called Ape,
Is very like you in size and in shape,
But he lives in the jungle
with black hair for clothes
And he gets very naughty the older he grows.

Nursery Rhymes

This cute little brother and sister you see
Seated cosily high on the limb of a tree
Are the Marmoset twins,
whose appealing round eyes
Look from flower-like faces
in wond'ring surprise.

"I've climbed up here to smile at you
and, oh, what do you think?
I've scattered master's papers
and upset all of his ink,
But then if little Monkeys
always were so very good
They'd not be little monkeys who
just can't act as they should."

Nursery Rhymes

He is so very lazy that he is even loath
To walk upon his own feet—
this funny boy named Sloth.
He swings upon the branches
from morning until night,
And eats the leaves about him
with laziest delight.

He works on tunnels night and day,
This Marmot boy from far away.
When winter comes then in he creeps,
And there until the spring he sleeps.

Nursery Rhymes

The woodchuck resides in a hole in the ground,
He is surly and cross, and he never is found
Out in the bright sunlight unless it's to see
If he can't make more winter
for you and for me.

This naughty boy just eats and eats
until he is a sight,
He eats until he cannot hold another tiny bite.
Of course, he's just an animal—
they call him Wolverine—
But does he make you think of boys
that you have ever seen?

Nursery Rhymes

Old Mr. Walrus climbs out of the deep
For a breath of air and an hour of sleep.
You will note that he isn't much on looks
But his skin we make into pocket-books.

He sits on the top of a gay wooden stand,
He stands on his head or he shakes your hand,
He dances a jig or he trumps a chant—
This jolly old circus Elephant.

Nursery Rhymes

Naughty, naughty Squirrel baby,
just as mother has you dressed
In your ribbons and your laces
and your go-to-meeting best,
Then to run and grab an apple
and get yourself all mussed!
Are you not afraid that mother
will be very, very fussed?

To market, to market, with baskets of eggs,
Jack Rabbit goes hurrying on his long legs;
He'll buy him some colors—
red, green, yellow, blue,
And when Easter comes 'round
you know what he'll do.

Nursery Rhymes

Chipmunk is a jolly lad,
Always friendly—never sad,
Shares with friends his wheat grains yellow,
He's a genuine good fellow.

The coney lives in Palestine
But he is very seldom seen.
You see he is so small and shy
He hides when folks are passing by.

Nursery Rhymes

They call this boy the Coati,
His name is strange, and so is he.
He laps to drink, digs with his snout.
On ground or trees he runs about.

The cute little dogs that live on the prairie
Were having a party and making quite merry,
When Big Dog, on watch,
heard a noise and called "Hush!"
And into their holes went the guests in a rush!

Nursery Rhymes

What do you suppose is in Gray Wolf's pack
He carries so stealthily over his back?
Some chickens, a lamb and an old mother hen
He has stolen to hide away in his den.

His manners are so charming
and his eyes so very bright,
I do believe that we might call
young Fox a gallant knight;
But then when he is cunning
and just a little pert,
I'm not so sure but we should call
this same young fox a flirt.

Nursery Rhymes

We just want to ask if you ever have seen a
Much dirtier boy than this little Hyena?
He has played in the street at making mud pies
Till nothing is clean save the whites of his eyes.

Beau coyote sings a nightly tune
To his lady fair in the big, round moon.
She smiles and throws moonbeams to him
And he serenades till her light is dim.

Nursery Rhymes

Tommie and Tillie Badger
went out in the field to play.
Said Tommie: "Here, I'll teach you—
put down your head this way,
Then toss your heels into the air
and give a little twirl—
You can't help turning somersaults
although you are a girl."

Miss Leopard Spermophilus,
with her high-sounding name,
Says just to be called "Gopher"
is really a shame,
And she's right here to tell you—
if this knowledge you should lack—
She's the only one who wears
the stars and stripes upon her back.

Nursery Rhymes

Doggy barked and said: "What fun
To make that Porcupine girl run;
Girls for boys to tease were meant."—
But girls with pins are different.

Sir Knight Armadillo, from tail tip to nose
In armor that's sure to bring terror to foes,
Goes forth with his weapons
to his battle ground,
And looks like a pineapple walking around.

Nursery Rhymes

Away in Australia the Echidna stays.
He is noted because of his strange little ways;
His claws are so sharp
that in manner quite tragic,
When frightened he sinks in
the ground as by magic.

Miss Ant Eater's mouth is so dreadfully small
It scarce seems it could be a real mouth at all,
And her long, furry tail is her blanket at night,
It covers and tucks her in all snug and tight.

Nursery Rhymes

This queer little Mole has a star for a nose
Just the shade of the pink in a dew-wet rose.
He lives down in the ground
where 'tis always like night,
So perhaps his star nose is to twinkle for light.

Here we have Mr. Duckbill of no little fame;
His mouth, you will see,
is what gives him his name.
He can walk, swim or burrow
and (so we have heard)
His wife, Mrs. Duckbill, lays eggs like a bird.

Nursery Rhymes

Such a dainty little person
in her coat of pale, clear gray,
Is this maiden, Miss Chinchilla,
and the hunter-folks all say
She is so clean she's exquisite
and never dreams of harm
When they go to take her silken fur
which helps to keep her warm.

The circus fat lady is big Mrs. Whale
With her very large head and her very long tail,
And her ears and her eyes
almost covered from sight
In the folds of thick skin
that wraps her up tight.

Nursery Rhymes

The Giant Book of Bedtime
Stories

LITTLE RED RIDING HOOD

There was once a sweet little maid who lived with her father and mother in a pretty little cottage at the edge of the village. At the further end of the wood was another pretty cottage and in it lived her grandmother.
    Everybody loved this little girl, her grandmother perhaps loved her most of all and gave her a great many pretty things. Once she gave her a red cloak with a hood which she always wore, so people called her Little Red Riding Hood.

Stories

One morning Little Red Riding Hood's mother said, "Put on your things and go to see your grandmother. She has been ill; take along this basket for her. I have put in it eggs, butter and cake, and other dainties."

It was a bright and sunny morning. Red Riding Hood was so happy that at first she wanted to dance through the wood. All around her grew pretty wild flowers which she loved so well and she stopped to pick a bunch for her grandmother.

Little Red Riding Hood wandered from her path and was stooping to pick a flower when from behind her a gruff voice said, "Good morning, Little Red Riding Hood." Little Red Riding Hood turned around and saw a great big wolf, but Little Red Riding Hood did not know what a wicked beast the wolf was, so she was not afraid.

"What have you in that basket, Little Red Riding Hood?"

"Eggs and butter and cake, Mr. Wolf."

"Where are you going with them, Little Red Riding Hood?"

"I am going to my grandmother, who is ill, Mr. Wolf."

"Where does your grandmother live, Little Red Riding Hood?"

"Along that path, past the wild rose bushes, then through the gate at the end of the wood, Mr. Wolf."

Then Mr. Wolf again said "Good morning" and set off, and Little Red Riding Hood again went in search of wild flowers.

At last he reached the porch covered with flowers and knocked at the door of the cottage.

"Who is there?" called the grandmother.

"Little Red Riding Hood," said the wicked wolf.

"Press the latch, open the door, and walk in," said the grandmother.

The wolf pressed the latch, and walked in where the grandmother lay in bed. He made one jump at her, but she jumped out of bed into a closet. Then the wolf put on the cap which she had dropped and crept under the bedclothes.

In a short while Little Red Riding Hood knocked at the door, and walked in, saying, "Good morning, Grandmother, I have brought you eggs, butter and cake, and here is a bunch of flowers I gathered in the wood." As she came nearer the bed she said, "What big ears you have, Grandmother."

"All the better to hear you with, my dear."

"What big eyes you have, Grandmother."

"All the better to see you with, my dear."

"But, Grandmother, what a big nose you have."

"All the better to smell with, my dear."

"But, Grandmother, what a big mouth you have."

"All the better to eat you up with, my dear," he said as he sprang at Little Red Riding Hood.

Just at that moment Little Red Riding Hood's father was passing the cottage and heard her scream. He rushed in and with his axe chopped off Mr. Wolf's head.

Everybody was happy that Little Red Riding Hood had escaped the wolf. Then Little Red Riding Hood's father carried her home and they lived happily ever after.

THE GOOSE-GIRL

There was once an old Queen who had a very beautiful daughter. The time came when the maiden was to go into a distant country to be married. The old Queen packed up everything suitable to a royal outfit.

She also sent a Waiting-woman with her. When the hour of departure came they bade each other a sorrowful farewell

221

and set out for the bridegroom's country.

When they had ridden for a time the Princess became very thirsty, and said to the Waiting-woman, "Go down and fetch me some water in my cup from the stream. I must have something to drink."
"If you are thirsty," said the Waiting-woman, "dismount yourself, lie down by the water and drink. I don't choose to be your servant."

Being very thirsty, the Princess dismounted, and knelt by the flowing water.

Now, when she was about to mount her horse again, the Waiting-woman said, "By rights your horse belongs to me; this jade will do for you!"

The poor little Princess was obliged to give way. Then the Waiting-woman, in a harsh voice, ordered her to take off her royal robes, and to put on her own mean garments. Finally she forced her to swear that she would not tell a person at the

Court what had taken place. Had she not taken the oath she would have been killed on the spot.

There was great rejoicing when they arrived at the castle. The Prince hurried towards them, and lifted the Waiting-woman from her horse, thinking she was his bride. She was led upstairs, but the real Princess had to stay below.

The old King looked out of the window and saw the delicate, pretty little creature standing in the courtyard; so he asked the bride about her companion.

"I picked her up on the way, and brought her with me for company. Give the girl something to do to keep her from idling."

The old King said, "I have a little lad who looks after the geese; she may help him."

The boy was called little Conrad, and the real bride was sent with him to look after the geese. When they reached the meadow, the Princess sat down on the grass and let down her hair, and when Conrad saw it he was so delighted that he wanted to pluck some out; but she said—

"Blow, blow, little breeze,
And Conrad's hat seize.
Let him join in the chase
While away it is whirled,
Till my tresses are curled
And I rest in my place."

Then a strong wind sprang up, which blew away Conrad's hat right over the fields, and he had to run after it. When he came back her hair was all put up again.

When they got home Conrad went to the King and said, "I won't tend the geese with that maiden again."

"Why not?" asked the King.

Then Conrad went on to tell the King all that had happened in the field. The King ordered Conrad to go next day as usual and he followed into the field and hid behind a bush. He saw it happen just as Conrad had told him. Thereupon he went away unnoticed; and in the evening, when the Goose-girl came home, he asked her why she did all these things.

"That I may not tell you," she answered.

Then he said, "If you won't tell me, then tell the iron stove there;" and he went away.

She crept up to the stove and unburdened her heart to it. The King stood outside by the pipes of the stove and heard all she said. Then he came back, and caused royal robes to be put upon her, and her beauty was a marvel. Then he called his son and told him that he had a false bride, but that the true bride was here.

The Prince was charmed with her beauty and a great banquet was prepared. The bridegroom sat at the head of the table, with the Princess on one side and the Waiting-woman at the other; but she did not recognize the Princess.

When they had eaten, the King put a riddle to the Waiting-woman. "What does a person deserve that deceives his master?"

The false bride answered, "He must be put into a barrel and dragged along by two white horses till he is dead."

"That is your doom," said the King, "and the judgment shall be carried out."

When the sentence was fulfilled, the young Prince married his true bride, and they lived together in peace and happiness.

THE SLEEPING BEAUTY

Once upon a time there was a king and queen who for a very long time had no children, and when at length a little daughter was born to them they were so pleased that they gave a christening feast to which they invited a number of fairies. But, unfortunately, they left out one rather cross old fairy, and she was so angry that she said the princess should die when she reached the age of sixteen, by pricking her hand with a spindle.

All the other fairies present, except one, had already given the princess their beautiful gifts, and this last one said she could not prevent part of the wicked wish coming true; but her gift should be that the princess should not really die, but only fall into a deep sleep, which should last for a hundred years, and at the end of that time she should be awakened by a king's son.

It all happened as the fairies had predicted. When the princess was sixteen years old she saw an old woman spinning and took the spindle from her to try this strange new work. Instantly she pricked her hand and fell into a deep sleep, as did everyone else in the palace. There she lay in a bower of roses, year after year, and the hedge around the palace garden grew so tall and thick that at last you could not have told that there was a castle at all.

At the end of the hundred years a king's son heard of the castle and the enchanted princess who lay asleep there and determined to rescue her. So he cut his way through the thick prickly hedge and at length he came to the princess.

When he saw how lovely and how sweet she looked he fell in love with her and, stooping, kissed her lips.

At once she awoke and with her the king and queen and all the courtiers, who had fallen asleep at the same time.

As the princess was as much taken with the prince's appearance as he was with hers, they decided to be married. And so the wedding was celebrated the same day with great pomp and ceremony.

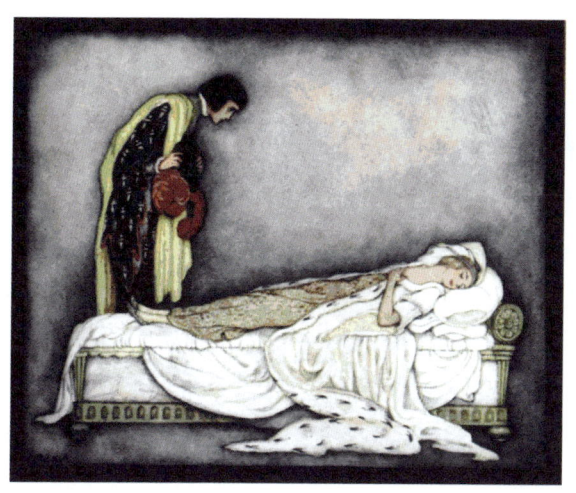

SNOWDROP AND SEVEN LITTLE DWARFS

Once upon a time there was a little princess called Snowdrop, who had a cruel stepmother who was jealous of her. The Queen had a magic mirror, which could speak to her, and when she looked into it and asked who was the fairest lady in

the land the mirror told her she was, for she was very beautiful; but as Snowdrop grew up she became still more lovely than her stepmother and the mirror did not fail to tell the Queen this.

So she ordered one of her huntsmen to take Snowdrop away and kill her; but he was too tender-hearted to do this and left the maiden in the wood and went home again. Snowdrop wandered about until she came to the house of seven little dwarfs, and they were so kind as to take her in and let her live with them. She used to make their seven little beds, and prepare the meals for the seven little men, and they were all quite happy until the Queen found out from her mirror that Snowdrop was alive still, for, as it always told the truth, it still told her Snowdrop was the fairest lady in the land.

She decided that Snowdrop must die, so she dyed her face and dressed up like an old peddler,  and in this disguise she went to the home of the seven Dwarfs and called out, "Laces for sale."

Snowdrop peeped out of the window and said, "Good-day, mother; what have you to sell?"

"Good laces, fine laces, laces of every color," and she held out one that was made of gay silk.

Snowdrop opened the door and bought the pretty lace.

"Child," said the old woman, "you are a sight, let me lace you properly for once."

Snowdrop placed herself before the old woman, who laced her so quickly and so tightly that she took away Snowdrop's breath and she fell down as though dead.

235

Not long after the seven dwarfs came home they found that she was laced too tight and cut the lace, whereupon Snowdrop began to breathe and soon came back to life again.

When the Queen got home and found by asking her mirror that Snowdrop was still alive, she planned to make an end of her for good, so she made a poisoned comb and disguised herself to look like a different old woman.

She journeyed to the dwarfs' home and induced Snowdrop to let her comb her hair. The minute she put the poisoned comb in her hair Snowdrop fell down as though dead.

When the seven dwarfs came home they found their poor Snowdrop on the floor, and suspecting the bad Queen began to look for the cause, soon finding the comb. No sooner had they removed it than Snowdrop came to life again.

Upon the Queen's return home she found by asking her mirror that Snowdrop still lived, so she disguised herself a third time and came to the dwarfs' little house and gave Snowdrop a poisoned apple. As soon as the little princess took a bite it stuck in her throat and choked her.

Oh! how grieved were the good little dwarfs. They made a fine glass coffin, and put Snowdrop into it and were carrying her away to bury her when they met a prince, who fell in love with the little dead maiden, and begged the dwarfs to give her to him.

The dwarfs were so sorry for him they consented, and the prince's servants were about to carry the coffin away when they stumbled and fell over the root of a tree. Snowdrop received such a violent jerk that the poisonous apple was jerked right out of her throat and she sat up alive and well again.

Of course she married the prince, and she, her husband and the good little dwarfs lived happily ever after, but the cruel step-mother came to a bad end, and no one was even sorry for her.

CINDERELLA, OR THE LITTLE GLASS SLIPPER

Once upon a time there was a gentleman who married, for his second wife, the proudest and most haughty woman that ever was seen. She had two daughters of her own, who were, indeed, exactly like her in all things. The gentleman had also a young daughter, of rare goodness and sweetness of temper, which she took from her mother, who was the best creature in the world.

The wedding was scarcely over, when the stepmother's bad temper began to show itself. She could not bear the goodness of this young girl, because it made her own daughters appear the more odious. The stepmother gave her the meanest work in the house to do; she had to scour the dishes, tables, etc., and to scrub the floors and clean out the bedrooms. The poor girl had to sleep in the garret, upon a wretched straw bed, while her sisters lay in fine rooms with inlaid floors, upon beds of the very newest fashion, and where they had looking-glasses so large that they [Pg 2]might see themselves at their full length. The poor girl bore all patiently, and dared not complain to her father, who would have scolded her if she had done so, for his wife governed him entirely.

When she had done her work, she used to go into the chimney corner, and sit down among the cinders, hence she was called Cinderwench. The younger sister of the two, who was not so rude and uncivil as the elder, called her Cinderella. However, Cinderella, in spite of her mean apparel, was a hundred times more handsome than her sisters, though they were always richly dressed.

It happened that the King's son gave a ball, and invited to it all persons of fashion. Our young misses were also invited, for they cut a very grand figure among the people of the country-side. They were highly delighted with the invitation, and wonderfully busy in choosing the gowns, petticoats, and head-dresses which might best become them. This made Cinderella's lot still harder, for it was she who ironed her sisters' linen and plaited their ruffles. They talked all day long of nothing but how they should be dressed.

"For my part," said the elder, "I will wear my red velvet suit with French trimmings."

"And I," said the younger, "shall wear my usual skirt; but then, to make amends for that [Pg 3]I will put on my gold-flowered mantle, and my diamond stomacher, which is far from being the most ordinary one in the world." They sent for the best hairdressers they could get to make up their hair in fashionable style, and bought patches for their cheeks. Cinderella was consulted in all these matters, for she had good taste. She advised them always for the best, and even offered her services to dress their hair, which they were very willing she should do.

As she was doing this, they said to her:—

241

"Cinderella, would you not be glad to go to the ball?"

"Young ladies," she said, "you only jeer at me; it is not for such as I am to go there."

"You are right," they replied; "people would laugh to see a Cinderwench at a ball."

Any one but Cinderella would have dressed their hair awry, but she was good-natured, and arranged it perfectly well. They were almost two days without eating, so much were they transported with joy. They broke above a dozen laces in trying to lace themselves tight, that they might have a fine, slender shape, and they were continually at their looking-glass.

At last the happy day came; they went to Court, and Cinderella followed them with her eyes as long as she could, and when she had lost sight of them, she fell a-crying.

Her godmother, who saw her all in tears, asked her what was the matter.

"I wish I could—I wish I could—" but she could not finish for sobbing.

Her godmother, who was a fairy, said to her, "You wish you could go to the ball; is it not so?"

"Alas, yes," said Cinderella, sighing.

"Well," said her godmother, "be but a good girl, and I will see that you go." Then she took her into her chamber, and said to her, "Run into the garden, and bring me a pumpkin."

Cinderella went at once to gather the finest she could get, and brought it to her godmother, not being able to imagine how this pumpkin could help her to go to the ball. Her godmother scooped out all the inside of it, leaving nothing but the rind. Then she struck it with her wand, and the pumpkin was instantly turned into a fine gilded coach.

She then went to look into the mouse-trap, where she found six mice, all alive. She ordered Cinderella to lift the trap-door, when, giving each mouse, as it went out, a little tap with her wand, it was that moment turned into a fine horse, and the six mice made a fine set of six horses of a beautiful mouse-colored, dapple gray.

Being at a loss for a coachman, Cinderella said, "I will go and see if there is not a rat in the rat-trap—we may make a coachman of him."

"You are right," replied her godmother; "go and look."

Cinderella brought the rat-trap to her, and in it there were three huge rats. The fairy chose the one which had the largest beard, and, having touched him with her wand, he was turned into a fat coachman with the finest mustache and whiskers ever seen.

After that, she said to her:—

"Go into the garden, and you will find six lizards behind the watering-pot; bring them to me."

She had no sooner done so than her godmother turned them into six footmen, who skipped up immediately behind the coach, with their liveries all trimmed with gold and silver, and they held on as if they had done nothing else their whole lives.

The fairy then said to Cinderella, "Well, you see here a carriage fit to go to the ball in; are you not pleased with it?"

"Oh, yes!" she cried; "but must I go as I am in these rags?"

Her godmother simply touched her with her wand, and, at the same moment, her clothes were turned into cloth of gold and silver, all decked with jewels. This done, she gave her a pair of the prettiest glass slippers in the whole world. Being thus attired, she got into the carriage, her god mother commanding her, above all things, not to stay till after midnight, and telling her, at the same time, that if she stayed one moment longer, the coach would be a pumpkin again, her horses mice, her coachman a rat, her footmen lizards, and her clothes would become just as they were before.

She promised her godmother she would not fail to leave the ball before midnight. She drove away, scarce able to contain herself for joy. The King's son, who was told that a great princess, whom nobody knew, was come, ran out to receive her. He gave her his hand as she alighted from the coach, and led her into the hall where the company were assembled. There was at once a profound silence; every one left off dancing, and the violins ceased to play, so attracted was every one by the singular beauties of the unknown newcomer. Nothing was then heard but a confused sound of voices saying:—

"Ha! how beautiful she is! Ha! how beautiful she is!"

The King himself, old as he was, could not keep his eyes off her, and he told the Queen under his breath that it was a long time since he had seen so beautiful and lovely a creature.

All the ladies were busy studying her clothes and head-dress, so that they might have theirs made next day after the same pattern, provided [Pg 7]they could meet with such fine materials and able hands to make them.

The King's son conducted her to the seat of honor, and afterwards took her out to dance with him. She danced so very gracefully that they all admired her more and more. A fine collation was served, but the young Prince ate not a morsel, so intently was he occupied with her.

She went and sat down beside her sisters, showing them a thousand civilities, and giving them among other things part of the oranges and citrons with which the Prince had regaled her. This very much surprised them, for they had not been presented to her.

Cinderella heard the clock strike a quarter to twelve. She at once made her adieus to the company and hastened away as fast as she could.

Stories

As soon as she got home, she ran to find her godmother, and, after having thanked her, she said she much wished she might go to the ball the next day, because the King's son had asked her to do so. As she was eagerly telling her godmother all that happened at the ball, her two sisters knocked at the door; Cinderella opened it. "How long you have stayed!" said she, yawning, rubbing her eyes, and stretching herself as if she had been just awakened. She had not, however, had any desire to sleep since they went from home.

"If you had been at the ball," said one of her sisters, "you would not have been tired with it. There came thither the finest princess, the most beautiful ever was seen with mortal eyes. She showed us a thousand civilities, and gave us oranges and citrons."

Cinderella did not show any pleasure at this. Indeed, she asked them the name of the princess; but they told her they did not know it, and that the King's son was very much concerned, and would give all the world to know who she was. At this Cinderella, smiling, replied:—

"Was she then so very beautiful? How fortunate you have been! Could I not see her? Ah!

dear Miss Charlotte, do lend me your yellow suit of clothes which you wear every day."

"Ay, to be sure!" cried Miss Charlotte; "lend my clothes to such a dirty Cinderwench as thou art! I should be out of my mind to do so." Cinderella, indeed, expected such an answer and was very glad of the refusal; for she would have been sadly troubled if her sister had lent her what she jestingly asked for. The next day the two sisters went to the ball, and so did Cinderella, but dressed more magnificently than before. The King's son was always by her side, and his pretty speeches to her never ceased. These by no means annoyed the young lady. Indeed, she quite forgot her godmother's orders [Pg 9]to her, so that she heard the clock begin to strike twelve when she thought it could not be more than eleven. She then rose up and fled, as nimble as a deer. The Prince followed, but could not overtake her. She left behind one of her glass slippers, which the Prince took up most carefully. She got home, but quite out of breath, without her carriage, and in her old clothes, having nothing left her of all her finery but one of the little slippers, fellow to the one she had dropped. The guards at the palace gate were asked if they had not seen a princess go out, and they replied they had seen nobody go out but a young girl, very meanly dressed, and who had more the air of a poor country girl than of a young lady.

When the two sisters returned from the ball, Cinderella asked them if they had had a pleasant time, and if the fine lady had been there. They told her, yes; but that she hurried away the moment it struck twelve, and with so much haste that she dropped one of her little glass slippers, the prettiest in the world, which the King's son had taken up. They said, further, that he had done nothing but look at her all the time, and that most certainly he was very much in love with the beautiful owner of the glass slipper.

What they said was true; for a few days after the King's son caused it to be proclaimed, by sound of trumpet, that he would marry her whose [Pg 10]foot this slipper would fit exactly. They began to try it on the princesses, then on the duchesses, and then on all the ladies of the Court; but in vain. It was brought to the two sisters, who did all they possibly could to thrust a foot into the slipper, but they could not succeed. Cinderella, who saw this, and knew her slipper, said to them, laughing:—
"Let me see if it will not fit me."

Her sisters burst out a-laughing, and began to banter her. The gentleman who was sent to try the slipper looked earnestly at Cinderella, and, finding her very handsome, said it was but just that she should try, and that he had orders to let every lady try it on.

He obliged Cinderella to sit down, and, putting the slipper to her little foot, he found it went on very easily, and fitted her as if it had been made of wax. The astonishment of her two sisters was great, but it was still greater when Cinderella pulled out of her pocket the other slipper and put it on her foot. Thereupon, in came her godmother, who, having touched Cinderella's clothes with her wand, made them more magnificent than those she had worn before.

Stories

And now her two sisters found her to be that beautiful lady they had seen at the ball. They threw themselves at her feet to beg pardon for all their ill treatment of her. Cinderella took [Pg 12] them up, and, as she embraced them, said that she forgave them with all her heart, and begged them to love her always.

She was conducted to the young Prince, dressed as she was. He thought her more charming than ever, and, a few days after, married her. Cinderella, who was as good as she was beautiful, gave her two sisters a home in the palace, and that very same day married them to two great lords of the Court.

BLUE BEARD

Once upon a time there was a man who had fine houses, both in town and country, a deal of silver and gold plate, carved furniture, and coaches gilded all over. But unhappily this man had a blue beard, which made him so ugly and so terrible that all the women and girls ran away from him.

One of his neighbors, a lady of quality, had two daughters who were perfect beauties. He asked for one of them in marriage, leaving to her the choice of which she would bestow on him. They would neither of them have him, and they sent him backward and forward from one to the other, neither being able to make up her mind to marry a man who had a blue beard. Another thing which made them averse to him was that he had already married several wives, and nobody knew what had become of them.

Blue Beard, to become better acquainted, took them, with their mother and three or four of their best friends, with some young people of the neighborhood to one of his country seats, where they stayed a whole week.

There was nothing going on but pleasure parties, hunting, fishing, dancing, mirth, and feasting. Nobody went to bed, but all passed the night in playing pranks on each other. In short, everything succeeded so well that the youngest daughter began to think that the beard of the master of the house was not so very blue, and that he was a very civil gentleman. So as soon as they returned home, the marriage was concluded.

About a month afterward Blue Beard told his wife that he was obliged to take a country journey for six weeks at least, upon business of great importance. He desired her to amuse herself well in his absence, to send for her friends, to take them into the country, if she pleased, and to live well wherever she was.

"Here," said he, "are the keys of the two great warehouses wherein I have my best furniture: these are of the room where I keep my silver and gold plate, which is not in everyday use; these open my safes, which hold my money, both gold and silver; these my caskets of jewels; and this is the master-key to all my apartments.

But as for this little key, it is the key of the closet at the end of the great gallery on the ground floor. Open them all; go everywhere; but as for that little closet, I forbid you to enter it, and I promise you surely that, if you open it, there's nothing that you may not expect from my anger."

She promised to obey exactly all his orders; and he, after having embraced her, got into his coach and proceeded on his journey.

Her neighbors and good friends did not stay to be sent for by the new-married lady, so great was their impatience to see all the riches of her house, not daring to come while her husband was there, because of his blue beard, which frightened them. They at once ran through all the rooms, closets, and wardrobes, which were so fine and rich, and each seemed to surpass all others. They went up into the warehouses, where was the best and richest furniture; and they could not sufficiently admire the number and beauty of the tapestry, beds, couches, cabinets, stands, tables, and looking-glasses, in which you might see yourself from head to foot. Some of them were framed with glass, others with silver, plain and gilded, the most beautiful and the most magnificent ever seen.

They ceased not to praise and envy the happiness of their friend, who, in the meantime, was not at all amused by looking upon all these rich things, because of her impatience to go and open the closet on the ground floor. Her curiosity was so great that, without considering how uncivil it was to leave her guests, she went down a little back staircase, with such excessive haste that twice or thrice she came near breaking her neck. Having reached the closet-door, she stood still for some time, thinking of her husband's orders, and considering that unhappiness might attend her if she was disobedient; but the temptation was so strong she could not overcome it. She then took the little key, and opened the door, trembling. At first she could not see anything plainly, because the windows were shut. After some moments she began to perceive that several dead women were scattered about the floor. (These were all the wives whom Blue Beard had married and murdered, one after the other, because they did not obey his orders about the closet on the ground floor.) She thought she surely would die for fear, and the key, which she pulled out of the lock, fell out of her hand.

After having somewhat recovered from the shock, she picked up the key, locked the door, and went upstairs into her chamber to compose herself; but she could not rest, so much was she frightened.

Having observed that the key of the closet was stained, she tried two or three times to wipe off the stain, but the stain would not come out. In vain did she wash it, and even rub it with soap and sand. The stain still remained, for the key was a magic key, and she could never make it quite clean; when the stain was gone off from one side, it came again on the other.

Blue Beard returned from his journey that same evening, and said he had received letters upon the road, informing him that the business which called him away was ended to his advantage. His wife did all she could to convince him she was delighted at his speedy return.

Next morning he asked her for the keys, which she gave him, but with such a trembling hand that he easily guessed what had happened.

"How is it," said he, "that the key of my closet is not among the rest?"

"I must certainly," said she, "have left it upstairs upon the table."

"Do not fail," said Blue Beard, "to bring it to me presently."

After having put off doing it several times, she was forced to bring him the key. Blue Beard, having examined it, said to his wife:—

"How comes this stain upon the key?"

"I do not know," cried the poor woman, paler than death.

"You do not know!" replied Blue Beard. "I very well know. You wished to go into the cabinet? Very well, madam; you shall go in, and take your place among the ladies you saw there."

She threw herself weeping at her husband's feet, and begged his pardon with all the signs of a true repentance for her disobedience. She would have melted a rock, so beautiful and sorrowful was she; but Blue Beard had a heart harder than any stone.

"You must die, madam," said he, "and that at once."

"Since I must die," answered she, looking upon him with her eyes all bathed in tears, "give me some little time to say my prayers."

"I give you," replied Blue Beard, "half a quarter of an hour, but not one moment more."

When she was alone she called out to her sister, and said to her:—

"Sister Anne,"—for that was her name,— "go up, I beg you, to the top of the tower, and look if my brothers are not coming; they promised me they would come to-day, and if you see them, give them a sign to make haste."

Her sister Anne went up to the top of the tower, and the poor afflicted wife cried out from time to time:—

"Anne, sister Anne, do you see any one coming?"

And sister Anne said:—

"I see nothing but the sun, which makes a dust, and the grass, which looks green."

In the meanwhile Blue Beard, holding a great saber in his hand, cried to his wife as loud as he could:—

"Come down instantly, or I shall come up to you."

"One moment longer, if you please," said his wife; and then she cried out very softly, "Anne, sister Anne, dost thou see anybody coming?"

And sister Anne answered:—

"I see nothing but the sun, which makes a dust, and the grass, which is green."

"Come down quickly," cried Blue Beard, "or I will come up to you."

"I am coming," answered his wife; and then she cried, "Anne, sister Anne, dost thou not see any one coming?"

"I see," replied sister Anne, "a great dust, which comes from this side."

"Are they my brothers?"

"Alas! no, my sister, I see a flock of sheep."

"Will you not come down?" cried Blue Beard.

"One moment longer," said his wife, and then she cried out, "Anne, sister Anne, dost thou see nobody coming?"

"I see," said she, "two horsemen, but they are yet a great way off."

"God be praised," replied the poor wife, joyfully; "they are my brothers; I will make them a sign, as well as I can, for them to make haste."

Then Blue Beard bawled out so loud that he made the whole house tremble. The distressed wife came down and threw herself at his feet, all in tears, with her hair about her shoulders.

"All this is of no help to you," says Blue Beard: "you must die"; then, taking hold of her hair with one hand, and lifting up his sword in the air with the other, he was about to take off her head. The poor lady, turning about to him, and looking at him with dying eyes, desired him to afford her one little moment to her thoughts.

"No, no," said he, "commend thyself to God," and again lifting his arm—

At this moment there was such a loud knocking at the gate that Blue Beard stopped suddenly. The gate was opened, and presently entered two horsemen, who, with sword in hand, ran directly to Blue Beard. He knew them to be his wife's brothers, one a dragoon, the other a musketeer. He ran away immediately, but the two brothers pursued him so closely that they overtook him before he could get to the steps of the porch. There they ran their swords through his body, and left him dead. The poor wife was almost as dead as her husband, and had not strength enough to arise and welcome her brothers.

Blue Beard had no heirs, and so his wife became mistress of all his estate. She made use of one portion of it to marry her sister Anne to a young gentleman who had loved her a long while; another portion to buy captains' commissions for her brothers; and the rest to marry herself to a very worthy gentleman, who made her forget the sorry time she had passed with Blue Beard.

THE STORY OF THE THREE BEARS

Once upon a time there were three Bears, who lived together in a house of their own, in a wood. One of them was a Little Wee Bear, and one was a Middle-sized Bear, and the other was a Great Big Bear. They had each a bowl for their porridge; a little bowl for the Little Wee Bear; and a middle-sized bowl for the Middle-sized Bear; and a great bowl for the Great Big Bear. And they had each a chair to sit in; a little chair for the Little Wee Bear; and a middle-sized chair for the Middle-sized Bear; and a great chair for the Great Big Bear. And they had each a bed to sleep in; a little bed for the Little Wee Bear; and a middle-sized bed for the Middle-sized Bear; and a great bed for the Great Big Bear.

One day, after they had made the porridge for their breakfast, and poured it into their porridge-bowls, they walked out into the wood while the porridge was cooling, that they might not burn their mouths by beginning too soon, for they were polite, well-brought-up Bears. And while they were away a little girl called Goldilocks, who lived at the other side of the wood and had been sent on an errand by her mother, passed by the house, and looked in at the window. And then she peeped in at the keyhole, for she was not at all a well-brought-up little girl. Then seeing nobody in the house she lifted the latch. The door was not fastened, because the Bears were good Bears, who did nobody any harm, and never suspected that anybody would harm them. So Goldilocks opened the door and went in; and well pleased was she when she saw the porridge on the table. If she had been a well-brought-up little girl she would have waited till the Bears came home, and then, perhaps, they would have asked her to breakfast; for they were good Bears—a little rough or so, as the manner of Bears is, but for all that very good-natured and hospitable. But she was an impudent, rude little girl, and so she set about helping herself.

First she tasted the porridge of the Great Big Bear, and that was too hot for her. Next she tasted the porridge of the Middle-sized Bear, but that was too cold for her. And then she went to the porridge of the Little Wee Bear, and tasted it, and that was neither too hot nor too cold, but just right, and she liked it so well that she ate it all up, every bit!

Then Goldilocks, who was tired, for she had been catching butterflies instead of running on her errand, sate down in the chair of the Great Big Bear, but that was too hard for her. And then she sate down in the chair of the Middle-sized Bear, and that was too soft for her. But when she sat down in the chair of the Little Wee Bear, that was neither too hard nor too soft, but just right. So she seated herself in it, and there she sate till the bottom of the chair came out, and down she came, plump upon the ground; and that made her very cross, for she was a bad-tempered little girl.

Now, being determined to rest, Goldilocks went upstairs into the bedchamber in which the Three Bears slept. And first she lay down upon the bed of the Great Big Bear, but that was too high at the head for her. And next she lay down upon the bed of the Middle-sized Bear, and that was too high at the foot for her. And then she lay down upon the bed of the Little Wee Bear, and that was neither too high at the head nor at the foot, but just right. So she covered herself up comfortably, and lay there till she fell fast asleep.

By this time the Three Bears thought their porridge would be cool enough for them to eat it properly; so they came home to breakfast. Now careless Goldilocks had left the spoon of the Great Big Bear standing in his porridge.

Stories

"SOMEBODY HAS BEEN AT MY PORRIDGE!" said the Great Big Bear in his great, rough, gruff voice.

Then the Middle-sized Bear looked at his porridge and saw the spoon was standing in it too.

"SOMEBODY HAS BEEN AT MY PORRIDGE!" said the Middle-sized Bear in his middle-sized voice.

Then the Little Wee Bear looked at his, and there was the spoon in the porridge-bowl, but the porridge was all gone!

"SOMEBODY HAS BEEN AT MY PORRIDGE, AND HAS EATEN IT ALL UP!" said the Little Wee Bear in his little wee voice.

Upon this the Three Bears, seeing that some one had entered their house, and eaten up the Little Wee Bear's breakfast, began to look about them. Now the careless Goldilocks had not put the hard cushion straight when she rose from the chair of the Great Big Bear.

"SOMEBODY HAS BEEN SITTING IN MY CHAIR!" said the Great Big Bear in his great, rough, gruff voice.

And the careless Goldilocks had squatted down the soft cushion of the Middle-sized Bear.
"SOMEBODY HAS BEEN SITTING IN MY CHAIR!" said the Middle-sized Bear in his middle-sized voice.

"SOMEBODY HAS BEEN SITTING IN MY CHAIR, AND HAS SATE THE BOTTOM THROUGH!" said the Little Wee Bear in his little wee voice.

Then the Three Bears thought they had better make further search in case it was a burglar, so they went upstairs into their bedchamber. Now Goldilocks had pulled the pillow of the Great Big Bear out of its place.

"SOMEBODY HAS BEEN LYING IN MY BED!" said the Great Big Bear in his great, rough, gruff voice.

And Goldilocks had pulled the bolster of the Middle-sized Bear out of its place.

"SOMEBODY HAS BEEN LYING IN MY BED!" said the Middle-sized Bear in his middle-sized voice.

But when the Little Wee Bear came to look at his bed, there was the bolster in its place! And the pillow was in its place upon the bolster!

And upon the pillow——?

There was Goldilocks' yellow head—which was not in its place, for she had no business there.

Stories

"SOMEBODY HAS BEEN LYING IN MY BED,—AND HERE SHE IS STILL!" said the Little Wee Bear in his little wee voice.

Now Goldilocks had heard in her sleep the great, rough, gruff voice of the Great Big Bear; but she was so fast asleep that it was no more to her than the roaring of wind, or the rumbling of thunder. And she had heard the middle-sized voice of the Middle-sized Bear, but it was only as if she had heard some one speaking in a dream. But when she heard the little wee voice of the Little Wee Bear, it was so sharp, and so shrill, that it awakened her at once. Up she started, and when she saw the Three Bears on one side of the bed, she tumbled herself out at the other, and ran to the window. Now the window was open, because the Bears, like good, tidy Bears, as they were, always opened their bedchamber window when they got up in the morning. So naughty, frightened little Goldilocks jumped; and whether she broke her neck in the fall, or ran into the wood and was lost there, or found her way out of the wood and got whipped for being a bad girl and playing truant, no one can say. But the Three Bears never saw anything more of her.

TATTERCOATS

In a great Palace by the sea there once dwelt a very rich old lord, who had neither wife nor children living, only one little granddaughter, whose face he had never seen in all her life. He hated her bitterly, because at her birth his favorite daughter died; and when the old nurse brought him the baby he swore that it might live or die as it liked, but he would never look on its face as long as it lived.

So he turned his back, and sat by his window looking out over the sea, and weeping great tears for his lost daughter, till his white hair and beard grew down over his shoulders and twined round his chair and crept into the chinks of the floor, and his tears, dropping on to the window-ledge, wore a channel through the stone, and ran away in a little river to the great sea. Meanwhile, his granddaughter grew up with no one to care for her, or clothe her; only the old nurse, when no one was by, would sometimes give her a dish of scraps from the kitchen, or a torn petticoat from the rag-bag; while the other servants of the palace would drive her from the house with blows and mocking words, calling her "Tattercoats," and pointing to her bare feet and shoulders, till she ran away, crying, to hide among the bushes.

So she grew up, with little to eat or to wear, spending her days out of doors, her only companion a crippled gooseherd, who fed his flock of geese on the common. And this gooseherd was a queer, merry little chap, and when she was hungry, or cold, or tired, he would play to her so gaily on his little pipe, that she forgot all her troubles, and would fall to dancing with his flock of noisy geese for partners.

Now one day people told each other that the King was traveling through the land, and was to give a great ball to all the lords and ladies of the country in the town near by, and that the Prince, his only son, was to choose a wife from amongst the maidens in the company. In due time one of the royal invitations to the ball was brought to the Palace by the sea, and the servants carried it up to the old lord, who still sat by his window, wrapped in his long white hair and weeping into the little river that was fed by his tears.

But when he heard the King's command, he dried his eyes and bade them bring shears to cut him loose, for his hair had bound him a fast prisoner, and he could not move. And then he sent them for rich clothes, and jewels, which he put on; and he ordered them to saddle the white horse, with gold and silk, that he might ride to meet the King; but he quite forgot he had a granddaughter to take to the ball.

Meanwhile Tattercoats sat by the kitchen-door weeping, because she could not go to see the grand doings. And when the old nurse heard her crying she went to the Lord of the Palace, and begged him to take his granddaughter with him to the King's ball.

But he only frowned and told her to be silent; while the servants laughed and said, "Tattercoats is happy in her rags, playing with the gooseherd! Let her be—it is all she is fit for."

A second, and then a third time, the old nurse begged him to let the girl go with him, but she was answered only by black looks and fierce words, till she was driven from the room by the jeering servants, with blows and mocking words.

Weeping over her ill-success, the old nurse went to look for Tattercoats; but the girl had been turned from the door by the cook, and had run away to tell her friend the gooseherd how unhappy she was because she could not go to the King's ball.

Now when the gooseherd had listened to her story, he bade her cheer up, and proposed that they should go together into the town to see the King, and all the fine things; and when she looked sorrowfully down at her rags and bare feet he played a note or two upon his pipe, so gay and merry, that she forgot all about her tears and her troubles, and before she well knew, the gooseherd had taken her by the hand, and she and he, and the geese before them, were dancing down the road towards the town.

"Even cripples can dance when they choose," said the gooseherd.

Before they had gone very far a handsome young man, splendidly dressed, riding up, stopped to ask the way to the castle where the King was staying, and when he found that they too were going thither, he got off his horse and walked beside them along the road.

"You seem merry folk," he said, "and will be good company."

"Good company, indeed," said the gooseherd, "and played a new tune that was not a dance."

It was a curious tune, and it made the strange young man stare and stare and stare at Tattercoats till he couldn't see her rags—till he couldn't, to tell the truth, see anything but her beautiful face.

Then he said, "You are the most beautiful maiden in the world. Will you marry me?"

Then the gooseherd smiled to himself, and played sweeter than ever.

But Tattercoats laughed. "Not I," said she; "you would be finely put to shame, and so would I be, if you took a goose-girl for your wife! Go and ask one of the great ladies you will see to-night at the King's ball, and do not flout poor Tattercoats."

But the more she refused him the sweeter the pipe played, and the deeper the young man fell in love; till at last he begged her to come that night at twelve to the King's ball, just as she was, with the gooseherd and his geese, in her torn petticoat and bare feet, and see if he wouldn't dance with her before the King and the lords and ladies, and present her to them all, as his dear and honored bride.

Now at first Tattercoats said she would not; but the gooseherd said, "Take fortune when it comes, little one."

So when night came, and the hall in the castle was full of light and music, and the lords and ladies were dancing before the King, just as the clock struck twelve, Tattercoats and the gooseherd, followed by his flock of noisy geese, hissing and swaying their heads, entered at the great doors, and walked straight up the ball-room, while on either side the ladies whispered, the lords laughed, and the King seated at the far end stared in amazement.

But as they came in front of the throne Tattercoats' lover rose from beside the King, and came to meet her. Taking her by the hand, he kissed her thrice before them all, and turned to the King.

"Father!" he said—for it was the Prince himself—"I have made my choice, and here is my bride, *the* loveliest girl in all the land, and the sweetest as well!"

Before he had finished speaking, the gooseherd had put his pipe to his lips and played a few no*t*es that sounded like a bird singing far off in the w*oo*ds; and as he played Tattercoats' rags were cha*n*ged to shining robes sewn with glittering jewels, a *g*olden crown lay upon her golden hair, and the *fl*ock of geese behind her became a crowd of dainty *p*ages, bearing her long train.

And as the King rose to g*ree*t her as his hter the trumpets sounded lou*dl*y in honor of the new Princess, and the people outside in the street said to each other:

"Ah! now the Prince has chosen for his wife the loveliest girl in all the land!"

But the gooseherd was never seen again, and no one knew what became of him; while the old lord went home once more to his Palace by the sea, for he could not stay at Court, when he had sworn never to look on his granddaughter's face.

So there he still sits by his window,—if you could only see him, as you may some day—weeping more bitterly than ever. And his white hair has bound him to the stones, and the river of his tears runs away to the great sea.

JACK THE GIANT-KILLER

I

When good King Arthur reigned with Guinevere his Queen, there lived, near the Land's End in Cornwall, a farmer who had one only son called Jack. Now Jack was brisk and ready; of such a lively wit that none nor nothing could worst him.

In those days, the Mount of St. Michael in Cornwall was the vastness of a huge giant whose name was Cormoran.

He was full eighteen feet in height, some three yards about his middle, of a grim fierce face, and he was the terror of all the country-side. He lived in a cave amidst the rocky Mount, and when he desired victuals he would wade across the tides to the mainland and furnish himself forth with all that came in his way. The poor folk and the rich folk alike ran out of th

Stories

houses and hid themselves when they heard the swish-swash of his big feet in the water; for if he saw them, he would think nothing of broiling half-a-dozen or so of them for breakfast. As it was, he seized their cattle by the score, carrying off half-a-dozen fat oxen on his back at a time, and hanging sheep and pigs to his waistbelt like bunches of dip-candles. Now this had gone on for long years, and the poor folk of Cornwall were in despair, for none could put an end to the giant Cormoran.

It so happened that one market day Jack, then quite a young lad, found the town upside down over some new exploit of the giant's. Women were weeping, men were cursing, and magistrates were sitting in Council over what was to be done. But none could suggest a plan. Then Jack, blithe and gay, went up to the magistrates, and with a fine courtesy—for he was ever polite—asked them what reward would be given to him who killed the giant Cormoran.

"The treasures of the Giant's Cave," said they.

"Every whit of it?" said Jack, who was never to be done.

"To the last farthing," said they.

"Then will I undertake the task," said Jack, and forthwith set about the business.

It was winter-time, and having got himself a horn, a pickaxe, and a shovel, he went over to the Mount in the dark evening, set to work, and before dawn he had dug a pit, no less than twenty-two feet deep and nigh as big across. This he covered with long thin sticks and straw, sprinkling a little loose mould over all to make it look like solid ground. So, just as dawn was breaking, he planted himself fair and square on the side of the pit that was farthest from the giant's cave, raised the horn to his lips, and with full blast sounded:

"Tantivy! Tantivy! Tantivy!"

just as he would have done had he been hunting a fox.

Of course this woke the giant, who rushed in a rage out of his cave, and seeing little Jack, fair and square blowing away at his horn, as calm and cool as may be, he became still more angry, and made for the disturber of his rest, bawling out, "I'll teach you to wake a giant, you little whipper-snapper. You shall pay dearly for your tantivys, I'll take you and broil you whole for break—"

He had only got as far as this when crash—he fell into the pit! So there was a break indeed; such an one that it caused the very foundations of the Mount to shake.

But Jack shook with laughter. "Ho, ho!" he cried, "how about breakfast now, Sir Giant? Will you have me broiled or baked? And will no diet serve you but poor little Jack? Faith! I've got you in Lob's pound now! You're in the stocks for bad behavior, and I'll plague you as I like. Would I had rotten eggs; but this will do as well." And with that he up with his pickaxe and dealt the giant Cormoran such a most weighty knock on the very crown of his head, that he killed him on the spot.

Whereupon Jack calmly filled up the pit with earth again and went to search the cave, where he found much treasure.

Now when the magistrates heard of Jack's great exploit, they proclaimed that henceforth he should be known as—JACK THE GIANT-KILLER.

And they presented him with a sword and belt, on which these words were embroidered in gold:
> Here's the valiant Cornishman
> Who slew the giant Cormoran.

II

Of course the news of Jack's victory soon spread over all England, so that another giant named Blunderbore who lived to the north, hearing of it, vowed if ever he came across Jack he would be revenged upon him. Now this giant Blunderbore was lord of an enchanted castle that stood in the middle of a lonesome forest.

It so happened that Jack, about four months after he had killed Cormoran, had occasion to journey into Wales, and on the road he passed this forest. Weary with walking, and finding a pleasant fountain by the wayside, he lay down to rest and was soon fast asleep.

Now the giant Blunderbore, coming to the well for water, found Jack sleeping, and knew by the lines embroidered on his belt that here was the far-famed giant-killer. Rejoiced at his luck, the giant, without more ado, lifted Jack to his shoulder and began to carry him through the wood to the enchanted castle.

But the rustling of the boughs awakened Jack, who, finding himself already in the clutches of the giant, was terrified; nor was his alarm decreased by seeing the courtyard of the castle all strewn with men's bones.

"Yours will be with them ere long," said Blunderbore as he locked poor Jack into an immense chamber above the castle gateway. It had a high-pitched, beamed roof, and one window that looked down the road. Here poor Jack was to stay while Blunderbore went to fetch his brother-giant, who lived in the same wood, that he might share in the feast.

Now, after a time, Jack, watching through the window, saw the two giants tramping hastily down the road, eager for their dinner.

"Now," said Jack to himself, "my death or my deliverance is at hand." For he had thought out a plan. In one corner of the room he had seen two strong cords. These he took, and making a cunning noose at the end of each, he hung

275

them out of the window, and, as the giants were unlocking the iron door of the gate, managed to slip them over their heads without their noticing it. Then, quick as thought, he tied the other ends to a beam, so that as the giants moved on the nooses tightened and throttled them until they grew black in the face. Seeing this, Jack slid down the ropes, and drawing his sword, slew them both.

So, taking the keys of the castle, he unlocked all the doors and set free three beauteous ladies who, tied by the hair of their heads, he found almost starved to death. "Sweet ladies," said Jack, kneeling on one knee—for he was ever polite—"here are the keys of this enchanted castle. I have destroyed the giant Blunderbore and his brutish brother, and thus have restored to you your liberty. These keys should bring you all else you require."

So saying he proceeded on his journey to Wales.

III

He traveled as fast as he could; perhaps too fast, for, losing his way, he found himself benighted and far from any habitation. He wandered on always in hopes, until on entering a narrow valley he came on a very large, dreary-looking house standing alone. Being anxious for shelter he went up to the door and knocked. You may imagine his surprise and alarm when the summons was answered by a giant with two heads. But though this monster's look was exceedingly fierce, his manners were quite polite; the truth being that he was a Welsh giant, and as such double-faced and smooth, given to gaining his malicious ends by a show of false friendship.

So he welcomed Jack heartily in a strong Welsh accent, and prepared a bedroom for him, where he was left with kind wishes for a good rest. Jack, however, was too tired to sleep well, and as he lay awake, he overheard his host muttering to himself in the next room. Having very keen ears he was able to make out these words, or something like them:

"Though here you lodge with me this night,
You shall not see the morning light.
My club shall dash your brains outright."

"Say'st thou so!" said Jack to himself, starting up at once, "So that is your Welsh trick, is it? But I will be even with you." Then, leaving his bed, he laid a big billet of wood among the blankets, and taking one of these to keep himself warm, made himself snug in a corner of the room, pretending to snore, so as to make Mr. Giant think he was asleep.

And sure enough, after a little time, in came the monster on tiptoe as if treading on eggs, and carrying a big club. Then—WHACK! WHACK! WHACK!

Jack could hear the bed being belabored until the Giant, thinking every bone of his guest's skin must be broken, stole out of the room again; whereupon Jack went calmly to bed once more and slept soundly! Next morning the giant couldn't believe his eyes when he saw Jack coming down the stairs fresh and hearty.

Stories

"Odds splutter hur nails!" he cried, astonished. "Did she sleep well? Was there not nothing felt in the night?"

"Oh," replied Jack, laughing in his sleeve, "I think a rat did come and give me two or three flaps of his tail."

On this the giant was dumbfounded, and led Jack to breakfast, bringing him a bowl which held at least four gallons of hasty-pudding, and bidding him, as a man of such mettle, eat the lot. Now Jack when traveling wore under his cloak a leathern bag to carry his things withal; so, quick as thought, he hitched this round in front with the opening just under his chin; thus, as he ate, he could slip the best part of the pudding into it without the giant's being any the wiser. So they sate down to breakfast, the giant gobbling down his own measure of hasty-pudding, while Jack made away with his.

"See," says crafty Jack when he had finished. "I'll show you a trick worth two of yours," and with that he up with a carving-knife and, ripping up the leathern bag, out fell all the hasty-pudding on the floor!

"Odds splutter hur nails!" cried the giant, not to be outdone. "Hur can do that hurself!" Whereupon he seized the carving-knife, and ripping open his own belly fell down dead.

Thus was Jack quit of the Welsh giant.

Stories
IV

Now it so happened that in those days, when gallant knights were always seeking adventures, King Arthur's only son, a very valiant Prince, begged of his father a large sum of money to enable him to journey to Wales, and there strive to set free a certain beautiful lady who was possessed by seven evil spirits. In vain the King denied him; so at last he gave way and the Prince set out with two horses, one of which he rode, the other laden with gold pieces. Now after some days' journey the Prince came to a market-town in Wales where there was a great commotion. On asking the reason for it he was told that, according to law, the corpse of a very generous man had been arrested on its way to the grave, because, in life, it had owed large sums to the money-lenders.

"That is a cruel law," said the young Prince. "Go, bury the dead in peace, and let the creditors come to my lodgings; I will pay the debts of the dead."

So the creditors came, but they were so numerous that by evening the Prince had but twopence left for himself, and could not go further on his journey.

Now it so happened that Jack the Giant-Killer on his way to Wales passed through the town, and, hearing of the Prince's plight, was so taken with his kindness and generosity that he determined to be the Prince's servant. So this was agreed upon, and next morning, after Jack had paid the reckoning with his last farthing, the two set out together. But as they were leaving the town, an old woman ran after the Prince and called out, "Justice! Justice! The dead man owed me twopence these seven years. Pay me as well as the others."

And the Prince, kind and generous, put his hand to his pocket and gave the old woman the twopence that was left to him. So now they had not a penny between them, and when the sun grew low the Prince said:

"Jack! Since we have no money, how are we to get a night's lodging?"

Then Jack replied, "We shall do well enough, Master; for within two or three miles of this place there lives a huge and monstrous giant with three heads, who can fight four hundred men in armor and make them fly from him like chaff before the wind."

"And what good will that be to us?" said the Prince. "He will for sure chop us up in a mouthful."

"Nay," said Jack, laughing. "Let me go and prepare the way for you. By all accounts this giant is a dolt. Mayhap I may manage better than that."

So the Prince remained where he was, and Jack pricked his steed at full speed till he came to the giant's castle, at the gate of which he knocked so loud that he made the neighboring hills resound.

On this the giant roared from within in a voice like thunder:

"Who's there?"

Then said Jack as bold as brass, "None but your poor cousin Jack."

"Cousin Jack!" said the giant, astounded. "And what news with my poor cousin Jack?" For, see you, he was quite taken aback; so Jack made haste to reassure him.

"Dear coz, heavy news, God wot!"

"Heavy news," echoed the giant, half afraid. "God wot, no heavy news can come to me. Have I not three heads? Can I not fight five hundred men in armor? Can I not make them fly like chaff before the wind?"

"True," replied crafty Jack, "but I came to warn you because the great King Arthur's son with a thousand men in armor is on his way to kill you."

At this the giant began to shiver and to shake. "Ah! Cousin Jack! Kind cousin Jack! This is heavy news indeed," said he. "Tell me, what am I to do?"

"Hide yourself in the vault," says crafty Jack, "and I will lock and bolt and bar you in; and keep the key till the Prince has gone. So you will be safe."

Then the giant made haste and ran down into the vault, and Jack locked, and bolted, and barred him in. Then being thus secure, he went and fetched his master, and the two made themselves heartily merry over what the giant was to have had for supper, while the miserable monster shivered and shook with fright in the underground vault.

Well, after a good night's rest Jack woke his master in early morn, and having furnished him well with gold and silver from the giant's treasure, bade him ride three miles forward on his journey. So when Jack judged that the Prince was pretty well out of the smell of the giant, he took the key and let his prisoner out. He was half dead with cold and damp, but very grateful; and he begged Jack to let him know what he would be given as a reward for saving the giant's life and castle from destruction, and he should have it.

"You're very welcome," said Jack, who always had his eyes about him. "All I want is the old coat and cap, together with the rusty old sword and slippers which are at your bed-head."

When the giant heard this he sighed and shook his head. "You don't know what you are asking," said he. "They are the most precious things I possess, but as I have promised, you must have them. The coat will make you invisible, the cap will tell you all you want to know, the sword will cut asunder whatever you strike, and the slippers will take you wherever you want to go in the twinkling of an eye!"

So Jack, overjoyed, rode away with the coat and cap, the sword and the slippers, and soon overtook his master; and they rode on together until they reached the castle where the beautiful lady lived whom the Prince sought.

Now she was very beautiful, for all she was possessed of seven devils, and when she heard the Prince sought her as a suitor, she smiled and ordered a splendid banquet to be prepared for his reception. And she sate on his right hand, and plied him with food and drink.

And when the repast was over she took out her own handkerchief and wiped his lips gently, and said, with a smile:

"I have a task for you, my lord! You must show me that kerchief to-morrow morning or lose your head."

And with that she put the handkerchief in her bosom and said, "Good-night!"

The Prince was in despair, but Jack said nothing till his master was in bed. Then he put on the old cap he had got from the giant, and lo! in a minute he knew all that he wanted to know. So, in the dead of the night, when the beautiful lady called on one of her familiar spirits to carry her to Lucifer himself, Jack was beforehand with her, and putting on his coat of darkness and his slippers of swiftness, was there as soon as she was. And when she gave the handkerchief to the Devil, bidding him keep it safe, and he put it away on a high shelf, Jack just up and nipped it away in a trice!

So the next morning, when the beauteous enchanted lady looked to see the Prince crest-fallen, he just made a fine bow and presented her with the handkerchief.

At first she was terribly disappointed, but, as the day drew on, she ordered another and still more splendid repast to be got ready. And this time, when the repast was over, she kissed the Prince full on the lips and said:

"I have a task for you, my lover. Show me to-morrow morning the last lips I kiss to-night or you lose your head."

Then the Prince, who by this time was head over ears in love, said tenderly, "If you will kiss none but mine, I will." Now the beauteous lady, for all she was possessed by seven devils, could not but see that the Prince was a very handsome young man; so she blushed a little, and said:

"That is neither here nor there: you must show me them, or death is your portion."

So the Prince went to his bed, sorrowful as before; but Jack put on the cap of knowledge and knew in a moment all he wanted to know.

Thus when, in the dead of the night, the beauteous lady called on her familiar spirit to take her to Lucifer himself, Jack in his coat of darkness and his shoes of swiftness was there before her.

"Thou hast betrayed me once," said the beauteous lady to Lucifer, frowning, "by letting go my handkerchief. Now will I give thee something none can steal, and so best the Prince, King's son though he be."

With that she kissed the loathly demon full on the lips, and left him. Whereupon Jack with one blow of the rusty sword of strength cut off Lucifer's head, and, hiding it under his coat of darkness, brought it back to his master.

Thus next morning when the beauteous lady, with malice in her beautiful eyes, asked the Prince to show her the lips she had last kissed, he pulled out the demon's head by the horns. On that the seven devils, which possessed the poor lady, gave seven dreadful shrieks and left her. Thus the enchantment being broken, she appeared in all her perfect beauty and goodness.

So she and the Prince were married the very next morning. After which they journeyed back to the court of King Arthur, where Jack the Giant-Killer, for his many exploits, was made one of the Knights of the Round Table.

Stories
V

This, however, did not satisfy our hero, who was soon on the road again searching for giants. Now he had not gone far when he came upon one, seated on a huge block of timber near the entrance to a dark cave. He was a most terrific giant. His goggle eyes were as coals of fire, his countenance was grim and gruesome; his cheeks, like huge flitches of bacon, were covered with a stubbly beard, the bristles of which resembled rods of iron wire, while the locks of hair that fell on his brawny shoulders showed like curled snakes or hissing adders. He held a knotted iron club, and breathed so heavily you could hear him a mile away. Nothing daunted by this fearsome sight, Jack alighted from his horse and, putting on his coat of darkness, went close up to the giant and said softly: "Hullo! is that you? It will not be long before I have you fast by your beard."

So saying he made a cut with the sword of strength at the giant's head, but, somehow, missing his aim, cut off the nose instead, clean as a whistle! My goodness! How the giant roared! It was like claps of thunder, and he began to lay about him with the knotted iron club, like one possessed. But Jack in his coat of darkness easily dodged the blows, and running in behind, drove the sword up to the hilt into the giant's back, so that he fell stone dead.

Jack then cut off the head and sent it to King Arthur by a waggoner whom he hired for the purpose. After which he began to search the giant's cave to find his treasure. He passed through many windings and turnings until he came to a huge hall paved and roofed with freestone. At the upper end of this was an immense fireplace where hung an iron cauldron, the like of which, for size, Jack had never seen before. It was boiling and gave out a savory steam; while beside it, on the right hand, stood a big massive table set out with huge platters and mugs. Here it was that the giants used to dine. Going a little further he came upon a sort of window barred with iron, and looking within beheld a vast number of miserable captives.

"Alas! Alack!" they cried on seeing him. "Art come, young man, to join us in this dreadful prison?"

"That depends," said Jack: "but first tell me wherefore you are thus held imprisoned?"

"Through no fault," they cried at once. "We are captives of the cruel giants and are kept here and well nourished until such time as the monsters desire a feast. Then they choose the fattest and sup off them."

On hearing this Jack straightway unlocked the door of the prison and set the poor fellows free. Then, searching the giants' coffers, he divided the gold and silver equally amongst the captives as some redress for their sufferings, and taking them to a neighboring castle gave them a right good feast.

VI

Now as they were all making merry over their deliverance, and praising Jack's prowess, a messenger arrived to say that one Thunderdell, a huge giant with two heads, having heard of the death of his kinsman, was on his way from the northern dales to be revenged, and was already within a mile or two of the castle, the country folk with their flocks and herds flying before him like chaff before the wind.

Now the castle with its gardens stood on a small island that was surrounded by a moat twenty feet wide and thirty feet deep, having very steep sides. And this moat was spanned by a drawbridge. This, without a moment's delay, Jack ordered should be sawn on both sides at the middle, so as to only leave one plank uncut over which he in his invisible coat of darkness passed swiftly to meet his enemy, bearing in his hand the wonderful sword of strength.

Now though the giant could not, of course, see Jack, he could smell him, for giants have keen noses. Therefore Thunderdell cried out in a voice like his name:

"Fee, fi, fo, fum!
I smell the blood of an Englishman.
Be he alive, or be he dead,
I'll grind his bones to make my bread!"

"Is that so?" said Jack, cheerful as ever. "Then art thou a monstrous miller for sure!"

On this the giant, peering round everywhere for a glimpse of his foe, shouted out:

"Art thou, indeed, the villain who hath killed so many of my kinsmen? Then, indeed, will I tear thee to pieces with my teeth, suck thy blood, and grind thy bones to powder."

"Thou'lt have to catch me first," said Jack, laughing, and throwing off his coat of darkness and putting on his slippers of swiftness, he began nimbly to lead the giant a pretty dance, he leaping and doubling light as a feather, the monster following heavily like a walking tower, so that the very foundations of the earth seemed to shake at every step. At this game the onlookers nearly split their sides with laughter, until Jack, judging there had been enough of it, made for the drawbridge, ran neatly over the single plank, and reaching the other side waited in teasing fashion for his adversary.

On came the giant at full speed, foaming at the mouth with rage, and flourishing his club. But when he came to the middle of the bridge his great weight, of course, broke the plank, and there he was fallen headlong into the moat, rolling and wallowing like a whale, plunging from place to place, yet unable to get out and be revenged.

The spectators greeted his efforts with roars of laughter, and Jack himself was at first too overcome with merriment to do more than scoff. At last, however, he went for a rope, cast it over the giant's two heads, so, with the help of a team of horses, drew them shoreward, where two blows from the sword of strength settled the matter.

VII

After some time spent in mirth and pastimes, Jack began once more to grow restless, and taking leave of his companions set out for fresh adventures.

He traveled far and fast, through woods, and vales, and hills, till at last he came, late at night, on a lonesome house set at the foot of a high mountain. Knocking at the door, it was opened by an old man whose head was white as snow.

"Father," said Jack, ever courteous, "can you lodge a benighted traveler?"

"Ay, that will I, and welcome to my poor cottage," replied the old man.

Whereupon Jack came in, and after supper they sate together chatting in friendly fashion. Then it was that the old man, seeing by Jack's belt that he was the famous Giant-Killer, spoke in this wise:

"My son! You are the great conqueror of evil monsters. Now close by there lives one well worthy of your prowess. On the top of yonder high hill is an enchanted castle kept by a giant named Galligantua, who, by the help of a wicked old magician, inveigles many beautiful ladies and valiant knights into the castle, where they are transformed into all sorts of birds and beasts, yea, even into fishes and insects. There they live pitiably in confinement; but most of all do I grieve for a duke's daughter whom they kidnapped in her father's garden, bringing her hither in a burning chariot drawn by fiery dragons. Her form is that of a white hind; and though many valiant knights have tried their utmost to break the spell and work her deliverance, none have succeeded; for, see you, at the entrance to the castle are two dreadful griffins who destroy every one who attempts to pass them by."

Now Jack bethought him of the coat of darkness which had served him so well before, and he put on the cap of knowledge, and in an instant he knew what had to be done. Then the very next morning, at dawn-time, Jack arose and put on his invisible coat and his slippers of swiftness. And in the twinkling of an eye there he was on the top of the mountain! And there were the two griffins guarding the castle gates—horrible creatures with forked tails and tongues. But they could not see him because of the coat of darkness, so he passed them by unharmed.

And hung to the doors of the gateway he found a golden trumpet on a silver chain, and beneath it was engraved in red lettering:

> Whoever shall this trumpet blow
> Will cause the giant's overthrow.
> The black enchantment he will break,
> And gladness out of sadness make.

No sooner had Jack read these words than he put the horn to his lips and blew a loud

"Tantivy! Tantivy! Tantivy!"

Now at the very first note the castle trembled to its vast foundations, and before he had finished the measure, both the giant and the magician were biting their thumbs and tearing their hair, knowing that their wickedness must now come to an end. But the giant showed fight and took up his club to defend himself; whereupon Jack, with one clean cut of the sword of strength, severed his head from his body, and would doubtless have done the same to the magician, but that the latter was a coward, and, calling up a whirlwind, was swept away by it into the air, nor has he ever been seen or heard of since. The enchantments being thus broken, all the valiant knights and beautiful ladies, who had been transformed into birds and beasts and fishes and reptiles and insects, returned to their proper shapes, including the duke's daughter, who, from being a white hind, showed as the most beauteous maiden upon whom the sun ever shone. Now, no sooner had this occurred than the whole castle vanished away in a cloud of smoke, and from that moment giants vanished also from the land.

So Jack, when he had presented the head of Galligantua to King Arthur, together with all the lords and ladies he had delivered from enchantment, found he had nothing more to do. As a reward for past services, however, King Arthur bestowed the hand of the duke's daughter upon honest Jack the Giant-Killer. So married they were, and the whole kingdom was filled with joy at their wedding. Furthermore, the King bestowed on Jack a noble castle with a magnificent estate belonging thereto, whereon he, his lady, and their children lived in great joy and content for the rest of their days.

Stories

JACK AND THE BEANSTALK

A long long time ago, when most of the world was young and folk did what they liked because all things were good, there lived a boy called Jack.

His father was bed-ridden, and his mother, a good soul, was busy early morns and late eyes planning and placing how to support her sick husband and her young son by selling the milk and butter which Milky-White, the beautiful cow, gave them without stint. For it was summer-time. But winter came on; the herbs of the fields took refuge from the frosts in the warm earth, and though his mother sent Jack to gather what fodder he could get in the hedgerows, he came back as often as not with a very empty sack; for Jack's eyes were so often full of wonder at all the things he saw that sometimes he forgot to work!

So it came to pass that one morning Milky-White gave no milk at all—not one drain! Then the good hard-working mother threw her apron over her head and sobbed:

"What shall we do? What shall we do?"

Now Jack loved his mother; besides, he felt just a bit sneaky at being such a big boy and doing so little to help, so he said, "Cheer up! Cheer up! I'll go and get work somewhere." And he felt as he spoke as if he would work his fingers to the bone; but the good woman shook her head mournfully.

"You've tried that before, Jack," she said, "and nobody would keep you. You are quite a good lad but your wits go a-wool-gathering. No, we must sell Milky-White and live on the money. It is no use crying over milk that is not here to spill!"

You see, she was a wise as well as a hard-working woman, and Jack's spirits rose.

"Just so," he cried. "We will sell Milky-White and be richer than ever. It's an ill wind that blows no one good. So, as it is market-day, I'll just take her there and we shall see what we shall see."

"But—" began his mother.

"But doesn't butter parsnips," laughed Jack. "Trust me to make a good bargain."

So, as it was washing-day, and her sick husband was more ailing than usual, his mother let Jack set off to sell the cow.

"Not less than ten pounds," she bawled after him as he turned the corner.

Ten pounds, indeed! Jack had made up his mind to twenty! Twenty solid golden sovereigns!

He was just settling what he should buy his mother as a fairing out of the money, when he saw a queer little old man on the road who called out, "Good-morning, Jack!"

"Good-morning," replied Jack, with a polite bow, wondering how the queer little old man happened to know his name; though, to be sure, Jacks were as plentiful as blackberries.

"And where may you be going?" asked the queer little old man. Jack wondered again—he was always wondering, you know—what the queer little old man had to do with it; but, being always polite, he replied:

"I am going to market to sell Milky-White—and I mean to make a good bargain."

"So you will! So you will!" chuckled the queer little old' man. "You look the sort of chap for it. I bet you know how many beans make five?"

"Two in each hand and one in my mouth," answered Jack readily. He really was sharp as a needle.

"Just so, just so!" chuckled the queer little old man; and as he spoke he drew out of his pocket five beans. "Well, here they are, so give us Milky-White."

Jack was so flabbergasted that he stood with his mouth open as if he expected the fifth bean to fly into it.

"What!" he said at last. "My Milky-White for five common beans! Not if I know it!"

"But they aren't common beans," put in the queer little old man, and there was a queer little smile on his queer little face. "If you plant these beans over-night, by morning they will have grown up right into the very sky."

Jack was too flabbergasted this time even to open his mouth; his eyes opened instead.

"Did you say right into the very sky?" he asked at last; for, see you, Jack had wondered more about the sky than about anything else.

"*RIGHT UP INTO THE VERY SKY*" repeated the queer old man, with a nod between each word. "It's a good bargain, Jack; and, as fair play's a jewel, if they don't—why! meet me here to-morrow morning and you shall have Milky-White back again. Will that please you?"

"Right as a trivet," cried Jack, without stopping to think, and the next moment he found himself standing on an empty road.

"Two in each hand and one in my mouth," repeated Jack. "That is what I said, and what I'll do. Everything in order, and if what the queer little old man said isn't true, I shall get Milky-White back to-morrow morning."

So whistling and munching the bean he trudged home cheerfully, wondering what the sky would be like if he ever got there.

"What a long time you've been!" exclaimed his mother, who was watching anxiously for him at the gate. "It is past sun-setting; but I see you have sold Milky-White. Tell me quick how much you got for her."

"You'll never guess," began Jack.

"Laws-a-mercy! You don't say so," interrupted the good woman. "And I worriting all day lest they should take you in. What was it? Ten pounds—fifteen—sure it *can't* be twenty!"

Jack held out the beans triumphantly.

"There," he said. "That's what I got for her, and a jolly good bargain too!"

It was his mother's turn to be flabbergasted; but all she said was:

"What! Them beans!"

"Yes," replied Jack, beginning to doubt his own wisdom; "but they're *magic* beans. If you plant them over-night, by morning they—grow—right up—into—the—sky—Oh! Please don't hit so hard!"

For Jack's mother for once had lost her temper, and was belaboring the boy for all she was worth. And when she had finished scolding and beating, she flung the miserable beans out of window and sent him, supperless, to bed.

If this was the magical effect of the beans, thought Jack ruefully, he didn't want any more magic, if you please.

However, being healthy and, as a rule, happy, he soon fell asleep and slept like a top.

When he woke he thought at first it was moonlight, for everything in the room showed greenish. Then he stared at the little window. It was covered as if with a curtain by leaves. He was out of bed in a trice, and the next moment, without waiting to dress, was climbing up the biggest beanstalk you ever saw. For what the queer little old man had said was true! One of the beans which his mother had chucked into the garden had found soil, taken root, and grown in the night....

Where?...

Up to the very sky? Jack meant to see at any rate.

So he climbed, and he climbed, and he climbed. It was easy work, for the big beanstalk with the leaves growing out of each side was like a ladder; for all that he soon was out of breath. Then he got his second wind, and was just beginning to wonder if he had a third when he saw in front of him a wide, shining white road stretching away, and away, and away.

So he took to walking, and he walked, and walked, and walked, till he came to a tall, shining white house with a wide white doorstep.

And on the doorstep stood a great big woman with a black porridge-pot in her hand. Now Jack, having had no supper, was hungry as a hunter, and when he saw the porridge-pot he said quite politely:

"Good-morning, 'm. I wonder if you *could* give me some breakfast?"

"Breakfast!" echoed the woman, who, in truth, was an ogre's wife. "If it is breakfast you're wanting, it's breakfast you'll likely be; for I expect my man home every instant, and there is nothing he likes better for breakfast than a boy—a fat boy grilled on toast."

Now Jack was not a bit of a coward, and when he wanted a thing he generally got it, so he said cheerful-like:

"I'd be fatter if I'd had my breakfast!" Whereat the ogre's wife laughed and bade Jack come in; for she was not, really, half as bad as she looked. But he had hardly finished the great bowl of porridge and milk she gave him when the whole house began to tremble and quake. It was the ogre coming home!

Thump! THUMP!! THUMP!!!

"Into the oven with you, sharp!" cried the ogre's wife; and the iron oven door was just closed when the ogre strode in. Jack could see him through the little peep-hole slide at the top where the steam came out.

He was a big one for sure. He had three sheep strung to his belt, and these he threw down on the table. "Here, wife," he cried, "roast me these snippets for breakfast; they are all I've been able to get this morning, worse luck! I hope the oven's hot?" And he went to touch the handle, while Jack burst out all of a sweat, wondering what would happen next.

"Roast!" echoed the ogre's wife. "Pooh! the little things would dry to cinders. Better boil them."

So she set to work to boil them; but the ogre began sniffing about the room. "They don't smell—mutton meat," he growled. Then he frowned horribly and began the real ogre's rhyme:

*"Fee-fi-fo-fum,
I smell the blood of an Englishman.
Be he alive, or be he dead,
I'll grind his bones to make my bread."*

"Don't be silly!" said his wife. "It's the bones of the little boy you had for supper that

I'm boiling down for soup! Come, eat your breakfast, there's a good ogre!"

So the ogre ate his three sheep, and when he had done he went to a big oaken chest and took out three big bags of golden pieces. These he put on the table, and began to count their contents while his wife cleared away the breakfast things. And by and by his head began to nod, and at last he began to snore, and snored so loud that the whole house shook.

Then Jack nipped out of the oven and, seizing one of the bags of gold, crept away, and ran along the straight, wide, shining white road as fast as his legs would carry him till he came to the beanstalk. He couldn't climb down it with the bag of gold, it was so heavy, so he just flung his burden down first, and, helter-skelter, climbed after it.

And when he came to the bottom, there was his mother picking up gold pieces out of the garden as fast as she could; for, of course, the bag had burst.

"Laws-a-mercy me!" she says. "Wherever have you been? See! It's been rainin' gold!"

"No, it hasn't," began Jack. "I climbed up—"

Then he turned to look for the beanstalk; but, lo and behold! it wasn't there at all! So he knew, then, it was all real magic.

After that they lived happily on the gold pieces for a long time, and the bed-ridden father got all sorts of nice things to eat; but, at last, a day came when Jack's mother showed a doleful face as she put a big yellow sovereign into Jack's hand and bade him be careful marketing, because there was not one more in the coffer. After that they must starve.

That night Jack went supperless to bed of his own accord. If he couldn't make money, he thought, at any rate he could eat less money. It was a shame for a big boy to stuff himself and bring no grist to the mill.

He slept like a top, as boys do when they don't overeat themselves, and when he woke....

Hey, presto! the whole room showed greenish, and there was a curtain of leaves over the window! Another bean had grown in the night, and Jack was up it like a lamp-lighter before you could say knife.

This time he didn't take nearly so long climbing until he reached the straight, wide, white road, and in a trice he found himself before the tall white house, where on the wide white steps the ogre's wife was standing with the black porridge-pot in her hand.

And this time Jack was as bold as brass.

"Good-morning, 'm," he said. "I've come to ask you for breakfast, for I had no supper, and I'm as hungry as a hunter."

"Go away, bad boy!" replied the ogre's wife. "Last time I gave a boy breakfast my man missed a whole bag of gold. I believe you are the same boy."

"Maybe I am, maybe I'm not," said Jack, with a laugh. "I'll tell you true when I've had my breakfast; but not till then."

So the ogre's wife, who was dreadfully curious, gave him a big bowl full of porridge; but before he had half finished it he heard the ogre coming—

Thump! THUMP! THUMP!

"In with you to the oven," shrieked the ogre's wife. "You shall tell me when he has gone to sleep."

This time Jack saw through the steam peep-hole that the ogre had three fat calves strung to his belt.

"Better luck to-day, wife!" he cried, and his voice shook the house. "Quick! Roast these trifles for my breakfast! I hope the oven's hot?"

And he went to feel the handle of the door, but his wife cried out sharply:

"Roast! Why, you'd have to wait hours before they were done! I'll broil them—see how bright the fire is!"

"Umph!" growled the ogre. And then he began sniffing and calling out:

"Fee-fi-fo-fum,
I smell the blood of an Englishman.
Be he alive, or be he dead,
I'll grind his bones to make my bread."

"Twaddle!" said the ogre's wife. "It's only the bones of the boy you had last week that I've put into the pig-bucket!"

"Umph!" said the ogre harshly; but he ate the broiled calves, and then he said to his wife, "Bring me my hen that lays the magic eggs. I want to see gold."

So the ogre's wife brought him a great big black hen with a shiny red comb. She plumped it down on the table and took away the breakfast things.

Then the ogre said to the hen, "Lay!" and it promptly laid—what do you think?—a beautiful, shiny, yellow, golden egg!

"None so dusty, henny-penny," laughed the ogre. "I shan't have to beg as long as I've got you." Then he said, "Lay!" once more; and, lo and behold! there was another beautiful, shiny, yellow, golden egg!

Jack could hardly believe his eyes, and made up his mind that he would have that hen, come what might. So, when the ogre began to doze, he just out like a flash from the oven, seized the hen, and ran for his life! But, you see, he reckoned without his prize; for hens, you know, always cackle when they leave their nests after laying an egg, and this one set up such a scrawing that it woke the ogre.

"Where's my hen?" he shouted, and his wife came rushing in, and they both rushed to the door; but Jack had got the better of them by a good start, and all they could see was a little figure right away down the wide white road, holding a big, scrawing, cackling, fluttering black hen by the legs!

How Jack got down the beanstalk he never knew. It was all wings, and leaves, and feathers, and cacklings; but get down he did, and there was his mother wondering if the sky was going to fall!

But the very moment Jack touched ground he called out, "Lay!" and the black hen ceased cackling and laid a great, big, shiny, yellow, golden egg.

So every one was satisfied; and from that moment everybody had everything that money could buy. For, whenever they wanted anything, they just said, "Lay!" and the black hen provided them with gold.

But Jack began to wonder if he couldn't find something else besides money in the sky. So one fine moonlight midsummer night he refused his supper, and before he went to bed stole out to the garden with a big watering-can and watered the ground under his window; for, thought he, "there must be two more beans somewhere, and perhaps it is too dry for them to grow." Then he slept like a top.

And, lo and behold! when he woke, there was the green light shimmering through his room, and there he was in an instant on the beanstalk, climbing, climbing, climbing for all he was worth.

But this time he knew better than to ask for his breakfast; for the ogre's wife would be sure to recognize him. So he just hid in some bushes beside the great white house, till he saw her in the scullery, and then he slipped out and hid himself in the copper; for he knew she would be sure to look in the oven first thing.

And by and by he heard—

Thump! THUMP! THUMP!

And peeping through a crack in the copper-lid, he could see the ogre stalk in with three huge oxen strung at his belt. But this time, no sooner had the ogre got into the house than he began shouting:

"Fee-fi-fo-fum,
I smell the blood of an Englishman.
Be he alive, or be he dead,

Stories

I'll grind his bones to make my bread."

    For, see you, the copper-lid didn't fit tight like the oven door, and ogres have noses like a dog's for scent.

    "Well, I declare, so do I!" exclaimed the ogre's wife. "It will be that horrid boy who stole the bag of gold and the hen. If so, he's hid in the oven!"

    But when she opened the door, lo and behold! Jack wasn't there! Only some joints of meat roasting and sizzling away. Then she laughed and said, "You and me be fools for sure. Why, it's the boy you caught last night as I was getting ready for your breakfast. Yes, we be fools to take dead meat for live flesh! So eat your breakfast, there's a good ogre!"

    But the ogre, though he enjoyed roast boy very much, wasn't satisfied, and every now and then he would burst out with "*Fee-fi-fo-fum,*" and get up and search the cupboards, keeping Jack in a fever of fear lest he should think of the copper.

    But he didn't. And when he had finished his breakfast he called out to his wife, "Bring me my magic harp! I want to be amused."

    So she brought out a little harp and put it on the table. And the ogre leant back in his chair and said lazily:

"Sing!"

    And, lo and behold! the harp began to sing. If you want to know what it sang about? Why! It sang about everything! And it sang so beautifully that Jack forgot to be frightened, and

the ogre forgot to think of "*Fee-fi-fo-fum*," and fell asleep and
did
NOT
SNORE.

Then Jack stole out of the copper like a mouse and crept hands and knees to the table, raised himself up ever so softly and laid hold of the magic harp; for he was determined to have it.

But, no sooner had he touched it, than it cried out quite loud, "Master! Master!" So the ogre woke, saw Jack making off, and rushed after him.

My goodness, it was a race! Jack was nimble, but the ogre's stride was twice as long. So, though Jack turned, and twisted, and doubled like a hare, yet at last, when he got to the beanstalk, the ogre was not a dozen yards behind him. There wasn't time to think, so Jack just flung himself on to the stalk and began to go down as fast as he could, while the harp kept calling, "Master! Master!" at the very top of its voice. He had only got down about a quarter of the way when there was the most awful lurch you can think of, and Jack nearly fell off the beanstalk. It was the ogre beginning to climb down, and his weight made the stalk sway like a tree in a storm. Then Jack knew it was life or death, and he climbed down faster and faster, and as he climbed he shouted, "Mother! Mother! Bring an axe! Bring an axe!"

Now his mother, as luck would have it, was in the backyard chopping wood, and she ran out thinking that this time the sky must have fallen. Just at that moment Jack touched ground, and he flung down the harp—which immediately began to sing of all sorts of beautiful things—and he seized the axe and gave a great chop at the beanstalk, which shook and swayed and bent like barley before a breeze.

"Have a care!" shouted the ogre, clinging on as hard as he could. But Jack *did* have a care, and he dealt that beanstalk such a shrewd blow that the whole of it, ogre and all, came toppling down, and, of course, the ogre broke his crown, so that he died on the spot.

After that everyone was quite happy. For they had gold to spare and if the bedridden father was dull, Jack just brought out the harp and said, "Sing!" And lo and behold, it sang about everything under the sun. So Jack ceased wondering so much and became quite a useful person.

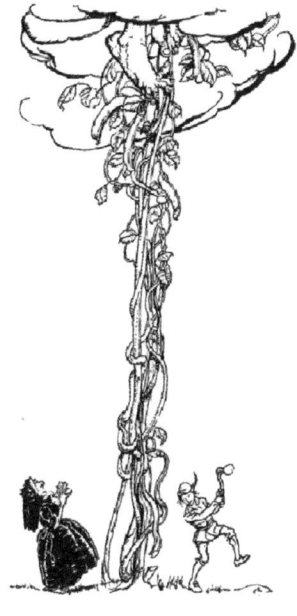

And the last bean still hasn't grown yet. It is still in the garden. I wonder if it will ever grow? And what little child will climb it's beanstalk into the sky? And what will that child find? Goody me!

THE THREE LITTLE PIGS

Once upon a time there was an old sow who had three little pigs, and as she had not enough for them to eat, she said they had better go out into the world and seek their fortunes.

Now the eldest pig went first, and as he trotted along the road he met a man carrying a bundle of straw. So he said very politely:
"If you please, sir, could you give me that straw to build me a house?"

And the man, seeing what good manners the little pig had, gave him the straw, and the little pig set to work and built a beautiful house with it.

Now, when it was finished, a wolf happened to pass that way; and he saw the house, and *he smelt the pig inside.*

So he knocked at the door and said:

"*Little pig! Little pig! Let me in! Let me in!*"

But the little pig saw the wolf's big paws through the keyhole, so he answered back:

"*No! No! No! by the hair of my chinny chin chin!*"

Then the wolf showed his teeth and said:

"*Then I'll huff and I'll puff and I'll blow your house in.*"

So he huffed and he puffed and he blew the house in. Then he ate up little piggy and went on his way.

Now, the next piggy, when he started, met a man carrying a bundle of furze, and, being very polite, he said to him:

"If you please, sir, could you give me that furze to build me a house?"

And the man, seeing what good manners the little pig had, gave him the furze, and the little pig set to work and built himself a beautiful house.

Now it so happened that when the house was finished the wolf passed that way; and he saw the house, and *he smelt the pig inside.*

So he knocked at the door and said:

"*Little pig! Little pig! Let me in! Let me in!*"

But the little pig peeped through the keyhole and saw the wolf's great ears, so he answered back:

"*No! No! No! by the hair of my chinny chin chin!*"

Then the wolf showed his teeth and said:

"*Then I'll huff and I'll puff and I'll blow your house in!*"

So he huffed and he puffed and he blew the house in. Then he ate up little piggy and went on his way.

Now the third little piggy, when he started, met a man carrying a load of bricks, and, being very polite, he said:

"If you please sir, could you give me those bricks to build me a house?"

And the man, seeing that he had been well brought up, gave him the bricks, and the little pig set to work and built himself a beautiful house.

And once again it happened that when it was finished the wolf chanced to come that way; and he saw the house, and he *smelt the pig inside.*

So he knocked at the door and said:

"*Little pig! Little pig! Let me in! Let me in!*"

But the little pig peeped through the keyhole and saw the wolf's great eyes, so he answered:

"*No! No! No! by the hair of my chinny chin chin!*"

"*Then I'll huff and I'll puff and I'll blow your house in!*" says the wolf, showing his teeth.

Well! he huffed and he puffed. He puffed and he huffed. And he huffed, huffed, and he puffed, puffed; but he could *not* blow the house down. At last he was so out of breath that he couldn't huff and he couldn't puff any more. So he thought a bit. Then he said:

"Little pig! I know where there is ever such a nice field of turnips."

"Do you," says little piggy, "and where may that be?"

"I'll show you," says the wolf; "if you will be ready at six o'clock to-morrow morning, I will call round for you, and we can go together to Farmer Smith's field and get turnips for dinner."

"Thank you kindly," says the little piggy. "I will be ready at six o'clock sharp."

But, you see, the little pig was not one to be taken in with chaff, so he got up at five, trotted off to Farmer Smith's field, rooted up the turnips, and was home eating them for breakfast when the wolf clattered at the door and cried:

"Little pig! Little pig! Aren't you ready?"

"Ready?" says the little piggy. "Why! what a sluggard you are! I've been to the field and come back again, and I'm having a nice potful of turnips for breakfast."

Then the wolf grew red with rage; but he was determined to eat little piggy, so he said, as if he didn't care:

"I'm glad you like them; but I know of something better than turnips."

"Indeed," says little piggy, "and what may that be?"

"A nice apple tree down in Merry gardens with the juiciest, sweetest apples on it! So if you will be ready at five o'clock to-morrow morning I will come round for you and we can get the apples together."

"Thank you kindly," says little piggy. "I will sure and be ready at five o'clock sharp."

Now the next morning he bustled up ever so early, and it wasn't four o'clock when he started to get the apples; but, you see, the wolf had been taken in once and wasn't going to be taken in again, so he also started at four o'clock, and the little pig had but just got his basket half full of apples when he saw the wolf coming down the road licking his lips.

"Hullo!" says the wolf, "here already! You *are* an early bird! Are the apples nice?"

"Very nice," says little piggy; "I'll throw you down one to try."

And he threw it so far away, that when the wolf had gone to pick it up, the little pig was able to jump down with his basket and run home.

Well, the wolf was fair angry; but he went next day to the little piggy's house and called through the door, as mild as milk:

"Little pig! Little pig! You are so clever, I should like to give you a fairing; so if you will come with me to the fair this afternoon you shall have one."

"Thank you kindly," says little piggy. "What time shall we start?"

"At three o'clock sharp," says the wolf, "so be sure to be ready."

Stories

"I'll be ready before three," sniggered the little piggy. And he was! He started early in the morning and went to the fair, and rode in a swing, and enjoyed himself ever so much, and bought himself a butter-churn as a fairing, and trotted away towards home long before three o'clock. But just as he got to the top of the hill, what should he see but the wolf coming up it, all panting and red with rage!

Well, there was no place to hide in but the butter-churn; so he crept into it, and was just pulling down the cover when the churn started to roll down the hill—

Bumpety, bumpety, bump!

Of course piggy, inside, began to squeal, and when the wolf heard the noise, and saw the butter-churn rolling down on top of him—

Bumpety, bumpety, bump!

—he was so frightened that he turned tail and ran away.

But he was still determined to get the little pig for his dinner; so he went next day to the house and told the little pig how sorry he was not to have been able to keep his promise of going to the fair, because of an awful, dreadful, terrible Thing that had rushed at him, making a fearsome noise.

"Dear me!" says the little piggy, "that must have been me! I hid inside the butter-churn when I saw you coming, and it started to roll! I am sorry I frightened you!"

But this was too much. The wolf danced about with rage and swore he would come down the chimney and eat up the little pig for his supper. But while he was climbing on to the roof the little pig made up a blazing fire and put on a big pot full of water to boil. Then, just as the wolf was coming down the chimney, the little piggy off with the lid, and plump! in fell the wolf into the scalding water.

So the little piggy put on the cover again, boiled the wolf up, and ate *him* for supper.

HANSEL AND GRETHEL

Once upon a time there dwelt near a large wood a poor wood cutter, with his wife, and two children by his former marriage, a little boy called Hansel, and a girl named Grethel. He had little enough to break or bite; and once, when there was a great famine in the land, he could hardly procure even his daily bread; and as he lay thinking in his bed one night, he sighed, and said to his wife, "What will become of us? How can we feed our children, when we have no more than we can eat ourselves?"

"Know then, my husband," answered she, "we will lead them away, quite early in the morning, into the thickest part of the wood, and there make them a fire, and give them each a little piece of bread, then we will go to our work, and leave them alone, so they will not find the way home again, and we shall be freed from them."

"No, wife," replied he, "that I can never do; how can you bring your heart to leave my children all alone in the wood; for the wild beasts will soon come and tear them to pieces?"

"Oh, you simpleton!" said she, "then we must all four die of hunger; you had better plane the coffins for us." But she left him no peace till he consented, saying, "Ah, but I shall miss the poor children."

The two children, however, had not gone to sleep, for very hunger, and so they overheard what the stepmother said to their father. Grethel wept bitterly, and said to Hansel, "What will become of us?"

"Be quiet, Grethel," said he; "do not cry—I will help you." And as soon as their parents had gone to sleep, he got up, put on his coat, and, unbarring the back door, went out. The moon shone brightly, and the white pebbles which lay before the door seemed like silver pieces, they glittered so brightly. Hansel stooped down, and put as many into his pocket as it would hold; and then going back he said to Grethel, "Be of good cheer, dear sister, and sleep in peace; God will not forsake us." And so saying, he went to bed again.

The next morning, before the sun arose, the wife went and awoke the two children. "Get up, you lazy things; we are going into the forest to chop wood." Then she gave them each a piece of bread, saying, "There is something for your dinner; do not eat it before the time, for you will get nothing else." Grethel took the bread in her apron, for Hansel's pocket was full of pebbles;

and so they all set out upon their way. When they had gone a little distance, Hansel stood still, and peeped back at the house; and this he repeated several times, till his father said, "Hansel, what are you looking at, and why do you lag behind? Take care, and remember your legs."

"Ah, father," said Hansel, "I am looking at my white cat sitting upon the roof of the house, and trying to say good-bye."

"You simpleton!" said the wife, "that is not a cat; it is only the sun shining on the white chimney." But in reality Hansel was not looking at a cat; but every time he stopped, he dropped a pebble out of his pocket upon the path.

When they came to the middle of the forest, the father told the children to collect wood, and he would make them a fire, so that they should not be cold. So Hansel and Grethel gathered together quite a little mount of twigs. Then they set fire to them; and as the flame burnt up high, the wife said, "Now, you children, lie down near the fire, and rest yourselves, whilst we go into the forest and chop more wood; when we are ready we will come and call you."

Hansel and Grethel sat down by the fire, and when it was noon, each ate the piece of bread; and because they could hear the blows of an axe they thought their father was near; but it was not an axe, but a branch which he had bound to an old tree, so as to be blown to and fro by the wind. They waited so long, that at last their eyes closed from weariness, and they fell fast asleep. When they awoke, it was quite dark, and Grethel began to cry. "How shall we get out of the wood?" But Hansel tried to comfort her by saying, "Wait

Stories

a little while till the moon rises, and then we will quickly find the way." The moon shone forth, and Hansel, taking his sister's hand, followed the pebbles, which glittered like new-coined silver pieces, and showed them the way. All night long they walked on, and as day broke they came to their father's house. They knocked at the door, and when the wife opened it, and saw Hansel and Grethel, she exclaimed, "You wicked children! Why did you sleep so long in the wood? We thought you were never coming home again." But their father was extremely glad, for it had grieved his heart to leave them all alone.

Not long afterwards there was again great scarcity in every corner of the land; and one night the children overheard their mother saying to their father, "Everything is once more consumed; we have only half a loaf left, and then the song is ended: the children must be sent away. We will take them deeper into the wood, so that they may not find the way out again; it is the only means of escape for us."

But her husband felt heavy at heart, and thought, "It were better to share the last crust with the children." His wife, however, would listen to nothing that he said, and scolded and reproached him without end.

He who says A must say B too; and he who consents the first time must also the second.

The children, however, had heard the conversation as they lay awake, and as soon as their parents went to sleep Hansel got up, intending to pick up some pebbles as before; but the wife had locked the door, so that he could not get out. Nevertheless he comforted Grethel, saying, "Do not weep; sleep in quiet; the good God will not forsake us."

Early in the morning the stepmother came and pulled them out of bed, and gave them each a slice of bread, which was still smaller than the former piece. On the way Hansel broke his in his pocket, and stopping every now and then, dropped a crumb upon the path. "Hansel, why do you stop and look about?" said the father, "keep in the path." "I am looking at my little dove," answered Hansel, "nodding a good-bye to me." "Simpleton!" said the wife, "that is no dove, but only the sun shining on the chimney." But Hansel kept still dropping crumbs as he went along.

The mother led the children deep into the wood, where they had never been before, and there making a gigantic fire, she said to them, "Sit down here and rest, and when you feel tired you can sleep for a little while. We are going into the forest to hew wood, and in the evening, when we are ready, we will come and fetch you again."

When noon came, Grethel shared her bread with Hansel, who had strewn his on the path. They then went to sleep; but the evening arrived and no one came to visit the poor children, and in the dark night they awoke, and Hansel comforted his sister by saying, "Only wait, Grethel, till the moon comes out, then we shall see the crumbs of bread which I have dropped, and they will show us the way home." The moon shone and they got up, but they could not see any crumbs, for the thousands of birds which had been flying about in the woods and fields had picked them all up. Hansel kept saying to Grethel, "We will soon find the way;" but they did not, and they walked the whole night long and the next day, but still they did not come out of the wood; and they got very hungry, for they had nothing to eat but the berries which they found upon the bushes. Soon they were so tired that they could not drag themselves along, then they lay down under a tree and again went to sleep.

It was now the third morning since they had left their father's house, and they still walked on; but they only got deeper, and deeper, and deeper into the wood, and Hansel felt that if help did not come very soon they must die of hunger. As soon as it was noon they saw a beautiful, snow-white bird sitting upon a bough, singing so sweetly that they stood still and listened to it. It soon ceased, and spreading its wings flew off; and they followed it until it arrived at a cottage, upon the roof of which it perched; and when they went close up to it they saw that the cottage was made of bread and cakes, and the window-panes were of clear sugar.

"We will go in here," said Hansel, "and have a glorious feast. I will eat a piece of the roof, and you can eat the window. Will they not be sweet?" So Hansel reached up and broke a piece off the roof, in order to see how it tasted; while Grethel stepped up to the window and began to bite it. Then a sweet voice called out in the room, "Tip-tap, tip-tap, who knocks at my door?" and the children answered, "The wind, the wind, the child of heaven;" and they went on eating without interruption. Hansel thought the roof tasted very nice, and so he tore off a great piece; while Grethel broke a large round pane out of the window, and sat down quite contentedly. Just then the door opened, and a very old woman, walking upon crutches, came out. Hansel and Grethel were so much frightened that they let fall what they had in their hands; but the old woman nodding her head, said, "Ah, you dear children, what has brought you here? Come in and stop with me, and no harm shall come to you;" and so saying she took them both by the hand, and led them into her cottage. A good meal of milk and pancakes, with sugar, apples and nuts, was spread on the table, and in the back room were two nice little beds, covered with white, where Hansel and Grethel laid themselves down, and were happy as could be.

The old woman behaved very kindly to them, but in reality she was a wicked old witch who way-laid children, and built the breadhouse in order to entice them in; but as soon as they were in her power she killed them, cooked and ate them, and made a great festival of the day. Witches have red eyes, and cannot see very far; but they have a fine sense of smelling, like wild beasts, so that they know when children approach them. When Hansel and Grethel came near the witch's house she laughed wickedly, saying, "Here come two who shall not escape me." And early in the morning, before they awoke, she went up to them, and saw how lovingly they lay sleeping, with their chubby red cheeks; and she mumbled to herself, "That will be a good bite." Then she took up Hansel with her rough hand, and shut him up in a little cage with a lattice-door; and although he screamed loudly it was of no use. Grethel came next, and shaking her till she awoke, she said, "Get up, you lazy brat, and fetch some water to cook something good for your brother, who must remain in that stall and get fat; and when he is fat enough I shall eat him." Grethel began to cry, but it was all useless, for the old witch made her do as she wanted. So a nice meal was cooked for Hansel, but Grethel got nothing else but a crab's claw.

Every morning the old witch came to the cage and said, "Hansel, stretch out your finger that I may feel whether you are getting fat." But Hansel used to stretch out a bone, and the old woman, having very bad sight, thought it was his finger, and wondered very much why he did not get fat. When four weeks had passed, and Hansel still kept quite lean, she lost all her patience, and would not wait any longer. "Grethel," she cried in a passion, "get some water quickly; be Hansel fat or lean, this morning I will kill and cook him." Oh, how the poor little sister grieved, as she was forced to fetch the water, and fast the tears ran down her cheeks! "Dear good God, help us now!" she prayed. "Had we only been eaten by the wild beasts in the wood, then we should have died together." But the old witch called out, "Leave off that noise; it will not help you a bit."

So early in the morning Grethel was compelled to go out and fill the kettle, and make a fire. "First, we will bake, however," said the old woman; "I have already heated the oven and kneaded the dough;" and so saying, she pushed poor Grethel up to the oven, out of which the flames were burning fiercely. "Creep in," said the witch, "and see if it is hot enough, and then we will put in the bread," but she intended when Grethel got in, to shut up the oven and let her bake, so that she might eat her as well as Hansel. Grethel perceived her wicked thoughts and said, "I do not know how to do it; how shall I get in?" "You stupid goose," said she, "the opening is big enough. See, I could even get in myself!" and she got up, and put her head into the oven. Then Grethel gave her a push, so that she fell right in, and shutting the iron door bolted it. Oh! how horribly the witch howled; but Grethel ran away, and left her to burn to ashes.

Now she ran to Hansel, and, opening the door, called out, "Hansel we are saved; the old witch is dead?"

So he sprang out, like a bird from his cage when the door was opened; and they were so glad that they fell upon each other's neck, and kissed each other over and over again. And now, as there was nothing to fear, they went back to the witch's [pg 68] house, where in every corner were caskets full of pearls and precious stones. "These are better than pebbles," said Hansel, putting as many into his pocket as it would hold; while Grethel thought, "I will take some home too," and filled her apron full.

"We must be off now," said Hansel, "and get out of this enchanted forest;" but when they had walked for two hours they came to a large piece of water.

"We cannot get over," said Hansel; "I can see no bridge at all." "And there is no boat either," said Grethel, "but there swims a white duck, I will ask her to help us over;" and she sang,

"Little Duck, good little Duck,
Grethel and Hansel, together we stand;
There is neither stile nor bridge,
Take us on your back to land."

So the Duck came to them, and Hansel sat himself on, and bade his sister sit beside him. "No," replied Grethel, "that will be too much for the Duck, she shall take us over one at a time."

This the good little bird did, and when both were happily arrived on the other

325

side, and had gone a little way, they came to a well-known wood, which they knew the better every step they went, and at last they perceived their father's house. Then they began to run, and rushing into the house, they fell upon their father's neck. He had not had one happy hour since he had left the children in the forest; and his wife was dead. Grethel shook her apron, and the pearls and precious stones rolled out upon the floor, and Hansel threw down one handful after the other out of his pocket. Then all their sorrows were ended, and they lived together in great happiness.

SNOW-WHITE AND ROSE-RED

A poor widow once lived in a little cottage. In front of the cottage was a garden, in which were growing two rose trees; one of these bore white roses, and the other red.

She had two children, who resembled the rose trees. One was called Snow-White, and the other Rose-Red; and they were as religious and loving, busy and untiring, as any two children ever were.

Snow-White was more gentle, and quieter than her sister, who liked better skipping about the fields, seeking flowers, and catching summer birds; while Snow-White stayed at home with her mother, either helping her in her work, or, when that was done, reading aloud.

The two children had the greatest affection the one for the other. They were always seen hand in hand; and should Snow-White say to her sister, "We will never separate," the other would reply, "Not while we live," the mother adding, "That which one has, let her always share with the other."

They constantly ran together in the woods, collecting ripe berries; but not a single animal would have injured them; quite the reverse, they all felt the greatest esteem for the young creatures. The hare came to eat parsley from their hands, the deer grazed by their side, the stag bounded past them unheeding; the birds, likewise, did not stir from the bough, but sang in entire security. No mischance befell them; if benighted in the wood, they lay down on the moss to repose and sleep till the morning; and their mother was satisfied as to their safety, and felt no fear about them.

Once, when they had spent the night in the wood, and the bright sunrise awoke them, they saw a beautiful child, in a snow-white robe, shining like diamonds, sitting close to the spot where they had reposed. She arose when they opened their eyes, and looked kindly at them; but said no word, and passed from their sight into the wood. When the children looked around they saw they had been sleeping on the edge of a precipice, and would surely have fallen over if they had gone forward two steps further in the darkness. Their mother said the beautiful child must have been the angel who watches over good children.

Snow-White and Rose-Red kept their mother's cottage so clean that it gave pleasure only to look in. In summer-time Rose-Red attended to the house, and every morning, before her mother awoke, placed by her bed a bouquet which had in it a rose from each of the rose-trees. In winter-time Snow-White set light to the fire, and put on the kettle, after polishing it until it was like gold for brightness. In the evening, when snow was falling, her mother would bid her bolt the door, and then, sitting by the hearth, the good widow would read aloud to them from a big book while the little girls were spinning. Close by them lay a lamb, and a white pigeon, with its head tucked under its wing, was on a perch behind.

One evening, as they were all sitting cozily together like this, there was a knock at the door, as if someone wished to come in.

"Make haste, Rose-Red!" said her mother; "open the door; it is surely some traveler seeking shelter." Rose-Red accordingly pulled back the bolt, expecting to see some poor man. But it was nothing of the kind; it was a bear, that thrust his big head in at the open door. Rose-Red cried out and sprang back, the lamb bleated, the dove fluttered her wings and Snow-White hid herself behind her mother's bed. The bear began speaking, and said, "Do not be afraid: I will not do you any harm; I am half-frozen, and would like to warm myself a little at your fire."

"Poor bear!" the mother replied; "come in and lie by the fire; only be careful that your hair is not burnt." Then she called Snow-White and Rose-Red, telling them that the bear was kind, and would not harm them. They came, as she bade them, and presently the lamb and the dove drew near also without fear.

"Children," begged the bear; "knock some of the snow off my coat." So they brought the broom and brushed the bear's coat quite clean. After that he stretched himself out in front of the fire, and pleased himself by growling a little, only to show that he was happy and comfortable. Before long they were all quite good friends, and the children began to play with their unlooked

for visitor, pulling his thick fur, or placing their feet on his back, or rolling him over and over. Then they took a slender hazel twig, using it upon his thick coat, and they laughed when he growled. The bear permitted them to amuse themselves in this way, only occasionally calling out, when it went a little too far, "Children, spare me an inch of life!"

When it was night, and all were making ready to go to bed, the widow told the bear, "You may stay here and lie by the hearth, if you like, so that you will be sheltered from the cold and from the bad weather."

The offer was accepted, but when morning came, as the day broke in the east, the two children let him out, and over the snow he went back into the wood.

After this, every evening at the same time the bear came, lay by the fire, and allowed the children to play with him; so they became quite fond of their curious playmate, and the door was not ever bolted in the evening until he had appeared.

When springtime came, and all around began to look green and bright, one morning the bear said to Snow-White, "Now I must leave you, and all the summer long I shall not be able to come back."

"Where, then, are you going, dear bear?" asked Snow-White. "I have to go to the woods to protect my treasure from the bad dwarfs. In winter time when the earth is frozen hard, they must remain underground, and cannot make their way through; but now that the sunshine has thawed the earth they can come to the surface, and whatever gets into their hands, or is brought to their caves, seldom, if ever, again sees daylight."

Snow-White was very sad when she said good-bye to the good-natured beast, and unfastened the door, that he might go; but in going out he was caught by a hook in the lintel, and a scrap of his fur being torn, Snow-White thought there was something shining like gold through the rent; but he went out so quickly that she could not feel certain what it was, and soon he was hidden among the trees.

One day the mother sent her children into the wood to pick up sticks. They found a big tree lying on the ground. It had been felled, and towards the roots they noticed something skipping and springing, which they could not make out, as it was sometimes hidden in the grasses. As they came nearer they could see it was a dwarf, with a shriveled up face and a snow-white beard an ell long. The beard was fixed in a gash in the tree trunk, and the tiny fellow was hopping to and fro, like a dog at the end of a string, but he could not manage to free himself. He stared at the children, with his red, fiery eyes, and called out, "Why are you standing there? Can't you come and try to help me?"

"What were you doing, little fellow?" enquired Rose-Red.

"Stupid, inquisitive goose!" replied the dwarf; "I meant to split the trunk, so that I could chop it up for kitchen sticks; big logs would burn up the small quantity of food we cook, for people like us do not consume great heaps of food, as you heavy, greedy folk do. The bill-hook I had driven in, and soon I should have done what I required; but the tool suddenly sprang from the cleft, which so quickly shut up again that it caught my handsome white beard; and here I must stop, for I cannot set myself free. You stupid, pale-faced creatures! You laugh, do you?"

In spite of the dwarf's bad temper, the girls took all possible pains to release the little man, but without avail; the beard could not be moved, it was wedged too tightly.

"I will run and get someone else," said Rose-Red.

"Idiot!" cried the dwarf. "Who would go and get more people? Already there are two too many. Can't you think of something better?"

"Don't be so impatient," said Snow-White. "I will try to think." She clapped her hands as if she had discovered a remedy, took out her scissors, and in a moment set the dwarf free by cutting off the end of his beard.

Immediately the dwarf felt that he was free he seized a sack full of gold that was hidden among the tree roots, and, lifting it up, grumbled out, "Clumsy creatures, to cut off a bit of my beautiful beard, of which I am so proud! I leave the cuckoos to pay you for what you did." Saying this, he swung the sack across his shoulder and went off without even casting a glance at the children.

Not long afterwards the two sisters went to angle in the brook, meaning to catch fish for dinner. As they were drawing near the water they perceived something, looking like a large grasshopper, springing towards the stream, as if it were going in. They hurried up to see what it might be, and found that it was the dwarf. "Where are you going?" said Rose-Red. "Surely you will not jump into the water?"

"I'm not such a simpleton as that!" yelled the little man. "Don't you see that a wretch of a fish is pulling me in?"

The dwarf had been sitting angling from the side of the stream when, by ill-luck, the wind had entangled his beard in his line, and just afterwards a big fish taking the bait, the unamiable little fellow had not sufficient strength to pull it out; so the fish had the advantage, and was dragging the dwarf after it. Certainly he caught at every stalk and spray near him, but that did not assist him greatly; he was forced to follow all the twistings of the fish, and was perpetually in danger of being drawn into the brook.

The girls arrived just in time. They caught hold of him firmly, and endeavored to untwist his beard from the line, but in vain; it was too tightly entangled. There was nothing left but again to make use of the scissors; so they were taken out, and the tangled portion was cut off.

When the dwarf noticed what they were about, he exclaimed, in a great rage, "Is this how you damage my beard? Not content with making it shorter before, you are now making it still smaller, and completely spoiling it. I shall not ever dare to show my face to my friends. I wish you had missed your way before you took this road." Then he fetched a sack of pearls that lay among the rushes, and saying not another word, hobbled off and disappeared behind a large stone.

Soon after this it chanced that the poor widow sent her children to the town to purchase cotton, needles, ribbon and tape. The way to the town ran over a common on which in every direction large masses of rocks were scattered about. The children's attention was soon attracted to a big bird that hovered in the air. They remarked that after circling slowly for a time, and gradually getting nearer to the ground, it all of a sudden pounced down amongst a mass of rock. Instantly a heart-rending cry reached their ears, and, running quickly to the place, they saw, with horror, that the eagle had seized their former acquaintance, the dwarf, and was just about to carry him off. The kind children did not hesitate for an instant. They took a firm hold of the little man, they strove so stoutly with the eagle for possession of his contemplated prey, that, after much rough treatment on both sides, the dwarf was left in the hands of his brave little friends, and the eagle took to flight.

As soon as the little man had in some measure recovered from his alarm, his small, squeaky, cracked voice was heard saying, "Couldn't you have held me more gently? See my little coat; you have rent and damaged it in a fine manner, you clumsy, officious things!" Then he picked up a sack of jewels, and slipped out of sight behind a piece of rock.

The maidens by this time were quite used to his ungrateful, ungracious ways; so they took no notice of it, but went on their way, made their purchases, and then were ready to return to their happy home.

On their way back, suddenly, once more they ran across their dwarf friend.

Upon a clear space he had turned out his sack of jewels, so that he could count and admire them, for he had not imagined that anybody would at so late an hour be coming across the common. The setting sun was shining upon the brilliant stones, and their changing hues and sparkling rays caused the children to pause to admire them also.

"What are you gazing at?" cried the dwarf, at the same time becoming red with rage; "and what are you standing there for, making ugly faces?"

It is probable that he might have proceeded in the same complimentary manner, but suddenly a great growl was heard near by them, and a big bear joined the party. Up jumped the dwarf in extreme terror, but could not get to his hiding-place, the bear was too close to him; so he cried out in very evident anguish—"Dear Mr. Bear, forgive me, I pray! I will render to you all my treasure. Just see those precious stones lying there! Grant me my life! What would you do with such an insignificant little fellow? You would not notice me between your teeth. See, though, those two children, they would be delicate morsels, and are as plump as partridges; I beg of you to take them, good Mr. Bear, and let me go."

But the bear would not be moved by his speeches. He gave the ill-disposed creature a blow with his paw, and he lay lifeless on the ground. Meanwhile, the maidens were running away, making off for home as well as they could; but all of a sudden they were stopped by a well-known voice that called out, "Snow-White, Rose-Red, stay! Do not fear. I will accompany you."

The bear quickly came towards them, but as he reached their side, suddenly the bear-skin slipped to the ground, and there before them was standing a handsome man, completely garmented in gold, who said, "I am a king's son, who was enchanted by the wicked dwarf lying over there. He stole my treasure, and compelled me to roam the woods transformed into a big bear until his death should set me free. Therefore he has only received a well-deserved punishment."

Then Rose-Red and Snow-White and the Prince all went back to the cottage, and some time afterwards Snow-White married the Prince, and Rose-Red, his brother, who shared between them the enormous treasure which the dwarf had collected in his cave.

The old mother spent many happy years with her children. The two rose-trees she took with her when she left the cottage, and they grew in front of her window, where they continued to bear each year the most beautiful roses, red and white.

Stories
RUMPELSTILTSKIN

There was once a poor Miller who had a beautiful daughter, and one day, having to go to speak with the King, he said, in order to make himself appear of consequence, that he had a daughter who could spin straw into gold. The King was very fond of gold, and thought to himself, "That is an art which would please me very well"; and so he said to the Miller, "If your daughter is so very clever, bring her to the castle in the morning, and I will put her to the proof."

As soon as she arrived the King led her into a chamber which was full of straw; and, giving her a wheel and a reel, he said, "Now set yourself to work, and if you have not spun this straw into gold by an early hour to-morrow, you must die." With these words he shut the room door, and left the maiden alone.

There she sat for a long time, thinking how to save her life; for she understood nothing of the art whereby straw might be spun into gold; and her perplexity increased more and more, till at last she began to weep. All at once the door opened, and in stepped a little Man, who said, "Good evening, fair maiden; why do you weep so sore?" "Ah," she replied, "I must spin this straw into gold, and I am sure I do not know how."

The little Man asked, "What will you give me if I spin it for you?"

"My necklace," said the maiden.

The Dwarf took it, placed himself in front of the wheel, and whirr, whirr, whirr, three times round, and the bobbin was full. Then he set up another, and whir, whir, whir, thrice round again, and a second bobbin was full; and so he went all night long, until all the straw was spun, and the bobbins were full of gold. At sunrise the King came, very much astonished to see the gold; the sight of which gladdened him, but did not make his heart less covetous. He caused the maiden to be led into another room, still larger, full of straw; and then he bade her spin it into gold during the night if she valued her life. The maiden was again quite at a loss what to do; but while she cried the door opened suddenly, as before, and the Dwarf appeared and asked her what she would give him in return for his assistance. "The ring off my finger," she replied. The little Man took the ring and began to spin at once, and by morning all the straw was changed to glistening gold. The King was rejoiced above measure at the sight of this, but still he was not satisfied, but, leading the maiden into another still larger room, full of straw as the others, he

said, "This you must spin during the night; but if you accomplish it you shall be my bride." "For," thought he to himself, "a richer wife thou canst not have in all the world."

When the maiden was left alone, the Dwarf again appeared and asked, for the third time, "What will you give me to do this for you?"

"I have nothing left that I can give you,"

replied the maiden.

"Then promise me your first-born child if you become Queen," said he.

The Miller's daughter thought, "Who can tell if that will ever happen?" and, ignorant how else to help herself out of her trouble, she promised the Dwarf what he desired; and he immediately set about and finished the spinning. When morning came, and the King found all he had wished for done, he celebrated his wedding, and the Miller's fair daughter became Queen.

The gay times she had at the King's Court caused her to forget that she had made a very foolish promise.

About a year after the marriage, when she had ceased to think about the little Dwarf, she brought a fine child into the world; and, suddenly, soon after its birth, the very man appeared and demanded what she had promised. The frightened Queen offered him all the riches of the kingdom if he would leave her her child; but the Dwarf answered, "No; something human is dearer to me than all the wealth of the world."

The Queen began to weep and groan so much that the Dwarf pitied her, and said, "I will leave you three days to consider; if you in that time discover my name you shall keep your child."

All night long the Queen racked her brains for all the names she could think of, and sent a messenger through the country to collect far and wide any new names. The following morning came the Dwarf, and she began with "Caspar," "Melchior," "Balthassar," and all the odd names she knew; but at each the little Man exclaimed, "That is not my name." The second day the

Queen inquired of all her people for uncommon and curious names, and called the Dwarf "Ribs-of-Beef," "Sheep-shank," "Whalebone," but at each he said, "This is not my name." The third day the messenger came back and said, "I have not found a single name; but as I came to a high mountain near the edge of a forest, where foxes and hares say good night to each other, I saw there a little house, and before the door a fire was burning, and round this fire a very curious little Man was dancing on one leg, and shouting:

"'To-day I stew, and then I'll bake,
To-morrow I shall the Queen's child take;
Ah! how famous it is that nobody knows
That my name is Rumpelstiltskin.'"

When the Queen heard this she was very glad, for now she knew the name; and soon after came the Dwarf, and asked, "Now, my lady Queen, what is my name?"

First she said, "Are you called Conrade?"

"No."

"Are you called Hal?" "No."

"Are you called Rumpelstiltskin?"

"A witch has told you! a witch has told you!" shrieked the little Man, and stamped his

right foot so hard in the ground with rage that he could not draw it out again. Then he took hold of his left leg with both his hands, and pulled away so hard that his right came off in the struggle, and he hopped away howling terribly.

And from that day to this the Queen has heard no more of her troublesome visitor.

BEAUTY AND THE BEAST

Once upon a time, a long while ago, there was a Beast.

He was a Great Beast, and lived in a Great Castle that stood in the middle of a Great Park, and everybody in the country held the Beast in great fear. In fact everything about the Beast was great; his roar was great and terrific and could be heard for miles around the park, and when he roared the people trembled.

Nobody ever saw the Beast, which was by no means remarkable, for the Beast never came out of his Park, and no one, I can assure you, ever ventured on to his estate.

But matters were not allowed to remain like this for ever, for [pg 110] something very wonderful happened to the Beast and to somebody else, and if that something had not happened this story would never have been written.

About two miles and three quarters from the Castle gates there lived a rich merchant and his three daughters. The two elder girls were ugly disagreeable things, and although they had all they could wish for to make them happy they were always grumbling; but the youngest daughter, whose name was Beauty, was very pretty, and her nature was happy and good, her presence was sunshine, and she was the joy of her father's heart.

Well, one day the two elder sisters had something to grumble about with a vengeance, for a telegram arrived to say that the merchant was no longer a rich merchant, for he had lost all his money.

So the horses and carriages had to be sold, and everything that was of value was got rid of, the servants were sent away, and the merchant and his daughters had to do their own work.

Dear me, it was shocking, the way those two sisters grumbled, but Beauty, oh dear no, she was all smiles, for her heart was as sunny as ever, as she rolled up the sleeves of her print frock, and cooked the dinner, and scrubbed the floors, and made herself useful, here, there, and everywhere.

Things had been going on like this for about three months, when one fine morning another telegram boy came with another telegram to say that somebody who owed the merchant a great deal of money was ready to pay the debt, and all the merchant had to do was to go to the city and get it.

Of course, everybody was delighted at this good news, and the merchant didn't waste any time, but started off to the city at once.

"Mind you bring me something back," said the eldest daughter as he was starting.

"What shall it be?" asked the merchant.

"A white satin dress trimmed with lace and pearls," said his eldest daughter.

"And you must bring me something too, please, father," said the second daughter.

"And what do you want," asked the merchant.

"A purse full of gold so that I can buy what I want myself," said the second daughter.

"I will try and do what you both ask," he said, "and what shall I bring for my Beauty?"

"I will wait a little for my dresses and things," replied the smiling Beauty, as she helped her father on with his cloak, "but I should like you to bring me home a rose, a lovely red rose, if you can."

So her father kissed her, and promised he would bring her the rose, and went on his way full of hopes.

What a pity it is that our hopes cannot be always realized, and that we are so often doomed to disappointment! When the merchant arrived at the city, to his dismay he found that the man who owed him the money was still unable to pay him, the man had been disappointed himself at the last moment.

So the unhappy father had to return home without the white satin dress trimmed with lace and pearls, and without the bag of money, and he dreaded meeting his two daughters, for he knew they would be terribly angry.

Now on his way home from the station to his house he had to pass by part of the wall that surrounded the Great Park where the Great Beast lived in his Great [pg 112] Castle; and as he passed by a corner of the wall what should he see hanging just over the top, and just within his reach if he stood on his toes, but a lovely red rose.

"At any rate I can take my Beauty what she asked for," he said to himself, and, without so much as giving a thought to the wrong he was doing, he stood on his toes and plucked the rose.

He was sorry he did it.

Of a sudden there was a roar, such a roar that the very ground shook, and as to the poor merchant he quivered like a leaf.

Enough to make him quiver indeed, for a gate in the wall suddenly opened, and out rushed the *Beast*.

Yes, the Beast, if you please, and he seized the merchant by the scruff of his neck, and dragged him into the Park, and shut the gate after him.

"Don't you know it's a sin to steal?" roared the Beast. "How dare you steal my roses? I am going to kill you."

"Oh, mercy, Mr. Beast," cried the unhappy man, flinging himself on his knees before the monster.

"I'm going to kill you," roared the Beast still more loudly. "It's

Stories

taken years to cultivate this sort of rose, and—and I'm going to kill you. Unless," he added after a pause, "you send me one of your daughters here instead."

"All right," said the merchant and got on his feet again.

"She must be here to-morrow by breakfast time, and I breakfast early," said the Beast, as he let the merchant out of the gate. "If she is not here, I shall come for you, and don't you forget it."

It was by no means likely that he would forget it, in fact he could think of nothing else. He hurried home and told his dreadful news, and received a dreadful scolding from his two elder daughters, who were angry at not getting their presents.

"And it is Beauty's fault that you have got into this trouble," they said. "Beauty and her stupid rose. Beauty had better get you out of the trouble." Beauty said little, but smiled on, with sunshine in her heart, and trust in her loving nature, and cooked the dinner.

Early next morning when the dawn was breaking she left her father's house, leaving a little note behind her begging him not to be anxious but that she had gone to the Beast's castle.

When she came to the gate in the wall she knocked upon it three times and it opened as if by magic, for she could see no one. And she stepped into the garden of red roses, and in the distance across the Park she saw the Castle, and she thought she had never seen anything so beautiful. For it was built of mother-of-pearl, and the red and yellow gleams of the rising sun shone upon its glistening walls, and lit them up with a thousand radiant lights.

Beauty marveled at the loveliness and walked on. And when she arrived at this beautiful Castle, the huge gates opened as if by magic, and the doors opened as if by magic, for never a soul did she see, nor living thing of any sort.

And in the great hall was the breakfast table laid for two. It was a nice breakfast with steaming hot dishes, and jams, honey, and hot rolls, and brightly polished silver, and sweet flowers.

Then the Beast appeared suddenly from behind a curtain; oh, he was an awful Beast, and Beauty's heart beat fast! But he seemed a polite Beast for all that.

He handed Beauty a chair, and when she had sat down said:

"I bid you welcome; which do you take, tea or coffee?"

"Tea please," answered Beauty.

"Then pour it out," he said, "and I'll take tea too, please. Eggs, do you like eggs hard or soft?"

"I always cook mine three minutes and a half," replied Beauty.

"Half a minute too much, I think. But you shall have just what you like."

And so she had; not only at the breakfast table but in everything. She had only to express a wish and it was immediately gratified. She had ponies to ride, and dogs and cats, and pet birds, and the most beautiful dresses ever worn by real princesses.

And if it had not been that she was away from her father she would really have been happy.

The Beast was most kind and attentive to her, and told her that he loved her, and three times a day he asked her to marry him, but

Beauty shook her head and said, oh no, she couldn't.

Well, Beauty had been at the great Castle some time when she began to pine to go home and see her father, and she begged the Beast to let her go.

"Very good," he said with a great sigh, "you may go home to-day, but promise me that you will be back early to-morrow morning. If you do not come back early I am sure I shall die for I love you so dearly."

So Beauty promised and went home, and she took presents for her father and her sisters, and when the sisters heard of all the wonderful things at the great Castle, they were envious and jealous, and made up their minds to do Beauty and the Beast a great injury.

So they mixed something in Beauty's supper that made her sleep nearly all the next day, and so she did not keep her promise. It was evening when she arrived at the gate in the wall, instead of early morning.

But she knocked three times and the gate opened by magic, and she went through the garden and hurried to the Castle, that shone like fire in the light of the setting sun. And the huge gates opened by magic, and the doors opened by magic, and she stood in the great hall, but there was no Beast there. She searched in all the rooms but he was not there; with fear and anxiety in her heart she ran into the gardens, and there she found him at last. Found him lying stretched out on the grass, and she thought he was dead.

"Oh, dear darling Beast," she cried, as she threw herself on her knees beside him, and raised his ugly head, "dear Beast, do not die, for I love you with all my heart, and will marry you to-morrow." And she kissed him. Then of a sudden he sprang to his feet, but no longer the Beast, no longer a hideous monster, but a beautiful prince most beautifully dressed. "Dearest," he said, "a wicked fairy turned me into this brute form until a day should come when a good girl like you should tell me that she loved me. And you will marry me to-morrow."

"Oh, yes," answered Beauty, "but the wicked fairy could not change your nature. I would have married you if you had remained just as you were."

And so they married and lived happy ever afterwards, and they took care of Beauty's father until the end of his days; so he was happy, and they forgave the two sisters and gave them fine dresses and jewels, and the two sisters turned over a new leaf and were less selfish, and they were happy, so this is a very happy ending to the story.

What a pity all stories can't end the same way!

THE VALIANT LITTLE TAILOR

One fine day a Tailor was sitting on his bench by the window in very high spirits, sewing away most diligently, and presently up the street came a country woman, crying, "Good jams for sale! Good jams for sale!" This cry sounded nice in the Tailor's ears, and, poking his diminutive head out of the window, he called, "Here, my good woman, just bring your jams in here!" The woman mounted the three steps up to the Tailor's house with her large basket, and began to open all the pots together before him. He looked at them all, held them up to the light, smelt them, and at last said, "These jams seem to me to be very nice, so you may weigh me out two ounces, my good woman; I don't object even if you make it a quarter of a pound." The woman, who hoped to have met with a good customer, gave him all he wished, and went off grumbling, and in a very bad temper.

"Now!" exclaimed the Tailor, "Heaven will send me a blessing on this jam, and give me fresh strength and vigor;" and, taking the bread from the cupboard, he cut himself a slice the size of the whole loaf, and spread the jam upon it. "That will taste very nice," said he; "but, before I take a bite, I will just finish this waistcoat." So he put the bread on the table and stitched away, making larger and larger stitches every time for joy. Meanwhile the smell of the jam rose to the ceiling, where many flies were sitting, and enticed them down, so that soon a great swarm of them had pitched on the bread. "Holloa! who asked you?" exclaimed the Tailor, driving away the uninvited visitors; but the flies, not understanding his words, would not be driven off, and came back in greater numbers than before. This put the little man in a great passion, and, snatching up in his anger a bag of cloth, he brought it down with a merciless swoop

Stories

upon them. When he raised it again he counted as many as seven lying dead before him with outstretched legs. "What a fellow you are!" said he to himself, astonished at his own bravery. "The whole town must hear of this." In great haste he cut himself out a band, hemmed it, and then put on it in large letters, "SEVEN AT ONE BLOW!" "Ah," said he, "not one city alone, the whole world shall hear it!" and his heart danced with joy, like a puppy-dog's tail.

The little Tailor bound the belt around his body, and made ready to travel forth into the wide world, feeling the workshop too small for his great deeds. Before he set out, however, he looked about his house to see if there were anything he could carry with him, but he found only an old cheese, which he pocketed, and observing a bird which was caught in the bushes before the door, he captured it, and put that in his pocket also. Soon after he set out boldly on his travels; and, as he was light and active, he felt no fatigue. His road led him up a hill, and when he arrived at the highest point of it he found a great Giant sitting there, who was gazing about him very composedly.

But the little Tailor went boldly up, and said, "Good day, friend; truly you sit there and see the whole world stretched below you. I also am on my way thither to seek my fortune. Are you willing to go with me?"

The Giant looked with scorn at the little Tailor, and said, "You rascal! you wretched creature!"

"Perhaps so," replied the Tailor; "but here may be seen what sort of a man I am;" and, unbuttoning his coat, he showed the Giant his belt. The Giant read, "SEVEN AT ONE BLOW"; and supposing they were men whom the Tailor had killed, he felt some respect for him. Still he meant to try him first; so taking up a pebble, he squeezed it so hard that water dropped out of it. "Do as well as that," said he to the other, "if you have the strength."

"If it be nothing harder than that," said the Tailor, "that's child's play." And, diving into his pocket, he pulled out the cheese and squeezed it till the whey ran out of it, and said, "Now, I fancy that I have done better than you."

The Giant wondered what to say, and could not believe it of the little man; so, catching up another pebble, he flung it so high that it almost went out of sight, saying, "There, you pigmy, do that if you can."

"Well done," said the Tailor; "but your pebble will fall down again to the ground. I will throw one up which will not come down;" and, dipping into his pocket, he took out the bird and threw it into the air. The bird, glad to be free, flew straight up, and then far away, and did not come back. "How does that little performance please you, friend?" asked the Tailor.

"You can throw well," replied the giant; "now truly we will see if you are able to carry something uncommon." So saying, he took him to a large oak tree, which lay upon the ground, and said, "If you are strong enough, now help me to carry this tree out of the forest."

"With pleasure," replied the Tailor; "you may hold the trunk upon your shoulder, and I will lift the boughs and branches, they are the heaviest, and carry them."

The Giant took the trunk upon his shoulder, but the Tailor sat down on one of the branches, and the Giant, who could not look round, was compelled to carry the whole tree and the Tailor also. He being behind, was very cheerful, and laughed at the trick, and presently began to sing the song, "There rode three tailors out at the gate," as if the carrying of trees were a trifle. The Giant, after he had staggered a very short distance with his heavy load, could go no further, and called out, "Do you hear? I must drop the tree." The Tailor, jumping down, quickly embraced the tree with both arms, as if he had been carrying it, and said to the Giant, "Are you such a big fellow, and yet cannot you carry a tree by yourself?"

Then they traveled on further, and as they came to a cherry-tree, the Giant seized the top of the tree where the ripest cherries hung, and, bending it down, gave it to the Tailor to hold, telling him to eat. But the Tailor was far too weak to hold the tree down, and when the Giant let go, the tree flew up in the air, and the Tailor was taken with it. He came down on the other side, however, unhurt, and the Giant said, "What does that mean? Are you not strong enough to hold that twig?" "My strength did not fail me," said the Tailor; "do you imagine that that was a hard task for one who has slain seven at one blow? I sprang over the tree simply because the hunters were shooting down here in the thicket. Jump after me if you can." The Giant made the attempt, but could not clear the tree, and stuck fast in the branches; so that in this affair, too, the Tailor had the advantage.

Then the Giant said, "Since you are such a brave fellow, come with me to my house, and stop a night with me." The Tailor agreed, and followed him; and when they came to the cave, there sat by the fire two other Giants, each with a roast sheep in his hand, of which he was eating. The Tailor sat down thinking. "Ah, this is very much more like the world than is my workshop." And soon the Giant pointed out a bed where he could lie down and go to sleep. The bed, however, was too large for him, so he crept out of it, and lay down in a corner. When midnight came, and the Giant fancied the Tailor would be in a sound sleep, he got up, and taking a heavy iron bar, beat the bed right through at one stroke, and believed he had thereby given the Tailor his death-blow. At the dawn of day the Giants went out into the forest, quite forgetting the Tailor, when presently up he came, quite cheerful, and showed himself before them. The Giants were frightened, and, dreading he might kill them all, they ran away in a great hurry.

The Tailor traveled on, always following his nose, and after he had journeyed some long distance, he came into the courtyard of a royal palace; and feeling very tired he laid himself down on the ground and went to sleep. Whilst he lay there the people came and viewed him on all sides, and read upon his belt, "Seven at one blow." "Ah," they said, "what does this great warrior here in time of peace? This must be some valiant hero." So they went and told the King, knowing that, should war break out, here was a valuable and useful man, whom one ought not to part with at any price. The King took advice, and sent one of his courtiers to the Tailor to beg for his fighting services, if he should be awake. The messenger stopped at the sleeper's side, and waited till he stretched out his limbs and unclosed his eyes, and then he mentioned to him his message. "Solely for that reason did I come here," was his answer; "I am quite willing to enter into the King's service." Then he was taken away with great honor, and a fine house was appointed him to dwell in.

The courtiers, however, became jealous of the Tailor, and wished him at the other end of the world. "What will happen?" said they to one another. "If we go to war with him, when he strikes out seven will fall at one stroke, and nothing will be left for us to do." In their anger they came to the determination to resign, and they went all together to the King, and asked his permission, saying, "We are not prepared to keep company with a man who kills seven at one blow." The King was sorry to lose all his devoted servants for the sake of one, and wished that he had never seen the Tailor, and would gladly have now been rid of him. He dared not, however dismiss him, because he feared the Tailor might kill him and all his subjects, and seat himself upon the throne. For a long time he deliberated, till finally he came to a decision; and, sending for the Tailor, he told him that, seeing he was so great a hero, he wished to beg a favor of him. "In a certain forest in my kingdom," said the King, "there are two Giants, who, by murder, rapine, fire, and robbery, have committed great damage, and no one approaches them without endangering his own life. If you overcome and slay both these Giants, I will give you my only daughter in marriage, and half of my kingdom for a dowry: a hundred knights shall accompany you, too, in order to render you assistance."

"Ah, that is something for a man like me," thought the Tailor to himself: "a lovely Princess and half a kingdom are not offered to one every day." "Oh, yes," he replied, "I will soon settle these two Giants, and a hundred horsemen are not needed for that purpose; he who kills seven at one blow has no fear of two."

Speaking thus, the little Tailor set out, followed by the hundred knights, to whom he said, immediately they came to the edge of the forest, "You must stay here; I prefer to meet these Giants alone."

Then he ran off into the forest, peering about him on all sides; and after a while he saw the two Giants sound asleep under a tree, snoring so loudly that the branches above them shook violently. The Tailor, bold as a lion, filled both his pockets with stones and climbed up the tree. When he got to the middle of it he crawled along a bough, so that he sat just above the sleepers, and then he let fall one stone after another upon the body of one of them. For some time the Giant did not move, until, at last awaking, he pushed his companion, and said, "Why are you hitting me?"

"You have been dreaming," he answered; "I did not touch you." So they laid themselves down again to sleep, and presently the Tailor threw a stone down upon the other. "What is that?" he cried. "Why are you knocking me about?"

"I did not touch you; you are dreaming," said the first. So they argued for a few minutes; but, both being very weary with the day's work, they soon went to sleep again. Then the Tailor began his fun again, and, picking out the largest stone, threw it with all his strength upon the chest of the first Giant. "This is too bad!" he exclaimed; and, jumping up like a madman, he fell upon his companion, who considered himself equally injured, and they set to in such good earnest, that they rooted up trees and beat one another about until they both fell dead upon the ground. Then the Tailor jumped down, saying, "What a piece of luck they did not pull up the tree on which I sat, or else I must have jumped on another like a squirrel, for I am not used to flying." Then he drew his sword, and, cutting a deep wound in the breast of both, he went to the horsemen and said, "The deed is done; I have given each his death-stroke; but it was a tough job, for in their defense they uprooted trees to protect themselves with; still, all that is of no use when such an one as I come, who slew seven at one stroke."

"And are you not wounded?" they asked.

"How can you ask me that? they have not injured a hair of my head," replied the little man. The knights could hardly believe him, till, riding into the forest, they found the Giants lying dead, and the uprooted trees around them.

Then the Tailor demanded the promised reward of the King; but he repented of his promise, and began to think of some new plan to shake off the hero. "Before you receive my daughter and the half of my kingdom," said he to him, "you must execute another brave deed. In the forest there lives a unicorn that commits great damage, you must first catch him."

"I fear a unicorn less than I did two Giants! Seven at one blow is my motto," said the Tailor. So he carried with him a rope and an axe and went off to the forest, ordering those, who were told to accompany him, to wait on the outskirts. He had not to hunt long, for soon the unicorn approached, and prepared to rush at him as if it would pierce him on the spot. "Steady! steady!" he exclaimed, "that is not done so easily"; and, waiting till the animal was close upon him, he sprang nimbly behind a tree. The unicorn, rushing with all its force against the tree, stuck its horn so fast in the trunk that it could not pull it out again, and so it remained prisoner.

"Now I have got him," said the Tailor; and coming from behind the tree, he first bound the rope around its neck, and then cutting the horn out of the tree with his axe, he arranged everything, and, leading the unicorn, brought it before the King.

The King, however, would not yet deliver over the promised reward, and made a third demand, that, before the marriage, the Tailor should capture a wild boar which did much damage, and he should have the huntsmen to help him. "With pleasure," was the reply; "it is a mere nothing." The huntsmen, however, he left behind, to their great joy, for this wild boar had already so often hunted them, that they saw no fun in now hunting it. As soon as the boar perceived the Tailor, it ran at him with gaping mouth and glistening teeth, and tried to throw him down on the ground; but our flying hero sprang into a little chapel which stood near, and out again at a window, on the other side, in a moment. The boar ran after him, but he, skipping around, closed the door behind it, and there the furious beast was caught, for it was much too unwieldy and heavy to jump out of the window.

The Tailor now ordered the huntsmen up, that they might see his prisoner with their own eyes; but our hero presented himself before the King, who was obliged at last, whether he would or no, to keep his word, and surrender his daughter and the half of his kingdom.

If he had known that it was no warrior, but only a Tailor, who stood before him, it would have grieved him still more.

So the wedding was celebrated with great magnificence, though with little rejoicing, and out of a Tailor there was made a King.

A short time afterwards the young Queen heard her husband talking in his sleep, saying, "Boy, make me a coat, and then stitch up these trousers, or I will lay the yard-measure over your shoulders!" Then she understood of what condition her husband was, and complained in the morning to her father, and begged he would free her from her husband, who was nothing more than a tailor. The King comforted her by saying, "This night leave your chamber-door open: my servants shall stand outside, and when he is asleep they shall come in, bind him, and carry him away to a ship, which shall take him out into the wide world." The wife was pleased with the proposal; but the King's armor-bearer, who had overheard all, went to the young King and revealed the whole plot. "I will soon put an end to this affair," said the valiant little Tailor. In the evening at their usual time they went to bed, and when his wife thought he slept she got up, opened the door, and laid herself down again.

The Tailor, however, only pretended to be asleep, and began to call out in a loud voice, "Boy, make me a coat, and then stitch up these trousers, or I will lay the yard-measure about your shoulders. Seven have I slain with one blow, two Giants have I killed, a unicorn have I led captive, and a wild boar have I caught, and shall I be afraid of those who stand outside my room?"

When the men heard these words spoken by the Tailor, a great fear came over them, and they ran away as if wild huntsmen were following them; neither afterwards dared any man venture to oppose him. Thus the Tailor became a King, and so he lived for the rest of his life.

RAPUNZEL

There were once a man and a woman who had long but in vain wished for a child. At length the woman hoped that God was about to grant her desire. These people had a little window at the back of their house from which a splendid garden could be seen, which was full of the most beautiful flowers and herbs. It was, however, surrounded by a high wall, and no one dared to go into it because it belonged to an enchantress, who had great power and was dreaded by all the world. One day the woman was standing by this window and looking down into the garden, when she saw a bed which was planted with the most beautiful rampion (rapunzel), and it looked so fresh and green that she longed for it, and had the greatest desire to eat some. This desire increased every day, and as she knew that she could not get any of it, she quite pined away, and looked pale and miserable. Then her husband was alarmed, and asked, "What ails you, dear wife?" "Ah," she replied, "if I can't get some of the rampion which is in the garden behind our house, to eat, I shall die." The man, who loved her, thought, "Sooner than let your wife die, bring her some of the rampion yourself, let it cost you what it will." In the twilight of evening, he clambered down over the wall into the garden of the enchantress, hastily clutched a handful of rampion, and took it to his wife. She at once made herself a salad of it, and ate it with much relish. She, however, liked it so much, so very much, that the next day she longed for it three times as much as before. If he was to have any rest, her husband must once more descend into the garden. In the gloom of evening, therefore, he let himself down again; but when he had clambered down the wall he was terribly afraid, for he saw the enchantress standing before him. "How can you dare," said she with angry look, "to descend into my garden and steal my rampion like a thief? You shall suffer for it!" "Ah," answered he, "let mercy take the place of justice. I only made up my mind to do it out of necessity. My wife saw your rampion from the window, and felt such a longing for it that she would have died if she had not got some to eat." Then the enchantress allowed her anger to be softened, and said to him, "If the case be as you say, I will

Stories

allow you to take away with you as much rampion as you will, only I make one condition, you must give me the child which your wife will bring into the world; it shall be well treated, and I will care for it like a mother." The man in his terror consented to everything, and when the little one came to them, the enchantress appeared at once, gave the child the name of Rapunzel, and took it away with her.

Rapunzel grew into the most beautiful child beneath the sun. When she was twelve years old, the enchantress shut her into a tower, which lay in a forest, and had neither stairs nor door, but quite at the top was a little window. When the enchantress wanted to go in, she placed herself beneath this, and cried,

"Rapunzel, Rapunzel,
Let down your hair to me."

Rapunzel had magnificent long hair, fine as spun gold, and when she heard the voice of the enchantress she unfastened her braided tresses, wound them round one of the hooks of the window above, and then the hair fell twenty yards down, and the enchantress climbed up by it.

After a year or two, it came to pass that the King's son rode through the forest and went by the tower. Then he heard a song, which was so charming that he stood still and listened. This was Rapunzel, who in her solitude passed her time in letting her sweet voice resound. The King's son wanted to climb up to her, and looked for the door of the tower, but none was to be found. He rode home, but the singing had so deeply touched his heart, that every day he went out into the forest and listened to it. Once when he was thus standing behind a tree, he saw that an enchantress came there, and he heard how she cried,

"Rapunzel, Rapunzel,
Let down your hair."

Then Rapunzel let down the braids of her hair, and the enchantress climbed up

to her. "If that is the ladder by which one mounts, I will for once try my fortune," said he, and the next day, when it began to grow dark, he went to the tower and cried.

"Rapunzel, Rapunzel,
Let down your hair."

Immediately the hair fell down, and the King's son climbed up.

At first Rapunzel was terribly frightened when a man such as her eyes had never yet beheld came to her; but the King's son began to talk to her quite like a friend, and told her that his heart had been so stirred that it had let him have no rest, and he had been forced to see her. Then Rapunzel lost her fear, and when he asked her if she would take him for a husband, and she saw that he was young and handsome, she thought, "He will love me more than old Dame Gothel does;" and she said yes, and laid her hand in his. She said, "I will willingly go away with you, but I do not know how to get down. Bring with you a skein of silk every time that you come, and I will weave a ladder with it, and when that is ready I will descend, and you will take me on your horse." They agreed that until that time he should come to her every evening, for the old woman came by day. The enchantress remarked nothing of this, until once Rapunzel said to her, "Tell me, Dame Gothel, how it happens that you are so much heavier for me to draw up than the young King's son—he is with me in a moment." "Ah! you wicked child," cried the enchantress, "what do I hear you say! I thought I had separated you from all the world, and yet you have deceived me!" In her anger she clutched Rapunzel's beautiful tresses, wrapped them twice round her left hand, seized a pair of scissors with the right, and snip, snip, they were cut off, and the lovely braids lay on the ground. And she was so pitiless that she took poor Rapunzel into a desert, where she had to live in great grief and misery.

On the same day, however, that she cast out Rapunzel, the enchantress in the evening fastened the braids of hair which she had cut off to the hook of the window, and when the King's son came and cried,

"Rapunzel, Rapunzel,
Let down your hair,"

she let the hair down. The King's son ascended, but he did not find his dearest Rapunzel above, but the enchantress, who gazed at him with wicked and venomous looks. "Aha!" she cried mockingly. "You would fetch your dearest, but the beautiful bird sits no longer singing in the nest; the cat has got it, and will scratch out your eyes as well. Rapunzel is lost to you; you will never see her more." The King's son was beside himself with pain, and in his despair he leapt down from the tower. He escaped with his life, but the thorns into which he fell pierced his eyes. Then he wandered quite blind about the forest, ate nothing but roots and berries, and did nothing but lament and weep over the loss of his dearest wife. Thus he roamed about I in misery for some years, and at length came to the desert where Rapunzel lived in wretchedness. He heard a voice, and it seemed so familiar to him that he went towards it, and when he approached, Rapunzel knew him and fell on his neck and wept. Two of her tears wetted his eyes, and they grew clear again, and he could see with them as before. He led her to his kingdom, where he was joyfully received, and they lived for a long time afterwards, happy and contented.

THE FROG PRINCE

In the olden time, when wishing was having, there lived a King, whose daughters were all beautiful; but the youngest was so exceedingly beautiful that the Sun himself, although he saw her very, very often, was delighted every time she came out into the sunshine.

Near the castle of this King was a large and gloomy forest, where in the midst stood an old lime-tree, beneath whose branches splashed a little fountain; so, whenever it was very hot, the King's youngest daughter ran off into this wood, and sat down by the side of the fountain; and, when she felt dull, would often divert herself by throwing a golden ball up into the air and catching it again. And this was her favorite amusement.

Now, one day it happened that this golden ball, when the King's daughter threw it into the air, did not fall down into her hand, but on to the grass; and then it rolled right into the fountain. The King's daughter followed the ball with her eyes, but it disappeared beneath the water, which was so deep that she could not see to the bottom. Then she began to lament, and to cry more loudly and more loudly; and, as she cried, a voice called out, "Why weepest thou, O King's daughter? thy tears would melt even a stone to pity." She looked around to the spot whence the voice came, and saw a frog stretching his thick, ugly head out of the water. "Ah! you old water-paddler," said she, "was it you that spoke? I am weeping for my golden ball which bounced away from me into the water."

"Be quiet, and do not cry," replied the Frog; "I can give thee good assistance. But what wilt thou give me if I succeed in fetching thy plaything up again?"

"What would you like, dear Frog?" said she. "My dresses, my pearls and jewels, or the golden crown which I wear?"

The Frog replied, "Dresses, or jewels, or golden crowns, are not for me; but if thou wilt love me, and let me be thy companion and playmate, and sit at thy table, and eat from thy little golden plate, and drink out of thy cup, and sleep in thy little bed,—if thou wilt promise me all these things, then I will dive down and fetch up thy golden ball."

"Oh, I will promise you all," said she, "if you will only get me my golden ball." But she thought to herself, "What is the silly Frog chattering about? Let him stay in the water with his equals; he cannot enter into society." Then the Frog, as soon as he had received her promise, drew his head under the water and dived down. Presently he swam up again with the golden ball in his mouth, and threw it on to the grass. The King's daughter was full of joy when she again saw her beautiful plaything; and, taking it up, she ran off immediately. "Stop! stop!" cried the Frog; "take me with thee. I cannot run as thou canst."

But this croaking was of no avail; although it was loud enough, the King's daughter did not hear it, but, hastening home, soon forgot the poor Frog, who was obliged to leap back into the fountain.

The next day, when the King's daughter was sitting at table with her father and all his courtiers, and was eating from her own little golden plate, something was heard coming up the marble stairs, splish-splash, splish-splash; and when it arrived at the top, it knocked at the door, and a voice said—

"Open the door, thou youngest daughter of the King!"

So she arose and went to see who it was that called to her; but when she opened the door and caught sight of the Frog, she shut it again very quickly and with great passion, and sat down at the table, looking exceedingly pale.
But the King perceived that her heart was beating violently, and asked her whether it were a giant who had come to fetch her away who stood at the door. "Oh, no!" answered she; "it is no giant, but an ugly Frog."

"What does the Frog want with you?" said the King.

"Oh, dear father, yesterday when I was playing by the fountain, my golden ball fell into the water, and this Frog fetched it up again because I cried so much: but first, I must tell you, he pressed me so much, that I promised him he should be my companion. I never thought that he could come out of the water, but somehow he has managed to jump out, and now he wants to come in here."

At that moment there was another knock, and a voice said—
"King's daughter, youngest,
Open the door.
Hast thou forgotten
Thy promises made
At the fountain so clear
'Neath the lime-tree's shade?
King's daughter, youngest.
Open the door."

Then the King said, "What you have promised, that you must perform; go and let him in." So the King's daughter went and opened the door, and the Frog hopped in after her right up to her chair: and as soon as she was seated, he said, "Lift me up;" but she hesitated so long that the King had to order her to obey. And as soon as the Frog sat on the chair he jumped on to the table and said, "Now push thy plate near me, that we may eat together." And she did so, but as every one noticed, very unwillingly. The Frog seemed to relish his dinner very much, but every bit that the King's daughter ate nearly choked her, till at last the Frog said, "I have satisfied my hunger, and feel very tired; wilt thou carry me upstairs now into thy chamber, and make thy bed ready that we may sleep together?" At this speech the King's daughter began to cry, for she was afraid of the cold Frog, and dared not touch him; and besides, he actually wanted to sleep in her own beautiful, clean bed!

But her tears only made the King very angry, and he said, "He who helped you in the time of your trouble must not now be despised!" So she took the Frog up with two fingers, and put him into a corner of her chamber. But as she lay in her bed, he crept up to it, and said, "I am so very tired that I shall sleep well; do take me up, or I will tell thy father." This speech put the King's daughter into a terrible passion, and catching the Frog up, she threw him with all her strength against the wall, saying "Now will you be quiet, you ugly Frog!"

But as he fell he was changed from a Frog into a handsome Prince with beautiful eyes, who after a little while became her dear companion and betrothed. One morning, Henry, trusted servant of the Prince, came for them with a carriage. When his master was changed into a frog, trusty Henry had grieved so much that he had bound three iron bands around his heart, for fear it should break with grief and sorrow. The faithful Henry (who was also the trusty Henry) helped in the bride and bridegroom, and placed himself in the seat behind, full of joy at his master's release. They had not proceeded far when the Prince heard a crack as if something had  broken behind the carriage; so he put his head out of the window and asked trusty Henry what was broken, and faithful Henry answered, "It was not the carriage, my master, but an iron band which I bound around my heart when it was in such grief because you were changed into a frog."

Twice afterwards on the journey there was the same noise, and each time the Prince thought that it was some part of the carriage that had given way; but it was only the breaking of the bands which bound the heart of the trusty Henry (who was also the faithful Henry), and who was thenceforward free and happy.

THE TRAVELS OF TOM THUMB

There lived a tailor who had only one son, and he was extremely small, not any larger than your thumb, and so was called Tom Thumb.

However, he was a courageous little fellow, and he told his father, "Father, I am determined to go into the world to seek my fortune."

"Very well, my son," answered the old man, and taking a big darning needle, he made a top to it of sealing wax, and gave it to Tom Thumb, saying:

"There is a sword for you to use to defend yourself on your journeying."

Then the little fellow, desiring to dine once more with his parents, popped into the kitchen to find out what his mother was preparing for his last dinner at home. All the dishes were ready to be taken in, and they were standing upon the hearth.

"What is it you have for dinner, dear mother?" he inquired.

"You can look for yourself," she replied.

Then Tom sprang up on to the hob, and peeped into all the dishes, but over one he leant so far, that he was carried up by the steam through the chimney, and then for some distance he floated on the smoke, but after a while he fell upon the ground once more.

Now, at last, Tom Thumb was really out in the wide world, and he went on cheerily, and after a time was engaged by a master tailor; but here the food was not so good as his mother's, and it was not to his taste.

So he said, "Mistress, if you will not give me better things to eat, I shall chalk upon your door, 'Too many potatoes, and not enough meat. Good-bye, potato-mill.'"

"I should like to know what you want, you little grasshopper!" cried the woman very angrily, and she seized a shred of cloth to strike him; however, the tiny tailor popped under a thimble, and from it he peeped, putting out his tongue at the mistress.

So she took up the thimble, meaning to catch him, but Tom Thumb hid himself amongst the shreds of cloth, and when she began to search through those, he slipped into a crack in the table, but put out his head to laugh at her; so she tried again to hit him with the shred, but did not succeed in doing so, for he slipped through the crack into the table drawer.

At last, though, he was caught, and driven out of the house.

So the little fellow continued his travels, and presently entering a thick forest, he encountered a company of robbers who were plotting to steal the king's treasure.

As soon as they saw the little tailor, they said to themselves, "A little fellow like this could creep through a keyhole, and aid us greatly." So one called out—

"Hullo, little man, will you come with us to the king's treasury? Certainly a Goliath like you could creep in with ease, and throw out the coins to us."

After considering awhile, Tom Thumb consented, and accompanied them to the king's treasury.

From top to bottom they inspected the door to discover a crack large enough for him to get through, and soon found one. He was for going in directly, but one of the sentinels happening to catch sight of him, exclaimed: "Here is indeed an ugly spider; I will crush it with my foot."

"Leave the poor creature alone," the other said; "it has not done you any harm."

So Tom Thumb slipped through the crack, and made his way to the treasury. Then he opened the window, and cast out the coins to the robbers who were waiting below. While the little tailor was engaged in this exciting employment, he heard the king coming to inspect his treasure, so as quickly as possible he crept out of sight. The king noticed that his treasure had been disarranged, and soon observed that coins were missing: but he was utterly unable to think how they could have been stolen, for the locks and bolts had not been tampered with, and everything was well fastened.

On going from the treasury, he warned the two sentinels, saying—

"Be on the watch, some one is after the money," and quite soon, on Tom Thumb setting to work again, they heard very clearly the coins ringing, chink, chank, as they struck one against the other.

As quickly as possible they unfastened the building and went in, hoping to take the thief. But Tom Thumb was too quick for them, he sprang into a corner, and hiding himself behind a coin, so that nothing of him was visible, he made fun of the sentinels; crying "I am here!" Then when the men hurried to the spot where the voice came from, he was no longer there, but from a different place cried out: "Ha, Ha! here I am!"

So the sentinels kept jumping about, but so cleverly did Tom move from one spot to another, that they were obliged to run around the whole time, hoping to find somebody, until at length, quite tired out, they went off.

Then Tomb Thumb went on with his work, and one after another he threw all the coins out of the window, but the very last he sounded and rang with all his might and springing nimbly upon it, so flew through the window.

The robbers were loud in their praises.

"Indeed you are a brave fellow," they said, "will you be our captain?"

Tom Thumb, thanking them, declined this honor, for he was anxious to see more of the world. Then the booty was apportioned out, but only a ducat was given to the little tailor, for that was as much as he could carry.

So Tom girded on his sword again, and bidding farewell to the robbers, continued his travels.

He tried to get work under various masters, but they would have nothing to do with him, so after a while he took service at an inn. But the maids there disliked him, for he was about everywhere, and saw all that went on, without being seen himself; and he told their mistress of their dishonest ways, of what was taken off the plates, and from out the cellars.

So they threatened they would drown him, if they caught him, and determined to do him some harm. Then, one day, a maid mowing in the garden saw Tom Thumb running in and out between the blades of grass, so she cut the grass, in great haste, just where he chanced to be, tied it all in a bundle, and, without anyone knowing, threw it to the cows.

Then one big black cow took up a mouthful of grass directly, with Tom in it, and swallowed it down; without doing him any damage, however.

But Tom did not approve of his position, for it was pitch dark down there, with no light burning.

When milking time came, he shouted—

"Drip, drap, drop,

Will the milking soon stop?"

but the sound of the milk trickling into the pail prevented his voice being heard.

Not long afterwards the master came into the shed, and said:

"I will have that cow killed to-morrow."

This put Tom Thumb into a great fright, and he called out loudly:

"Please let me out, here I am inside."

This the master heard plainly enough, but could not make out where the voice came from.

"Where are you?" he inquired.

"In the black cow," was the reply.

However, the master could not understand what was meant, and so went away.

The following morning the cow was killed, but fortunately in the cutting up the knife did not touch Tom Thumb, who was put aside with the meat that was to be made into sausages.

When the butcher began chopping, he cried as loudly as he could—

"Don't chop far, I am down beneath," but the chopper made so much noise, that he attracted no attention.

It was indeed a terrible situation for poor Tom. But being in danger brightens one's wits, and he sprang so nimbly, this way and that, keeping clear of the chopper, that not a blow struck him, and he did not get even a scratch.

However, he could not escape, there was no help for it, he was forced into a skin with the sausage meat, so was compelled to make himself as comfortable as might be. It was very close quarters, and besides that, the sausages were suspended to smoke in the chimney, which was by no means entertaining, and the time passed slowly.

When winter came, he was taken down for a guest's meal, and while the hostess was slicing the sausage he had to be on his guard, lest if he stretched out his head it might be cut off.
Watching his opportunity, at last he was able to jump out of the sausage, and right glad was he to be once again in the company of his fellow-men.

STORIES

It was not very long, however, that he stayed in this house, where he had been met by so many misfortunes, and again he set forth on his travels, rejoicing in his freedom, but this did not long continue.

Swiftly running across the field came a fox, who, in an instant, had snapped up poor little Tom.

"Oh, Mr. Fox," called out the little tailor, "it is I who am in your throat; please let me out."

"Certainly," answered Reynard, "you are not a bit better than nothing at all, you don't in the least satisfy me; make me a promise, that I shall have the hens in your father's yard, and you shall regain your liberty."

"Willingly, you shall have all the hens; I make you a faithful promise," responded Tom Thumb.

So the fox coughed and set him free, and himself carried Tom home.

Then when the father had his dear little son once more he gave the fox all his hens, with the greatest of pleasure.

"Here, father, I am bringing you a golden coin from my travels," said the little fellow, and he brought out the ducat the thieves had apportioned to him.

"But how was it that the fox was given all the poor little hens?"

379

"Foolish little one, don't you think your father would rather have you, than all the hens he ever had in his yard?"

THE BOGEY-BEAST

There was once a woman who was very, very cheerful, though she had little to make her so; for she was old, and poor, and lonely. She lived in a little bit of a cottage and earned a scant living by running errands for her neighbors, getting a bite here, a sup there, as reward for her services. So she made shift to get on, and always looked as spry and cheery as if she had not a want in the world.

Now one summer evening, as she was trotting, full of smiles as ever, along the high road to her hovel, what should she see but a big black pot lying in the ditch!

"Goodness me!" she cried, "that would be just the very thing for me if I only had something to put in it! But I haven't! Now who could have left it in the ditch?"

And she looked about her expecting the owner would not be far off; but she could see nobody.

"Maybe there is a hole in it," she went on, "and that's why it has been cast away. But it would do fine to put a flower in for my window; so I'll just take it home with me."

And with that she lifted the lid and looked inside. "Mercy me!" she cried, fair amazed. "If it isn't full of gold pieces. Here's luck!"

And so it was, brimful of great gold coins. Well, at first she simply stood stock-still, wondering if she was standing on her head or her heels. Then she began saying:

"Lawks! But I do feel rich. I feel awful rich!"

After she had said this many times, she began to wonder how she was to get her treasure home. It was too heavy for her to carry, and she could see no better way than to tie the end of her shawl to it and drag it behind her like a go-cart.

"It will soon be dark," she said to herself as she trotted along. "So much the better! The neighbors will not see what I'm bringing home, and I shall have all the night to myself, and be able to think what I'll do! Mayhap I'll buy a grand house and just sit by the fire with a cup o' tea and do no work at all like a queen. Or maybe I'll bury it at the garden foot and just keep a bit in the old china teapot on the chimney-piece. Or maybe—Goody! Goody! I feel that grand I don't know myself."

By this time she was a bit tired of dragging such a heavy weight, and, stopping to rest a while, turned to look at her treasure.

And lo! it wasn't a pot of gold at all! It was nothing but a lump of silver.

She stared at it, and rubbed her eyes, and stared at it again.

"Well! I never!" she said at last. "And me thinking it was a pot of gold! I must have been dreaming. But this is luck! Silver is far less trouble—easier to mind, and not so easy stolen. Them gold pieces would have been the death o' me, and with this great lump of silver—"

So she went off again planning what she would do, and feeling as rich as rich, until becoming a bit tired again she stopped to rest and gave a look round to see if her treasure was safe; and she saw nothing but a great lump of iron!

"Well! I never!" says she again. "And I mistaking it for silver! I must have been dreaming. But this is luck! It's real convenient. I can get penny pieces for old iron, and penny pieces are a deal handier for me than your gold and silver. Why! I should never have slept a wink for fear of being robbed. But a penny piece comes in useful, and I shall sell that iron for a lot and be real rich—rolling rich."

So on she trotted full of plans as to how she would spend her penny pieces, till once more she stopped to rest and looked round to see her treasure was safe. And this time she saw nothing but a big stone.

"Well! I never!" she cried, full of smiles. "And to think I mistook it for iron. I must have been dreaming. But here's luck indeed, and me wanting a stone terrible bad to stick open the gate. Eh my! but it's a change for the better! It's a fine thing to have good luck."

So, all in a hurry to see how the stone would keep the gate open, she trotted off down the hill till she came to her own cottage. She unlatched the gate and then turned to unfasten her shawl from the stone which lay on the path behind her. Aye! It was a stone sure enough. There was plenty light to see it lying there, douce and peaceable as a stone should.

So she bent over it to unfasten the shawl end, when—"Oh my!" All of a sudden it gave a jump, a squeal, and in one moment was as big as a haystack. Then it let down four great lanky legs and threw out two long ears, nourished a great long tail and romped off, kicking and squealing and whinnying and laughing like a naughty, mischievous boy!

The old woman stared after it till it was fairly out of sight, then she burst out laughing too.

"Well!" she chuckled, "I am in luck! Quite the luckiest body hereabouts. Fancy my seeing the Bogey-Beast all to myself; and making myself so free with it too! My goodness! I do feel that uplifted—that *GRAND*!"—

So she went into her cottage and spent the evening chuckling over her good luck.

The Giant Book of Bedtime Stories
Fables

THE FOX AND THE GRAPES

A hungry Fox saw some fine bunches of Grapes hanging from a vine that was trained along a high trellis, and did his best to reach them by jumping as high as he could into the air. But it was all in vain, for they were just out of reach: so he gave up trying, and walked away with an air of dignity and unconcern, remarking, "I thought those Grapes were ripe, but I see now they are quite sour."

THE GOOSE THAT LAID THE GOLDEN EGGS

A Man and his Wife had the good fortune to possess a Goose which laid a Golden Egg every day. Lucky though they were, they soon began to think they were not getting rich fast enough, and, imagining the bird must be made of gold inside, they decided to kill it in order to secure the whole store of precious metal at once. But when they cut it open they found it was just like any other goose. Thus, they neither got rich all at once, as they had hoped, nor enjoyed any longer the daily addition to their wealth.

Much wants more and loses all.

THE CAT AND THE MICE

There was once a house that was overrun with Mice. A Cat heard of this, and said to herself, "That's the place for me," and off she went and took up her quarters in the house, and caught the Mice one by one and ate them. At last the Mice could stand it no longer, and they determined to take to their holes and stay there. "That's awkward," said the Cat to herself: "the only thing to do is to coax them out by a trick." So she considered a while, and then climbed up the wall and let herself hang down by her hind legs from a peg, and pretended to be dead. By and by a Mouse peeped out and saw the Cat hanging there. "Aha!" it cried, "you're very clever, madam, no doubt: but you may turn yourself into a bag of meal hanging there, if you like, yet you won't catch us coming anywhere near you."

If you are wise you won't be deceived by the innocent airs of those whom you have once found to be dangerous.

THE MISCHIEVOUS DOG

There was once a Dog who used to snap at people and bite them without any provocation, and who was a great nuisance to every one who came to his master's house. So his master fastened a bell round his neck to warn people of his presence. The Dog was very proud of the bell, and strutted about tinkling it with immense satisfaction. But an old dog came up to him and said, "The fewer airs you give yourself the better, my friend. You don't think, do you, that your bell was given you as a reward of merit? On the contrary, it is a badge of disgrace."

Notoriety is often mistaken for fame.

THE CHARCOAL-BURNER AND THE FULLER

There was once a Charcoal-burner who lived and worked by himself. A Fuller, however, happened to come and settle in the same neighborhood; and the Charcoal-burner, having made his acquaintance and finding he was an agreeable sort of fellow, asked him if he would come and share his house: "We shall get to know one another better that way," he said, "and, beside, our household expenses will be diminished." The Fuller thanked him, but replied, "I couldn't think of it, sir: why, everything I take such pains to whiten would be blackened in no time by your charcoal."

THE MICE IN COUNCIL

Once upon a time all the Mice met together in Council, and discussed the best means of securing themselves against the attacks of the cat. After several suggestions had been debated, a Mouse of some standing and experience got up and said, "I think I have hit upon a plan which will ensure our safety in the future, provided you approve and carry it out. It is that we should fasten a bell round the neck of our enemy the cat, which will by its tinkling warn us of her approach." This proposal was warmly applauded, and it had been already decided to adopt it, when an old Mouse got upon his feet and said, "I agree with you all that the plan before us is an admirable one: but may I ask who is going to bell the cat?"

THE BAT AND THE WEASELS

A Bat fell to the ground and was caught by a Weasel, and was just going to be killed and eaten when it begged to be let go. The Weasel said he couldn't do that because he was an enemy of all birds on principle. "Oh, but," said the Bat, "I'm not a bird at all: I'm a mouse." "So you are," said the Weasel, "now I come to look at you"; and he let it go. Some time after this the Bat was caught in just the same way by another

Weasel, and, as before, begged for its life. "No," said the Weasel, "I never let a mouse go by any chance." "But I'm not a mouse," said the Bat; "I'm a bird." "Why, so you are," said the Weasel; and he too let the Bat go.

Look and see which way the wind blows before you commit yourself.

THE DOG AND THE SOW

A Dog and a Sow were arguing and each claimed that its own young ones were finer than those of any other animal. "Well," said the Sow at last, "mine can see, at any rate, when they come into the world: but yours are born blind."

THE FOX AND THE CROW

A Crow was sitting on a branch of a tree with a piece of cheese in her beak when a Fox observed her and set his wits to work to discover some way of getting the cheese. Coming and standing under the tree he looked up and said, "What a noble bird I see above me! Her beauty is without equal, the hue of her plumage exquisite. If only her voice is as sweet as her looks are fair, she ought without doubt to be Queen of the Birds."

The Crow was hugely flattered by this, and just to show the Fox that she could sing she gave a loud caw. Down came the cheese, of course, and the Fox, snatching it up, said, "You have a voice, madam, I see: what you want is wits."

THE HORSE AND THE GROOM

There was once a Groom who used to spend long hours clipping and combing the Horse of which he had charge, but who daily stole a portion of his allowance of oats, and sold it for his own profit. The Horse gradually got into worse and worse condition, and at last cried to the Groom, "If you really want me to look sleek and well, you must comb me less and feed me more."

THE WOLF AND THE LAMB

A Wolf came upon a Lamb straying from the flock, and felt some compunction about taking the life of so helpless a creature without some plausible excuse; so he cast about for a grievance and said at last, "Last year, sirrah, you grossly insulted me." "That is impossible, sir," bleated the Lamb, "for I wasn't born then." "Well," retorted the Wolf, "you feed in my pastures." "That cannot be," replied the Lamb, "for I have never yet tasted grass." "You drink from my spring, then," continued the Wolf. "Indeed, sir," said the poor Lamb, "I have never yet drunk anything but my mother's milk." "Well, anyhow," said the Wolf, "I'm not going without my dinner": and he sprang upon the Lamb and devoured it without more ado.

Fables
THE PEACOCK AND THE CRANE

A Peacock taunted a Crane with the dullness of her plumage. "Look at my brilliant colors," said she, "and see how much finer they are than your poor feathers." "I am not denying," replied the Crane, "that yours are far gayer than mine; but when it comes to flying I can soar into the clouds, whereas you are confined to the earth like any dunghill cock."

THE CAT AND THE BIRDS

A Cat heard that the Birds in an aviary were ailing. So he got himself up as a doctor, and, taking with him a set of the instruments proper to his profession, presented himself at the door, and inquired after the health of the Birds. "We shall do very well," they replied, without letting him in, "when we've seen the last of you."

A villain may disguise himself, but he will not deceive the wise.

THE SPENDTHRIFT AND THE SWALLOW

A Spendthrift, who had wasted his fortune, and had nothing left but the clothes in which he stood, saw a Swallow one fine day in early spring. Thinking that summer had come, and that he could now do without his coat, he went and sold it for what it would fetch. A change, however, took place in the weather, and there came a sharp frost which killed the unfortunate Swallow. When the Spendthrift saw its dead body he cried, "Miserable bird! Thanks to you I am perishing of cold myself."

One swallow does not make summer.

THE OLD WOMAN AND THE DOCTOR

An Old Woman became almost totally blind from a disease of the eyes, and, after consulting a Doctor, made an agreement with him in the presence of witnesses that she should pay him a high fee if he cured her, while if he failed he was to receive nothing. The Doctor accordingly prescribed a course of treatment, and every time he paid her a visit he took away with him some article out of the house, until at last, when he visited her for the last time, and the cure was complete, there was nothing left. When the Old Woman saw that the house was empty she refused to pay him his fee; and, after repeated refusals on her part, he sued her before the magistrates for payment of her debt. On being brought into court she was ready with her defense. "The claimant," said she, "has stated the facts about our agreement correctly. I undertook to pay him a fee if he cured me, and he, on his part, promised to charge nothing if he failed. Now, he says I am cured; but I say that I am blinder than ever, and I can prove what I say. When my eyes were bad I could at any rate see well enough to be aware that my house contained a certain amount of furniture and other things; but now, when according to him I am cured, I am entirely unable to see anything there at all."

THE MOON AND HER MOTHER

The Moon once begged her Mother to make her a gown. "How can I?" replied she; "there's no fitting your figure. At one time you're a New Moon, and at another you're a Full Moon; and between whiles you're neither one nor the other."

MERCURY AND THE WOODMAN

A Woodman was felling a tree on the bank of a river, when his axe, glancing off the trunk, flew out of his hands and fell into the water. As he stood by the water's edge lamenting his loss, Mercury appeared and asked him the reason for his grief; and on learning what had happened, out of pity for his distress he dived into the river and, bringing up a golden axe, asked him if that was the one he had lost. The Woodman replied that it was not, and Mercury then dived a second time, and, bringing up a silver axe, asked if that was his. "No, that is not mine either," said the Woodman. Once more Mercury dived into the river, and brought up the missing axe. The Woodman was overjoyed at recovering his property, and thanked his benefactor warmly; and the latter was so pleased with his honesty that he made him a present of the other two axes. When the Woodman told the story to his companions, one of these was filled with envy of his good fortune and determined to try his luck for himself. So he went and began to fell a tree at the edge of the river, and presently contrived to let his axe drop into the water. Mercury appeared as before, and, on learning that his axe had fallen in, he dived and brought up a golden axe, as he had done on the previous occasion. Without waiting to be asked whether it was his or not the fellow cried, "That's mine, that's mine," and stretched out his hand eagerly for the prize: but Mercury was so disgusted at his dishonesty that he not only declined to give him the golden axe, but also refused to recover for him the one he had let fall into the stream.

Honesty is the best policy.

Fables
THE ASS, THE FOX, AND THE LION

An Ass and a Fox went into partnership and sallied out to forage for food together. They hadn't gone far before they saw a Lion coming their way, at which they were both dreadfully frightened. But the Fox thought he saw a way of saving his own skin, and went boldly up to the Lion and whispered in his ear, "I'll manage that you shall get hold of the Ass without the trouble of stalking him, if you'll promise to let me go free." The Lion agreed to this, and the Fox then rejoined his companion and contrived before long to lead him by a hidden pit, which some hunter had dug as a trap for wild animals, and into which he fell. When the Lion saw that the Ass was safely caught and couldn't get away, it was to the Fox that he first turned his attention, and he soon finished him off, and then at his leisure proceeded to feast upon the Ass.

Betray a friend, and you'll often find you have ruined yourself.

THE LION AND THE MOUSE

A Lion asleep in his lair was waked up by a Mouse running over his face. Losing his temper he seized it with his paw and was about to kill it. The Mouse, terrified, piteously entreated him to spare its life. "Please let me go," it cried, "and one day I will repay you for your kindness." The idea of so insignificant a creature ever being able to do anything for him amused the Lion so much that he laughed aloud, and good-humouredly let it go. But the Mouse's chance came, after all.

One day the Lion got entangled in a net which had been spread for game by some hunters, and the Mouse heard and recognized his roars of anger and ran to the spot. Without more ado it set to work to gnaw the ropes with its teeth, and succeeded before long in setting the Lion free. "There!" said the Mouse, "you laughed at me when I promised I would repay you: but now you see, even a Mouse can help a Lion."

THE CROW AND THE PITCHER

A thirsty Crow found a Pitcher with some water in it, but so little was there that, try as she might, she could not reach it with her beak, and it seemed as though she would die of thirst within sight of the remedy. At last she hit upon a clever plan. She began dropping pebbles into the Pitcher, and with each pebble the water rose a little higher until at last it reached the brim, and the knowing bird was enabled to quench her thirst.

Necessity is the mother of invention.

THE BOYS AND THE FROGS

Some mischievous Boys were playing on the edge of a pond, and, catching sight of some Frogs swimming about in the shallow water, they began to amuse themselves by pelting them with stones, and they killed several of them. At last one of the Frogs put his head out of the water and said, "Oh, stop! stop! I beg of you: what is sport to you is death to us."

THE NORTH WIND AND THE SUN

A dispute arose between the North Wind and the Sun, each claiming that he was stronger than the other. At last they agreed to try their powers upon a traveler, to see which could soonest strip him of his cloak. The North Wind had the first try; and, gathering up all his force for the attack, he came whirling furiously down upon the man, and caught up his cloak as though he would wrest it from him by one single effort: but the harder he blew, the more closely the man wrapped it round himself. Then came the turn of the Sun. At first he beamed gently upon the traveler, who soon unclasped his cloak and walked on with it hanging loosely about his shoulders: then he shone forth in his full strength, and the man, before he had gone

many steps, was glad to throw his cloak right off and complete his journey more lightly clad.

Persuasion is better than force

THE MISTRESS AND HER SERVANTS

A Widow, thrifty and industrious, had two servants, whom she kept pretty hard at work. They were not allowed to lie long abed in the mornings, but the old lady had them up and doing as soon as the cock crew. They disliked intensely having to get up at such an hour, especially in winter-time: and they thought that if it were not for the cock waking up their Mistress so horribly early, they could sleep longer. So they caught it and wrung its neck. But they weren't prepared for the consequences. For what happened was that their Mistress, not hearing the cock crow as usual, waked them up earlier than ever, and set them to work in the middle of the night.

THE GOODS AND THE ILLS

There was a time in the youth of the world when Goods and Ills entered equally into the concerns of men, so that the Goods did not prevail to make them altogether blessed, nor the Ills to make them wholly miserable. But owing to the foolishness of mankind the Ills multiplied greatly in number and increased in strength, until it seemed as though they would deprive the Goods of all share in human affairs, and banish them from the earth. The latter, therefore, betook themselves to heaven and complained to Jupiter of the treatment they had received, at the same

Fables

time praying him to grant them protection from the Ills, and to advise them concerning the manner of their intercourse with men. Jupiter granted their request for protection, and decreed that for the future they should not go among men openly in a body, and so be liable to attack from the hostile Ills, but singly and unobserved, and at infrequent and unexpected intervals. Hence it is that the earth is full of Ills, for they come and go as they please and are never far away; while Goods, alas! come one by one only, and have to travel all the way from heaven, so that they are very seldom seen.

THE HARES AND THE FROGS

The Hares once gathered together and lamented the unhappiness of their lot, exposed as they were to dangers on all sides and lacking the strength and the courage to hold their own. Men, dogs, birds and beasts of prey were all their enemies, and killed and devoured them daily: and sooner than endure such persecution any longer, they one and all determined to end their miserable lives. Thus resolved and desperate, they rushed in a body towards a neighboring pool, intending to drown themselves. On the bank were sitting a number of Frogs, who, when they heard the noise of the Hares as they ran, with one accord leaped into the water and hid themselves in the depths. Then one of the older Hares who was wiser than the rest cried out to his companions, "Stop, my friends, take heart; don't let us destroy ourselves after all: see, here are creatures who are afraid of us, and who must, therefore, be still more timid than ourselves."

THE FOX AND THE STORK

A Fox invited a Stork to dinner, at which the only fare provided was a large flat dish of soup. The Fox lapped it up with great relish, but the Stork with her long bill tried in vain to partake of the savory broth. Her evident distress caused the sly Fox much amusement.

But not long after the Stork invited him in turn, and set before him a pitcher with a long and narrow neck, into which she could get her bill with ease. Thus, while she enjoyed her dinner, the Fox sat by hungry and helpless, for it was impossible for him to reach the tempting contents of the vessel.

Fables
THE WOLF IN SHEEP'S CLOTHING

A Wolf resolved to disguise himself in order that he might prey upon a flock of sheep without fear of detection. So he clothed himself in a sheepskin, and slipped among the sheep when they were out at pasture. He completely deceived the shepherd, and when the flock was penned for the night he was shut in with the rest. But that very night as it happened, the shepherd, requiring a supply of mutton for the table, laid hands on the Wolf in mistake for a Sheep, and killed him with his knife on the spot.

THE STAG IN THE OX-STALL

A Stag, chased from his lair by the hounds, took refuge in a farmyard, and, entering a stable where a number of oxen were stalled, thrust himself under a pile of hay in a vacant stall, where he lay concealed, all but the tips of his horns. Presently one of the Oxen said to him, "What has induced you to come in here? Aren't you aware of the risk you are running of being captured by the herdsmen?" To which he replied, "Pray let me stay for the present. When night comes I shall easily escape under cover of the dark." In the course of the afternoon more than one of the farm-hands came in, to attend to the wants of the cattle, but not one of them noticed the presence of the Stag, who accordingly began to congratulate himself on his escape and to express his gratitude to the Oxen. "We wish you well," said the one who had spoken before, "but you are not out of danger yet. If the master comes, you will certainly be found out, for nothing ever escapes his keen eyes." Presently, sure enough, in he came, and made a great to-do about the way the Oxen were kept. "The beasts are starving," he cried; "here, give them more hay, and put plenty of litter under them." As he spoke, he seized an armful himself from the pile where the Stag lay concealed, and at once detected him. Calling his men, he had him seized at once and killed for the table.

THE MILKMAID AND HER PAIL

A farmer's daughter had been out to milk the cows, and was returning to the dairy carrying her pail of milk upon her head. As she walked along, she fell a-musing after this fashion: "The milk in this pail will provide me with cream, which I will make into butter and take to market to sell. With the money I will buy a number of eggs, and these, when hatched, will produce chickens, and by and by I shall have quite a large poultry-yard. Then I shall sell some of my fowls, and with the money which they will bring in I will buy myself a new gown, which I shall wear when I go to the fair; and all the young fellows will admire it, and come and make love to me, but I shall toss my head and have nothing to say to them." Forgetting all about the pail, and suiting the action to the word, she tossed her head. Down went the pail, all the milk was spilled, and all her fine castles in the air vanished in a moment!

Do not count your chickens before
they are hatched.

THE DOLPHINS, THE WHALES, AND THE SPRAT

The Dolphins quarreled with the Whales, and before very long they began fighting with one another. The battle was very fierce, and had lasted some time without any sign of coming to an end, when a Sprat thought that perhaps he could stop it; so he stepped in and tried to persuade them to give up fighting and make friends. But one of the Dolphins said to him contemptuously, "We would rather go on fighting till we're all killed than be reconciled by a Sprat like you!"

THE FOX AND THE MONKEY

A Fox and a Monkey were on the road together, and fell into a dispute as to which of the two was the better born. They kept it up for some time, till they came to a place where the road passed through a cemetery full of monuments, when the Monkey stopped and looked about him and gave a great sigh. "Why do you sigh?" said the Fox. The Monkey pointed to the tombs and replied, "All the monuments that you see here were put up in honor of my forefathers, who in their day were eminent men." The Fox was speechless for a moment, but quickly recovering he said, "Oh! don't stop at any lie, sir; you're quite safe: I'm sure none of your ancestors will rise up and expose you."

> *Boasters brag most when they cannot be detected.*

THE ASS AND THE LAP-DOG

There was once a man who had an Ass and a Lap-dog. The Ass was housed in the stable with plenty of oats and hay to eat and was as well off as an ass could be. The little Dog was made a great pet of by his master, who fondled him and often let him lie in his lap; and if he went out to dinner, he would bring back a tit-bit or two to give him when he ran to meet him on his return. The Ass had, it is true, a good deal of work to do, carting or grinding the corn, or carrying the burdens of the farm: and ere long he became very jealous, contrasting his own life of labor with the ease and idleness of the Lap-dog. At last one day he broke his halter, and frisking into the house just as his master sat down to dinner, he pranced and capered about, mimicking the frolics of the little favorite, upsetting the table and smashing the crockery with his clumsy efforts. Not content with that, he even tried to jump on his master's lap, as he had so often seen the dog allowed to do. At that the servants, seeing the danger their master was in, belabored the silly Ass with sticks and cudgels, and drove him back to his stable half dead with his beating. "Alas!" he cried, "all this I have brought on myself. Why could I not be satisfied with my natural and honorable position, without wishing to imitate the ridiculous antics of that useless little Lap-dog?"

THE FIR-TREE AND THE BRAMBLE

A Fir-tree was boasting to a Bramble, and said, somewhat contemptuously, "You poor creature, you are of no use whatever. Now, look at me: I am useful for all sorts of things, particularly when men build houses; they can't do without me then." But the Bramble replied, "Ah, that's all very well: but you wait till they come with axes and saws to cut you down, and then you'll wish you were a Bramble and not a Fir."

Better poverty without a care than wealth with its many obligations.

THE FROGS' COMPLAINT AGAINST THE SUN

Once upon a time the Sun was about to take to himself a wife. The Frogs in terror all raised their voices to the skies, and Jupiter, disturbed by the noise, asked them what they were croaking about. They replied, "The Sun is bad enough even while he is single, drying up our marshes with his heat as he does. But what will become of us if he marries and begets other Suns?"

THE DOG, THE COCK, AND THE FOX

A Dog and a Cock became great friends, and agreed to travel together. At nightfall the Cock flew up into the branches of a tree to roost, while the Dog curled himself up inside the trunk, which was hollow. At break of day the Cock woke up and crew, as usual. A Fox heard, and, wishing to make a breakfast of him, came and stood under the tree and begged him to come down. "I should so like," said he, "to make the acquaintance of one who has such a beautiful voice." The Cock replied, "Would you just wake my porter who sleeps at the foot of the tree? He'll open the door and let you in." The Fox accordingly rapped on the trunk, when out rushed the Dog and tore him in pieces.

Fables
THE GNAT AND THE BULL

A Gnat alighted on one of the horns of a Bull, and remained sitting there for a considerable time. When it had rested sufficiently and was about to fly away, it said to the Bull, "Do you mind if I go now?" The Bull merely raised his eyes and remarked, without interest, "It's all one to me; I didn't notice when you came, and I shan't know when you go away."

We may often be of more consequence in our own eyes than in the eyes of our neighbors.

THE BEAR AND THE TRAVELLERS

Two Travelers were on the road together, when a Bear suddenly appeared on the scene. Before he observed them, one made for a tree at the side of the road, and climbed up into the branches and hid there. The other was not so nimble as his companion; and, as he could not escape, he threw himself on the ground and pretended to be dead. The Bear came up and sniffed all round him, but he kept perfectly still and held his breath: for they say that a bear will not touch a dead body. The Bear took him for a corpse, and went away. When the coast was clear, the Traveler in the tree came down, and asked the other what it was the Bear had whispered to him when he put his mouth to his ear. The other replied, "He told me never again to travel with a friend who deserts you at the first sign of danger."

Misfortune tests the sincerity of friendship.

THE SLAVE AND THE LION

A Slave ran away from his master, by whom he had been most cruelly treated, and, in order to avoid capture, betook himself into the desert. As he wandered about in search of food and shelter, he came to a cave, which he entered and found to be unoccupied. Really, however, it was a Lion's den, and almost immediately, to the horror of the wretched fugitive, the Lion himself appeared. The man gave himself up for lost: but, to his utter astonishment, the Lion, instead of springing upon him and devouring him, came and fawned upon him, at the same time whining and lifting up his paw. Observing it to be much swollen and inflamed, he examined it and found a large thorn embedded in the ball of the foot. He accordingly removed it and dressed the wound as well as he could: and in course of time it healed up completely. The Lion's gratitude was unbounded; he looked upon the man as his friend, and they shared the cave for some time together. A day came, however, when the Slave began to long for the society of his fellow-men, and he bade farewell to the Lion and returned to the town. Here he was presently recognized and carried off in chains to his former master, who resolved to make an example of him, and ordered that he should be thrown to the beasts at the next public spectacle in the theatre. On the fatal day the beasts were loosed into the arena, and among the rest a Lion of huge bulk and ferocious aspect; and then the wretched Slave was cast in among them. What was the amazement of the spectators, when the Lion after one glance bounded up to him and lay down at his feet with every expression of affection and delight! It was his old friend of the cave! The audience clamored that the Slave's life should be spared: and the governor of the town, marveling at such gratitude and fidelity in a beast, decreed that both should receive their liberty.

THE FLEA AND THE MAN

A Flea bit a Man, and bit him again, and again, till he could stand it no longer, but made a thorough search for it, and at last succeeded in catching it. Holding it between his finger and thumb, he said—or rather shouted, so angry was he—"Who are you, pray, you wretched little creature, that you make so free with my person?" The Flea, terrified, whimpered in a weak little voice, "Oh, sir! pray let me go; don't kill

me! I am such a little thing that I can't do you much harm." But the Man laughed and said, "I am going to kill you now, at once: whatever is bad has got to be destroyed, no matter how slight the harm it does."

Do not waste your pity on a scamp.

THE BEE AND JUPITER

A Queen Bee from Hymettus flew up to Olympus with some fresh honey from the hive as a present to Jupiter, who was so pleased with the gift that he promised to give her anything she liked to ask for. She said she would be very grateful if he would give stings to the bees, to kill people who robbed them of their honey. Jupiter was greatly displeased with this request, for he loved mankind: but he had given his word, so he said that stings they should have. The stings he gave them, however, were of such a kind that whenever a bee stings a man the sting is left in the wound and the bee dies.

Evil wishes, like fowls, come home to roost.

THE OAK AND THE REEDS

An Oak that grew on the bank of a river was uprooted by a severe gale of wind, and thrown across the stream. It fell among some Reeds growing by the water, and said to them, "How is it that you, who are so frail and slender, have managed to weather the storm, whereas I, with all my strength, have been torn up by the roots and hurled into the river?" "You were stubborn," came the reply, "and fought against the storm, which proved stronger than you: but we bow and yield to every breeze, and thus the gale passed harmlessly over our heads."

THE BLIND MAN AND THE CUB

There was once a Blind Man who had so fine a sense of touch that, when any animal was put into his hands, he could tell what it was merely by the feel of it. One day the Cub of a Wolf was put into his hands, and he was asked what it was. He felt it for some time, and then said, "Indeed, I am not sure whether it is a Wolf's Cub or a Fox's: but this I know—it would never do to trust it in a sheepfold."

Evil tendencies are early shown.

THE BOY AND THE SNAILS

A Farmer's Boy went looking for Snails, and, when he had picked up both his hands full, he set about making a fire at which to roast them; for he meant to eat them. When it got well alight and the Snails began to feel the heat, they gradually withdrew more and more into their shells with the hissing noise they always make when they do so. When the Boy heard it, he said, "You abandoned creatures, how can you find heart to whistle when your houses are burning?"

THE APES AND THE TWO TRAVELLERS

Two men were traveling together, one of whom never spoke the truth, whereas the other never told a lie: and they came in the course of their travels to the land of Apes. The King of the Apes, hearing of their arrival, ordered them to be brought before him; and by way of impressing them with his magnificence, he received them sitting on a throne, while the Apes, his subjects, were ranged in long rows on either side of him. When the Travelers came into his presence he asked them what they thought of him as a King. The lying Traveler said, "Sire, every one must see that you are a most noble and mighty monarch." "And what do you think of my subjects?" continued the King. "They," said the Traveler, "are in every way worthy of their royal master." The Ape was so delighted with his answer that he gave him a very handsome present. The other Traveler thought that if his companion was rewarded so splendidly for telling a lie, he himself would certainly receive a still greater reward for telling the truth; so, when the Ape turned to him and said, "And what, sir, is your opinion?" he replied, "I think you are a very fine Ape, and all your subjects are fine Apes too." The King of the Apes was so enraged at his reply that he ordered him to be taken away and clawed to death.

THE ASS AND HIS BURDENS

A Peddler who owned an Ass one day bought a quantity of salt, and loaded up his beast with as much as he could bear. On the way home the Ass stumbled as he was crossing a stream and fell into the water. The salt got thoroughly wetted and much of it melted and drained away, so that, when he got on his legs again, the Ass found his load had become much less heavy. His master, however, drove him back to town and bought more salt, which he added to what remained in the panniers, and started out again. No sooner had they reached a stream than the Ass lay down in it, and rose, as before, with a much lighter load. But his master detected the trick, and turning back once more, bought a large number of sponges, and piled them on the back of the Ass. When they came to the stream the Ass again lay down: but this time, as the sponges soaked up large quantities of water, he found, when he got up on his legs, that he had a bigger burden to carry than ever.

You may play a good card once too often.

THE SHEPHERD'S BOY AND THE WOLF

A Shepherd's Boy was tending his flock near a village, and thought it would be great fun to hoax the villagers by pretending that a Wolf was attacking the sheep: so he shouted out, "Wolf! wolf!" and when the people came running up he laughed at them for their pains. He did this more than once, and every time the villagers found they had been hoaxed, for there was no Wolf at all. At last a Wolf really did come, and the Boy cried, "Wolf! wolf!" as loud as he could: but the people were so used to hearing him call that they took no notice of his cries for help. And so the Wolf had it all his own way, and killed off sheep after sheep at his leisure.

You cannot believe a liar even when he tells the truth.

THE FOX AND THE GOAT

A Fox fell into a well and was unable to get out again. By and by a thirsty Goat came by, and seeing the Fox in the well asked him if the water was good. "Good?" said the Fox, "it's the best water I ever tasted in all my life. Come down and try it yourself." The Goat thought of nothing but the prospect of quenching his thirst, and jumped in at once. When he had had enough to drink, he looked about, like the Fox, for some way of getting out, but could find none. Presently the Fox said, "I have an idea. You stand on your hind legs, and plant your forelegs firmly against the side of the well, and then I'll climb on to your back, and, from there, by stepping on your horns, I can get out. And when I'm out, I'll help you out too." The Goat did as he was requested, and the Fox climbed on to his back and so out of the well; and then he coolly walked away. The Goat called loudly after him and reminded him of his promise to help him out: but the Fox merely turned and said, "If you had as much sense in your head as you have hair in your beard you wouldn't have got into the well without making certain that you could get out again."

Look before your leap.

THE FISHERMAN AND THE SPRAT

A Fisherman cast his net into the sea, and when he drew it up again it contained nothing but a single Sprat that begged to be put back into the water. "I'm only a little fish now," it said, "but I shall grow big one day, and then if you come and catch me again I shall be of some use to you." But the Fisherman replied, "Oh, no, I shall keep you now I've got you: if I put you back, should I ever see you again? Not likely!"

THE BOASTING TRAVELLER

A Man once went abroad on his travels, and when he came home he had wonderful tales to tell of the things he had done in foreign countries. Among other things, he said he had taken part in a jumping-match at Rhodes, and had done a wonderful jump which no one could beat. "Just go to Rhodes and ask them," he said; "every one will tell you it's true." But one of those who were listening said, "If you can jump as well as all that, we needn't go to Rhodes to prove it. Let's just imagine this is Rhodes for a minute: and now—jump!"

Deeds, not words.

THE CRAB AND HIS MOTHER

An Old Crab said to her son, "Why do you walk sideways like that, my son? You ought to walk straight." The Young Crab replied, "Show me how, dear mother, and I'll follow your example." The Old Crab tried, but tried in vain, and then saw how foolish she had been to find fault with her child.

Example is better than precept.

Fables
THE ASS AND HIS SHADOW

A certain man hired an Ass for a journey in summertime, and started out with the owner following behind to drive the beast. By and by, in the heat of the day, they stopped to rest, and the traveler wanted to lie down in the Ass's Shadow; but the owner, who himself wished to be out of the sun, wouldn't let him do that; for he said he had hired the Ass only, and not his Shadow: the other maintained that his bargain secured him complete control of the Ass for the time being. From words they came to blows; and while they were belaboring each other the Ass took to his heels and was soon out of sight.

THE FARMER AND HIS SONS

A Farmer, being at death's door, and desiring to impart to his Sons a secret of much moment, called them round him and said, "My sons, I am shortly about to die; I would have you know, therefore, that in my vineyard there lies a hidden treasure. Dig, and you will find it." As soon as their father was dead, the Sons took spade and fork and turned up the soil of the vineyard over and over again, in their search for the treasure which they supposed to lie buried there. They found none, however: but the vines, after so thorough a digging, produced a crop such as had never before been seen.

THE DOG AND THE COOK

A rich man once invited a number of his friends and acquaintances to a banquet. His dog thought it would be a good opportunity to invite another Dog, a friend of his; so he went to him and said, "My master is giving a feast: there'll be a fine spread, so come and dine with me to-night." The Dog thus invited came, and when he saw the preparations being made in the kitchen he said to himself, "My word, I'm in luck: I'll take care to eat enough to-night to last me two or three days." At the same time he wagged his tail briskly, by way of showing his friend how delighted he was to have been asked. But just then the Cook caught sight of him, and, in his annoyance at seeing a strange Dog in the kitchen, caught him up by the hind legs and threw him out of the window. He had a nasty fall, and limped away as quickly as he could, howling dismally. Presently some other dogs met him, and said, "Well, what sort of a dinner did you get?" To which he replied, "I had a splendid time: the wine was so good, and I drank so much of it, that I really don't remember how I got out of the house!"

Be shy of favors bestowed at the expense of others.

THE MONKEY AS KING

At a gathering of all the animals the Monkey danced and delighted them so much that they made him their King. The Fox, however, was very much disgusted at the promotion of the

Monkey: so having one day found a trap with a piece of meat in it, he took the Monkey there and said to him, "Here is a dainty morsel I have found, sire; I did not take it myself, because I thought it ought to be reserved for you, our King. Will you be pleased to accept it?" The Monkey made at once for the meat and got caught in the trap. Then he bitterly reproached the Fox for leading him into danger; but the Fox only laughed and said, "O Monkey, you call yourself King of the Beasts and haven't more sense than to be taken in like that!"

THE THIEVES AND THE COCK

Some Thieves broke into a house, and found nothing worth taking except a Cock, which they seized and carried off with them. When they were preparing their supper, one of them caught up the Cock, and was about to wring his neck, when he cried out for mercy and said, "Pray do not kill me: you will find me a most useful bird, for I rouse honest men to their work in the morning by my crowing." But the Thief replied with some heat, "Yes, I know you do, making it still harder for us to get a livelihood. Into the pot you go!"

THE FARMER AND FORTUNE

A Farmer was plowing one day on his farm when he turned up a pot of golden coins with his plough. He was overjoyed at his discovery, and from that time forth made an offering daily at the shrine of the Goddess of the Earth. Fortune was displeased at this, and came to him and said, "My man, why do you give Earth the credit for the gift which I bestowed upon you? You never thought of thanking me for your good luck; but should you be unlucky enough to lose what you have gained I know very well that I, Fortune, should then come in for all the blame."

Show gratitude where gratitude is due.

JUPITER AND THE MONKEY

Jupiter issued a proclamation to all the beasts, and offered a prize to the one who, in his judgment, produced the most beautiful offspring. Among the rest came the Monkey, carrying a baby monkey in her arms, a hairless, flat-nosed little fright. When they saw it, the gods all burst into peal on peal of laughter; but the Monkey hugged her little one to her, and said, "Jupiter may give the prize to whomsoever he likes: but I shall always think my baby the most beautiful of them all."

Fables
FATHER AND SONS

A certain man had several Sons who were always quarrelling with one another, and, try as he might, he could not get them to live together in harmony. So he determined to convince them of their folly by the following means. Bidding them fetch a bundle of sticks, he invited each in turn to break it across his knee. All tried and all failed: and then he undid the bundle, and handed them the sticks one by one, when they had no difficulty at all in breaking them. "There, my boys," said he, "united you will be more than a match for your enemies: but if you quarrel and separate, your weakness will put you at the mercy of those who attack you."

Union is strength.

THE LAMP

A Lamp, well filled with oil, burned with a clear and steady light, and began to swell with pride and boast that it shone more brightly than the sun himself. Just then a puff of wind came and blew it out. Some one struck a match and lit it again, and said, "You just keep alight, and never mind the sun. Why, even the stars never need to be relit as you had to be just now."

THE OWL AND THE BIRDS

The Owl is a very wise bird; and once, long ago, when the first oak sprouted in the forest, she called all the other Birds together and said to them, "You see this tiny tree? If you take my advice, you will destroy it now when it is small: for when it grows big, the mistletoe will appear upon it, from which birdlime will be prepared for your destruction." Again, when the first flax was sown, she said to them, "Go and eat up that seed, for it is the seed of the flax,  out of which men will one day make nets to catch you." Once more, when she saw the first archer, she warned the Birds that he was their deadly enemy, who would wing his arrows with their own feathers and shoot them. But they took no notice of what she said: in fact, they thought she was rather mad, and laughed at her. When, however, everything turned out as she had foretold, they changed their minds and conceived a great respect for her wisdom. Hence, whenever she appears, the Birds attend upon her in the hope of hearing something that may be for their good. She, however, gives them advice no longer, but sits moping and pondering on the folly of her kind.

THE ASS IN THE LION'S SKIN

An Ass found a Lion's Skin, and dressed himself up in it. Then he went about frightening every

one he met, for they all took him to be a lion, men and beasts alike, and took to their heels when they saw him coming. Elated by the success of his trick, he loudly brayed in triumph. The Fox heard him, and recognized him at once for the Ass he was, and said to him, "Oho, my friend, it's you, is it? I, too, should have been afraid if I hadn't heard your voice."

THE SHE-GOATS AND THEIR BEARDS

Jupiter granted beards to the She-Goats at their own request, much to the disgust of the he-Goats, who considered this to be an unwarrantable invasion of their rights and dignities. So they sent a deputation to him to protest against his action. He, however, advised them not to raise any objections. "What's in a tuft of hair?" said he. "Let them have it if they want it. They can never be a match for you in strength."

THE OLD LION

A Lion, enfeebled by age and no longer able to procure food for himself by force, determined to do so by cunning. Betaking himself to a cave, he lay down inside and feigned to be sick: and whenever any of the other animals entered to inquire after his health, he sprang upon them and devoured them. Many lost their lives in this way, till one day a Fox called at the cave, and, having a suspicion of the truth, addressed the Lion from outside instead of going in, and asked him how he did. He replied that he was in a very bad way: "But," said he, "why do you stand outside? Pray come in." "I should have done so," answered the Fox, "if I hadn't noticed that all the footprints point towards the cave and none the other way."

THE BOY BATHING

A Boy was bathing in a river and got out of his depth, and was in great danger of being drowned. A man who was passing along a road heard his cries for help, and went to the riverside and began to scold him for being so careless as to get into deep water, but made no attempt to help him. "Oh, sir," cried the Boy, "please help me first and scold me afterwards."

Give assistance, not advice, in a crisis.

Fables
THE QUACK FROG

Once upon a time a Frog came forth from his home in the marshes and proclaimed to all the world that he was a learned physician, skilled in drugs and able to cure all diseases. Among the crowd was a Fox, who called out, "You a doctor! Why, how can you set up to heal others when you cannot even cure your own lame legs and blotched and wrinkled skin?"

Physician, heal thyself.

THE SWOLLEN FOX

A hungry Fox found in a hollow tree a quantity of bread and meat, which some shepherds had placed there against their return. Delighted with his find he slipped in through the narrow aperture and greedily devoured it all. But when he tried to get out again he found himself so swollen after his big meal that he could not squeeze through the hole, and fell to whining and groaning over his misfortune. Another Fox, happening to pass that way, came and asked him what the matter was; and, on learning the state of the case, said, "Well, my friend, I see nothing for it but for you to stay where you are till you shrink to your former size; you'll get out then easily enough."

THE MOUSE, THE FROG, AND THE HAWK

A Mouse and a Frog struck up a friendship; they were not well mated, for the Mouse lived entirely on land, while the Frog was equally at home on land or in the water. In order that they might never be separated, the Frog tied himself and the Mouse together by the leg with a piece of thread. As long as they kept on dry land all went fairly well; but, coming to the edge of a pool, the Frog jumped in, taking the Mouse with him, and began swimming about and croaking with pleasure. The unhappy Mouse, however, was soon drowned, and floated about on the surface in the wake of the Frog. There he was spied by a Hawk, who pounced down on him and seized him in his talons. The Frog was unable to loose the knot which bound him to the Mouse, and thus was carried off along with him and eaten by the Hawk.

THE BOY AND THE NETTLES

A Boy was gathering berries from a hedge when his hand was stung by a Nettle. Smarting with the pain, he ran to tell his mother, and said to her between his sobs, "I only touched it ever so lightly, mother." "That's just why you got stung, my son," she said; "if you had grasped it firmly, it wouldn't have hurt you in the least."

THE PEASANT AND THE APPLE-TREE

A Peasant had an Apple-tree growing in his garden, which bore no fruit, but merely served to provide a shelter from the heat for the sparrows and grasshoppers which sat and chirped in its branches. Disappointed at its barrenness he determined to cut it down, and went and fetched his axe for the purpose. But when the sparrows and the grasshoppers saw what he was about to do, they begged him to spare it, and said to him, "If you destroy the tree we shall have to seek shelter elsewhere, and you will no longer have our merry chirping to enliven your work in the garden." He, however, refused to listen to them, and set to work with a will to cut through the trunk. A few strokes showed that it was hollow inside and contained a swarm of bees and a large store of honey. Delighted with his find he threw down his axe, saying, "The old tree is worth keeping after all."

Utility is most men's test of worth.

THE JACKDAW AND THE PIGEONS

A Jackdaw, watching some Pigeons in a farmyard, was filled with envy when he saw how well they were fed, and determined to disguise himself as one of them, in order to secure a share of the good things they enjoyed. So he painted himself white from head to foot and joined the flock; and, so long as he was silent, they never suspected that he was not a pigeon like themselves. But one day he was unwise enough to start chattering, when they at once saw through his disguise and pecked him so unmercifully that he was glad to escape and join his own kind again. But the other jackdaws did not recognize him in his white dress, and would not let him feed with them, but drove him away: and so he became a homeless wanderer for his pains.

JUPITER AND THE TORTOISE

Jupiter was about to marry a wife, and determined to celebrate the event by inviting all the animals to a banquet. They all came except the Tortoise, who did not put in an appearance, much to Jupiter's surprise. So when he next saw the Tortoise he asked him why he had not been at the banquet. "I don't care for going out," said the Tortoise; "there's no place like home." Jupiter was so much annoyed by this reply that he decreed that from that time forth the Tortoise should carry his house upon his back, and never be able to get away from home even if he wished to.

THE DOG IN THE MANGER

A Dog was lying in a Manger on the hay which had been put there for the cattle, and when they came and tried to eat, he growled and snapped at them and wouldn't let them get at their food. "What a selfish beast," said one of them to his companions; "he can't eat himself and yet he won't let those eat who can."

THE TWO BAGS

Every man carries Two Bags about with him, one in front and one behind, and both are packed full of faults. The Bag in front contains his neighbors' faults, the one behind his own. Hence it is that men do not see their own faults, but never fail to see those of others.

THE OXEN AND THE AXLETREES

A pair of Oxen were drawing a heavily loaded wagon along the highway, and, as they tugged and strained at the yoke, the Axletrees creaked and groaned terribly. This was too much for the Oxen, who turned round indignantly and said,

"Hullo, you there! Why do you make such a noise when we do all the work?"

They complain most who suffer least.

THE BOY AND THE FILBERTS

A Boy put his hand into a jar of Filberts, and grasped as many as his fist could possibly hold. But when he tried to pull it out again, he found he couldn't do so, for the neck of the jar was too small to allow of the passage of so large a handful. Unwilling to lose his nuts but unable to withdraw his hand, he burst into tears. A bystander, who saw where the trouble lay, said to him, "Come, my boy, don't be so greedy: be content with half the amount, and you'll be able to get your hand out without difficulty."

Do not attempt too much at once.

THE FROGS ASKING FOR A KING

Time was when the Frogs were discontented because they had no one to rule over them: so they sent a deputation to Jupiter to ask him to give them a King. Jupiter, despising the folly of their request, cast a

log into the pool where they lived, and said that that should be their King. The Frogs were terrified at first by the splash, and scuttled away into the deepest parts of the pool; but by and by, when they saw that the log remained motionless, one by one they ventured to the surface again, and before long, growing bolder, they began to feel such contempt for it that they even took to sitting upon it. Thinking that a King of that sort was an insult to their dignity, they sent to Jupi-

ter a second time, and begged him to take away the sluggish King he had given them, and to give them another and a better one. Jupiter, annoyed at being pestered in this way, sent a Stork to rule over them, who no sooner arrived among them than he began to catch and eat the Frogs as fast as he could.

THE OLIVE-TREE AND THE FIG-TREE

An Olive-tree taunted a Fig-tree with the loss of her leaves at a certain season of the year. "You," she said, "lose your leaves every autumn, and are bare till the spring: whereas I, as you see, remain green and flourishing all the year round." Soon afterwards there came a heavy fall of snow, which settled on the leaves of the Olive so that she bent and broke under the weight; but the flakes fell harmlessly through the bare branches of the Fig, which survived to bear many another crop.

THE LION AND THE BOAR

One hot and thirsty day in the height of summer a Lion and a Boar came down to a little spring at the same moment to drink. In a trice they were quarrelling as to who should drink first. The quarrel soon became a fight and they attacked one another with the utmost fury. Presently, stopping for a moment to take breath, they saw some vultures seated on a rock above evidently waiting for one of them to be killed, when they would fly down and feed upon the carcass. The sight sobered them at once, and they made up their quarrel, saying, "We had much better be friends than fight and be eaten by vultures."

THE WALNUT-TREE

A Walnut-tree, which grew by the roadside, bore every year a plentiful crop of nuts. Every one who passed by pelted its branches with sticks and stones, in order to bring down the fruit, and the tree suffered severely. "It is hard," it cried, "that the very persons who enjoy my fruit should thus reward me with insults and blows."

THE MAN AND THE LION

A Man and a Lion were companions on a journey, and in the course of conversation they began to boast about their prowess, and each claimed to be superior to the other in strength and courage. They were still arguing with some heat when they came to a cross-road where there was a statue of a Man strangling a Lion. "There!" said the Man triumphantly, "look at that! Doesn't that prove to you that we are stronger than you?" "Not so fast, my friend," said the Lion: "that is only your view of the case. If we Lions could make statues, you may be sure that in most of them you would see the Man underneath."

There are two sides to every question.

THE TORTOISE AND THE EAGLE

A Tortoise, discontented with his lowly life, and envious of the birds he saw disporting themselves in the air, begged an Eagle to teach him to fly. The Eagle protested that it was idle for him to try, as nature had not provided him with wings; but the Tortoise pressed him with entreaties and promises of treasure, insisting that it could only be a question of learning the craft of the air. So at length the Eagle consented to do the best he could for him, and picked him up in his talons. Soaring with him to a great height in the sky he then let him go, and the wretched Tortoise fell headlong and was dashed to pieces on a rock.

THE KID ON THE HOUSETOP

A Kid climbed up on to the roof of an outhouse, attracted by the grass and other things that grew in the thatch; and as he stood there browsing away, he caught sight of a Wolf passing below, and jeered at him because he couldn't reach him. The Wolf only looked up and said, "I hear you, my young friend; but it is not you who mock me, but the roof on which you are standing."

THE FOX WITHOUT A TAIL

A fox once fell into a trap, and after a struggle managed to get free, but with the loss of his  brush. He was then so much ashamed of his appearance that he thought life was not worth living unless he could persuade the other Foxes to part with their tails also, and thus divert attention from his own loss. So he called a meeting of all the Foxes, and advised them to cut off their tails: "They're ugly things anyhow," he said, "and besides they're heavy, and it's tiresome to be always carrying them about with you." But one of the other Foxes said, "My friend, if you hadn't lost your own tail, you wouldn't be so keen on getting us to cut off ours."

THE VAIN JACKDAW

Jupiter announced that he intended to appoint a king over the birds, and named a day on which they were to appear before his throne, when he would select the most beautiful of them all to be their ruler. Wishing to look their best on the occasion they repaired to the banks of a stream, where they busied themselves in washing and preening their feathers. The Jackdaw was there along with the rest, and realized that, with his ugly plumage, he would have no chance of being chosen as he was: so he waited till they were all gone, and then picked up the most gaudy of the feathers they had dropped, and fastened them about his own body, with the result that he looked gayer than any of them. When the appointed day came, the birds assembled before Jupiter's throne; and, after passing them in review, he was about to make the Jackdaw king, when all the rest set upon the king-elect, stripped him of his borrowed plumes, and exposed him for the Jackdaw that he was.

THE TRAVELLER AND HIS DOG

A Traveler was about to start on a journey, and said to his Dog, who was stretching himself by the door, "Come, what are you yawning for? Hurry up and get ready: I mean you to go with me." But the Dog merely wagged his tail and said quietly, "I'm ready, master: it's you I'm waiting for."

THE SHIPWRECKED MAN AND THE SEA

A Shipwrecked Man cast up on the beach fell asleep after his struggle with the waves. When he woke up, he bitterly reproached the Sea for its treachery in enticing men with its smooth and smiling surface, and then, when they were well embarked, turning in fury upon them and sending both ship and sailors to destruction. The Sea arose in the form of a woman, and replied, "Lay not the blame on me, O sailor, but on the Winds. By nature I am as calm and safe as the land itself: but the Winds fall upon me with their gusts and gales, and lash me into a fury that is not natural to me."

THE WILD BOAR AND THE FOX

A Wild Boar was engaged in whetting his tusks upon the trunk of a tree in the forest when a Fox came by and, seeing what he was at, said to him, "Why are you doing that, pray? The huntsmen are not out to-day, and there are no other dangers at hand that I can see." "True, my friend," replied the Boar, "but the instant my life is in danger I shall need to use my tusks. There'll be no time to sharpen them then."

MERCURY AND THE SCULPTOR

Mercury was very anxious to know in what estimation he was held by mankind; so he disguised himself as a man and walked into a Sculptor's studio, where there were a number of statues finished and ready for sale. Seeing a statue of Jupiter among the rest, he inquired the price of it. "A crown," said the Sculptor. "Is that all?" said he, laughing; "and" (pointing to one of Juno) "how much is that one?" "That," was the reply, "is half a crown." "And how much might you be wanting for that one over there, now?" he continued, pointing to a statue of himself. "That one?" said the Sculptor; "Oh, I'll throw him in for nothing if you'll buy the other two."

THE FAWN AND HIS MOTHER

A Hind said to her Fawn, who was now well grown and strong, "My son, Nature has given you a powerful body and a stout pair of horns, and I can't think why you are such a coward as to run away from the hounds." Just then they both heard the sound of a pack in full cry, but at a considerable distance. "You stay where you are," said the Hind; "never mind me": and with that she ran off as fast as her legs could carry her.

THE FOX AND THE LION

A Fox who had never seen a Lion one day met one, and was so terrified at the sight of him that he was ready to die with fear. After a time he met him again, and was still rather frightened, but not nearly so much as he had been when he met him first. But when he saw him for the third time he was so far from being afraid that he went up to him and began to talk to him as if he had known him all his life.

THE EAGLE AND HIS CAPTOR

A Man once caught an Eagle, and after clipping his wings turned him loose among the fowls in his hen-house, where he moped in a corner, looking very dejected and forlorn. After a while his Captor was glad enough to sell him to a neighbor, who took him home and let his wings grow again. As soon as he had recovered the use of them, the Eagle flew out and caught a hare, which he brought home and presented to his benefactor. A fox observed this, and said to the Eagle, "Don't waste your gifts on him! Go and give them to the man who first caught you; make _him_ your friend, and then perhaps he won't catch you and clip your wings a second time."

THE BLACKSMITH AND HIS DOG

A Blacksmith had a little Dog, which used to sleep when his master was at work, but was very wide awake indeed when it was time for meals. One day his master pretended to be disgusted at this, and when he had thrown him a bone as usual, he said, "What on earth is the good of a lazy cur like you? When I am hammering away at my anvil, you just curl up and go to sleep: but no sooner do I stop for a mouthful of food than you wake up and wag your tail to be fed."

Those who will not work deserve to starve.

THE STAG AT THE POOL

A thirsty Stag went down to a pool to drink. As he bent over the surface he saw his own reflection in the water, and was struck with admiration for his fine spreading antlers, but at the same time he felt nothing but disgust for the weakness and slenderness of his legs. While he stood there looking at himself, he was seen and attacked by a Lion; but in the chase which ensued, he soon drew away from his pursuer, and kept his lead as long as the ground over which he ran was open and free of trees. But coming presently to a wood, he was caught by his antlers in the branches, and fell a victim to the teeth and claws of his enemy. "Woe is me!" he cried with his last breath; "I despised my legs, which might have saved my life: but I gloried in my horns, and they have proved my ruin."

What is worth most is often valued least.

THE DOG AND THE SHADOW

A Dog was crossing a plank bridge over a stream with a piece of meat in his mouth, when he happened to see his own reflection in the water. He thought it was another dog with a piece of meat twice as big; so he let go his own, and flew at the other dog to get the larger piece. But, of course, all that happened was that he got neither; for one was only a shadow, and the other was carried away by the current.

MERCURY AND THE TRADESMEN

When Jupiter was creating man, he told Mercury to make an infusion of lies, and to add a little of it to the other ingredients which went to the making of the Tradesmen. Mercury did so, and introduced an equal amount into each in turn—the tallow-chandler, and the greengrocer, and the haberdasher, and all, till he came to the horse-dealer, who was last on the list, when, finding that he had a quantity of the infusion still left, he put it all into him. This is why all

Tradesmen lie more or less, but they none of them lie like a horse-dealer.

THE MICE AND THE WEASELS

There was war between the Mice and the Weasels, in which the Mice always got the worst of it, numbers of them being killed and eaten by the Weasels. So they called a council of war, in which an old Mouse got up and said, "It's no wonder we are always beaten, for we have no generals to plan our battles and direct our movements in the field." Acting on his advice, they chose the biggest Mice to be their leaders, and these, in order to be distinguished from the rank and file, provided themselves with helmets bearing large plumes of straw. They then led out the Mice to battle, confident of victory: but they were defeated as usual, and were soon scampering as fast as they could to their holes. All made their way to safety without difficulty except the leaders, who were so hampered by the badges of their rank that they could not get into their holes, and fell easy victims to their pursuers.

Greatness carries its own penalties.

THE PEACOCK AND JUNO

The Peacock was greatly discontented because he had not a beautiful voice like the nightingale, and he went and complained to Juno about it. "The nightingale's song," said he, "is the envy of all the birds; but whenever I utter a sound I become a laughing-stock." The goddess tried to console him by saying, "You have not, it is true, the power of song, but then you far excel all the rest in beauty: your neck flashes like the emerald and your splendid tail is a marvel of gorgeous color." But the Peacock was not appeased. "What is the use," said he, "of being beautiful, with a voice like mine?" Then Juno replied, with a shade of sternness in her tones, "Fate has allotted to all their destined gifts: to yourself beauty, to the eagle strength, to the nightingale song, and so on to all the rest in their degree; but you alone are dissatisfied with your portion. Make, then, no more complaints. For, if your present wish were granted, you would quickly find cause for fresh discontent."

THE BEAR AND THE FOX

A Bear was once bragging about his generous feelings, and saying how refined he was compared with other animals. (There is, in fact, a tradition that a Bear will never touch a dead body.) A Fox, who heard him talking in this strain, smiled and said, "My friend, when you are hungry, I only wish you _would_ confine your attention to the dead and leave the living alone."

A hypocrite deceives no one but himself.

Fables
THE ASS AND THE OLD PEASANT

An old Peasant was sitting in a meadow watching his Ass, which was grazing close by, when all of a sudden he caught sight of armed men stealthily approaching. He jumped up in a moment, and begged the Ass to fly with him as fast as he could, "Or else," said he, "we shall both be captured by the enemy." But the Ass just looked round lazily and said, "And if so, do you think they'll make me carry heavier loads than I have to now?" "No," said his master. "Oh, well, then," said the Ass, "I don't mind if they do take me, for I shan't be any worse off."

THE OX AND THE FROG

Two little Frogs were playing about at the edge of a pool when an Ox came down to the water to drink, and by accident trod on one of them and crushed the life out of him. When the old Frog missed him, she asked his brother where he was. "He is dead, mother," said the little Frog; "an enormous big creature with four legs came to our pool this morning and trampled him down in the mud." "Enormous, was he? Was he as big as this?" said the Frog, puffing herself out to look as big as possible. "Oh! yes, _much_ bigger," was the answer. The Frog puffed herself out still more. "Was he as big as this?" said she. "Oh! yes, yes, mother, _MUCH_ bigger," said the little Frog. And yet again she puffed and puffed herself out till she was almost as round as a ball. "As big as...?" she began—but then she burst.

THE MAN AND THE IMAGE

A poor Man had a wooden Image of a god, to which he used to pray daily for riches. He did this for a long time, but remained as poor as ever, till one day he caught up the Image in disgust and hurled it with all his strength against the wall. The force of the blow split open the head and a quantity of gold coins fell out upon the floor. The Man gathered them up greedily, and said, "O you old fraud, you! When I honored you, you did me no good whatever: but no sooner do I treat you to insults and violence than you make a rich man of me!"

HERCULES AND THE WAGGONER

A Waggoner was driving his team along a muddy lane with a full load behind them, when the wheels of his wagon sank so deep in the mire that no efforts of his horses could move them. As he stood there, looking helplessly on, and calling loudly at intervals upon Hercules for assistance, the god himself appeared, and said to him, "Put your shoulder to the wheel, man, and goad on your horses, and then you may call on Hercules to assist you. If you won't lift a finger to help yourself, you can't expect Hercules or any one else to come to your aid."

Heaven helps those who help themselves.

Fables

THE POMEGRANATE, THE APPLE-TREE, AND THE BRAMBLE

A Pomegranate and an Apple-tree were disputing about the quality of their fruits, and each claimed that its own was the better of the two. High words passed between them, and a violent quarrel was imminent, when a Bramble impudently poked its head out of a neighboring hedge and said, "There, that's enough, my friends; don't let us quarrel."

THE LION, THE BEAR, AND THE FOX

A Lion and a Bear were fighting for possession of a kid, which they had both seized at the same moment. The battle was long and fierce, and at length both of them were exhausted, and lay upon the ground severely wounded and gasping for breath. A Fox had all the time been prowling round and watching the fight: and when he saw the combatants lying there too weak to move, he slipped in and seized the kid, and ran off with it. They looked on helplessly, and one said to the other, "Here we've been mauling each other all this while, and no one the better for it except the Fox!"

THE TWO SOLDIERS AND THE ROBBER

Two Soldiers traveling together were set upon by a Robber. One of them ran away, but the other stood his ground, and laid about him so lustily with his sword that the Robber was fain to fly and leave him in peace. When the coast was clear the timid one ran back, and, flourishing his weapon, cried in a threatening voice, "Where is he? Let me get at him, and I'll soon let him know whom he's got to deal with." But the other replied, "You are a little late, my friend: I only wish you had backed me up just now, even if you had done no more than speak, for I should have been encouraged, believing your words to be true. As it is, calm yourself, and put up your sword: there is no further use for it. You may delude others into thinking you're as brave as a lion: but I know that, at the first sign of danger, you run away like a hare."

THE LION AND THE WILD ASS

A Lion and a Wild Ass went out hunting together: the latter was to run down the prey by his superior speed, and the former would then come up and dispatch it. They met with great success; and when it came to sharing the spoil the Lion divided it all into three equal portions. "I will take the first," said he, "because I am King of the beasts; I will also take the second, because, as your partner, I am entitled to half of what remains; and as for the third—well, unless you give it up to me and take yourself off pretty quick, the third, believe me, will make you feel very sorry for yourself!"

Might makes right.

THE MAN AND THE SATYR

A Man and a Satyr became friends, and determined to live together. All went well for a while, until one day in wintertime the Satyr saw the Man blowing on his hands. "Why do you do that?" he asked. "To warm my hands," said the Man. That same day, when they sat down to supper together, they each had a steaming hot bowl of porridge, and the Man raised his bowl to his mouth and blew on it. "Why do you do that?" asked the Satyr. "To cool my porridge," said the Man. The Satyr got up from the table. "Good-bye," said he, "I'm going: I can't be friends with a man who blows hot and cold with the same breath."

THE IMAGE-SELLER

A certain man made a wooden Image of Mercury, and exposed it for sale in the market. As no one offered to buy it, however, he thought he would try to attract a purchaser by proclaiming the virtues of the Image. So he cried up and down the market, "A god for sale! a god for sale! One who'll bring you luck and keep you lucky!" Presently one of the bystanders stopped him and said, "If your god is all you make him out to be, how is it you don't keep him and make the most of him yourself?" "I'll tell you why," replied he; "he brings gain, it is true, but he takes his time about it; whereas I want money at once."

THE EAGLE AND THE ARROW

An Eagle sat perched on a lofty rock, keeping a sharp look-out for prey. A huntsman, concealed in a cleft of the mountain and on the watch for game, spied him there and shot an Arrow at him. The shaft struck him full in the breast and pierced him through and through. As he lay in the agonies of death, he turned his eyes upon the Arrow. "Ah! cruel fate!" he cried, "that I should perish thus: but oh! fate more cruel still, that the Arrow which kills me should be winged with an Eagle's feathers!"

THE RICH MAN AND THE TANNER

A Rich Man took up his residence next door to a Tanner, and found the smell of the tan-yard so extremely unpleasant that he told him he must go. The Tanner delayed his departure, and the

Rich Man had to speak to him several times about it; and every time the Tanner said he was making arrangements to move very shortly. This went on for some time, till at last the Rich Man got so used to the smell that he ceased to mind it, and troubled the Tanner with his objections no more.

THE WOLF, THE MOTHER, AND HER CHILD

A hungry Wolf was prowling about in search of food. By and by, attracted by the cries of a Child, he came to a cottage. As he crouched beneath the window, he heard the Mother say to the Child, "Stop crying, do! or I'll throw you to the Wolf." Thinking she really meant what she said, he waited there a long time in the expectation of satisfying his hunger. In the evening he heard the Mother fondling her Child and saying, "If the naughty Wolf comes, he shan't get my little one: Daddy will kill him." The Wolf got up in much disgust and walked away: "As for the people in that house," said he to himself, "you can't believe a word they say."

THE OLD WOMAN AND THE WINE-JAR

An old Woman picked up an empty Wine-jar which had once contained a rare and costly wine, and which still retained some traces of its exquisite bouquet. She raised it to her nose and

sniffed at it again and again. "Ah," she cried, "how delicious must have been the liquid which has left behind so ravishing a smell."

THE LIONESS AND THE VIXEN

A Lioness and a Vixen were talking together about their young, as mothers will, and saying how healthy and well-grown they were, and what beautiful coats they had, and how they were the image of their parents. "My litter of cubs is a joy to see," said the Fox; and then she added, rather maliciously, "But I notice you never have more than one." "No," said the Lioness grimly, "but that one's a lion."

Quality, not quantity.

THE VIPER AND THE FILE

A Viper entered a carpenter's shop, and went from one to another of the tools, begging for something to eat. Among the rest, he addressed himself to the File, and asked for the favor of a meal. The File replied in a tone of pitying contempt, "What a simpleton you must be if you imagine you will get anything from me, who invariably take from every one and never give anything in return."

The covetous are poor givers.

THE CAT AND THE COCK

A Cat pounced on a Cock, and cast about for some good excuse for making a meal off him, for

Cats don't as a rule eat Cocks, and she knew she ought not to. At last she said, "You make a great nuisance of yourself at night by crowing and keeping people awake: so I am going to make an end of you." But the Cock defended himself by saying that he crowed in order that men might wake up and set about the day's work in good time, and that they really couldn't very well do without him. "That may be," said the Cat, "but whether they can or not, I'm not going without my dinner"; and she killed and ate him.

The want of a good excuse never kept a villain from crime.

THE HARE AND THE TORTOISE

A Hare was one day making fun of a Tortoise for being so slow upon his feet. "Wait a bit," said the Tortoise; "I'll run a race with you, and I'll wager that I win." "Oh, well," replied the Hare, who was much amused at the idea, "let's try and see"; and it was soon agreed that the fox should set a course for them, and be the judge. When the time came both started off together, but the Hare was soon so far ahead that he thought he might as well have a rest: so down he lay and fell fast asleep. Meanwhile the Tortoise kept plodding on, and in time reached the goal. At last the Hare woke up with a start, and dashed on at his fastest, but only to find that the Tortoise had already won the race.

Slow and steady wins the race.

THE SOLDIER AND HIS HORSE

A Soldier gave his Horse a plentiful supply of oats in time of war, and tended him with the utmost care, for he wished him to be strong to endure the hardships of the field, and swift to bear his master, when need arose, out of the reach of danger. But when the war was over he employed him on all sorts of drudgery, bestowing but little attention upon him, and giving him, moreover, nothing but chaff to eat. The time came when war broke out again, and the Soldier saddled and bridled his Horse, and, having put on his heavy coat of mail, mounted him to ride off and take the field. But the poor half-starved beast sank down under his weight, and said to his rider, "You will have to go into battle on foot this time. Thanks to hard work and bad food, you have turned me from a Horse into an ass; and you cannot in a moment turn me back again into a Horse."

THE OXEN AND THE BUTCHERS

Once upon a time the Oxen determined to be revenged upon the Butchers for the havoc they wrought in their ranks, and plotted to put them to death on a given day. They were all gathered together discussing how best to carry out the plan, and the more violent of them were engaged in sharpening their horns for the fray, when an old Ox got up upon his feet and said, "My brothers, you have good reason, I know, to hate these Butchers, but, at any rate, they understand their trade and do what they have to do without causing unnecessary pain. But if we kill them, others, who have no experience, will be set to slaughter us, and will by their bungling inflict great sufferings upon us. For you may be sure that, even though all the Butchers perish, mankind will never go without their beef."

THE WOLF AND THE LION

A wolf stole a lamb from the flock, and was carrying it off to devour it at his leisure when he met a Lion, who took his prey away from him and walked off with it. He dared not resist, but when the Lion had gone some distance he said, "It is most unjust of you to take what's mine away from me like that." The Lion laughed and called out in reply, "It was justly yours, no doubt! The gift of a friend, perhaps, eh?"

THE SHEEP, THE WOLF, AND THE STAG

A Stag once asked a Sheep to lend him a measure of wheat, saying that his friend the Wolf would be his surety. The Sheep, however, was afraid that they meant to cheat her; so she excused herself, saying, "The Wolf is in the habit of seizing what he wants and running off with it without paying, and you, too, can run much faster than I. So how shall I be able to come up with either of you when the debt falls due?"

Fables

Two blacks do not make a white.

THE LION AND THE THREE BULLS

Three Bulls were grazing in a meadow, and were watched by a Lion, who longed to capture and devour them, but who felt that he was no match for the three so long as they kept together. So he began by false whispers and malicious hints to foment jealousies and distrust among them. This stratagem succeeded so well that ere long the Bulls grew cold and unfriendly, and finally avoided each other and fed each one by himself apart. No sooner did the Lion see this than he fell upon them one by one and killed them in turn.

The quarrels of friends are the opportunities of foes.

THE HORSE AND HIS RIDER

A Young Man, who fancied himself something of a horseman, mounted a Horse which had not been properly broken in, and was exceedingly difficult to control. No sooner did the Horse feel his weight in the saddle than he bolted, and nothing would stop him. A friend of the Rider's met him in the road in his headlong career, and called out, "Where are you off to in such a hurry?" To which he, pointing to the Horse, replied, "I've no idea: ask him."

THE GOAT AND THE VINE

A Goat was straying in a vineyard, and began to browse on the tender shoots of a Vine which bore several fine bunches of grapes. "What have I done to you," said the Vine, "that you should harm me thus? Isn't there grass enough for you to feed on? All the same, even if you eat up every leaf I have, and leave me quite bare, I shall produce wine enough to pour over you when you are led to the altar to be sacrificed."

THE TWO POTS

Two Pots, one of earthenware and the other of brass, were carried away down a river in flood. The Brazen Pot urged his companion to keep close by his side, and he would protect him. The other thanked him, but begged him not to come near him on any account: "For that," he said, "is just what I am most afraid of. One touch from you and I should be broken in pieces."

equals make the best friends.

THE OLD HOUND

A Hound who had served his master well for years, and had run down many a quarry in his time, began to lose his strength and speed owing to age. One day, when out hunting, his master started a powerful wild boar and set the Hound at him. The latter seized the beast by the ear, but his teeth were gone and he could not retain his hold; so the boar escaped. His master began to scold him severely, but the Hound interrupted him with these words: "My will is as strong as ever, master, but my body is old and feeble. You ought to honor me for what I have been instead of abusing me for what I am."

THE CLOWN AND THE COUNTRYMAN

A Nobleman announced his intention of giving a public entertainment in the theatre, and offered splendid prizes to all who had any novelty to exhibit at the performance. The announcement attracted a crowd of conjurers, jugglers, and acrobats, and among the rest a Clown, very popular with the crowd, who let it be known that he was going to give an entirely new turn. When the day of the performance came, the theatre was filled from top to bottom some time before the entertainment began. Several performers exhibited their tricks, and then the popular favorite came on empty-handed and alone. At once there was a hush of expectation: and he, letting his head fall upon his breast, imitated the squeak of a pig to such perfection that the audience insisted on his producing the animal, which, they said, he must have somewhere concealed about his person. He, however, convinced them that there was no pig there, and then the applause was deafening. Among the spectators was a Countryman, who disparaged the Clown's performance and announced that he would give a much superior exhibition of the same trick on the following day. Again the theatre was filled to overflowing, and again the Clown gave his imitation amidst the cheers of the crowd. The Countryman, meanwhile, before going on the stage, had secreted a young porker under his smock; and when the spectators derisively bade him do better if he could, he gave it a pinch in the ear and made it squeal loudly. But they all with one voice shouted out that the Clown's imitation was much more true to life. Thereupon he produced the pig from under his smock and said sarcastically, "There, that shows what sort of judges you are!"

THE LARK AND THE FARMER

A Lark nested in a field of corn, and was rearing her brood under cover of the ripening grain. One day, before the young were fully fledged, the Farmer came to look at the crop, and, finding it yellowing fast, he said, "I must send round word to my neighbors to come and help me reap this field." One of the young Larks overheard him, and was very much frightened, and asked her mother whether they hadn't better move house at once. "There's no hurry," replied she; "a man who looks to his friends for help will take his time about a thing." In a few days the Farmer came by again, and saw that the grain was overripe and falling out of the ears upon the ground. "I must put it off no longer," he said; "This very day I'll hire the men and set them to work at once." The Lark heard him and said to her young, "Come, my children, we must be off: he talks no more of his friends now, but is going to take things in hand himself."

Self-help is the best help.

Fables
THE LION AND THE ASS

A Lion and an Ass set up as partners and went a-hunting together. In course of time they came to a cave in which there were a number of wild goats. The Lion took up his stand at the mouth of the cave, and waited for them to come out; while the Ass went inside and brayed for all he was worth in order to frighten them out into the open. The Lion struck them down one by one as they appeared; and when the cave was empty the Ass came out and said, "Well, I scared them pretty well, didn't I?" "I should think you did," said the Lion: "why, if I hadn't known you were an Ass, I should have turned and run myself."

THE PROPHET

A Prophet sat in the market-place and told the fortunes of all who cared to engage his services. Suddenly there came running up one who told him that his house had been broken into by thieves, and that they had made off with everything they could lay hands on. He was up in a moment, and rushed off, tearing his hair and calling down curses on the miscreants. The bystanders were much amused, and one of them said, "Our friend professes to know what is going to happen to others, but it seems he's not clever enough to perceive what's in store for himself."

THE HOUND AND THE HARE

A young Hound started a Hare, and, when he caught her up, would at one moment snap at her with his teeth as though he were about to kill her, while at another he would let go his hold and frisk about her, as if he were playing with another dog. At last the Hare said, "I wish you would show yourself in your true colors! If you are my friend, why do you bite me? If you are my enemy, why do you play with me?"

He is no friend who plays double.

THE LION, THE MOUSE, AND THE FOX

A Lion was lying asleep at the mouth of his den when a Mouse ran over his back and tickled him so that he woke up with a start and began looking about everywhere to see what it was that had disturbed him. A Fox, who was looking on, thought he would have a joke at the expense of the Lion; so he said, "Well, this is the first time I've seen a Lion afraid of a Mouse." "Afraid of a Mouse?" said the Lion testily: "not I! It's his bad manners I can't stand."

THE TRUMPETER TAKEN PRISONER

A Trumpeter marched into battle in the van of the army and put courage into his comrades by his warlike tunes. Being captured by the enemy, he begged for his life, and said, "Do not put me to death; I have killed no one: indeed, I have no weapons, but carry with me only my trumpet here." But his captors replied, "That is only the more reason why we should take your life; for, though you do not fight yourself, you stir up others to do so."

THE WOLF AND THE CRANE

A Wolf once got a bone stuck in his throat. So he went to a Crane and begged her to put her long bill down his throat and pull it out. "I'll make it worth your while," he added. The Crane did as she was asked, and got the bone out quite easily. The Wolf thanked her warmly, and was just turning away, when she cried, "What about that fee of mine?" "Well, what about it?" snapped the Wolf, baring his teeth as he spoke; "you can go about boasting that you once put your head into a Wolf's mouth and didn't get it bitten off. What more do you want?"

THE EAGLE, THE CAT, AND THE WILD SOW

An Eagle built her nest at the top of a high tree; a Cat with her family occupied a hollow in the trunk half-way down; and a Wild Sow and her young took up their quarters at the foot. They might have got on very well as neighbors had it not been for the evil cunning of the Cat. Climbing up to the Eagle's nest she said to the Eagle, "You and I are in the greatest possible danger. That dreadful creature, the Sow, who is always to be seen grubbing away at the foot of the tree, means to uproot it, that she may devour your family and mine at her ease." Having thus driven the Eagle almost out of her senses with terror, the Cat climbed down the tree, and said to the Sow, "I must warn you against that dreadful bird, the Eagle. She is only waiting her chance to fly down and carry off one of your little pigs when you take them out, to feed her brood with." She succeeded in frightening the Sow as much as the Eagle. Then she returned to her hole in the trunk, from which, feigning to be afraid, she never came forth by day. Only by night did she creep out unseen to procure food for her kittens. The Eagle, meanwhile was afraid to stir from her nest, and the Sow dared not leave her home among the roots: so that in time both they and their families perished of hunger, and their dead bodies supplied the Cat with ample food for her growing family.

Fables
THE WOLF AND THE SHEEP

A Wolf was worried and badly bitten by dogs, and lay a long time for dead. By and by he began to revive, and, feeling very hungry, called out to a passing Sheep and said, "Would you kindly bring me some water from the stream close by? I can manage about meat, if only I could get something to drink." But this Sheep was no fool. "I can quite understand", said he, "that if I brought you the water, you would have no difficulty about the meat. Good-morning."

THE TUNNY-FISH AND THE DOLPHIN

A Tuna-fish was chased by a Dolphin and splashed through the water at a great rate, but the Dolphin gradually gained upon him, and was just about to seize him when the force of his flight carried the Tuna on to a sandbank. In the heat of the chase the Dolphin followed him, and there they both lay out of the water, gasping for dear life. When the Tuna saw that his enemy was doomed like himself, he said, "I don't mind having to die now: for I see that he who is the cause of my death is about to share the same fate."

THE THREE TRADESMEN

The citizens of a certain city were debating about the best material to use in the fortifications which were about to be erected for the greater security of the town. A Carpenter got up and advised the use of wood, which he said was readily procurable and easily worked. A Stone-mason objected to wood on the ground that it was so inflammable, and recommended stones instead. Then a Tanner got on his legs and said, "In my opinion there's nothing like leather."

Every man for himself.

THE MOUSE AND THE BULL

A Bull gave chase to a Mouse which had bitten him in the nose: but the Mouse was too quick for him and slipped into a hole in a wall. The Bull charged furiously into the wall again and again until he was tired out, and sank down on the ground exhausted with his efforts. When all was quiet, the Mouse darted out and bit him again. Beside himself with rage he started to his feet, but by that time the Mouse was back in his hole again, and he could do nothing but bellow and fume in helpless anger. Presently he heard a shrill little voice say from inside the wall, "You big fellows don't always have it your own way, you see: sometimes we little ones come off best."

The battle is not always to the strong.

THE HARE AND THE HOUND

A Hound started a Hare from her form, and pursued her for some distance; but as she gradually gained upon him, he gave up the chase. A rustic who had seen the race met the Hound as he was returning, and taunted him with his defeat. "The little one was too much for you," said he. "Ah, well," said the Hound, "don't forget it's one thing to be running for your dinner, but quite another to be running for your life."

THE TOWN MOUSE AND THE COUNTRY MOUSE

A Town Mouse and a Country Mouse were acquaintances, and the Country Mouse one day invited his friend to come and see him at his home in the fields. The Town Mouse came, and they sat down to a dinner of barleycorns and roots, the latter of which had a distinctly earthy flavor. The fare was not much to the taste of the guest, and presently he broke out with "My poor dear friend, you live here no better than the ants. Now, you should just see how I fare! My larder is a regular horn of plenty. You must come and stay with me, and I promise you you shall live on the fat of the land." So when he returned to town he took the Country Mouse with him, and showed him into a larder containing flour and oatmeal and figs and honey and dates.

The Country Mouse had never seen anything like it, and sat down to enjoy the luxuries his friend provided: but before they had well begun, the door of the larder opened and some one came in. The two Mice scampered off and hid themselves in a narrow and exceedingly uncomfortable hole. Presently, when all was quiet, they ventured out again; but some one else came in, and off they scuttled again. This was too much for the visitor. "Good-bye," said he, "I'm off. You live in the lap of luxury, I can see, but you are surrounded by dangers; whereas at home I can enjoy my simple dinner of roots and corn in peace."

THE LION AND THE BULL

A Lion saw a fine fat Bull pasturing among a herd of cattle and cast about for some means of getting him into his clutches; so he sent him word that he was sacrificing a sheep, and asked if he would do him the honor of dining with him. The Bull accepted the invitation, but, on arriving at the Lion's den, he saw a great array of saucepans and spits, but no sign of a sheep; so he turned on his heel and walked quietly away. The Lion called after him in an injured tone to ask the reason, and the Bull turned round and said, "I have reason enough. When I saw all your preparations it struck me at once that the victim was to be a Bull and not a sheep."

The net is spread in vain in sight of the bird.

THE WOLF, THE FOX, AND THE APE

A Wolf charged a Fox with theft, which he denied, and the case was brought before an Ape to be tried. When he had heard the evidence on both sides, the Ape gave judgment as follows: "I do not think," he said, "that you, O Wolf, ever lost what you claim; but all the same I believe that you, Fox, are guilty of the theft, in spite of all your denials."

The dishonest get no credit, even if they act honestly.

THE EAGLE AND THE COCKS

There were two Cocks in the same farmyard, and they fought to decide who should be master. When the fight was over, the beaten one went and hid himself in a dark corner; while the victor flew up on to the roof of the stables and crowed lustily. But an Eagle espied him from high up in the sky, and swooped down and carried him off. Forthwith the other Cock came out of his corner and ruled the roost without a rival.

Pride comes before a fall.

THE ESCAPED JACKDAW

A Man caught a Jackdaw and tied a piece of string to one of its legs, and then gave it to his children for a pet. But the Jackdaw didn't at all like having to live with people; so, after a while, when he seemed to have become fairly tame and they didn't watch him so closely, he slipped away and flew back to his old haunts. Unfortunately, the string was still on his leg, and before long it got entangled in the branches of a tree and the Jackdaw couldn't get free, try as he would. He saw it was all up with him, and cried in despair, "Alas, in gaining my freedom I have lost my life."

THE FARMER AND THE FOX

A Farmer was greatly annoyed by a Fox, which came prowling about his yard at night and carried off his fowls. So he set a trap for him and caught him; and in order to be revenged upon him, he tied a bunch of tow to his tail and set fire to it and let him go. As ill-luck would have it, however, the Fox made straight for the fields where the corn was standing ripe and ready for cutting. It quickly caught fire and was all burnt up, and the Farmer lost all his harvest.

Revenge is a two-edged sword.

VENUS AND THE CAT

A Cat fell in love with a handsome young man, and begged the goddess Venus to change her into a woman. Venus was very gracious about it,

and changed her at once into a beautiful maiden, whom the young man fell in love with at first sight and shortly afterwards married. One day Venus thought she would like to see whether the Cat had changed her habits as well as her form; so she let a mouse run loose in the room where they were. Forgetting everything, the young woman had no sooner seen the mouse than up she jumped and was after it like a shot: at which the goddess was so disgusted that she changed her back again into a Cat.

THE CROW AND THE SWAN

A Crow was filled with envy on seeing the beautiful white plumage of a Swan, and thought it was due to the water in which the Swan constantly bathed and swam. So he left the neighborhood of the altars, where he got his living by picking up bits of the meat offered in sacrifice, and went and lived among the pools and streams. But though he bathed and washed his feathers many times a day, he didn't make them any whiter, and at last died of hunger into the bargain.

You may change your habits, but not your nature.

THE STAG WITH ONE EYE

A Stag, blind of one eye, was grazing close to the sea-shore and kept his sound eye turned towards the land, so as to be able to perceive the approach of the hounds, while the blind eye he turned towards the sea, never suspecting that any danger would threaten him from that quarter. As it fell out, however, some sailors, coasting along the shore, spied him and shot an arrow at him, by which he was mortally wounded. As he lay dying, he said to himself, "Wretch that I am! I bethought me of the dangers of the land, whence none assailed me: but I feared no peril from the sea, yet thence has come my ruin."

Misfortune often assails us from an unexpected quarter.

THE FLY AND THE DRAUGHT-MULE

A Fly sat on one of the shafts of a cart and said to the Mule who was pulling it, "How slow you are! Do mend your pace, or I shall have to use my sting as a goad." The Mule was not in the least disturbed. "Behind me, in the cart," said he, "sits my master. He holds the reins, and flicks me with his whip, and him I obey, but I don't want any of your impertinence. _I_ know when I may dawdle and when I may not."

THE COCK AND THE JEWEL

A Cock, scratching the ground for something to eat, turned up a Jewel that had by chance been dropped there. "Ho!" said he, "a fine thing you are, no doubt, and, had your owner found you, great would his joy have been. But for me! give me a single grain of corn before all the jewels in the world."

THE WOLF AND THE SHEPHERD

A Wolf hung about near a flock of sheep for a long time, but made no attempt to molest them. The Shepherd at first kept a sharp eye on him, for he naturally thought he meant mischief: but as time went by and the Wolf showed no inclination to meddle with the flock, he began to look upon him more as a protector than as an enemy: and when one day some errand took him to the city, he felt no uneasiness at leaving the Wolf with the sheep. But as soon as his back was turned the Wolf attacked them and killed the greater number. When the Shepherd returned and saw the havoc he had wrought, he cried, "It serves me right for trusting my flock to a Wolf."

THE FARMER AND THE STORK

A Farmer set some traps in a field which he had lately sown with corn, in order to catch the cranes which came to pick up the seed. When he returned to look at his traps he found several cranes caught, and among them a Stork, which begged to be let go, and said, "You ought not to kill me: I am not a crane, but a Stork, as you can easily see by my feathers, and I am the most honest and harmless of birds." But the Farmer replied, "It's nothing to me what you are: I find you among these cranes, who ruin my crops, and, like them, you shall suffer."

> *If you choose bad companions no one will believe that you are anything but bad yourself.*

Fables
THE CHARGER AND THE MILLER

A Horse, who had been used to carry his rider into battle, felt himself growing old and chose to work in a mill instead. He now no longer found himself stepping out proudly to the beating of the drums, but was compelled to slave away all day grinding the corn. Bewailing his hard lot, he said one day to the Miller, "Ah me! I was once a splendid war-horse, gaily caparisoned, and attended by a groom whose sole duty was to see to my wants. How different is my present condition! I wish I had never given up the battlefield for the mill." The Miller replied with asperity, "It's no use your regretting the past. Fortune has many ups and downs: you must just take them as they come."

THE GRASSHOPPER AND THE OWL

An Owl, who lived in a hollow tree, was in the habit of feeding by night and sleeping by day; but her slumbers were greatly disturbed by the chirping of a Grasshopper, who had taken up his abode in the branches. She begged him repeatedly to have some consideration for her comfort, but the Grasshopper, if anything, only chirped the louder. At last the Owl could stand it no longer, but determined to rid herself of the pest by means of a trick. Addressing herself to the Grasshopper, she said in her pleasantest manner, "As I cannot sleep for your song, which, believe me, is as sweet as the notes of Apollo's lyre, I have a mind to taste some nectar, which Minerva gave me the other day. Won't you come in and join me?" The Grasshopper was flattered by the praise of his song, and his mouth, too, watered at the mention of the delicious drink, so he said he would be delighted. No sooner had he got inside the hollow where the Owl was sitting than she pounced upon him and ate him up.

THE GRASSHOPPER AND THE ANTS

One fine day in winter some Ants were busy drying their store of corn, which had got rather damp during a long spell of rain. Presently up came a Grasshopper and begged them to spare her a few grains, "For," she said, "I'm simply starving." The Ants stopped work for a moment, though this was against their principles. "May we ask," said they, "what you were doing with yourself all last summer? Why didn't you collect a store of food for the winter?" "The fact is," replied the Grasshopper, "I was so busy singing that I hadn't the time." "If you spent the summer singing," replied the Ants, "you can't do better than spend the winter dancing." And they chuckled and went on with their work.

THE FARMER AND THE VIPER

One winter a Farmer found a Viper frozen and numb with cold, and out of pity picked it up and placed it in his bosom. The Viper was no sooner revived by the warmth than it turned upon its benefactor and inflicted a fatal bite upon him; and as the poor man lay dying, he cried, "I have only got what I deserved, for taking compassion on so villainous a creature."

Kindness is thrown away upon the evil.

THE TWO FROGS

Two Frogs were neighbors. One lived in a marsh, where there was plenty of water, which frogs love: the other in a lane some distance away, where all the water to be had was that which lay in the ruts after rain. The Marsh Frog warned his friend and pressed him to come and live with him in the marsh, for he would find his quarters there far more comfortable and—what was still more important—more safe. But the other refused, saying that he could not bring himself to move from a place to which he had become accustomed. A few days afterwards a heavy wagon came down the lane, and he was crushed to death under the wheels.

THE COBBLER TURNED DOCTOR

A very unskillful Cobbler, finding himself unable to make a living at his trade, gave up mending boots and took to doctoring instead. He gave out that he had the secret of a universal antidote against all poisons, and acquired no small reputation, thanks to his talent for puffing himself. One day, however, he fell very ill; and the King of the country bethought him that he would test the value of his remedy. Calling, therefore, for a cup, he poured out a dose of the antidote, and, under pretence of mixing poison with it, added a little water, and commanded him to drink it. Terrified by the fear of being poisoned, the Cobbler confessed that he knew nothing about medicine, and that his antidote was worthless. Then the King summoned his subjects and addressed them as follows: "What folly could be greater than yours? Here is this Cobbler to whom no one will send his boots to be mended, and yet you have not hesitated to entrust him with your lives!"

THE ASS, THE COCK, AND THE LION

An Ass and a Cock were in a cattle-pen together. Presently a Lion, who had been starving for days, came along and was just about to fall upon the Ass and make a meal of him when the Cock, rising to his full height and flapping his wings vigorously, uttered a tremendous crow. Now, if there is one thing that frightens a Lion, it is the crowing of a Cock: and this one had no sooner heard the noise than he fled. The Ass was mightily elated at this, and thought that, if the Lion couldn't face a Cock, he would be still less likely to stand up to an Ass: so he ran out and pursued him. But when the two had got well out of sight and hearing of the Cock, the Lion suddenly turned upon the Ass and ate him up.

False confidence often leads to disaster.

Fables
THE BELLY AND THE MEMBERS

The Members of the Body once rebelled against the Belly. "You," they said to the Belly, "live in luxury and sloth, and never do a stroke of work; while we not only have to do all the hard work there is to be done, but are actually your slaves and have to minister to all your wants. Now, we will do so no longer, and you can shift for yourself for the future." They were as good as their word, and left the Belly to starve. The result was just what might have been expected: the whole Body soon began to fail, and the Members and all shared in the general collapse. And then they saw too late how foolish they had been.

THE BALD MAN AND THE FLY

A Fly settled on the head of a Bald Man and bit him. In his eagerness to kill it, he hit himself a smart slap. But the Fly escaped, and said to him in derision, "You tried to kill me for just one little bite; what will you do to yourself now, for the heavy smack you have just given yourself?" "Oh, for that blow I bear no grudge," he replied, "for I never intended myself any harm; but as for you, you contemptible insect, who live by sucking human blood, I'd have borne a good deal more than that for the satisfaction of dashing the life out of you!"

THE ASS AND THE WOLF

An Ass was feeding in a meadow, and, catching sight of his enemy the Wolf in the distance, pretended to be very lame and hobbled painfully along. When the Wolf came up, he asked the Ass how he came to be so lame, and the Ass replied that in going through a hedge he had trodden on a thorn, and he begged the Wolf to pull it out with his teeth, "In case," he said, "when you eat me, it should stick in your throat and hurt you very much." The Wolf said he would, and told the Ass to lift up his foot, and gave his whole mind to getting out the thorn. But the Ass suddenly let out with his heels and fetched the Wolf a fearful kick in the mouth, breaking his teeth; and then he galloped off at full speed. As soon as he could speak the Wolf growled to himself, "It serves me right: my father taught me to kill, and I ought to have stuck to that trade instead of attempting to cure."

Fables
THE MONKEY AND THE CAMEL

At a gathering of all the beasts the Monkey gave an exhibition of dancing and entertained the company vastly. There was great applause at the finish, which excited the envy of the Camel and made him desire to win the favor of the assembly by the same means. So he got up from his place and began dancing, but he cut such a ridiculous figure as he plunged about, and made such a grotesque exhibition of his ungainly person, that the beasts all fell upon him with ridicule and drove him away.

THE SICK MAN AND THE DOCTOR

A Sick Man received a visit from his Doctor, who asked him how he was. "Fairly well, Doctor," said he, "but I find I sweat a great deal." "Ah," said the Doctor, "that's a good sign." On his next visit he asked the same question, and his patient replied, "I'm much as usual, but I've taken to having shivering fits, which leave me cold all over." "Ah," said the Doctor, "that's a good sign too." When he came the third time and inquired as before about his patient's health, the Sick Man said that he felt very feverish. "A very good sign," said the Doctor; "you are doing very nicely indeed." Afterwards a friend came to see the invalid, and on asking him how he did, received this reply: "My dear friend, I'm dying of good signs."

THE TRAVELLERS AND THE PLANE-TREE

Two Travelers were walking along a bare and dusty road in the heat of a summer's day. Coming presently to a Plane-tree, they joyfully turned aside to shelter from the burning rays of the sun in the deep shade of its spreading branches. As they rested, looking up into the tree, one of them remarked to his companion, "What a useless tree the Plane is! It bears no fruit and is of no service to man at all." The Plane-tree interrupted him with indignation. "You ungrateful creature!" it cried: "you come and take shelter under me from the scorching sun, and then, in the very act of enjoying the cool shade of my foliage, you abuse me and call me good for nothing!"

Many a service is met with ingratitude.

THE FLEA AND THE OX

A Flea once said to an Ox, "How comes it that a big strong fellow like you is content to serve mankind, and do all their hard work for them, while I, who am no bigger than you see, live on their bodies and drink my fill of their blood, and never do a stroke for it all?" To which the Ox replied, "Men are very kind to me, and so I am grateful to them: they feed and house me well, and every now and then they show their fondness for me by patting me on the head and neck." "They'd pat me, too," said the Flea, "if I let them: but I take good care they don't, or there would be nothing left of me."

THE BIRDS, THE BEASTS, AND THE BAT

The Birds were at war with the Beasts, and many battles were fought with varying success on either side. The Bat did not throw in his lot definitely with either party, but when things went well for the Birds he was found fighting in their ranks; when, on the other hand, the Beasts got the upper hand, he was to be found among the Beasts. No one paid any attention to him while the war lasted: but when it was over, and peace was restored, neither the Birds nor the Beasts would have anything to do with so double-faced a traitor, and so he remains to this day a solitary outcast from both.

THE MAN AND HIS TWO SWEETHEARTS

A Man of middle age, whose hair was turning grey, had two Sweethearts, an old woman and a young one. The elder of the two didn't like having a lover who looked so much younger than herself; so, whenever he came to see her, she used to pull the dark hairs out of his head to make him look old. The younger, on the other hand, didn't like him to look so much older than herself, and took every opportunity of pulling out the grey hairs, to make him look young. Between them, they left not a hair in his head, and he became perfectly bald.

THE EAGLE, THE JACKDAW, AND THE SHEPHERD

One day a Jackdaw saw an Eagle swoop down on a lamb and carry it off in its talons. "My word," said the Jackdaw, "I'll do that myself." So it flew high up into the air, and then came shooting down with a great whirring of wings on to the back of a big ram. It had no sooner alighted than its claws got caught fast in the wool, and nothing it could do was of any use: there it stuck, flapping away, and only making things worse instead of better. By and by up came the Shepherd. "Oho," he said, "so that's what you'd be doing, is it?" And he took the Jackdaw, and clipped its wings and carried it home to his children. It looked so odd that they didn't know what to make of it. "What sort of bird is it, father?" they asked. "It's a Jackdaw," he replied, "and nothing but a Jackdaw: but it wants to be taken for an Eagle."

> *If you attempt what is beyond your power, your trouble will be wasted and you court not only misfortune but ridicule.*

THE WOLF AND THE BOY

A Wolf, who had just enjoyed a good meal and was in a playful mood, caught sight of a Boy lying flat upon the ground, and, realizing that he was trying to hide, and that it was fear of himself that made him do this, he went up to him and said, "Aha, I've found you, you see; but if you can say three things to me, the truth of which cannot be disputed, I will spare your life." The Boy plucked up courage and thought for a moment, and then he said, "First, it is a pity you saw me; secondly, I was a fool to let myself be seen; and thirdly, we all hate wolves because they are always making unprovoked attacks upon our flocks." The Wolf replied, "Well, what you say is true enough from your point of view; so you may go."

THE MILLER, HIS SON, AND THEIR ASS

A Miller, accompanied by his young Son, was driving his Ass to market in hopes of finding a purchaser for him. On the road they met a troop of girls, laughing and talking, who exclaimed, "Did you ever see such a pair of fools? To be trudging along the dusty road when they might be riding!" The Miller thought there was sense in what they said; so he made his Son mount the Ass, and himself walked at the side. Presently they met some of his old cro-

nies, who greeted them and said, "You'll spoil that Son of yours, letting him ride while you toil along on foot! Make him walk, young lazybones! It'll do him all the good in the world." The Miller followed their advice, and took his Son's place on the back of the Ass while the boy trudged along behind. They had not gone far when they overtook a party of women and children, and the Miller heard them say, "What a selfish old man!

He himself rides in comfort, but lets his poor little boy follow as best he can on his own legs!" So he made his Son get up behind him.  Further along the road they met some travelers, who asked the Miller whether the Ass he was riding was his own property, or a beast hired for the occasion.

He replied that it was his own, and that he was taking it to market to sell.

"Good heavens!" said they, "with a load like that the poor beast will be so exhausted by the time he gets there that no one will look at him. Why, you'd do better to carry him!" "Anything to please you," said the old man, "we can but try." So they got off, tied the Ass's legs together with a rope and slung him on a pole, and at last reached the town, carrying him between them. This was so absurd a sight that the people ran out in crowds to laugh at it, and chaffed the Father and Son unmercifully, some even calling them lunatics.

They had then got to a bridge over the river, where the Ass, frightened by the noise and his unusual situation, kicked and struggled till he broke the ropes that bound him, and fell into the water and was drowned. Whereupon the unfortunate Miller, vexed and ashamed, made the best of his way home again, convinced that in trying to please all he had pleased none, and had lost his Ass into the bargain.

THE STAG AND THE VINE

A Stag, pursued by the huntsmen, concealed himself under cover of a thick Vine. They lost track of him and passed by his hiding-place without being aware that he was anywhere near. Supposing all danger to be over, he presently began to browse on the leaves of the Vine. The movement drew the attention of the returning huntsmen, and one of them, supposing some animal to be hidden there, shot an arrow at a venture into the foliage. The unlucky Stag was pierced to the heart, and, as he expired, he said,

"I deserve my fate for my treachery in feeding upon the leaves of my protector."

Ingratitude sometimes brings its own punishment.

THE LAMB CHASED BY A WOLF

A Wolf was chasing a Lamb, which took refuge in a temple. The Wolf urged it to come out of the precincts, and said, "If you don't, the priest is sure to catch you and offer you up in sacrifice on the altar." To which the Lamb replied, "Thanks, I think I'll stay where I am: I'd rather be sacrificed any day than be eaten up by a Wolf."

THE ARCHER AND THE LION

An Archer went up into the hills to get some sport with his bow, and all the animals fled at the sight of him with the exception of the Lion, who stayed behind and challenged him to fight. But he shot an arrow at the Lion and hit him, and said, "There, you see what my messenger can do: just you wait a moment and I'll tackle you myself."

The Lion, however, when he felt the sting of the arrow, ran away as fast as his legs could carry him. A fox, who had seen it all happen, said to the Lion, "Come, don't be a coward: why don't you stay and show fight?" But the Lion replied, "You won't get me to stay, not you: why, when he sends a messenger like that before him, he must himself be a terrible fellow to deal with."

Give a wide berth to those who can do damage at a distance.

THE WOLF AND THE GOAT

A Wolf caught sight of a Goat browsing above him on the scanty herbage that grew on the top of a steep rock; and being unable to get at her, tried to induce her to come lower down. "You are risking your life up there, madam, indeed you are," he called out: "pray take my advice and come down here, where you will find plenty of better food." The Goat turned a knowing eye upon him. "It's little you care whether I get good grass or bad," said she: "what you want is to eat me."

THE SICK STAG

A Stag fell sick and lay in a clearing in the forest, too weak to move from the spot. When the news of his illness spread, a number of the other beasts came to inquire after his health, and they one and all nibbled a little of the grass that grew round the invalid till at last there was not a blade within his reach. In a few days he began to mend, but was still too feeble to get up and go in search of fodder; and thus he perished miserably of hunger owing to the thoughtlessness of his friends.

THE ASS AND THE MULE

A certain man who had an Ass and a Mule loaded them both up one day and set out upon a journey. So long as the road was fairly level, the Ass got on very well: but by and by they came to a place among the hills where the road was very rough and steep, and the Ass was at his last gasp. So he begged the Mule to relieve him of a part of his load: but the Mule refused. At last, from sheer weariness, the Ass stumbled and fell down a steep place and was killed. The driver was in despair, but he did the best he could: he added the Ass's load to the Mule's, and he also flayed the Ass and put his skin on the top of the double load. The Mule could only just manage the extra weight, and, as he staggered painfully along, he said to himself, "I have only got what I deserved: if I had been willing to help the Ass at first, I should not now be carrying his load and his skin into the bargain."

BROTHER AND SISTER

A certain man had two children, a boy and a girl: and the boy was as good-looking as the girl was plain. One day, as they were playing together in their mother's chamber, they chanced upon a mirror and saw their own features for the first time. The boy saw what a handsome fellow he was, and began to boast to his Sister about his good looks: she, on her part, was ready to cry with vexation when she was aware of her plainness, and took his remarks as an insult to herself. Running to her father, she told him of her Brother's conceit, and accused him of meddling with his mother's things. He laughed and kissed them both, and said, "My children, learn from now onwards to make a good use of the glass. You, my boy, strive to be as good as it shows you to be handsome; and you, my girl, resolve to make up for the plainness of your features by the sweetness of your disposition."

THE HEIFER AND THE OX

A Heifer went up to an Ox, who was straining hard at the plough, and sympathized with him in a rather patronizing sort of way on the necessity of his having to work so hard. Not long afterwards there was a festival in the village and every one kept holiday: but, whereas the Ox was turned loose into the pasture, the Heifer was seized and led off to sacrifice. "Ah," said the Ox, with a grim smile, "I see now why you were allowed to have such an idle time: it was because you were always intended for the altar."

THE KINGDOM OF THE LION

When the Lion reigned over the beasts of the earth he was never cruel or tyrannical, but as gentle and just as a King ought to be. During his reign he called a general assembly of the beasts, and drew up a code of laws under which all were to live in perfect equality and harmony: the wolf and the lamb, the tiger and the stag, the leopard and the kid, the dog and the hare, all should dwell side by side in unbroken peace and friendship. The hare said, "Oh! how I have longed for this day when the weak take their place without fear by the side of the strong!"

THE ASS AND HIS DRIVER

An Ass was being driven down a mountain road, and after jogging along for a while sensibly enough he suddenly quitted the track and rushed to the edge of a precipice. He was just about to leap over the edge when his Driver caught hold of his tail and did his best to pull him back: but pull as he might he couldn't get the Ass to budge from the brink. At last he gave up, crying, "All right, then, get to the bottom your own way; but it's the way to sudden death, as you'll find out quick enough."

THE LION AND THE HARE

A Lion found a Hare sleeping in her form, and was just going to devour her when he caught sight of a passing stag. Dropping the Hare, he at once made for the bigger game; but finding, after a long chase, that he could not overtake the stag, he abandoned the attempt and came back for the Hare. When he reached the spot, however, he found she was nowhere to be seen, and he had to go without his dinner. "It serves me right," he said; "I should have been content with what I had got, instead of hankering after a better prize."

THE WOLVES AND THE DOGS

Once upon a time the Wolves said to the Dogs, "Why should we continue to be enemies any longer? You are very like us in most ways: the main difference between us is one of training only. We live a life of freedom; but you are enslaved to mankind, who beat you, and put heavy collars round your necks, and compel you to keep watch over their flocks and herds for them, and, to crown all, they give you nothing but bones to eat. Don't put up with it any longer, but hand over the flocks to us, and we will all live on the fat of the land and feast together." The Dogs allowed themselves to be persuaded by these words, and accompanied the Wolves into their den. But no sooner were they well inside than the Wolves set upon them and tore them to pieces.

Traitors richly deserve their fate.

THE BULL AND THE CALF

A full-grown Bull was struggling to force his huge bulk through the narrow entrance to a cow-house where his stall was, when a young Calf came up and said to him, "If you'll step aside a moment, I'll show you the way to get through." The Bull turned upon him an amused look. "I knew that way," said he, "before you were born."

Fables

THE TREES AND THE AXE

A Woodman went into the forest and begged of the Trees the favor of a handle for his Axe. The principal Trees at once agreed to so modest a request, and unhesitatingly gave him a young ash sapling, out of which he fashioned the handle he desired. No sooner had he done so than he set to work to fell the noblest Trees in the wood. When they saw the use to which he was putting their gift, they cried, "Alas! alas! We are undone, but we are ourselves to blame. The little we gave has cost us all: had we not sacrificed the rights of the ash, we might ourselves have stood for ages."

THE ASTRONOMER

There was once an Astronomer whose habit it was to go out at night and observe the stars. One night, as he was walking about outside the town gates, gazing up absorbed into the sky and not looking where he was going, he fell into a dry well. As he lay there groaning, some one passing by heard him, and, coming to the edge of the well, looked down and, on learning what had happened, said, "If you really mean to say that you were looking so hard at the sky that you didn't even see where your feet were carrying you along the ground, it appears to me that you deserve all you've got."

THE LABOURER AND THE SNAKE

A Laborer's little son was bitten by a Snake and died of the wound. The father was beside himself with grief, and in his anger against the Snake he caught up an axe and went and stood close to the Snake's hole, and watched for a chance of killing it. Presently the Snake came out, and the man aimed a blow at it, but only succeeded in cutting off the tip of its tail before it wriggled in again. He then tried to get it to come out a second time, pretending that he wished to make up the quarrel. But the Snake said, "I can never be your friend because of my lost tail, nor you mine because of your lost child."

Injuries are never forgotten in the presence of those who caused them.

THE CAGE-BIRD AND THE BAT

A Singing-bird was confined in a cage which hung outside a window, and had a way of singing at night when all other birds were asleep. One night a Bat came and clung to the bars of the cage, and asked the Bird why she was silent by day and sang only at night. "I have a very good reason for doing so," said the Bird: "it was once when I was singing in the daytime that a fowler was attracted by my voice, and set his nets for me and caught me. Since then I have never sung except by night." But the Bat replied, "It is no use your doing that now when you are a prisoner: if only you had done so before you were caught, you might still have been free."

Precautions are useless after the event.

THE ASS AND HIS PURCHASER

A Man who wanted to buy an Ass went to market, and, coming across a likely-looking beast, arranged with the owner that he should be allowed to take him home on trial to see what he was like. When he reached home, he put him into his stable along with the other asses. The newcomer took a look round, and immediately went and chose a place next to the laziest and greediest beast in the stable. When the master saw this he put a halter on him at once, and led him off and handed him over to his owner again.

The latter was a good deal surprised to see him back so soon, and said, "Why, do you mean to say you have tested him already?" "I don't want to put him through any more tests," replied the other: "I could see what sort of beast he is from the companion he chose for himself."

A man is known by the company he keeps.

THE KID AND THE WOLF

A Kid strayed from the flock and was chased by a Wolf. When he saw he must be caught he turned round and said to the Wolf, "I know, sir, that I can't escape being eaten by you: and so, as my life is bound to be short, I pray you let it be as merry as may be. Will you not play me a tune to dance to before I die?" The Wolf saw no objection to having some music before his dinner: so he took out his pipe and began to play, while the Kid danced before him. Before many minutes were passed the gods who guarded the flock heard the sound and came up to see what was going on. They no sooner clapped eyes on the Wolf than they gave chase and drove him away. As he ran off, he turned and said to the Kid, "It's what I thoroughly deserve: my trade is the butcher's, and I had no business to turn piper to please you."

THE DEBTOR AND HIS SOW

A Man of Athens fell into debt and was pressed for the money by his creditor; but he had no means of paying at the time, so he begged for delay. But the creditor refused and said he must pay at once. Then the Debtor fetched a Sow—the only one he had—and took her to market to offer her for sale. It happened that his creditor was there too. Presently a buyer came along and asked if the Sow produced good litters. "Yes," said the Debtor, "very fine ones; and the remarkable thing is that she produces females at the Mysteries and males at the Panathenea." (Festivals these were: and the Athenians always sacrifice a sow at one, and a boar at the other; while at the Dionysia they sacrifice a kid.) At that the creditor, who was standing by, put in, "Don't be surprised, sir; why, still better, at the Dionysia this Sow has kids!"

THE BALD HUNTSMAN

A Man who had lost all his hair took to wearing a wig, and one day he went out hunting. It was blowing rather hard at the time, and he hadn't gone far before a gust of wind caught his hat and carried it off, and his wig too, much to the amusement of the hunt. But he quite entered into the joke, and said, "Ah, well! the hair that wig is made of didn't stick to the head on which it grew; so it's no wonder it won't stick to mine."

THE HERDSMAN AND THE LOST BULL

A Herdsman was tending his cattle when he missed a young Bull, one of the finest of the herd. He went at once to look for him, but, meeting with no success in his search, he made a vow that, if he should discover the thief, he would sacrifice a calf to Jupiter. Continuing his search, he entered a thicket, where he presently espied a lion devouring the lost Bull. Terrified with fear, he raised his hands to heaven and cried, "Great Jupiter, I vowed I would sacrifice a calf to thee if I should discover the thief: but now a full-grown Bull I promise thee if only I myself escape unhurt from his clutches."

THE MULE

One morning a Mule, who had too much to eat and too little to do, began to think himself a very fine fellow indeed, and frisked about saying,

"My father was undoubtedly a high-spirited horse and I take after him entirely." But very soon afterwards he was put into the harness and compelled to go a very long way with a heavy load behind him. At the end of the day, exhausted by his unusual exertions, he said dejectedly to himself, "I must have been mistaken about my father; he can only have been an ass after all."

THE HOUND AND THE FOX

A Hound, roaming in the forest, spied a lion, and being well used to lesser game, gave chase, thinking he would make a fine quarry. Presently the lion perceived that he was being pursued; so, stopping short, he rounded on his pursuer and gave a loud roar. The Hound immediately turned tail and fled. A Fox, seeing him running away, jeered at him and said, "Ho! ho! There goes the coward who chased a lion and ran away the moment he roared!"

THE FATHER AND HIS DAUGHTERS

A Man had two Daughters, one of whom he gave in marriage to a gardener, and the other to a potter. After a time he thought he would go and see how they were getting on; and first he went to the gardener's wife. He asked her how she was, and how things were going with herself and her husband. She replied that on the whole they were doing very well: "But," she continued, "I do wish we could have some good heavy rain: the garden wants it badly." Then he went on to the potter's wife and made the same inquiries of her. She replied that she and her husband had nothing to complain of: "But," she went on, "I do wish we could have some nice dry weather, to dry the pottery." Her Father looked at her with a humorous expression on his face. "You want dry weather," he said, "and your sister wants rain. I was going to ask in my prayers that your wishes should be granted; but now it strikes me I had better not refer to the subject."

THE THIEF AND THE INNKEEPER

A Thief hired a room at an inn, and stayed there some days on the look-out for something to steal. No opportunity, however, presented itself, till one day, when there was a festival to be celebrated, the Innkeeper appeared in a fine new coat and sat down before the door of the inn for an airing. The Thief no sooner set eyes upon the coat than he longed to get possession of it. There was no business doing, so he went and took a seat by the side of the Innkeeper, and began talking to him. They conversed together for some time, and then the Thief suddenly yawned and howled like a wolf. The Innkeeper asked him in some concern what ailed him. The Thief replied, "I will tell you about myself, sir, but first I must beg you to take charge of my clothes for me, for I intend to leave them with you. Why I have these fits of yawning I cannot tell: maybe they are sent as a punishment for my misdeeds; but, whatever the reason, the facts are that when I have yawned three times I become a ravening wolf and fly at men's throats." As he finished speaking he yawned a second time and howled again as before. The Innkeeper, believing every word he said, and terrified at the prospect of being confronted with a wolf, got up hastily and started to run indoors; but the Thief caught him by the coat and tried to stop him, crying, "Stay, sir, stay, and take charge of my clothes, or else I shall never see them again." As he spoke he opened his mouth and began to yawn for the third time. The Innkeeper, mad with the fear of being eaten by a wolf, slipped out of his coat, which remained in the other's hands, and bolted into the inn and locked the door behind him; and the Thief then quietly stole off with his spoil.

THE PACK-ASS AND THE WILD ASS

A Wild Ass, who was wandering idly about, one day came upon a Pack-Ass lying at full length in a sunny spot and thoroughly enjoying himself. Going up to him, he said, "What a lucky beast you are! Your sleek coat shows how well you live: how I envy you!" Not long after the Wild Ass saw his acquaintance again, but this time he was carrying a heavy load, and his driver was following behind and beating him with a thick stick. "Ah, my friend," said the Wild Ass, "I don't envy you any more: for I see you pay dear for your comforts."

> *Advantages that are dearly bought
> are doubtful blessings.*

THE ASS AND HIS MASTERS

A Gardener had an Ass which had a very hard time of it, what with scanty food, heavy loads, and constant beating. The Ass therefore begged Jupiter to take him away from the Gardener and hand him over to another master. So Jupiter sent Mercury to the Gardener to bid him sell the Ass to a Potter, which he did. But the Ass was as discontented as ever, for he had to work harder than before: so he begged Jupiter for relief a second time, and Jupiter very obligingly arranged that he should be sold to a Tanner. But when the Ass saw what his new master's trade was, he cried in despair, "Why wasn't I content to serve either of my former masters, hard as I had to work and badly as I was treated? for they would have buried me decently, but now I shall come in the end to the tanning-vat."

*Servants don't know a good master
till they have served a worse.*

THE PACK-ASS, THE WILD ASS, AND THE LION

A Wild Ass saw a Pack-Ass jogging along under a heavy load, and taunted him with the condition of slavery in which he lived, in these words: "What a vile lot is yours compared with mine! I am free as the air, and never do a stroke of work; and, as for fodder, I have only to go to the hills and there I find far more than enough for my needs. But you! you depend on your master for food, and he makes you carry heavy loads every day and beats you unmercifully." At that moment a Lion appeared on the scene, and made no attempt to molest the Pack-Ass owing to the presence of the driver; but he fell upon the Wild Ass, who had no one to protect him, and without more ado made a meal of him.

*It is no use being your own master
unless you can stand up for yourself.*

Fables
THE ANT

Ants were once men and made their living by tilling the soil. But, not content with the results of their own work, they were always casting longing eyes upon the crops and fruits of their neighbors, which they stole, whenever they got the chance, and added to their own store. At last their covetousness made Jupiter so angry that he changed them into Ants. But, though their forms were changed, their nature remained the same: and so, to this day, they go about among the cornfields and gather the fruits of others' labor, and store them up for their own use.

You may punish a thief, but his bent remains.

THE FROGS AND THE WELL

Two Frogs lived together in a marsh. But one hot summer the marsh dried up, and they left it to look for another place to live in: for frogs like damp places if they can get them. By and by they came to a deep well, and one of them looked down into it, and said to the other, "This looks a nice cool place: let us jump in and settle here." But the other, who had a wiser head on his shoulders, replied, "Not so fast, my friend: supposing this well dried up like the marsh, how should we get out again?"

Think twice before you act.

THE CRAB AND THE FOX

A Crab once left the sea-shore and went and settled in a meadow some way inland, which looked very nice and green and seemed likely to be a good place to feed in. But a hungry Fox came along and spied the Crab and caught him. Just as he was going to be eaten up, the Crab said, "This is just what I deserve; for I had no business to leave my natural home by the sea and settle here as though I belonged to the land."

Be content with your lot.

THE FOX AND THE GRASSHOPPER

A Grasshopper sat chirping in the branches of a tree. A Fox heard her, and, thinking what a dainty morsel she would make, he tried to get her down by a trick. Standing below in full view of her, he praised her song in the most flattering terms, and begged her to descend, saying he would like to make the acquaintance of the owner of so beautiful a voice. But she was not to be taken in, and replied, "You are very much mistaken, my dear sir, if you imagine I am going to come down: I keep well out of the way of you and your kind ever since the day when I saw numbers of grasshoppers' wings strewn about the entrance to a fox's earth."

THE FARMER, HIS BOY, AND THE ROOKS

A Farmer had just sown a field of wheat, and was keeping a careful watch over it, for numbers of Rooks and starlings kept continually settling on it and eating up the grain. Along with him went his Boy, carrying a sling: and whenever the Farmer asked for the sling the starlings understood what he said and warned the Rooks and they were off in a moment. So the Farmer hit on a trick. "My lad," said he, "we must get the better of these birds somehow. After this, when I want the sling, I won't say 'sling,' but just 'humph!' and you must then hand me the sling quickly." Presently back came the whole flock. "Humph!" said the Farmer; but the starlings took no notice, and he had time to sling several stones among them, hitting one on the head, another in the legs, and another in the wing, before they got out of range. As they made all haste away they met some cranes, who asked them what the matter was. "Matter?" said one of the Rooks; "it's those rascals, men, that are the matter. Don't you go near them. They have a way of saying one thing and meaning another which has just been the death of several of our poor friends."

THE ASS AND THE DOG

An Ass and a Dog were on their travels together, and, as they went along, they found a sealed packet lying on the ground. The Ass picked it up, broke the seal, and found it contained some writing, which he proceeded to read out aloud to the Dog. As he read on it turned out to be all about grass and barley and hay—in short, all the kinds of fodder that Asses are fond of. The Dog was a good deal bored with listening to all this, till at last his impatience got the better of him, and he cried, "Just skip a few pages, friend, and see if there isn't something about meat and bones." The Ass glanced all through the packet, but found nothing of the sort, and said so. Then the Dog said in disgust, "Oh, throw it away, do: what's the good of a thing like that?"

THE ASS CARRYING THE IMAGE

A certain man put an Image on the back of his Ass to take it to one of the temples of the town. As they went along the road all the people they met uncovered and bowed their heads out of reverence for the Image; but the Ass thought they were doing it out of respect for himself, and began to give himself airs accordingly. At last he became so conceited that he imagined he could do as he liked, and, by way of protest against the load he was carrying, he came to a full stop and flatly declined to proceed any further. His driver, finding him so obstinate, hit him hard and long with his stick, saying the while, "Oh, you dunder-headed idiot, do you suppose it's come to this, that men pay worship to an Ass?"

Rude shocks await those who take to themselves the credit that is due to others.

THE ATHENIAN AND THE THEBAN

An Athenian and a Theban were on the road together, and passed the time in conversation, as is the way of travelers. After discussing a variety of subjects they began to talk about heroes, a topic that tends to be more fertile than edifying. Each of them was lavish in his praises of the heroes of his own city, until eventually the Theban asserted that Hercules was the greatest hero who had ever lived on earth, and now occupied a foremost place among the gods; while the Athenian insisted that Theseus was far superior, for his fortune had been in every way supremely blessed, whereas Hercules had at one time been forced to act as a servant. And he gained his point, for he was a very glib fellow, like all Athenians; so that the Theban, who was no match for him in talking, cried at last in some disgust, "All right, have your way; I only hope that, when our heroes are angry with us, Athens may suffer from the anger of Hercules, and Thebes only from that of Theseus."

THE GOATHERD AND THE GOAT

A Goatherd was one day gathering his flock to return to the fold, when one of his goats strayed and refused to join the rest. He tried for a long time to get her to return by calling and whistling to her, but the Goat took no notice of him at all; so at last he threw a stone at her and broke one of her horns. In dismay, he begged her not to tell his master: but she replied, "You silly fellow, my horn would cry aloud even if I held my tongue."

It's no use trying to hide what can't be hidden.

THE SHEEP AND THE DOG

Once upon a time the Sheep complained to the shepherd about the difference in his treatment of themselves and his Dog. "Your conduct," said they, "is very strange and, we think, very unfair. We provide you with wool and lambs and milk and you give us nothing but grass, and even that we have to find for ourselves: but you get nothing at all from the Dog, and yet you feed him with tit-bits from your own table." Their remarks were overheard by the Dog, who spoke up at once and said, "Yes, and quite right, too: where would you be if it wasn't for me? Thieves would steal you! Wolves would eat you! Indeed, if I didn't keep constant watch over you, you would be too terrified even

to graze!" The Sheep were obliged to acknowledge that he spoke the truth, and never again made a grievance of the regard in which he was held by his master.

THE SHEPHERD AND THE WOLF

A Shepherd found a Wolf's Cub straying in the pastures, and took him home and reared him along with his dogs. When the Cub grew to his full size, if ever a wolf stole a sheep from the flock, he used to join the dogs in hunting him down. It sometimes happened that the dogs failed to come up with the thief, and, abandoning the pursuit, returned home. The Wolf would on such occasions continue the chase by himself, and when he overtook the culprit, would stop and share the feast with him, and then return to the Shepherd. But if some time passed without a sheep being carried off by the wolves, he would steal one himself and share his plunder with the dogs. The Shepherd's suspicions were aroused, and one day he caught him in the act; and, fastening a rope round his neck, hung him on the nearest tree.

What's bred in the bone is sure to come out in the flesh.

THE LION, JUPITER, AND THE ELEPHANT

The Lion, for all his size and strength, and his sharp teeth and claws, is a coward in one thing: he can't bear the sound of a cock crowing, and runs away whenever he hears it. He complained bitterly to Jupiter for making him like that; but

Jupiter said it wasn't his fault: he had done the best he could for him, and, considering this was his only failing, he ought to be well content. The Lion, however, wouldn't be comforted, and was so ashamed of his timidity that he wished he might die. In this state of mind, he met the Elephant and had a talk with him. He noticed that the great beast cocked up his ears all the time, as if he were listening for something, and he asked him why he did so. Just then a gnat came humming by, and the Elephant said, "Do you see that wretched little buzzing insect? I'm terribly afraid of its getting into my ear: if it once gets in, I'm dead and done for." The Lion's spirits rose at once when he heard this: "For," he said to himself, "if the Elephant, huge as he is, is afraid of a gnat, I needn't be so much ashamed of being afraid of a cock, who is ten thousand times bigger than a gnat."

THE PIG AND THE SHEEP

A Pig found his way into a meadow where a flock of Sheep were grazing. The shepherd caught him, and was proceeding to carry him off to the butcher's when he set up a loud squealing and struggled to get free. The Sheep rebuked him for making such a to-do, and said to him, "The shepherd catches us regularly and drags us off just like that, and we don't make any fuss." "No, I dare say not," replied the Pig, "but my case and yours are altogether different: he only wants you for wool, but he wants me for bacon."

THE GARDENER AND HIS DOG

A Gardner's Dog fell into a deep well, from which his master used to draw water for the plants in his garden with a rope and a bucket. Failing to get the Dog out by means of these, the Gardener went down into the well himself in order to fetch him up. But the Dog thought he had come to make sure of drowning him; so he bit his master as soon as he came within reach, and hurt him a good deal, with the result that he left the Dog to his fate and climbed out of the well, remarking, "It serves me quite right for trying to save so determined a suicide."

THE RIVERS AND THE SEA

Once upon a time all the Rivers combined to protest against the action of the Sea in making their waters salt. "When we come to you," said they to the Sea, "we are sweet and drinkable: but when once we have mingled with you, our waters become as briny and unpalatable as your own." The Sea replied shortly, "Keep away from me and you'll remain sweet."

THE LION IN LOVE

A Lion fell deeply in love with the daughter of a cottager and wanted to marry her; but her father was unwilling to give her to so fearsome a husband, and yet didn't want to offend the Lion; so he hit upon the following expedient. He went to the Lion and said, "I think you will make a very good husband for my daughter: but I cannot consent to your union unless you let me draw your teeth and pare your nails, for my daughter is terribly afraid of them." The Lion was so much in love that he readily agreed that this should be done. When once, however, he was thus disarmed, the Cottager was afraid of him no longer, but drove him away with his club.

THE BEE-KEEPER

A Thief found his way into an apiary when the Bee-keeper was away, and stole all the honey. When the Keeper returned and found the hives empty, he was very much upset and stood staring at them for some time. Before long the bees came back from gathering honey, and, finding their hives overturned and the Keeper standing by, they made for him with their stings. At this he fell into a passion and cried, "You ungrateful scoundrels, you let the thief who stole my honey get off scot-free, and then you go and sting me who have always taken such care of you!"

When you hit back make sure you have got the right man.

THE WOLF AND THE HORSE

A Wolf on his rambles came to a field of oats, but, not being able to eat them, he was passing on his way when a Horse came along. "Look," said the Wolf, "here's a fine field of oats. For your sake I have left it untouched, and I shall greatly enjoy the sound of your teeth munching the ripe grain." But the Horse replied, "If wolves could eat oats, my fine friend, you would hardly have indulged your ears at the cost of your belly."

There is no virtue in giving to others what is useless to oneself.

THE BAT, THE BRAMBLE, AND THE SEAGULL

A Bat, a Bramble, and a Seagull went into partnership and determined to go on a trading voyage together. The Bat borrowed a sum of money for his venture; the Bramble laid in a stock of clothes of various kinds; and the Seagull took a quantity of lead: and so they set out. By and by a great storm came on, and their boat with all the cargo went to the bottom, but the three travelers managed to reach land. Ever since then the Seagull flies to and fro over the sea, and every now and then dives below the surface, looking for the lead he's lost; while the Bat is so afraid of meeting his creditors that he hides away by day and only comes out at night to feed; and the Bramble catches hold of the clothes of every one who passes by, hoping some day to recognize and recover the lost garments.

> *All men are more concerned to recover what they lose than to acquire what they lack.*

THE DOG AND THE WOLF

A Dog was lying in the sun before a farmyard gate when a Wolf pounced upon him and was just going to eat him up; but he begged for his life and said, "You see how thin I am and what a wretched meal I should make you now: but if you will only wait a few days my master is going to give a feast. All the rich scraps and pickings will fall to me and I shall get nice and fat: then will be the time for you to eat me." The Wolf thought this was a very good plan and went away. Some time afterwards he came to the farmyard again, and found the Dog lying out of reach on the stable roof. "Come down," he called, "and be eaten: you remember our agreement?" But the Dog said coolly, "My friend, if ever you catch me lying down by the gate there again, don't you wait for any feast."

Once bitten, twice shy.

THE WASP AND THE SNAKE

A Wasp settled on the head of a Snake, and not only stung him several times, but clung obstinately to the head of his victim. Maddened with pain the Snake tried every means he could think of to get rid of the creature, but without success. At last he became desperate, and crying, "Kill you I will, even at the cost of my own life," he laid his head with the Wasp on it under the wheel of a passing wagon, and they both perished together.

THE EAGLE AND THE BEETLE

An Eagle was chasing a hare, which was running for dear life and was at her wits' end to know where to turn for help. Presently she espied a Beetle, and begged it to aid her. So when the Eagle came up the Beetle warned her not to touch the hare, which was under its protection. But the Eagle never noticed the Beetle because it was so small, seized the hare and ate her up. The Beetle never forgot this, and used to keep an eye on the Eagle's nest, and whenever the Eagle laid an egg it climbed up and rolled it out of the nest and broke it. At last the Eagle got so worried over the loss of her eggs that she went up to Jupiter, who is the special protector of Eagles, and begged him to give her a safe place to nest in: so he let her lay her eggs in his lap. But the Beetle noticed this and made a ball of dirt the size of an Eagle's egg, and flew up and deposited it in Jupiter's lap. When Jupiter saw the dirt, he stood up to shake it out of his robe, and, forgetting about the eggs, he shook them out too, and they were broken just as before. Ever since then, they say, Eagles never lay their eggs at the season when Beetles are about.

The weak will sometimes find ways to avenge an insult, even upon the strong.

THE FOWLER AND THE LARK

A Fowler was setting his nets for little birds when a Lark came up to him and asked him what he was doing. "I am engaged in founding a city," said he, and with that he withdrew to a short distance and concealed himself. The Lark examined the nets with great curiosity, and presently, catching sight of the bait, hopped on to them in order to secure it, and became entangled in the meshes. The Fowler then ran up quickly and captured her. "What a fool I was!" said she: "but at any rate, if that's the kind of city you are founding, it'll be a long time before you find fools enough to fill it."

Fables
THE FISHERMAN PIPING

A Fisherman who could play the flute went down one day to the sea-shore with his nets and his flute; and, taking his stand on a projecting rock, began to play a tune, thinking that the music would bring the fish jumping out of the sea. He went on playing for some time, but not a fish appeared: so at last he threw down his flute and cast his net into the sea, and made a great haul of fish. When they were landed and he saw them leaping about on the shore, he cried, "You rascals! you wouldn't dance when I piped: but now I've stopped, you can do nothing else!"

THE WEASEL AND THE MAN

A Man once caught a Weasel, which was always sneaking about the house, and was just going to drown it in a tub of water, when it begged hard for its life, and said to him, "Surely you haven't the heart to put me to death? Think how useful I have been in clearing your house of the mice and lizards which used to infest it, and show your gratitude by sparing my life." "You have not been altogether useless, I grant you," said the Man: "but who killed the fowls? Who stole the meat? No, no! You do much more harm than good, and die you shall."

THE PLOUGHMAN, THE ASS, AND THE OX

A Ploughman yoked his Ox and his Ass together, and set to work to plough his field. It was a poor makeshift of a team, but it was the best he could do, as he had but a single Ox. At the end of the day, when the beasts were loosed from the yoke, the Ass said to the Ox, "Well, we've had a hard day: which of us is to carry the master home?" The Ox looked surprised at the question. "Why," said he, "you, to be sure, as usual."

DEMADES AND HIS FABLE

Demades the orator was once speaking in the Assembly at Athens; but the people were very inattentive to what he was saying, so he stopped and said, "Gentlemen, I should like to tell you one of Aesop's fables." This made every one listen intently. Then Demades began: "Demeter, a Swallow, and an Eel were once traveling together, and came to a river without a bridge: the Swallow flew over it, and the Eel swam across"; and then he stopped. "What happened to Demeter?" cried several people in the audience. "Demeter," he replied, "is very angry with you for listening to fables when you ought to be minding public business."

THE MONKEY AND THE DOLPHIN

When people go on a voyage they often take with them lap-dogs or monkeys as pets to wile away the time. Thus it fell out that a man returning to Athens from the East had a pet Monkey on board with him. As they neared the coast of Attica a  great storm burst upon them, and the ship capsized. All on board were thrown into the water, and tried to save themselves by swimming, the Monkey among the rest. A Dolphin saw him, and, supposing him to be a man, took him on his back and began swimming towards the shore. When they got near the Piraeus, which is the port of Athens, the Dolphin asked the Monkey if he was an Athenian. The Monkey replied that he was, and added that he came

of a very distinguished family. "Then, of course, you know the Piraeus," continued the Dolphin. The Monkey thought he was referring to some high official or other, and replied, "Oh, yes, he's a very old friend of mine." At that, detecting his hypocrisy, the Dolphin was so disgusted that he dived below the surface, and the unfortunate Monkey was quickly drowned.

THE CROW AND THE SNAKE

A hungry Crow spied a Snake lying asleep in a sunny spot, and, picking it up in his claws, he was carrying it off to a place where he could make a meal of it without being disturbed, when the Snake reared its head and bit him. It was a poisonous Snake, and the bite was fatal, and the dying Crow said, "What a cruel fate is mine! I thought I had made a lucky find, and it has cost me my life!"

THE DOGS AND THE FOX

Some Dogs once found a lion's skin, and were worrying it with their teeth. Just then a Fox came by, and said, "You think yourselves very brave, no doubt; but if that were a live lion you'd find his claws a good deal sharper than your teeth."

THE NIGHTINGALE AND THE HAWK

A Nightingale was sitting on a bough of an oak and singing, as her custom was. A hungry Hawk presently spied her, and darting to the spot seized her in his talons. He was just about to tear her in pieces when she begged him to spare her life: "I'm not big enough," she pleaded, "to make you a good meal: you ought to seek your prey among the bigger birds." The Hawk eyed her with some contempt. "You must think me very simple," said he, "if you suppose I am going to give up a certain prize on the chance of a better of which I see at present no signs."

THE ROSE AND THE AMARANTH

A Rose and an Amaranth blossomed side by side in a garden, and the Amaranth said to her neighbor, "How I envy you your beauty and your sweet scent! No wonder you are such a universal favorite." But the Rose replied with a shade of sadness in her voice, "Ah, my dear friend, I bloom but for a time: my petals soon wither and fall, and then I die. But your flowers never fade, even if they are cut; for they are everlasting."

THE MAN, THE HORSE, THE OX, AND THE DOG

One winter's day, during a severe storm, a Horse, an Ox, and a Dog came and begged for shelter in the house of a Man. He readily admitted them, and, as they were cold and wet, he lit a fire for their comfort: and he put oats before the Horse, and hay before the Ox, while he fed the Dog with the remains of his own dinner. When the storm abated, and they were about to depart, they determined to show their gratitude in the following way. They divided the life of Man among them, and each endowed one part of it with the qualities which were peculiarly his own.

The Horse took youth, and hence young men are high-mettled and impatient of restraint; the Ox took middle age, and accordingly men in middle life are steady and hard-working; while the Dog took old age, which is the reason why old men are so often peevish and ill-tempered, and, like dogs, attached chiefly to those who look to their comfort, while they are disposed to snap at those who are unfamiliar or distasteful to them.

THE WOLVES, THE SHEEP, AND THE RAM

The Wolves sent a deputation to the Sheep with proposals for a lasting peace between them, on condition of their giving up the sheep-dogs to instant death. The foolish Sheep agreed to the terms; but an old Ram, whose years had brought him wisdom, interfered and said, "How can we expect to live at peace with you? Why, even with the dogs at hand to protect us, we are never secure from your murderous attacks!"

THE SWAN

The Swan is said to sing but once in its life—when it knows that it is about to die. A certain man, who had heard of the song of the Swan, one day saw one of these birds for sale in the market, and bought it and took it home with him. A few days later he had some friends to dinner, and produced the Swan, and bade it sing for their entertainment: but the Swan remained silent. In course of time, when it was growing old, it became aware of its approaching end and broke into a sweet, sad song. When its owner heard it, he said angrily, "If the creature only sings when it is about to die, what a fool I was that day I wanted to hear its song! I ought to have wrung its neck instead of merely inviting it to sing."

THE SNAKE AND JUPITER

A Snake suffered a good deal from being constantly trodden upon by man and beast, owing partly to the length of his body and partly to his being unable to raise himself above the surface of the ground: so he went and complained to Jupiter about the risks to which he was exposed. But Jupiter had little sympathy for him. "I dare say," said he, "that if you had bitten the first that trod on you, the others would have taken more trouble to look where they put their feet."

THE WOLF AND HIS SHADOW

A Wolf, who was roaming about on the plain when the sun was getting low in the sky, was much impressed by the size of his shadow, and said to himself, "I had no idea I was so big. Fancy my being afraid of a lion! Why, I, not he, ought to be King of the beasts"; and, heedless of danger, he strutted about as if there could

be no doubt at all about it. Just then a lion sprang upon him and began to devour him. "Alas," he cried, "had I not lost sight of the facts, I shouldn't have been ruined by my fancies."

THE PLOUGHMAN AND THE WOLF

A Ploughman loosed his oxen from the plough, and led them away to the water to drink. While he was absent a half-starved Wolf appeared on the scene, and went up to the plough and began chewing the leather straps attached to the yoke. As he gnawed away desperately in the hope of satisfying his craving for food, he somehow got entangled in the harness, and, taking fright, struggled to get free, tugging at the traces as if he would drag the plough along with him. Just then the Ploughman came back, and seeing what was happening, he cried, "Ah, you old rascal, I wish you would give up thieving for good and take to honest work instead."

MERCURY AND THE MAN BITTEN BY AN ANT

A Man once saw a ship go down with all its crew, and commented severely on the injustice of the gods. "They care nothing for a man's character," said he, "but let the good and the bad go to their deaths together." There was an ant-heap close by where he was standing, and, just as he spoke, he was bitten in the foot by an Ant. Turning in a temper to the ant-heap he stamped upon it and crushed hundreds of unoffending ants. Suddenly Mercury appeared, and belabored him with his staff, saying as he did so,

"You villain, where's your nice sense of justice now?"

THE WILY LION

A Lion watched a fat Bull feeding in a meadow, and his mouth watered when he thought of the royal feast he would make, but he did not dare to attack him, for he was afraid of his sharp horns. Hunger, however, presently compelled him to do something: and as the use of force did not promise success, he determined to resort to artifice. Going up to the Bull in friendly fashion, he said to him, "I cannot help saying how much I admire your magnificent figure. What a fine head! What powerful shoulders and thighs! But, my dear friend, what in the world makes you wear those ugly horns? You must find them as awkward as they are unsightly. Believe me, you would do much better without them." The Bull was foolish enough to be persuaded by this flattery to have his horns cut off; and, having now lost his only means of defense, fell an easy prey to the Lion.

THE PARROT AND THE CAT

A Man once bought a Parrot and gave it the run of his house. It reveled in its liberty, and presently flew up on to the mantelpiece and screamed away to its heart's content. The noise disturbed the Cat, who was asleep on the hearthrug. Looking up at the intruder, she said, "Who may you be, and where have you come from?" The Parrot replied, "Your master has just bought me and brought me home with him."

"You impudent bird," said the Cat, "how dare you, a newcomer, make a noise like that? Why, I was born here, and have lived here all my life, and yet, if I venture to mew, they throw things at me and chase me all over the place." "Look here, mistress," said the Parrot, "you just hold your tongue. My voice they delight in; but yours—yours is a perfect nuisance."

THE STAG AND THE LION

A Stag was chased by the hounds, and took refuge in a cave, where he hoped to be safe from his pursuers. Unfortunately the cave contained a Lion, to whom he fell an easy prey. "Unhappy that I am," he cried, "I am saved from the power of the dogs only to fall into the clutches of a Lion."

Out of the frying-pan into the fire.

THE IMPOSTOR

A certain man fell ill, and, being in a very bad way, he made a vow that he would sacrifice a hundred oxen to the gods if they would grant him a return to health. Wishing to see how he would keep his vow, they caused him to recover in a short time. Now, he hadn't an ox in the world, so he made a hundred little oxen out of tallow and offered them up on an altar, at the same time saying, "Ye gods, I call you to witness that I have discharged my vow." The gods determined to be even with him, so they sent him a dream, in which he was bidden to go to the seashore and fetch a hundred crowns which he was to find there. Hastening in great excitement to the shore, he fell in with a band of robbers, who seized him and carried him off to sell as a slave: and when they sold him a hundred crowns was the sum he fetched.

Do not promise more than you can perform.

THE DOGS AND THE HIDES

Once upon a time a number of Dogs, who were famished with hunger, saw some Hides steeping in a river, but couldn't get at them because the water was too deep. So they put their heads together, and decided to drink away at the river till it was shallow enough for them to reach the Hides. But long before that happened they burst themselves with drinking.

THE LION, THE FOX, AND THE ASS

A Lion, a Fox, and an Ass went out hunting together. They had soon taken a large booty, which the Lion requested the Ass to divide between them. The Ass divided it all into three equal parts, and modestly begged the others to take their choice; at which the Lion, bursting with fury, sprang upon the Ass and tore him to pieces. Then, glaring at the Fox, he bade him make a fresh division. The Fox gathered almost the whole in one great heap for the Lion's share, leaving only the smallest possible morsel for himself. "My dear friend," said the Lion, "how did you get the knack of it so well?" The Fox replied, "Me? Oh, I took a lesson from the Ass."

Happy is he who learns from the misfortunes of others.

THE FOWLER, THE PARTRIDGE, AND THE COCK

One day, as a Fowler was sitting down to a scanty supper of herbs and bread, a friend dropped in unexpectedly. The larder was empty; so he went out and caught a tame Partridge, which he kept as a decoy, and was about to wring her neck when she cried, "Surely you won't kill me? Why, what will you do without me next time you go fowling? How will you get the birds to come to your nets?" He let her go at this, and went to his hen-house, where he had a plump young Cock. When the Cock saw what he was after, he too pleaded for his life, and said, "If you kill me, how will you know the time of night? and who will wake you up in the morning when it is time to get to work?" The Fowler, however, replied, "You are useful for telling the time, I know; but, for all that, I can't send my friend supperless to bed." And therewith he caught him and wrung his neck.

THE GNAT AND THE LION

A Gnat once went up to a Lion and said, "I am not in the least afraid of you: I don't even allow that you are a match for me in strength. What does your strength amount to after all? That you can scratch with your claws and bite with your teeth—just like a woman in a temper—and nothing more. But I'm stronger than you: if you don't believe it, let us fight and see." So saying, the Gnat sounded his horn, and darted in and bit the Lion on the nose. When the Lion felt the sting, in his haste to crush him he scratched his nose badly, and made it bleed, but failed altogether to hurt the Gnat, which buzzed off in triumph, elated by its victory. Presently, however, it got entangled in a spider's web, and was caught and eaten by the spider, thus falling a prey to an insignificant insect after having triumphed over the King of the Beasts.

THE FARMER AND HIS DOGS

A Farmer was snowed up in his farmstead by a severe storm, and was unable to go out and procure provisions for himself and his family. So he first killed his sheep and used them for food; then, as the storm still continued, he killed his goats; and, last of all, as the weather showed no signs of improving, he was compelled to kill his oxen and eat them. When his Dogs saw the various animals being killed and eaten in turn, they said to one another, "We had better get out of this or we shall be the next to go!"

THE EAGLE AND THE FOX

An Eagle and a Fox became great friends and determined to live near one another: they thought that the more they saw of each other the better friends they would be. So the Eagle built a nest at the top of a high tree, while the Fox settled in a thicket at the foot of it and produced a litter of cubs. One day the Fox went out foraging for food, and the Eagle, who also wanted food for her young, flew down into the thicket, caught up the Fox's cubs, and carried them up into the tree for a meal for herself and her family. When the Fox came back, and found out what had happened, she was not so much sorry for the loss of her cubs as furious because she couldn't get at the Eagle and pay her out for her treachery. So she sat down not far off and cursed her. But it wasn't long before she had her revenge. Some villagers happened to be sacrificing a goat on a neighboring altar, and the Eagle flew down and carried off a piece of burning flesh to her nest. There was a strong wind blowing, and the nest caught fire, with the result that her fledglings fell half-roasted to the ground. Then the Fox ran to the spot and devoured them in full sight of the Eagle.

> *False faith may escape human punishment, but cannot escape the divine.*

THE BUTCHER AND HIS CUSTOMERS

Two Men were buying meat at a Butcher's stall in the market-place, and, while the Butcher's back was turned for a moment, one of them snatched up a joint and hastily thrust it under the other's cloak, where it could not be seen. When the Butcher turned round, he missed the meat at once, and charged them with having stolen it: but the one who had taken it said he hadn't got it, and the one who had got it said he hadn't taken it. The Butcher felt sure they were deceiving him, but he only said, "You may cheat me with your lying, but you can't cheat the gods, and they won't let you off so lightly."

Prevarication often amounts to perjury.

HERCULES AND MINERVA

Hercules was once traveling along a narrow road when he saw lying on the ground in front of him what appeared to be an apple, and as he passed he stamped upon it with his heel. To his astonishment, instead of being crushed it doubled in size; and, on his attacking it again and smiting it with his club, it swelled up to an enormous size and blocked up the whole road. Upon this he dropped his club, and stood looking at it in amazement. Just then Minerva appeared, and said to him, "Leave it alone, my friend; that which you see before you is the apple of discord: if you do not meddle with it, it remains small as it was at first, but if you resort to violence it swells into the thing you see."

Fables
THE FOX WHO SERVED A LION

A Lion had a Fox to attend on him, and whenever they went hunting the Fox found the prey and the Lion fell upon it and killed it, and then they divided it between them in certain proportions. But the Lion always got a very large share, and the Fox a very small one, which didn't please the latter at all; so he determined to set up on his own account. He began by trying to steal a lamb from a flock of sheep: but the shepherd saw him and set his dogs on him. The hunter was now the hunted, and was very soon caught and dispatched by the dogs.

Better servitude with safety than freedom with danger.

THE QUACK DOCTOR

A certain man fell sick and took to his bed. He consulted a number of doctors from time to time, and they all, with one exception, told him that his life was in no immediate danger, but that his illness would probably last a considerable time. The one who took a different view of his case, who was also the last to be consulted, bade him prepare for the worst: "You have not twenty-four hours to live," said he, "and I fear I can do nothing." As it turned out, however, he was quite wrong; for at the end of a few days the sick man quitted his bed and took a walk abroad, looking, it is true, as pale as a ghost. In the course of his walk he met the Doctor who had prophesied his death. "Dear me," said the latter, "how do you do? You are fresh from the other world, no doubt. Pray, how are our departed friends getting on there?" "Most comfortably," replied the other, "for they have drunk the water of oblivion, and have forgotten all the troubles of life. By the way, just before I left, the authorities were making arrangements to prosecute all the doctors, because they won't let sick men die in the course of nature, but use their arts to keep them alive. They were going to charge you along with the rest, till I assured them that you were no doctor, but a mere impostor."

THE LION, THE WOLF, AND THE FOX

A Lion, infirm with age, lay sick in his den, and all the beasts of the forest came to inquire after his health with the exception of the Fox. The Wolf thought this was a good opportunity for paying off old scores against the Fox, so he called the attention of the Lion to his absence, and said, "You see, sire, that we have all come to see how you are except the Fox, who hasn't come near you, and doesn't care whether you are well or ill." Just then the Fox came in and heard the last words of the Wolf. The Lion roared at him in deep displeasure, but he begged to be allowed to explain his absence, and said, "Not one of them cares for you so much as I, sire, for all the time I have been going round to the doctors and trying to find a cure for your illness." "And may I ask if you have found one?" said the Lion. "I have, sire," said the Fox, "and it is this: you must flay a Wolf and wrap yourself in his skin while it is still warm." The Lion accordingly turned to the Wolf and struck him dead with one blow of his paw, in order to try the Fox's prescription; but the Fox laughed and said to himself, "That's what comes of stirring up ill-will."

HERCULES AND PLUTUS

When Hercules was received among the gods and was entertained at a banquet by Jupiter, he responded courteously to the greetings of all with the exception of Plutus, the god of wealth. When Plutus approached him, he cast his eyes upon the ground, and turned away and pretended not to see him. Jupiter was surprised at this conduct on his part, and asked why, after having been so cordial with all the other gods, he had behaved like that to Plutus. "Sire," said Hercules, "I do not like Plutus, and I will tell you why. When we were on earth together I always noticed that he was to be found in the company of scoundrels."

THE FOX AND THE LEOPARD

A Fox and a Leopard were disputing about their looks, and each claimed to be the more handsome of the two. The Leopard said, "Look at my smart coat; you have nothing to match that." But the Fox replied, "Your coat may be smart, but my wits are smarter still."

THE FOX AND THE HEDGEHOG

A Fox, in swimming across a rapid river, was swept away by the current and carried a long way downstream in spite of his struggles, until at last, bruised and exhausted, he managed to scramble on to dry ground from a backwater. As he lay there unable to move, a swarm of horseflies settled on him and sucked his blood undisturbed, for he was too weak even to shake them off. A Hedgehog saw him, and asked if he should brush away the flies that were tormenting him; but the Fox replied, "Oh, please, no, not on any account, for these flies have sucked their fill and are taking very little from me now; but, if you drive them off, another swarm of hungry ones will come and suck all the blood I have left, and leave me without a drop in my veins."

THE CROW AND THE RAVEN

A Crow became very jealous of a Raven, because the latter was regarded by men as a bird of omen which foretold the future, and was accordingly held in great respect by them. She was very anxious to get the same sort of reputation herself; and, one day, seeing some travelers approaching, she flew on to a branch of a tree at the roadside and cawed as loud as she could. The travelers were in some dismay at the sound, for they feared it might be a bad omen; till one of them, spying the Crow, said to his companions, "It's all right, my friends, we can go on without fear, for it's only a crow and that means nothing."

Fables

Those who pretend to be something they are not only make themselves ridiculous.

THE WITCH

A Witch professed to be able to avert the anger of the gods by means of charms, of which she alone possessed the secret; and she drove a brisk trade, and made a fat livelihood out of it. But certain persons accused her of black magic and carried her before the judges, and demanded that she should be put to death for dealings with the Devil. She was found guilty and condemned to death: and one of the judges said to her as she was leaving the dock, "You say you can avert the anger of the gods. How comes it, then, that you have failed to disarm the enmity of men?"

THE OLD MAN AND DEATH

An Old Man cut himself a bundle of faggots in a wood and started to carry them home. He had a long way to go, and was tired out before he had got much more than half-way. Casting his burden on the ground, he called upon Death to come and release him from his life of toil. The words were scarcely out of his mouth when, much to his dismay, Death stood before him and professed his readiness to serve him. He was almost frightened out of his wits, but he had enough presence of mind to stammer out, "Good sir, if you'd be so kind, pray help me up with my burden again."

THE MISER

A Miser sold everything he had, and melted down his hoard of gold into a single lump, which he buried secretly in a field. Every day he went to look at it, and would sometimes spend long hours gloating over his treasure. One of his men noticed his frequent visits to the spot, and one day watched him and discovered his secret. Waiting his opportunity, he went one night and dug up the gold and stole it. Next day the Miser visited the place as usual, and, finding his treasure gone, fell to tearing his hair and groaning over his loss. In this condition he was seen by one of his neighbors, who asked him what his trouble was. The Miser told him of his misfortune; but the other replied, "Don't take it so much to heart, my friend; put a brick into the hole, and take a look at it every day: you won't be any worse off than before, for even when you had your gold it was of no earthly use to you."

Fables
THE FOXES AND THE RIVER

A number of Foxes assembled on the bank of a river and wanted to drink; but the current was so strong and the water looked so deep and dangerous that they didn't dare to do so, but stood near the edge encouraging one another not to be afraid. At last one of them, to shame the rest, and show how brave he was, said, "I am not a bit frightened! See, I'll step right into the water!" He had no sooner done so than the current swept him off his feet. When the others saw him being carried down-stream they cried, "Don't go and leave us! Come back and show us where we too can drink with safety." But he replied, "I'm afraid I can't yet: I want to go to the seaside, and this current will take me there nicely. When I come back I'll show you with pleasure."

THE HORSE AND THE STAG

There was once a Horse who used to graze in a meadow which he had all to himself. But one day a Stag came into the meadow, and said he had as good a right to feed there as the Horse, and moreover chose all the best places for himself. The Horse, wishing to be revenged upon his unwelcome visitor, went to a man and asked if he would help him to turn out the Stag. "Yes," said the man, "I will by all means; but I can only do so if you let me put a bridle in your mouth and mount on your back." The Horse agreed to this, and the two together very soon turned the Stag out of the pasture: but when that was done, the Horse found to his dismay that in the man he had got a master for good.

THE FOX AND THE BRAMBLE

In making his way through a hedge a Fox missed his footing and caught at a Bramble to save himself from falling. Naturally, he got badly scratched, and in disgust he cried to the Bramble, "It was your help I wanted, and see how you have treated me! I'd sooner have fallen outright." The Bramble, interrupting him, replied, "You must have lost your wits, my friend, to catch at me, who am myself always catching at others."

THE FOX AND THE SNAKE

A Snake, in crossing a river, was carried away by the current, but managed to wriggle on to a bundle of thorns which was floating by, and was thus carried at a great rate down-stream. A Fox caught sight of it from the bank as it went whirling along, and called out, "Gad! the passenger fits the ship!"

THE LION, THE FOX, AND THE STAG

A Lion lay sick in his den, unable to provide himself with food. So he said to his friend the Fox, who came to ask how he did, "My good friend, I wish you would go to yonder wood and beguile the big Stag, who lives there, to come to my den: I have a fancy to make my dinner off a stag's heart and brains." The Fox went to the wood and found the Stag and said to him, "My dear sir, you're in luck. You know the Lion, our King: well, he's at the point of death, and has appointed you his successor to rule over the beasts. I hope you won't forget that I was the first to bring you the good news. And now I must be going back to him; and, if you take my advice, you'll come too and be with him at the last." The Stag was highly flattered, and followed the Fox to the Lion's den, suspecting nothing. No sooner had he got inside than the Lion sprang upon him, but he misjudged his spring, and the Stag got away with only his ears torn, and returned as fast as he could to the shelter of the wood. The Fox was much mortified, and the Lion, too, was dreadfully disappointed, for he was getting very hungry in spite of his illness. So he begged the Fox to have another try at coaxing the Stag to his den. "It'll be almost impossible this time," said the Fox, "but I'll try"; and off he went to the wood a second time, and found the Stag resting and trying to recover from his fright. As soon as he saw the Fox he cried, "You scoundrel, what do you mean by trying to lure me to my death like that? Take yourself off, or I'll do you to death with my horns." But the Fox was entirely shameless. "What a coward you were," said he; "surely you didn't think the Lion meant any harm? Why, he was only going to whisper some royal secrets into your ear when you went off like a scared rabbit. You have rather disgusted him, and I'm not sure he won't make the wolf King instead, unless you come back at once and show you've got some spirit. I promise you he won't hurt you, and I will be your faithful servant." The Stag was foolish enough to be persuaded to return, and this time the Lion made no mistake, but overpowered him, and feasted right royally upon his carcass. The Fox, meanwhile, watched his chance and, when the Lion wasn't looking, filched away the brains to reward him for his trouble. Presently the Lion began searching for them, of course without success: and the Fox, who was watching him, said, "I don't think it's much use your looking for the brains: a creature who twice walked into a Lion's den can't have got any."

THE MAN WHO LOST HIS SPADE

A Man was engaged in digging over his vineyard, and one day on coming to work he missed his Spade. Thinking it may have been stolen by one of his laborers, he questioned them closely, but they one and all denied any knowledge of it. He was not convinced by their denials, and insisted that they should all go to the town and take oath in a temple that they were not guilty of the theft. This was because he had no great opinion of the simple country deities, but thought that the thief would not pass undetected by the shrewder gods of the town. When they got inside the gates the first thing they heard was the town crier proclaiming a reward for information about a thief who had stolen something from the city temple. "Well," said the Man to himself, "it strikes me I had better go back home again. If these town gods can't detect the thieves who steal from their own temples, it's scarcely likely they can tell me who stole my Spade."

THE PARTRIDGE AND THE FOWLER

A Fowler caught a Partridge in his nets, and was just about to wring its neck when it made a piteous appeal to him to spare its life and said, "Do not kill me, but let me live and I will repay you for your kindness by decoying other partridges into your nets." "No," said the Fowler, "I will not spare you. I was going to kill you anyhow, and after that treacherous speech you thoroughly deserve your fate."

THE RUNAWAY SLAVE

A Slave, being discontented with his lot, ran away from his master. He was soon missed by the latter, who lost no time in mounting his horse and setting out in pursuit of the fugitive. He presently came up with him, and the Slave, in the hope of avoiding capture, slipped into a treadmill and hid himself there. "Aha," said his master, "that's the very place for you, my man!"

THE HUNTER AND THE WOODMAN

A Hunter was searching in the forest for the tracks of a lion, and, catching sight presently of a Woodman engaged in felling a tree, he went up to him and asked him if he had noticed a lion's footprints anywhere about, or if he knew where his den was. The Woodman answered, "If you will come with me, I will show you the lion himself." The Hunter turned pale with fear, and his teeth chattered as he replied, "Oh, I'm not looking for the lion, thanks, but only for his tracks."

THE SERPENT AND THE EAGLE

An Eagle swooped down upon a Serpent and seized it in his talons with the intention of carrying it off and devouring it. But the Serpent was too quick for him and had its coils round him in a moment; and then there ensued a life-and-death struggle between the two. A countryman, who was a witness of the encounter, came to the assistance of the Eagle, and succeeded in freeing him from the Serpent and enabling him to escape. In revenge the Serpent spat some of his poison into the man's drinking-horn. Heated with his exertions, the man was about to slake his thirst with a draught from the horn, when the Eagle knocked it out of his hand, and spilled its contents upon the ground.

One good turn deserves another.

THE ROGUE AND THE ORACLE

A Rogue laid a wager that he would prove the Oracle at Delphi to be untrustworthy by procuring from it a false reply to an inquiry by himself. So he went to the temple on the appointed day with a small bird in his hand, which he concealed under the folds of his cloak, and asked whether what he held in his hand were alive or dead. If the Oracle said "dead," he meant to produce the bird alive: if the reply was "alive," he intended to wring its neck and show it to be dead. But the Oracle was one too many for him, for the answer he got was this: "Stranger, whether the thing that you hold in your hand be alive or dead is a matter that depends entirely on your own will."

THE HORSE AND THE ASS

A Horse, proud of his fine harness, met an Ass on the high-road. As the Ass with his heavy burden moved slowly out of the way to let him pass, the Horse cried out impatiently that he could hardly resist kicking him to make him move faster. The Ass held his peace, but did not forget the other's insolence. Not long afterwards the Horse became broken-winded, and was sold by his owner to a farmer. One day, as he was drawing a dung-cart, he met the Ass again, who in turn derided him and said, "Aha! you never thought to come to this, did you, you who were so proud! Where are all your gay trappings now?"

THE DOG CHASING A WOLF

A Dog was chasing a Wolf, and as he ran he thought what a fine fellow he was, and what strong legs he had, and how quickly they covered the ground. "Now, there's this Wolf," he said to himself, "what a poor creature he is: he's no match for me, and he knows it and so he runs away." But the Wolf looked round just then and said, "Don't you imagine I'm running away from you, my friend: it's your master I'm afraid of."

GRIEF AND HIS DUE

When Jupiter was assigning the various gods their privileges, it so happened that Grief was not present with the rest: but when all had received their share, he too entered and claimed his due. Jupiter was at a loss to know what to do, for there was nothing left for him. However, at last he decided that to him should belong the tears that are shed for the dead. Thus it is the same with Grief as it is with the other gods. The more devoutly men render to him his due, the more lavish is he of that which he has to bestow. It is not well, therefore, to mourn long for the departed; else Grief, whose sole pleasure is in such mourning, will be quick to send fresh cause for tears.

THE HAWK, THE KITE, AND THE PIGEONS

The Pigeons in a certain dovecote were persecuted by a Kite, who every now and then swooped down and carried off one of their number. So they invited a Hawk into the dovecote to defend them against their enemy. But they soon repented of their folly: for the Hawk killed more of them in a day than the Kite had done in a year.

THE WOMAN AND THE FARMER

A Woman, who had lately lost her husband, used to go every day to his grave and lament her loss. A Farmer, who was engaged in plowing not far from the spot, set eyes upon the Woman and desired to have her for his wife: so he left his plough and came and sat by her side, and began to shed tears himself. She asked him why he wept; and he replied, "I have lately lost my wife, who was very dear to me, and tears ease my grief." "And I," said she, "have lost my husband." And so for a while they mourned in silence. Then he said, "Since you and I are in like case, shall we not do well to marry and live together? I shall take the place of your dead husband, and you, that of my dead wife." The Woman consented to the plan, which indeed seemed reasonable enough: and they dried their tears. Meanwhile, a thief had come and stolen the oxen which the Farmer had left with his plough. On discovering the theft, he beat his breast and loudly bewailed his loss. When the Woman heard his cries, she came and said, "Why, are you weeping still?" To which he replied, "Yes, and I mean it this time."

PROMETHEUS AND THE MAKING OF MAN

At the bidding of Jupiter, Prometheus set about the creation of Man and the other animals. Jupiter, seeing that Mankind, the only rational creatures, were far outnumbered by the irrational beasts, bade him redress the balance by turning some of the latter into men. Prometheus did as he was bidden, and this is the reason why some people have the forms of men but the souls of beasts.

THE SWALLOW AND THE CROW

A Swallow was once boasting to a Crow about her birth. "I was once a princess," said she, "the daughter of a King of Athens, but my husband used me cruelly, and cut out my tongue for a slight fault. Then, to protect me from further injury, I was turned by Juno into a bird." "You chatter quite enough as it is," said the Crow. "What you would have been like if you hadn't lost your tongue, I can't think."

THE HUNTER AND THE HORSEMAN

A Hunter went out after game, and succeeded in catching a hare, which he was carrying home with him when he met a man on horseback, who said to him, "You have had some sport I see, sir," and offered to buy it. The Hunter readily agreed; but the Horseman had no sooner got the hare in his hands than he set spurs to his horse and went off at full gallop. The Hunter ran after him for some little distance; but it soon dawned upon him that he had been tricked, and he gave up trying to overtake the Horseman, and, to save his face, called after him as loud as he could, "All right, sir, all right, take your hare: it was meant all along as a present."

THE GOATHERD AND THE WILD GOATS

A Goatherd was tending his goats out at pasture when he saw a number of Wild Goats approach and mingle with his flock. At the end of the day he drove them home and put them all into the pen together. Next day the weather was so bad that he could not take them out as usual: so he kept them at home in the pen, and fed them there. He only gave his own goats enough food to keep them from starving, but he gave the Wild Goats as much as they could eat and more; for he was very anxious for them to stay, and he thought that if he fed them well they wouldn't want to leave him. When the weather improved, he took them all out to pasture again; but no sooner had they got near the hills than the Wild Goats broke away from the flock and scampered off. The Goatherd was very much disgusted at this, and roundly abused them for their ingratitude. "Rascals!" he cried, "to run away like that after the way I've treated you!" Hearing this, one of them turned round and said, "Oh, yes, you treated us all right—too well, in fact; it was just that that put us on our guard. If you treat newcomers like ourselves so much better than your own flock, it's more than likely that, if another lot of strange goats joined yours, _we_ should then be neglected in favor of the last comers."

THE NIGHTINGALE AND THE SWALLOW

A Swallow, conversing with a Nightingale, advised her to quit the leafy coverts where she made her home, and to come and live with men, like herself, and nest under the shelter of their roofs. But the Nightingale replied, "Time was when I too, like yourself, lived among men: but the memory of the cruel wrongs I then suffered makes them hateful to me, and never again will I approach their dwellings."

The scene of past sufferings revives painful memories.

THE TRAVELLER AND FORTUNE

A Traveler, exhausted with fatigue after a long journey, sank down at the very brink of a deep well and presently fell asleep. He was within an ace of falling in, when Dame Fortune appeared to him and touched him on the shoulder, cautioning him to move further away. "Wake up, good sir, I pray you," she said; "had you fallen into the well, the blame would have been thrown not on your own folly but on me, Fortune."

THE AMBITIOUS FOX AND THE UNAPPROACHABLE GRAPES

A farmer built around his crop

Fables

A wall, and crowned his labors
By placing glass upon the top
To lacerate his neighbors,
Provided they at any time
Should feel disposed the wall to climb.

He also drove some iron pegs
Securely in the coping,
To tear the bare, defenseless legs
Of brats who, upward groping,
Might steal, despite the risk of fall,
The grapes that grew upon the wall.

One day a fox, on thieving bent,
A crafty and an old one,
Most shrewdly tracked the pungent scent
That eloquently told one
That grapes were ripe and grapes were good
And likewise in the neighborhood.

He threw some stones of divers shapes
The luscious fruit to jar off:
It made him ill to see the grapes
So near and yet so far off.
His throws were strong, his aim was fine,
But "Never touched me!" said the vine.

The farmer shouted, "Drat the boys!"
And, mounting on a ladder,
He sought the cause of all the noise;
No farmer could be madder,
Which was not hard to understand
Because the glass had cut his hand.

His passion he could not restrain,
But shouted out, "You're thievish!"

The fox replied, with fine disdain,
"Come, country, don't be peevish."
(Now "country" is an epithet
One can't forgive, nor yet forget.)

The farmer rudely answered back
With compliments unvarnished,
And downward hurled the *bric-a-brac*
With which the wall was garnished,
In view of which demeanor strange,
The fox retreated out of range.

"I will not try the grapes to-day,"
He said. "My appetite is
Fastidious, and, anyway,
I fear appendicitis."
(The fox was one of the *elite*
Who call it *site* instead of *seet*.)

The moral is that if your host
Throws glass around his entry
You know it isn't done by most
Who claim to be the gentry,
While if he hits you in the head
You may be sure he's underbred.

Fables

"THE FOX RETREATED OUT OF RANGE" [Page 5]

THE ARROGANT FROG AND THE SUPERIOR BULL

Once, on a time and in a place
Conducive to malaria,
There lived a member of the race
Of *Rana Temporaria*;
Or, more concisely still, a frog
Inhabited a certain bog.

A bull of Brobdingnagian size,

Too proud for condescension,
One morning chanced to cast his eyes
Upon the frog I mention;
And, being to the manner born,
Surveyed him with a lofty scorn.

Perceiving this, the Bactrian's frame
With anger was inflated,
Till, growing larger, he became
Egregiously elated;
For inspiration's sudden spell
Had pointed out a way to swell.

"Ha! ha!" he proudly cried, "a fig
For this, your mammoth torso!
Just watch me while I grow as big
As you--or even more so!"
To which magniloquential gush
His bullship simply answered "Tush!"

Alas! the frog's success was slight,
Which really was a wonder,
In view of how with main and might
He strove to grow rotunder!
And, standing patiently the while,
The bull displayed a quiet smile.

But ah, the frog tried once too oft
And, doing so, he busted;
Whereat the bull discreetly coughed
And moved away, disgusted,
As well he might, considering
The wretched taste that marked the thing.

THE MORAL: Everybody knows
How ill a wind it is that blows.

Fables

"HE STROVE TO GROW ROTUNDER"

THE PAMPERED LAPDOG AND THE MISGUIDED ASS

A woolly little terrier pup
Gave vent to yelps distressing,
Whereat his mistress took him up
And soothed him with caressing,
And yet he was not in the least
What one would call a handsome beast.

He might have been a Javanese,
He might have been a Jap dog,
And also neither one of these,
But just a common lapdog,
The kind that people send, you know,
Done up in cotton, to the Show.

At all events, whate'er his race,
The pretty girl who owned him
Caressed his unattractive face
And petted and cologned him,
While, watching her with mournful eye,
A patient ass stood silent by.

"If thus," he mused, "the feminine
And fascinating gender
Is led to love, I, too, can win
Her protestations tender."
And then the poor, misguided chap
Sat down upon the lady's lap.

Then, as her head with terror swam,
"This method seems to suit you,"
Observed the ass, "so here I am."
Said she, "Get up, you brute you!"

And promptly screamed aloud for aid:
No ass was ever more dismayed.

"SAID SHE, 'GET UP, YOU BRUTE YOU!'"

They took the ass into the yard
And there, with whip and truncheon,
They beat him, and they beat him hard,
From breakfast-time till luncheon.
He only gave a tearful gulp,

Though almost pounded to a pulp.

THE MORAL is (or seems, at least,
To be): In etiquette you
Will find that while enough's a feast
A surplus will upset you.
Toujours, toujours la politesse, if
The quantity be not excessive.

THE SYCOPHANTIC FOX AND THE GULLIBLE RAVEN

A raven sat upon a tree,
And not a word he spoke, for
His beak contained a piece of Brie,
Or, maybe, it was Roquefort:
We'll make it any kind you please--
At all events, it was a cheese.

Beneath the tree's umbrageous limb
A hungry fox sat smiling;
He saw the raven watching him,
And spoke in words beguiling.
"*J'admire*," said he, "*ton beau plumage.*"
(The which was simply persiflage.)

Two things there are, no doubt you know,
To which a fox is used:
A rooster that is bound to crow,
A crow that's bound to roost,
And whichsoever he espies
He tells the most unblushing lies.

"Sweet fowl," he said, "I understand
You're more than merely natty,
I hear you sing to beat the band

And Adelina Patti.
Pray render with your liquid tongue
A bit from 'Gotterdammerung.'"

"'J'ADMIRE,' SAID HE, 'TON BEAU PLUMAGE'"

This subtle speech was aimed to please
The crow, and it succeeded:

He thought no bird in all the trees
Could sing as well as he did.
In flattery completely doused,
He gave the "Jewel Song" from "Faust."

But gravitation's law, of course,
As Isaac Newton showed it,
Exerted on the cheese its force,
And elsewhere soon bestowed it.
In fact, there is no need to tell
What happened when to earth it fell.

I blush to add that when the bird
Took in the situation
He said one brief, emphatic word,
Unfit for publication.
The fox was greatly startled, but
He only sighed and answered "Tut."

THE MORAL is: A fox is bound
To be a shameless sinner.
And also: When the cheese comes round
You know it's after dinner.
But (what is only known to few)
The fox is after dinner, too.

THE CONFIDING PEASANT AND THE MALADROIT BEAR

A peasant had a docile bear,
A bear of manners pleasant,
And all the love she had to spare
She lavished on the peasant:
She proved her deep affection plainly
(The method was a bit ungainly).

Fables

The peasant had to dig and delve,
And, as his class are apt to,
When all the whistles blew at twelve
He ate his lunch, and napped, too,
The bear a careful outlook keeping
The while her master lay a-sleeping.

"AND SO A WEIGHTY ROCK SHE AIMED"

As thus the peasant slept one day,
The weather being torrid,

A gnat beheld him where he lay
And lit upon his forehead,
And thence, like all such winged creatures,
Proceeded over all his features.

The watchful bear, perceiving that
The gnat lit on her master,
Resolved to light upon the gnat
And plunge him in disaster;
She saw no sense in being lenient
When stones lay round her, most convenient.

And so a weighty rock she aimed
With much enthusiasm:
"Oh, lor'!" the startled gnat exclaimed,
And promptly had a spasm:
A natural proceeding this was,
Considering how close the miss was.

Now by his dumb companion's pluck,
Which caused the gnat to squall so,
The sleeping man was greatly struck
(And by the bowlder, also).
In fact, his friends who idolized him
Remarked they hardly recognized him.

Of course the bear was greatly grieved,
But, being just a dumb thing,
She only thought: "I was deceived,
But still, I did hit *something!*"
Which showed this masculine achievement
Had somewhat soothed her deep bereavement.

THE MORAL: If you prize your bones
Beware of females throwing stones.

The Giant Book of Bedtime Stories
Some Selected Proverbs

Afghan

- No rose is without thorns.
- One flower does not bring spring.
- There is a path to the top of highest mountain.

Chinese

- A man who pays respect to the great paves the way for his own greatness.
- An old woman is always uneasy when dry bones are mentioned in a proverb.
- If you don't stand for something, you will fall for something.

- Looking at a king's mouth one would never think he sucked his mother's breast.

- The faintest ink is more powerful than the strongest memory.

- The sun will shine on those who stand before it shines on those who kneel under them.

English

- A change is as good as a rest.

- A fool and his money are soon parted.

- A miss is as good as a mile.

- A rolling stone gathers no moss.

- Absence makes the heart grow fonder.

- Actions speak louder than words.

- All work and no play make Jack a dull boy.

- An apple a day keeps the doctor away.

- Any port in a storm.

- Beggars can't be choosers.

- Better late than never

Fables

- Caught between a rock and a hard place

- Different strokes for different folks.

- Don't count your chickens before they're hatched

- A stitch in time saves nine
- Eat, drink and be merry (for tomorrow we die).

- Every dog has its day.

- Great minds think alike.

- Half a loaf is better than no bread.

- He that fights and runs away, lives to fight another day.

- He who pays the piper calls the tune.

- Hell hath no fury like a woman scorned.

- Home is where the heart is.

- Honesty is the best policy.

- Hunger is the best sauce.

- If a job is worth doing, it's worth doing well.

- If at first you don't succeed, try, try again.

- If you can't stand the heat, get out of the kitchen.

- If you lie down with dogs, you'll get up with fleas.

- It never rains, but it pours.

- It's more blessed to give than to receive.

- Laughter is the best medicine.

- Let bygones be bygones.

- Let sleeping dogs lie.

- Lightning never strikes twice in the same place.

- Little strokes fell great oaks.

- Look after the pennies, and the dollars will look after themselves.

- Misfortunes always come in threes.

- Necessity is the mother of invention.

- Once a thief, always a thief.

- One man's meat is another man's poison.

- Out of the frying pan and into the fire

- Possession is nine tenths of the law.

- Sometimes the remedy is worse than the disease.

- The chickens have come home to roost.

- The early bird catches the worm.

- The grass looks greener on the other side of the fence.

- The pen is mightier than the sword.

- The walls have ears.

- There are plenty more fish in the sea.

- Time heals all wounds.

- To err is human, to forgive divine.

- Too many cooks spoil the broth.

- What can't be cured must be endured.

- Where there's smoke, there's fire.

- You can lead a horse to water, but you can't make it drink.

- You can't have your cake and eat it too.

- You can't make an omelet without breaking eggs.

- You have to strike while the iron is hot.

German

- A bird in the hand is worth two in the bush.
- An old broom knows the corners of the house.
- Barking dogs don't bite.
- Birds of a feather flock together.
- Blood is thicker than water.
- Can't see the forest for the trees.
- Clothes make the man.
- Dark bread makes cheeks red, white bread makes people dead.
- Don't cry "wolf."
- Don't look a gift horse in the mouth.
- Don't rock the boat.
- Dumb luck.
- Easy come, easy go.
- Haste makes waste.

- He hit the nail on the head.
- He who laughs last, laughs best.
- Kissin don't last but cookin do.
- Little drops of water, little grains of sand, make the mighty ocean and the pleasant land.
- Love is blind.
- Necessity is the mother of invention.
- Neither a borrower nor a lender be.
- Opposites attract.
- Out of sight, out of mind.
- Still waters run deep.
- The apple doesn't fall far from the tree.
- The first million is the hardest.
- Them that have, gets.
- There are two sides to everything.
- There is no fool like an old fool.
- There's no place like home.
- Time will tell.

- Trouble shared is trouble halved—joy shared is joy doubled.

- Use it or lose it.

- What you don't know won't hurt you.

- When the cat's away the mice will play.

- Work before pleasure.

Italian

- Better one day as a lion than a hundred as a sheep

  Love rules without rules

  Since the house is on fire let us warm ourselves

  He who scrubs the head of an ass wastes his soap
-
  The liar needs a good memory
-
  People in glass houses should not throw stones
-
  Every rule has an exception
-
  Don't judge a book by its cover
-
  You catch more flies with honey than a barrel of vinegar

- A fool and his money are soon parted

Kurdish

- A cup of coffee commits one to forty years of friendship.

- A fool dreams of wealth, a wise man, of happiness.

- A good companion shortens the longest road.

- A hungry stomach has no ears.
- A kind word warms a man through three winters.

- A knife-wound heals, but a tongue-wound festers.

- A neighbor's hen looks as big as a goose, and his wife as young as a girl.

- A small key opens big doors.

- A wise man does his own work.

- A wise man remembers his friends at all times; a fool, only when he has need of them.

- An illness comes by the pound and goes away by the ounce.

- Beauty passes; wisdom remains.

- Better a calf of one's own than a jointly owned cow.

- Do not roll up your trousers before reaching the stream.

- Dogs bark, but the caravan goes on.

- Eat and drink with your friends but do not trade with them.

- Every "bad" has its "worse".

- For every wise man there is one still wiser.
- God finds a low branch for the bird that cannot fly.

- Guests bring good luck with them.

- If God closes one door, He opens a thousand others.

- If you are an anvil, be patient; if you are a hammer, be strong.

- In a flat country a hillock thinks itself a mountain.

- Kind words will unlock an iron door.

- Listen a hundred times; ponder a thousand times; speak once.

- Many will show you the way once your cart has overturned.

- Once a friend, always a friend.

- One gives twice who gives quickly.

- Part with your head, but not with your secret.

- Patience is bitter, but it bears sweet fruit.

- Study from new books but from old teachers.

- Those who know do not talk; those who talk do not know.

- What is loaned goes away smiling but returns weeping.

- What you give away you keep.

- When a cat wants to eat her kittens, she says they look like mice.

- Whoever speaks evil to you of others will speak evil of you to others.

- Work as if you were to live forever; live as if you were to die tomorrow.

Nigerian

- A man who is trampled to death by an elephant is a man who is blind and deaf.

- If one were to remove every smoking wood from a fire and condemn it as bad, one would be killing the fire itself.

- The fish that can see that its water is getting shallower, cannot be stranded.

- It is not enough to run, one must arrive and know when one has arrived.

- A farmer does not conclude by the mere look of it that a corn is unripe; he tears it open for examination.
- An ant-hill that is destined to become a giant ant-hill will definitely become one, no matter how many times it is destroyed by elephants.

- He who is afraid of doing too much always does too little.

- We live by hope, but a reed never becomes an Iroko tree by dreaming.

- It is not only the fox, even the snail arrives at its destination.

- When an elephant falls, meat is sure to be surplus for those who follow the hunter.

- One finger cannot remove lice from the head.

- It is by the strength of their number that the ants in the field are able to carry their prey to the nest.

- If one imitates the upright, one becomes upright; if one imitates the crooked, one becomes crooked.

- The bottom of wealth is sometimes a dirty thing to behold.

- Rather than tell a lie to help a friend, it is better to assist him in paying the fine for his offense.
- The fowl perspires, but the feathers do not allow us to see the perspiration.
- Those who are carrying elephants home on their heads, need not use their toes to dig up crickets on the way.

- The leech that does not let go even when it is filled, dies on the dry land.

- It is one person in a street that kills a dog and the street is named a street of dog killers.

- A man who has one finger pointing at another has three pointing towards himself.

- Anyone who urinates in a stream should be warned because any of his relatives may drink from the water.

- When the roots of a tree begin to decay, it spreads death to the branches.

- Without retaliation evils would one day become extinct from the world.

- A person who has children does not die.

- A woman who is not successful in her own marriage has no advice to give to her younger generations.

- Criticism is easy but it does not create.

- It is the boast of every juju priest that unless he dies, no thief can ever come to steal his juju away.
- It is when there is a stampede, that a person with big buttocks knows that he carries a load.

Russian

- The sun will shine into our yard too.

- All are not cooks that walk with long knives.

- Any fish is good if it is on the hook.

- It is a bad workman that has a bad saw.

- You cannot break through a wall with your forehead.

- Idleness is the mother of all vices.

- A fly will not get into a closed mouth.

- Not everyone who has a cowl on is a monk.

- A wolf won't eat wolf.

- A man should not be struck when he is down.

- Eggs cannot teach a hen.

- An empty barrel makes the greatest sound.

- One is one's own master on one's own stove.

The Giant Book of Bedtime Stories
Bible Stories

The Story of Adam and Eve

The first man's name was Adam and his wife he called Eve. They lived in a beautiful Garden away in the East Country, which was called Eden, filled with beautiful trees and flowers of all kinds. But they did not live in Eden long for they did not obey God's command, but ate the fruit of a tree that had been forbidden them. They were driven forth by an angel and had to give up their beautiful home.

Therefore, Adam and his wife went out into the world to live and to work. For a time they were all alone, but after a while God gave them a little child of their own, the first baby that ever came into the world. Eve named him Cain; and after a time another baby came, whom she named Abel.

When the two boys grew up, they worked, as their father worked before them. Cain, the older brother, chose to work in the fields, and to

Bible Stories

raise grain and fruits. Abel, the younger brother, had a flock of sheep and became a shepherd.

They were driven forth by an angel

While Adam and Eve were living in the Garden of Eden, they could talk with God and hear God's voice speaking to them. But now that they were out in the world, they could no longer talk with God freely, as before. So when they came to God, they built an altar of stones heaped up, and upon it, they laid something as a gift to God, and burned it, to show that it was not their own, but was given to God, whom they could not see. Then before the altar they made their prayer to God, and asked God to forgive their sins, all that they had done was wrong; and prayed God to bless them and do good to them.

Each of these brothers, Cain and Abel, offered upon the altar to God his own gift. Cain brought the fruits and the grain that he had grown; and Abel brought a sheep from his flock, and killed it and burned it upon the altar. For some reason God was pleased with Abel and his offering, but was not pleased with Cain and his offering. Perhaps God wished Cain to offer something that had life, as Abel offered; perhaps Cain's heart was not right when he came before God.

God showed that He was not pleased with Cain; and Cain, instead of being sorry for his sin, and asking God to forgive him, was very angry with God, and angry toward his brother Abel. When they were out in the field together Cain struck his brother Abel and killed him. Therefore, the first baby in the world grew up to be the murderer of his own brother.

The Lord said to Cain, "Where is Abel, your brother?"

Cain answered, "I do not know; why should I take care of my brother?"

Then the Lord said to Cain, "What is this that you have done? Your brother's blood is like a voice crying to me from the ground. Do you see how the ground has opened, like a mouth, to drink your brother's blood? As long as you live, you shall be under God's curse for the murder of your brother. You shall wander over the earth, and shall never find a home, because you have done this wicked deed."

The Murder of Abel

Cain said to the Lord, "My punishment is greater than I can bear. Thou hast driven me out from among men; and thou hast hid thy face from me. If any man finds me he will kill me, because I shall be alone, and no one will be my friend."

God said to Cain, "If any one harms Cain, he shall be punished for it." And the Lord God placed a mark on Cain, so that whoever met him should know him and should know also that God had forbidden any man to harm him. Then Cain and his wife went away from Adam's home to live in a place by themselves, and there they had children. Cain's family built a city in that land; and Cain named the city after his first child, whom he had called Enoch.

The Story of Noah and the Ark

After Abel was slain, and his brother Cain had gone into another land, again God gave a child to Adam and Eve. This child they named Seth; and other sons and daughters were given to them; for Adam and Eve lived many years. At last they died, as God had said they must die, because they had eaten of the tree that God had forbidden them to eat.

By the time that Adam died, there were many people on the earth; for the children of Adam and Eve had many other children; and when these grew up they had other children; and these had children. These men, women, and children lived in tents. They owned sheep and cattle, and they moved about with them, wherever they could find pasture. The children played around the tent doors, and sat beside the campfires in the evenings, where they all sang together, and the older people told them stories.

After a time this land where Adam's sons lived began to be full of people.

It is sad to tell that as time went on more and more of these people became wicked, and fewer and fewer of them grew up to become good men and women. All the people lived near together, and few went away to other lands; so it happened that even the children of good men and women learned to be bad, like the people around them, and no longer did what was right and good.

As God looked down on the world that he had made, he saw how wicked the men in it had become, and that every thought and every act of man was evil and only evil continually.

While most of the people in the world were very wicked, there were some good people also, though they were very few. The best of all the men who lived at that time was a man whose name was Enoch. He was not the son of Cain, but another Enoch, who came from the family of Seth, the son of Adam, who was born after the death of Abel. While so many around Enoch were doing evil, this man did only what was right. He walked with God and God walked with him, and talked with him. At last, when Enoch was a very old man and weary with life, God took him away from earth to heaven. He did not die, as all the people have since Adam disobeyed God, but "he was not, for God took him." This means that Enoch was taken up from earth without dying.

Not all the people in the time of Enoch were shepherds. Some of them had learned how to make rude bows, arrows, axes, and plows. After a long time they melted iron, and they made knives, swords, and dishes to use in their homes. They sowed grain in the fields and reaped harvests, and they planted vines and fruit trees. God looked down on the earth and said:

"I will take away all men from the earth that I have made; because the men of the world are evil, and do evil continually."

Even in those bad times God saw one good man. His name was Noah. Noah tried to do right in the sight of God. As Enoch had walked with God, so Noah walked with God, and talked with him. Noah had three sons; their names were Shem, and Ham, and Japheth.

God said to Noah, "The time has come when all the men and women on the earth are to be destroyed. Every one must die, because they are all wicked. But you and your family shall be saved, because you alone are trying to do right."

Then God told Noah how he might save his life and the lives of his sons. He was to build a very large boat, as large as the largest ships that are made in our time; very long, and very wide and very deep; with a roof over it; and made like a long, wide house in three stories; but so built that it would float on the water. Such a ship as this was called "an ark." God told Noah to build this ark, and to have it ready for the time when he would need it.

"For," said God to Noah, "I am going to bring a great flood of water on the earth to cover all the land and to drown all the people on the earth. And as the animals on the earth will be drowned with the people, you must make the ark large enough to hold a pair of each kind of animals and several pairs of some animals that are needed by men, like sheep and goats and oxen; so that there will be animals as well as men to live upon the earth after the flood has passed away. And you must take in the ark food for yourself and your family, and for all the animals with you; enough food to last for a year, while the flood shall stay on the earth."

Noah did what God told him to do, although it must have seemed very strange to all the people around, to build this great ark where there was no water for it to sail upon. And it was a long time, because this ship was so big, that Noah and his sons were at work building the ark, which God had told them to build, while the wicked people around wondered, and no doubt laughed at Noah for building a great ship where there was no sea.

At last, the ark was finished, and stood like a great house on the land. There was a door on one side, and a window on the roof, to let in the light. Then God said to Noah:

"Come into the ark, you and your wife, and your three sons, and their wives with them; for the flood of waters will come very soon. And take with you animals of all kinds, and birds, and things that creep; seven pairs of these that will be needed by men, and one pair of all the rest, so that all kinds of animals may be kept alive upon the earth."

Noah and his wife, and his three sons, Shem, Ham and Japheth, with their wives, went into the ark. And God brought to the door of the ark the animals, and the birds, and the creeping things of all kinds; and they went into the ark. Noah and his sons put them in their places, and brought in food enough to feed them all for many days. Then the door of the ark was shut and no more people and no more animals could come in.

In a few days, the rain began to fall, as it had never rained before. It seemed as though the heavens were opened to pour great floods upon the earth. The streams filled, and the rivers rose higher and higher, and the ark began to float on the water. The people left their houses and ran up to the hills; but soon the hills were covered, and all the people on them were drowned.

Some had climbed up to the tops of higher mountains, but the water rose higher and higher, until even the mountains were covered and all the people, wicked as they had been, were drowned in the great sea that now rolled over all the earth where man had lived. All the animals, the tame animals, cattle, and sheep, and oxen, were drowned; and the wild animals, lions, and tigers, and all the rest were drowned. Even the birds were drowned, for their nests in the trees were swept away, and there was no place where they could fly from the terrible storm. For forty days and nights the rain kept on, until there was no breath of life remaining outside of the ark.

After forty days the rain stopped, but the water stayed upon the earth for more than six months, and the ark with all that were in it floated over the great sea that covered the land. Then God sent a wind to blow over the waters, and to dry them up; so by degrees the waters grew less and less. First mountains rose above the waters, then the hills rose up, and finally the ark ceased to float and lay aground on a mountain that is called Mount Ararat.

The water rose higher and higher

Noah could not see what had happened on the earth, because the door was shut, and the only window was up in the roof. But he felt that the ark was no longer moving, and he knew that the water must have gone down. After waiting for a time, Noah opened a window, and let loose a bird called a raven. Now the raven has strong wings; and this raven flew round and round until the waters had gone down, and it could find a place to rest, and it did not come back to the ark.

After Noah had waited for it awhile, he sent out a dove; but the dove could not find any place to rest, so it flew back to the ark, and Noah took it into the ark again. Then Noah waited a week longer, and afterward he sent out the dove again. At the evening, the dove came back to the ark, which was its home; and in its bill was a fresh leaf which it had picked off from an olive tree.

So Noah knew that the water had gone down enough to let the trees grow again. He waited another week, and sent out the dove again; but this time the dove flew away and never came back. Noah knew that the earth was becoming dry again. So he took off a part of the roof, and looked out, and saw that there was dry land all around the ark, and the waters were no longer everywhere.

Noah had now lived in the ark a little more than a year, and he was glad to see the green land and the trees once more. God said to Noah:

"Come out of the ark, with your wife, and your sons, and their wives, and all the living things that are with you in the ark."

Noah opened the door of the ark, and with his family came out, and stood once more on the ground. And the animals, and birds, and creeping things in the ark, came out also, and began again to bring life to the earth.

The first thing that Noah did when he came out of the ark was to give thanks to God for saving all his family when the rest of the people on the earth were destroyed. He built an altar, and laid upon it an offering to the Lord, and gave himself and his family to God and promised to do God's will.

God was pleased with Noah's offering, and God said:

"I will not again destroy the earth on account of men, no matter how bad they may be. From this time, no flood shall again cover the earth; but the seasons of spring and summer and fall and winter, shall remain without change. I give to you the earth; you shall be the rulers of the ground and of every living thing upon it."

Then God caused a rainbow to appear in the sky, and he told Noah and his sons that whenever they or the people after them should see the rainbow, they should remember that God had placed it in the sky and over the clouds as a sign of his promise, that he would always remember the earth, and the people upon it, and would never again send a flood to destroy man from the earth.

So as often as we see the beautiful rainbow, we are to remember that it is the sign of God's promise to the world.

The Tower Of Babel

The sons of Noah were named Shem, Ham and Japheth. These sons in turn became the fathers of children so that the descendants of Noah were very numerous.

One of these descendants, named Nimrod, was a mighty hunter and a man of power and authority in the land, and it has even been said that the people worshiped him as a god.

In those days men liked to build high towers reaching away up toward the heavens. Perhaps they were afraid of another flood, and perhaps they simply wished to show what they could do; but however that may be, ruins of towers can still be seen in various parts of the world, one of the most noted of which is that of the "Tower of Nimrod." It is forty feet high and stands on the top of a hill near the River Euphrates in Asia.

In the time of Nimrod, the people said, "Let us build us a city and a tower, whose top may reach unto Heaven; and let us make us a name, lest we be scattered abroad upon the face of the whole earth." So they began to build the tower, and they made it very strong indeed, and kept raising it higher and higher toward the heavens, thinking, Jewish tradition, or story, tells us, that they would have a shelter in which they would be perfectly safe from any flood which might come, or any fire. There were some of the people also who wished to use the tower as a temple for the idols that they worshiped. Six hundred thousand men worked upon this wonderful tower, so the story goes on to say, and they kept up the work until the tower rose to a height of seventy miles, so that, toward the last, it took a year to get materials for the work up to the top where the laborers were employed. Of course, this story is exaggerated, but without doubt, the tower rose to a great height and was a wonderful piece of work.

God was not pleased with what the people were doing, however, because they thought themselves so great and powerful that they had no need of Him, and so He put an end to their bold plans.

The Tower of Babel

Up to this time, all the people of the world had spoken the same language; but now, when they were working upon this wonderful tower, they commenced to talk in different tongues so that they could not understand each other, and there was great confusion. Owing to this, they were obliged to give up the building of the tower, and they separated themselves into groups, or divisions, each division speaking the same language, and then they spread out over the world, forming the various nations.

The tower was called the Tower of Babel because of the babble, or confusion, of tongues that had taken place there, and it was left unfinished to be a monument of God's power and man's weakness without Him.

The Story of Hagar and Ishmael

After the great flood the family of Noah and those who came after him grew in number, until, as the years went on, the earth began to be full of people once more. There was one great difference between the people who had lived before the flood and those who lived after it. Before the flood, all the people stayed close together, so that very many lived in one land, and no one lived in other lands. After the flood, families began to move from one place to another seeking new homes. Some went one way, and some another, so that as the number of people grew, they covered much more of the earth than those who had lived before the flood.

Part of the people went up to the north and built a city called Nineveh, which became the ruling city of a great land called Assyria, whose people were called Assyrians.

Another company went away to the west and settled by the great river Nile, and founded the land of Egypt, with its strange temples and pyramids, its sphinx and its monuments.

Another company wandered northwest until they came to the shore of the great sea, which they called the Mediterranean Sea. There they founded the cities of Sidon and Tyre, where the people were sailors, sailing to countries far away, and bringing home many things from other lands to sell to the people of Babylon, and Assyria, and Egypt, and other countries.

The destruction of Sodom

Among the many cities that the people built were two called Sodom and Gomorrah. The people in these cities were very wicked and were nearly all destroyed. One good man named Lot and his family escaped.

There was another good man named Abraham who did not live in these cities. He tried to do God's will and was promised a son to bring joy into his family.

After Sodom and Gomorrah were destroyed, Abraham moved his tent and his camp away from that part of the land, and went to live near a place called Gerar, in the southwest, not far from the Great Sea. There at last, the child whom God had promised to Abraham and Sarah, his wife, was born, when Abraham, his father, was a very old man.

They named this child Isaac, as the angel had told them he should be named. Abraham and Sarah were so happy to have a little boy, that after a time they gave a great feast and invited all the people to come and rejoice with them, and all in honor of the little Isaac.

Sarah had a maid named Hagar, an Egyptian woman, who ran away from her mistress, saw an angel by a well, and afterward came back to Sarah. She, too, had a child and his name was Ishmael. So now there were two boys in Abraham's tent, the older boy, Ishmael, the son of Hagar, and the younger boy, Isaac, the son of Abraham and Sarah.

Ishmael did not like the little Isaac, and did not treat him kindly. This made his mother Sarah very angry, and she said to her husband:

"I do not wish to have this boy Ishmael growing up with my son Isaac. Send away Hagar and her boy, for they are a trouble to me."

Abraham felt very sorry to have trouble come between Sarah and Hagar, and between Isaac and Ishmael; for Abraham was a kind and good man, and he was friendly to them all.

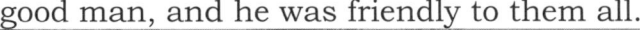

The expulsion of Hagar

The Lord said to Abraham, "Do not be troubled about Ishmael and his mother. Do as Sarah has asked you to do, and send them away. It is best that Isaac should be left alone in your tent, for he is to receive everything that is yours. I the Lord will take care of Ishmael, and will make a great people of his descendants, those who shall come from him."

The next morning Abraham sent Hagar and her boy away, expecting them to go back to the land of Egypt, from which Hagar had come. He gave them some food for the journey, and a bottle of water to drink by the way. The bottles in that country were not made of glass like ours. They are made from the skin of a goat. One of these skin-bottles Abraham filled with water and gave to Hagar.

Hagar went away from Abraham's tent, leading her little boy. But in some way she lost the road, and wandered over the desert, not knowing where she was, until all the water in the bottle was used up; and her poor boy in the hot sun and the burning sand had nothing to drink. She thought that he would die of his terrible thirst; and she laid him down under a little bush; and then she went away, for she said to herself:

"I cannot bear to look at my poor boy suffering and dying for want of water."

Just at that moment, while Hagar was crying, and her boy was moaning with thirst, she heard a voice saying to her:

"Hagar, what is your trouble? Do not be afraid. God has heard your cry and the cry of your child. God will take care of you both, and will make of your boy a great nation of people."

It was the voice of an angel from heaven; and then Hagar looked, and there, nearby, was a spring of water in the desert. How glad Hagar was as she filled the bottle with water and took it to her suffering boy under the bush!

Hagar in the wilderness

After this, Hagar did not go down to Egypt. She found a place where she lived and brought up her son in the wilderness, far from other people. Ishmael grew up in the desert and learned to shoot with the bow and arrow. He became a wild man, and his children after him grew up to be wild men also. They were the Arabians of the desert, who even to this day have never been ruled by any other people, but wander through the desert, and live as they please. Ishmael came to be the father of many people, and his descendants, the wild Arabians of the desert, are living unto this day in that land.

The Story of Abraham and Isaac

You remember that in those times of which we are telling, when men worshipped God, they built an altar of earth or of stone, and laid an offering upon it as a gift to God. The offering was generally a sheep, or a goat, or a young ox—some animal that was used for food. Such an offering was called "a sacrifice."

The people who worshipped idols often did what seems to us strange and very terrible. They thought that it would please their gods if they would offer as a sacrifice the most precious living things that were their own; and they would take their own little children and kill them upon their altars as offerings to the gods of wood and stone, that were no real gods, but only images.

God wished to show Abraham and all his descendants, those who should come after him, that he was not pleased with such offerings as those of living people, killed on the altars. God took a way to teach Abraham, so that he and his children after him would never forget it. At the same time, he wished to see how faithful and obedient Abraham would be to his commands; how fully Abraham would trust in God, or, as we would say, how great was Abraham's faith in God.

Therefore, God gave to Abraham a command that he did not mean to have obeyed, though this he did not tell to Abraham. He said:

"Take now your son, your only son Isaac, whom you love so greatly, and go to the land of Moriah, and there on a mountain that I will show you, offer him for a burnt-offering to me."

Though this command filled Abraham's heart with pain, yet he would not be as surprised to receive it as a father would in our day; for such offerings were very common among all those people in the land where Abraham lived. Abraham never for one moment doubted or disobeyed God's word. He knew that Isaac was the child whom God had promised, and that God had promised, too, that Isaac should have children, and that those coming from Isaac should be a great nation. He did not see how God could keep his promise with regard to Isaac, if Isaac should be killed as an offering; unless indeed God should raise him up from the dead afterward.

Abraham undertook at once to obey God's command. He took two young men with him and an ass laden with wood for the fire; and he went toward the mountain in the north, Isaac, his son, walking by his side. For two days they walked, sleeping under the trees at night in the open country. On the third day Abraham saw the mountain far away. And as they drew near to the mountain Abraham said to the young men:

"Stay here with the ass, while I go up yonder mountain with Isaac to worship; and when we have worshipped, we will come back to you." For Abraham believed that in some way God would bring back Isaac to life. He took the wood from the ass and placed it on Isaac, and they two walked up the mountain together. As they were walking, Isaac said:

The Trial of the faith of Abraham

"Father, here is the wood, but where is the lamb for the offering?"

Abraham said, "My son, God will provide himself a Lamb for a burnt offering."

Bible Stories

They came to the place on the top of the mountain. There Abraham built an altar of stones and earth heaped up; and on it, he placed the wood. Then he tied the hands and the feet of Isaac, and laid him on the altar, on the wood. Abraham lifted up his hand, holding a knife to kill his son. Another moment longer and Isaac would be slain by his own father's hand.

Just at that moment the angel of the Lord out of heaven called to Abraham, and said:

"Abraham! Abraham!"

Abraham answered, "Here I am, Lord." Then the angel of the Lord said:

"Do not lay your hand upon your son. Do no harm to him. Now I know that you love God more than you love your only son, and that you are obedient to God, since you are ready to give up your son, your only son, to God."

What a relief and a joy these words from heaven brought to the heart of Abraham! How glad he was to know that it was not God's will for him to kill his son! Then Abraham looked around, and there in the thicket was a ram caught by his horns. Abraham took the ram and offered him up for a burnt-offering in place of his son. So Abraham's words came true when he said that God would provide for himself a lamb.

The place where this altar was built Abraham named Jehovah-jireh, words in the language that Abraham spoke meaning, "The Lord will provide."

This offering, which seems so strange, did much good. It showed Abraham and Isaac that Isaac belonged to God, for to God he had been offered; and in Isaac all those who should come from him, his descendants, had been given to

God. Then it showed to Abraham and to all the people after him, that God did not wish children or men killed as offerings for worship; and while all the people around offered such sacrifices, the Israelites, who came from Abraham and from Isaac, never offered them, but offered oxen and sheep and goats instead.

These gifts expressed their thankfulness to God, but they were glad to be taught that God does not desire men's lives to be taken.

The Story of Jacob

After Abraham died, his son Isaac lived in the land of Canaan. Like his father, Isaac had his home in a tent; around him were the tents of his people, and many flocks of sheep and herds of cattle feeding wherever they could find grass to eat and water to drink.

Isaac and his wife Rebekah had two children. The older was named Esau and the younger Jacob.

Esau was a man of the woods and very fond of hunting; and he was rough and covered with hair.

Jacob was quiet and thoughtful, staying at home, dwelling in a tent, and caring for the flocks of his father.

Isaac loved Esau more than Jacob, because Esau brought to his father that which he had killed in his hunting; but Rebekah liked Jacob, because she saw that he was wise and careful in his work.

Among the people in those lands, when a man dies, his older son receives twice as much as the younger of what the father has owned.

This was called his "birthright," for it was his right as the oldest born. Esau, as the older, had a "birthright" to more of Isaac's possessions than Jacob. And besides this, there was the privilege of the promise of God that the family of Isaac should receive great blessings.

Now Esau, when he grew up, did not care for his birthright or the blessing that God had promised. But Jacob, who was a wise man, wished greatly to have the birthright which would come to Esau when his father died. Once, when Esau came home hungry and tired from hunting in the fields, he saw that Jacob had a bowl of something that he had just cooked for dinner. And Esau said:

"Give me some of that red stuff in the dish. Will you not give me some? I am hungry."

Jacob answered, "I will give it to you, if you will first of all sell to me your birthright."

Esau said, "What is the use of the birthright to me now, when I am almost starving to death? You can have my birthright if you will give me something to eat."

Then Esau made Jacob a solemn promise to give to Jacob his birthright, all for a bowl of food. It was not right for Jacob to deal so selfishly with his brother; but it was very wrong in Esau to care so little for his birthright and God's blessing.

Some time after this, when Esau was forty years old, he married two wives. Though this would be very wicked in our times, it was not supposed to be wrong then; for even good men then had more than one wife. But Esau's two wives were women from the people of Canaan, who worshipped idols, and not the true God, and they taught their children to pray to idols; so that those who came from Esau, the people who were his descendants, lost all knowledge of God, and became very wicked. But this was long after that time.

Isaac and Rebekah were very sorry to have their son Esau marry women who prayed to idols and not to God; but still Isaac loved his active son Esau more than his quiet son Jacob. But Rebekah loved Jacob more than Rebekah loved Esau.

Isaac became at last very old and feeble, and so blind that he could see scarcely anything. One day he said to Esau:

"My son, I am very old, and do not know how soon I must die. Before I die, I wish to give to you, as my older son, God's blessing upon you, and your children, and your descendants. Go out into the fields, and with your bow and arrows shoot some animal that is good for food, and make for me a dish of cooked meat such as you know I love; and after I have eaten it I will give you the blessing."

Now Esau ought to have told his father that the blessing did not belong to him, for he had sold it to his brother Jacob. However, he did not tell his father. He went out into the fields hunting, to find the kind of meat that his father liked the most.

Now Rebekah was listening, and heard all that Isaac had said to Esau. She knew that it would be better for Jacob to have the blessing than for Esau; and she loved Jacob more than she loved Esau. So she called to Jacob and told him what Isaac had said to Esau, and she said:

"Now, my son, do what I tell you, and you will get the blessing instead of your brother. Go to the flocks and bring to me two little kids from the goats, and I will cook them just like the meat which Esau cooks for your father. And you will bring it to your father, and he will think that you are Esau, and will give you the blessing; and it really belongs to you."

Jacob said, "You know that Esau and I are not alike. His neck and arms are covered with hairs, while mine are smooth. My father will feel of me, and he will find that I am not Esau; and then, instead of giving me a blessing, I am afraid that he will curse me."

Rebekah answered her son, "Never mind; you do as I have told you, and I will take care of you. If any harm comes it will come to me; so do not be afraid, but go and bring the meat."

Then Jacob went and brought a pair of little kids from the flocks, and from them his mother made a dish of food, so that it would be to the taste just as Isaac liked it. Then Rebekah found some of Esau's clothes, and dressed Jacob in them; and she placed on his neck and hands some of the skins of the kids, so that his neck and his hands would feel rough and hairy to the touch.

Then Jacob came into his father's tent, bringing the dinner

Isaac said, "Who are you, my son?"

And Jacob answered, "I am Esau, your oldest son; I have done as you bade me; now sit up and eat the dinner that I have made, and then give me your blessing as you promised me."

Isaac said, "How is it that you found it so quickly?"

Jacob answered, "Because the Lord your God showed me where to go and gave me good success."

Isaac blessing Jacob

Isaac did not feel certain that it was his son Esau, and he said, "Come near and let me feel you, so that I may know that you are really my son Esau."

Jacob went up close to Isaac's bed, and Isaac felt of his face, and his neck, and his hands, and he said:

"The voice sounds like Jacob, but the hands are the hands of Esau. Are you really my son Esau?"

Jacob told a lie to his father, and said, "I am."

Then the old man ate the food that Jacob had brought to him; and he kissed Jacob, believing him to be Esau; and he gave him the blessing, saying to him:

"May God give you the dew of heaven, and the richness of the earth, and plenty of grain and wine. May nations bow down to you and peoples become your servants. May you be the master over your brother, and may your family and descendants that shall come from you rule over his family and his descendants. Blessed be those that bless you, and cursed be those that curse you."

Just as soon as Jacob had received the blessing, he rose up and hastened away. He had scarcely gone out, when Esau came in from hunting, with the dish of food that he had cooked. And he said:

"Let my father sit up and eat the food that I have brought, and give me the blessing."

Isaac said, "Why, who are you?"

Esau answered, "I am your son; your oldest son, Esau."

Isaac trembled, and said, "Who then is the one that came in and brought to me food? and I have eaten his food and have blessed him; yes, and he shall be blessed."

When Esau heard this, he knew that he had been cheated; and he cried aloud, with a bitter cry, "O, my father, my brother has taken away my blessing, just as he took away my birthright! Can't you give me another blessing, too? Have you given everything to my brother?"

Isaac told him all that he had said to Jacob, making him the ruler over his brother.

But Esau begged for another blessing; and Isaac said:

"My son, your dwelling shall be of the riches of the earth and of the dew of heaven. You shall live by your sword and your descendants shall serve his descendants. But in time to come they shall break loose and shall shake off the yoke of your brother's rule and shall be free."

All this happened many years afterward. The people who came from Esau lived in a land called Edom, on the south of the land of Israel, where Jacob's descendants lived. After a time the Israelites became rulers over the Edomites; and later still, the Edomites made themselves free from the Israelites. But all this took place hundreds of years afterward.

It was better that Jacob's descendants, those who came after him, should have the blessing, than that Esau's people should have it; for Jacob's people worshipped God, and Esau's people walked in the way of the idols and became wicked.

Bible Stories
The Story of the Ladder That Reached To Heaven

After Esau found that he had lost his birthright and his blessing, he was very angry against his brother Jacob; and he said to himself, and told others:

"My father Isaac is very old and cannot live long. As soon as he is dead, then I shall kill Jacob for having robbed me of my right."

When Rebekah heard this, she said to Jacob, "Before it is too late, do you go away from home and get out of Esau's sight. Perhaps when Esau sees you no longer, he will forget his anger, and then you can come home again. Go and visit my brother Laban, your uncle, in Haran, and stay with him for a little while."

We must remember that Rebekah came from the family of Nahor, Abraham's younger brother, who lived in Haran, a long distance to the northeast of Canaan, and that Laban was Rebekah's brother.

Jacob went out of Beersheba, on the border of the desert, and walked alone, carrying his staff in his hand. One evening, just about sunset, he came to a place among the mountains, more than sixty miles distant from his home. As he had no bed to lie down upon, he took a stone and rested his head upon it for a pillow, and lay down to sleep.

On that night, Jacob had a wonderful dream. In his dream, he saw stairs leading from the earth where he lay up to heaven; and angels were going up and coming down upon the stairs. Above the stairs, he saw the Lord God standing. And God said to Jacob:

"I am the Lord, the God of Abraham, and the God of Isaac your father; and I will be your God, too. The land where you are lying all alone shall belong to you and to your children after you; and your children shall spread abroad over the lands, east and west, and north and south, like the dust of the earth; and in your family all the world shall receive a blessing. I am with you in your journey, and I will keep you where you are going, and will bring you back to this land. I will never leave you, and I will surely keep my promise to you."

In the morning Jacob awakened from his sleep, and he said:

"Surely, the Lord is in this place, and I did not know it! I thought that I was all alone, but God has been with me. This place is the house of God; it is the gate of heaven!"

Jacob took the stone on which his head had rested, and he set it up as a pillar, and poured oil on it as an offering to God. And Jacob named that place Bethel, which in the language that Jacob spoke means "The House of God."

Jacob made a promise to God at that time, and said:

"If God really will go with me and will keep me in the way that I go, and will give me bread to eat and will bring me to my father's house in peace, then the Lord shall be my God: and this stone shall be the house of God, and of all that God gives me I will give back to God one-tenth as an offering."

Then Jacob went onward in his long journey. He walked across the river Jordan in a shallow place, feeling his way with his staff; he climbed mountains and journeyed beside the great desert on the east, and at last came to the city of Haran. Beside the city was the well, where Abraham's servant had met Jacob's mother, Rebekah; and there, after Jacob had waited for a time, he saw a young woman coming with her sheep to give them water.

Then Jacob took off the flat stone that was over the mouth of the well, and drew water and gave it to the sheep. When he found that this young woman was his own cousin Rachel, the daughter of Laban, he was so glad that he wept for joy. And at that moment he began to love Rachel, and longed to have her for his wife.

Rachel's father, Laban, who was Jacob's uncle, gave a welcome to Jacob, and took him into his home.

Jacob asked Laban if he would give his daughter, Rachel, to him as his wife; and Jacob said, "If you give me Rachel, I will work for you seven years."

And Laban said, "It is better that you should have her, than that a stranger should marry her."

Jacob lived seven years in Laban's house, caring for his sheep and oxen and camels; but his love for Rachel made the time seem short.

At last, the day came for the marriage; and they brought in the bride, who, after the manner of that land, was covered with a thick veil, so that her face could not be seen. She was married to Jacob, and when Jacob lifted up her veil he found that he had married, not Rachel, but her older sister, Leah, who was not beautiful, and whom Jacob did not love at all.

Jacob was very angry that he had been deceived,—though that was just the way in which Jacob himself had deceived his father and cheated his brother Esau. His uncle Laban said:

"In our land we never allow the younger daughter to be married before the older daughter. Keep Leah for your wife, and work for me seven years longer, and you shall have Rachel also."

Jacob tending the sheep

For in those times, as we have seen, men often had two wives, or even more than two. Jacob stayed seven years more, fourteen years in all, before he received Rachel as his wife.

While Jacob was living at Haran, eleven sons were born to him. Only one of these was the child of Rachel, whom Jacob loved. This son was Joseph, who was dearer to Jacob than any of his other children, partly because he was the youngest, and because he was the child of his beloved Rachel.

The Story of Joseph and His Coat of Many Colors

After Jacob came back to the land of Canaan with his eleven sons, another son was born to him, the second child of his wife Rachel, whom Jacob loved so well. Soon after the baby came, his mother Rachel died, and Jacob was filled with sorrow. Even to this day, you can see the place where Rachel was buried, on the road between Jerusalem and Bethlehem. Jacob named the child whom Rachel left, Benjamin; and now Jacob had twelve sons. Most of them were grown-up men; but Joseph was a boy seventeen years old, and his brother Benjamin was almost a baby.

Of all his children, Jacob loved Joseph the best, because he was Rachel's child; because he was so much younger than most of his brothers; and because he was good, and faithful, and thoughtful. Jacob gave to Joseph a robe or coat of bright colors, made somewhat like a long cloak with wide sleeves. This was a special mark of Jacob's favor to Joseph, and it made his older brothers envious of him.

Then, too, Joseph did what was right, while his older brothers often did very wrong acts, of which Joseph sometimes told their father; and this made them very angry with Joseph. They hated him still more because of two strange dreams he had, and of which he told them. One day he said, "Listen to this dream that I have dreamed. I dreamed that we were out in the field binding sheaves, when suddenly my sheaf stood up, and all your sheaves came around it and bowed down to my sheaf!"

And they said scornfully, "Do you suppose that the dream means that you will some time rule over us, and that we shall bow down to you?"

Then, a few days after, Joseph said, "I have dreamed again. This time, I saw in my dream the sun, and the moon, and eleven stars, all come and bow to me!"

His father said to him, "I do not like you to dream such dreams. Shall I, and your mother, and your brothers, come and bow down before you as if you were a king?"

His brothers hated Joseph, and would not speak kindly to him; but his father thought much of what Joseph had said.

At one time, Joseph's ten brothers were taking care of the flock in the fields near Shechem, which was nearly fifty miles from Hebron, where Jacob's tents were spread. Jacob wished to send a message to his sons, and he called Joseph, and said to him:

"Your brothers are near Shechem with the flock. I wish that you would go to them, and take a message, and find if they are well and if the flocks are doing well; and bring me word from them."

That was quite an errand, for a boy to go alone over the country, find his way, for fifty miles, and then walk home again. But Joseph was a boy who could take care of himself, and could be trusted; so he went forth on his journey, walking northward over the mountains, past Bethlehem, and Jerusalem, and Bethel—though we are not sure those cities were then built, except Jerusalem, which was already a strong city.

When Joseph reached Shechem, he could not find his brothers, for they had taken their flocks to another place. A man met Joseph wandering in the field, and asked him, "Whom are you seeking?"

Joseph said, "I am looking for my brothers; the sons of Jacob. Can you tell me where I will find them?"

The man said, "They are at Dothan; for I heard them say that they were going there."

Then Joseph walked over the hills to Dothan, which was fifteen miles further. His brothers saw him afar off coming toward them. They knew him by his bright garment; and one said to another: "Look, that dreamer is coming! Come, let us kill him, and throw his body into a pit, and tell his father that some wild beast has eaten him; and then we will see what becomes of his dreams."

One of his brothers, whose name was Reuben, felt more kindly toward Joseph than the others.

"Let us not kill him, but let us throw him into this pit, in the wilderness, and leave him there to die."

Reuben intended, after they had gone away, to lift Joseph out of the pit, and take him home to his father. The brothers did as Reuben told them; they threw Joseph into the pit, which was empty. He cried, and begged them to save him; but they would not. They calmly sat down to eat their dinner on the grass, while their brother was calling to them from the pit.

After the dinner, Reuben chanced to go to another part of the field; so that he was not at hand when a company of men passed by with their camels, going from Gilead, on the east of the river Jordan, to Egypt, to sell spices and fragrant gum from trees to the Egyptians.

Then Judah, another of Joseph's brothers, said, "What good will it do us to kill our brother? Would it not be better for us to sell him to these men, and let them carry him away? After all, he is our brother, and we would better not kill him."

His brothers agreed with him; so they stopped the men who were passing, and drew up Joseph from the pit, and for twenty pieces of silver, they sold Joseph to these men; and they took him away with them down to Egypt.

After a while, Reuben came to the pit, where they had left Joseph, and looked into it; but Joseph was not there. Then Reuben was in great trouble; and he came back to his brothers, saying, "The boy is not there! What shall I do?"

Joseph sold into slavery

Then his brothers told Reuben what they had done; and they all agreed together to deceive their father. They killed one of the goats, and dipped Joseph's coat in its blood; and they brought it to their father, and they said to him, "We found this coat out in the wilderness. Look at it, father, and tell us if you think it was the coat of your son."

Jacob knew the coat at once. He said, "It is my son's coat. Some wild beast has eaten him. There is no doubt that Joseph has been torn in pieces!"

Jacob's heart was broken over the loss of Joseph, all the more because he had sent Joseph alone on the journey through the wilderness. They tried to comfort him, but he would not be comforted. He said, "I will go down to the grave mourning for my poor lost son."

So the old man sorrowed for his son Joseph; and all the time his wicked brothers knew that Joseph was not dead; but they would not tell their father the dreadful deed they had done to their brother, in selling him as a slave.

The Dreams of a King

The men who bought Joseph from his brothers were called Ishmaelites, because they belonged to the family of Ishmael, who, you remember, was the son of Hagar, the servant of Sarah. These men carried Joseph southward over the plain which lies beside the great sea on the west of Canaan; and after many days they brought Joseph to Egypt. How strange it must have seemed to the boy who had lived in tents to see the great river Nile, and the cities thronged with people, the temples, and the mighty pyramids!

The Ishmaelites sold Joseph as a slave to a man named Potiphar, who was an officer in the army of Pharaoh, the king of Egypt. Joseph was a beautiful boy, and cheerful and willing in his spirit, and able in all that he undertook; so that his master Potiphar became very friendly to him, and after a time, he placed Joseph in charge of his house, and everything in it. For some years, Joseph continued in the house of Potiphar, a slave in name, but in reality the master of all his affairs, and ruler over his fellow servants.

Potiphar's wife, who at first was very friendly to Joseph, afterward became his enemy, because Joseph would not do wrong to please her. She told her husband falsely, that Joseph had done a wicked deed. Her husband believed her, was very angry with Joseph, and put him in the prison with those who had been sent to that place for breaking the laws of the land. How hard it was for Joseph to be charged with a crime, when he had done no wrong, and to be thrust into a dark prison among wicked people!

Joseph had faith in God, that at some time all would come out right; and in the prison he was cheerful, and kind, and helpful, as he had always been. The keeper of the prison saw that Joseph was not like the other men around him, and he was kind to Joseph. In a very little while, Joseph was placed in charge of all his fellow-prisoners, and took care of them, just as he had taken care of everything in Potiphar's house. The keeper of the prison scarcely looked into the prison at all; for he had confidence that Joseph would be faithful and wise in doing the work given to him. Joseph did right, and served God, and God blessed Joseph in everything.

While Joseph was in the prison, two men were sent there by the king of Egypt, because he was displeased with them. One was the king's chief butler, who served the king with wine; the other was the chief baker, who served him with bread. These two men were under Joseph's care;

and Joseph waited on them, for they were men of rank.

One morning, when Joseph came into the room where the butler and the baker were kept, he found them looking quite sad. Joseph said to them:

"Why do you look so sad today?" Joseph was cheerful and happy in his spirit; and he wished others to be happy also, even in prison.

One of them said, "Each one of us dreamed last night a very strange dream, and there is no one to tell us what our dreams mean."

For in those times, before God gave the Bible to men, he often spoke to men in dreams; and there were wise men who could sometimes tell what the dreams meant.

"Tell me," said Joseph, "what your dreams are. Perhaps my God will help me to understand them."

Then the chief butler told his dream. He said, "In my dream I saw a grape-vine with three branches; and as I looked, the branches shot out buds; and the buds became blossoms; and the blossoms turned into clusters of ripe grapes. And I picked the grapes, and squeezed their juice into king Pharaoh's cup, and it became wine; and I gave it to king Pharaoh to drink, just as I used to do when I was beside his table."

Then Joseph said, "This is what your dream means. The three branches mean three days. In three days, king Pharaoh shall call you out of prison and shall put you back in your place; and you shall stand at his table, and shall give him his wine, as you have given it before. When you go out of prison, please to remember me, and try to find some way to get me, too, out of this prison. For I was stolen out of the land of Canaan, and sold as a slave; and I have done nothing wrong to deserve being put in this prison. Do speak to the king for me, that I may be set free."

Of course, the chief butler felt very happy to hear that his dream had so pleasant a meaning. The chief baker spoke, hoping to have an answer as good:

"In my dream," said the baker, "there were three baskets of white bread on my head, one above another, and on the topmost basket were all kinds of roasted meat and food for Pharaoh; and the birds came, and ate the food from the baskets on my head."

Joseph said to the baker:

"This is the meaning of your dream, and I am sorry to tell it to you. The three baskets are three days. In three days, by order of the king you shall be lifted up, and hanged upon a tree; and the birds shall eat your flesh from your bones as you are hanging in the air."

It came to pass just as Joseph had said. Three days after that, king Pharaoh sent his officers to the prison. They came and took out both the chief butler and the chief baker. The baker they hung up by his neck to die, and left his body for the birds to pick in pieces. The chief butler they brought back to his old place, where he waited at the king's table, and handed him his wine to drink.

You would have supposed that the butler would remember Joseph, who had given him the promise of freedom, and had shown such wisdom. In his gladness, he forgot all about Joseph.

And two full years passed by, while Joseph was still in prison, until he was a man thirty years old.

One night, king Pharaoh himself dreamed a dream—in fact, two dreams in one. And in the morning he sent for all the wise men of Egypt, and told to them his dreams; but there was not a man who could give the meaning of them. The king was troubled, for he felt that the dreams had some meaning which it was important for him to know.

Then suddenly the chief butler who was by the king's table remembered his own dream in the prison two years before, and remembered, too, the young man who had told its meaning so exactly. He said:

"I do remember my faults this day. Two years ago king Pharaoh was angry with his servants, with me and the chief baker; and he sent us to the prison. While we were in the prison, one night each of us dreamed a dream; and the next day a young man in the prison, a Hebrew from the land of Canaan, told us what our dreams meant; and in three days they came true, just as the young Hebrew had said. I think that if this young man is in the prison still, he could tell the king the meaning of his dreams."

You notice that the butler spoke of Joseph as "a Hebrew." The people of Israel, to whom Joseph belonged, were called Hebrews as well as Israelites. The word Hebrew means, "One who crossed over," and it was given to the Israelites because Abraham, their father, had come from a land on the other side of the great river Euphrates, and had crossed over the river on his way to Canaan.

Then king Pharaoh sent in haste to the prison for Joseph; and Joseph was taken out, and he was dressed in new garments, and was led in to Pharaoh in the palace. Pharaoh said:

"I have dreamed a dream; and there is no one who can tell what it means. And I have been told that you have power to understand dreams and what they mean."

Joseph Interpreting Pharaoh's Dream

Joseph answered Pharaoh:

"The power is not in me; but God will give Pharaoh a good answer. What is the dream that the king has dreamed?"

"In my first dream," said Pharaoh, "I was standing by the river: and I saw seven fat and handsome cows come up from the river to feed in the grass. While they were feeding, seven other cows followed them up from the river, very thin, and poor, and lean—such miserable creatures as I had never seen before. And the seven lean cows ate up the seven fat cows; and after they had eaten them up, they were as lean and miserable as before. Then I awoke.

"And I fell asleep again, and dreamed again. In my second dream, I saw seven heads of grain growing up on one stalk, large, strong, and good. Then seven heads came up after them, which were thin, poor, and withered. Moreover, the seven thin heads swallowed up the seven good heads; and afterward were as poor and withered as before.

"And I told these two dreams to all the wise men, and there is no one who can explain them. Can you tell me what these dreams mean?"

Joseph said to the king:

"The two dreams have the same meaning. God has been showing to king Pharaoh what he will do in this land. The seven good cows mean seven years, and the seven good heads of grain mean the same seven years. The seven lean cows and the seven thin heads of grain also mean seven years. The good cows and the good grain mean seven years of plenty, and the seven thin cows and thin heads of grain mean seven poor years. There are coming upon the land of Egypt seven years of such plenty as have never been seen; when the fields shall bring greater crops than ever before; and after those years shall come seven years when the fields shall bring no crops at all. Then for seven years, there shall be such need, that the years of plenty will be forgotten, for the people will have nothing to eat.

"Now, let king Pharaoh find some man who is able and wise, and let him set this man to rule over the land. During the seven years of plenty, let a part of the crops be put away for the years of need. If this shall be done, then when the years of need come, there will be plenty of food for all the people, and no one will suffer, for all will have enough."

King Pharaoh said to Joseph: "Since God has shown you all this, there is no other man as wise as you. I will appoint you to do this work, and to rule over the land of Egypt. All the people shall be under you; only on the throne of Egypt I will be above you."

Pharaoh took from his own hand the ring which held his seal, and put on Joseph's hand, so that he could sign for the king, and seal in the king's place. And he dressed Joseph in robes of fine linen, and put around his neck a gold chain. He made Joseph ride in a chariot which was next in rank to his own. They cried out before Joseph, "Bow the knee." Thus, Joseph was ruler over all the land of Egypt.

The Story of the Money in the Sacks

When Joseph was made ruler over the land of Egypt, he did just as he had always done. It was not Joseph's way to sit down, to rest and enjoy himself, and make others wait on him. He found his work at once, and began to do it faithfully and thoroughly. He went out over all the land of Egypt and saw how rich and abundant were the fields of grain, giving much more than the people could use for their own needs. He told the people not to waste it, but to save it for the coming time of need.

He called upon the people to give him for the king one bushel of grain out of every five, to be stored up. The people brought their grain, after taking for themselves as much as they needed, and Joseph stored it up in great storehouses in the cities; so much at last that no one could keep account of it.

The king of Egypt gave a wife to Joseph from the noble young women of his kingdom. Her name was Asenath; and to Joseph and his wife God gave two sons. The oldest son he named Manasseh, a word that means, "Making to Forget."

"For," said Joseph, "God has made me to forget all my troubles and my toil as a slave."

The second son he named Ephraim, a word that means "Fruitful." "Because," said Joseph, "God has not only made the land fruitful; but he has made me fruitful in the land of my troubles."

The seven years of plenty soon passed by, and then came the years of need. In all the lands around people were hungry, and there was no food for them to eat; but in the land of Egypt everybody had enough. Most of the people soon used up the grain that they had saved; many had saved none at all, and they all cried to the king to help them.

"Go to Joseph!" said king Pharaoh, "and do whatever he tells you to do."

Then the people came to Joseph, and Joseph opened the storehouses, and sold to the people all the grain that they wished to buy. Not only the people of Egypt came to buy grain, but people of all the lands around as well, for there was great need and famine everywhere. And the need was as great in the land of Canaan, where Jacob lived, as in other lands. Jacob was rich in flocks and cattle and gold and silver, but his fields gave no grain, and there was danger that his family and his people would starve. Jacob—who was now called Israel also—heard that there was food in Egypt and he said to his sons: "Why do you look at each other, asking what to do to find food? I have been told that there is grain in Egypt. Go down to that land, and take money with you, and bring grain, so that we may have bread, and may live."

Then the ten older brothers of Joseph went down to the land of Egypt. They rode upon asses, for horses were not much used in those times, and they brought money with them. But Jacob would not let Benjamin, Joseph's younger brother, go with them, for he was all the more dear to his father, now that Joseph was no longer with him; and Jacob feared that harm might come to him.

Then Joseph's brothers came to Joseph to buy food. They did not know him, grown up to be a man, dressed as a prince, and seated on a throne. Joseph was now nearly forty years old, and it had been almost twenty-three years since they had sold him. Joseph knew them all, as soon as he saw them. He wished to be sharp and stern with them, not because he hated them; but because he wished to see what their spirit was, and whether they were as selfish, and cruel, and wicked as they had been in other days.

They came before him, and bowed, with their faces to the ground. Then, no doubt, Joseph thought of the dream that had come to him while he was a boy, of his brothers' sheaves bending down around his sheaf. He spoke to them as a stranger, as if he did not understand their language, and he had their words explained to him in the language of Egypt.

"Who are you? And from what place do you come?" said Joseph, in a harsh, stern manner.

They answered him very meekly: "We have come from the land of Canaan to buy food."

"No," said Joseph, "I know what you have come for. You have come as spies, to see how helpless the land is, so that you can bring an army against us, and make war on us."

"No, no," said Joseph's ten brothers. "We are no spies. We are the sons of one man, who lives in the land of Canaan; and we have come for food, because we have none at home."

"You say that you are the sons of one man, who is your father? Is he living? Have you any more brothers? Tell me all about yourselves."

They said: "Our father is an old man in Canaan. We did have a younger brother, but he was lost; and we have one brother still, who is the youngest of all, but his father could not spare him to come with us."

"No," said Joseph. "You are not good, honest men. You are spies. I shall put you all in prison, except one of you; and he shall go and bring that youngest brother of yours; and when I see him, then I will believe that you tell the truth."

Joseph put all the ten men in prison, and kept them under guard for three days; then he sent for them again. They did not know that he could understand their language, and they said to each other, while Joseph heard, but pretended not to hear: "This has come upon us because of the wrong that we did to our brother Joseph, more than twenty years ago. We heard him cry, and plead with us, when we threw him into the pit, and we would not have mercy on him. God is giving us only what we have deserved."

Reuben, who had tried to save Joseph, said: "Did I not tell you not to harm the boy? and you would not listen to me. God is bringing our brother's blood upon us all."

When Joseph heard this, his heart was touched, for he saw that his brothers were sorry for the wrong that they had done to him. He turned away from them, so that they could not see his face, and he wept. Then he turned again to them and spoke roughly as before, and said:

"This I will do, for I serve God. I will let you all go home, except one man. One of you I will shut up in prison; but the rest of you can go home and take food for your people. And you must come back and bring your youngest brother with you, and I shall know then that you have spoken the truth."

Then Joseph gave orders, and his servants seized one of his brothers, whose name was Simeon, and bound him in their sight and took him away to prison. He ordered his servants to fill the men's sacks with grain, and to put every man's money back into the sack before it was tied up, so that they would find the money as soon as they opened the sack. Then the men loaded their asses with the sacks of grain, and started to go home, leaving their brother Simeon a prisoner.

When they stopped on the way to feed their asses, one of the brothers opened his sack, and there he found his money lying on the top of the grain. He called out to his brothers: "See, here is my money given again to me!" They were frightened, but they did not dare to go back to Egypt and meet the stern ruler of the land. They went home and told their old father all that had happened to them, and how their brother Simeon was in prison, and must stay there until they should return, bringing Benjamin with them.

When they opened their sacks of grain, there in the mouth of each sack was the money that they had given; and they were filled with fear. Then they spoke of going again to Egypt and taking Benjamin, but Jacob said to them:

"You are taking my sons away from me. Joseph is gone, Simeon is gone, and now you would take Benjamin away. All these things are against me!" Reuben said, "Here are my own two boys. You may kill them, if you wish, in case I do not bring Benjamin back to you." Jacob said: "My youngest son shall not go with you. His brother is dead, and he alone is left to me. If harm should come to him, it would bring down my gray hairs with sorrow to the grave."

The Mystery of the Lost Brother

The food that Jacob's sons had brought from Egypt did not last long, for Jacob's family was large. Most of his sons were married and had children of their own; so that the children and grandchildren were sixty-six, besides the servants who waited on them, and the men who cared for Jacob's flocks. So around the tent of Jacob was quite a camp of other tents and an army of people.

When the food that had come from Egypt was nearly eaten up, Jacob said to his sons:

"Go down to Egypt again, and buy some food for us."

Judah, Jacob's son, the man who years before had urged his brothers to sell Joseph to the Ishmaelites, said to his father: "It is of no use for us to go to Egypt, unless we take Benjamin with us. The man who rules in that land said to us, 'You shall not see my face, unless your youngest brother be with you'."

Israel said, "Why did you tell the man that you had a brother? You did me great harm when you told him."

"Why," said Jacob's sons, "we could not help telling him. The man asked us all about our family, 'Is your father yet living? Have you any more brothers?' And we had to tell him, his questions were so close. How should we know that he would say, 'Bring your brother here, for me to see him'?"

Judah said, "Send Benjamin with me, and I will take care of him. I promise you that I will bring him safely home. If he does not come back, let me bear the blame forever. He must go, or we shall die for want of food; and we might have gone down to Egypt and come home again, if we had not been kept back."

Jacob said, "If he must go, then he must. But take a present to the man, some of the choicest fruits of the land, some spices, and perfumes, and nuts, and almonds. And take twice as much money, besides the money that was in your sacks. Perhaps that was a mistake, when the money was given back to you. Take your brother Benjamin, and may the Lord God make the man kind to you, so that he will set Simeon free, and let you bring Benjamin back. But if it is God's will that I lose my children, I cannot help it."

So ten brothers of Joseph went down a second time to Egypt, Benjamin going in place of Simeon. They came to Joseph's office, the place where he sold grain to the people; and they stood before their brother, and bowed as before. Joseph saw that Benjamin was with them, and he said to his steward, the man who was over his house:

"Make ready a dinner, for all these men shall dine with me today."

When Joseph's brothers found that they were taken into Joseph's house, they were filled with fear. They said to each other:

"We have been taken here on account of the money in our sacks. They will say that we have stolen it, and then they will sell us all for slaves."

Joseph's steward, the man who was over his house, treated the men kindly; and when they spoke of the money in their sacks, he would not take it again, saying:

"Never fear; your God must have sent you this as a gift. I had your money."

The stewards received the men into Joseph's house, and washed their feet, according to the custom of the land. At noon, Joseph came in to meet them. They brought him the present from their father, and again they bowed before him, with their faces on the ground.

Joseph asked them if they were well, and said: "Is your father still living, the old man of whom you spoke? Is he well?"

They said, "Our father is well and he is living." And again they bowed to Joseph.

Joseph looked at his younger brother Benjamin, the child of his own mother Rachel, and said:

"Is this your youngest brother, of whom you spoke to me? God be gracious unto you, my son."

Joseph's heart was so full that he could not keep back the tears. He went in haste to his own room, and wept there. Then he washed his face, came out again, and ordered the table to be set for dinner. They set Joseph's table for himself, as the ruler, and another table for his Egyptian officers, and another for the eleven men from Canaan; for Joseph had brought Simeon out of the prison, and had given him a place with his brothers.

Joseph himself arranged the order of the seats for his brothers, the oldest at the head, and all in order of age down to the youngest. The men wondered at this, and could not see how the ruler of Egypt could know the order of their ages. Joseph sent dishes from his table to his brothers, and he gave to Benjamin five times as much as to the others. Perhaps he wished to see whether they were as jealous of Benjamin as in other days they had been toward him.

After dinner, Joseph said to his steward, "Fill the men's sacks with grain, as much as they can carry, and put each man's money in his sack. And put my silver cup in the sack of the youngest, with his money."

The steward did as Joseph had said; and early in the morning, the brothers started to go home. A little while afterward, Joseph said to his steward:

"Hasten, follow after the men from Canaan, and say, 'Why have you wronged me, after I had treated you kindly? You have stolen my master's silver cup, out of which he drinks'."

The steward followed the men, overtook them, and charged them with stealing. They said to him:

"Why should you talk to us in this manner? We have stolen nothing. Why, we brought back to you the money that we found in our sacks; and is it likely that we would steal from your lord his silver or gold? You may search us, and if you find your master's cup on any of us, let him die, and the rest of us may be sold as slaves."

They took down the sacks from the asses, and opened them; and in each man's sack was his money, for the second time. And when they came to Benjamin's sack, there was the ruler's silver cup! Then, in the greatest sorrow, they tied up their bags again, laid them on the asses, and came back to Joseph's palace.

Joseph said to them:

"What wicked thing is this that you have done? Did you not know that I would surely find out your deeds?"

Then Judah said, "O, my lord, what can we say? God has punished us for our sins; and now we must all be slaves, both we that are older, and the younger in whose sack the cup was found."

"No," said Joseph. "Only one of you is guilty; the one who has taken away my cup. I will hold him as a slave, and the rest of you can go home to your father.

Joseph wished to see whether his brothers were still selfish, and were willing to let Benjamin suffer, if they could escape.

Then Judah, the very man who had urged his brothers to sell Joseph as a slave, came forward, fell at Joseph's feet, and pleaded with him to let Benjamin go. He told again the whole story, how Benjamin was the one whom his father loved the most of all his children, now that his brother was lost. He said:

"I promised to bear the blame, if this boy was not brought home in safety. If he does not go back, it will kill my poor old father, who has seen much trouble. Now let my youngest brother go home to his father, and I will stay here as a slave in his place!"

Joseph Making Himself Known to His Brethren

Joseph knew now, what he had longed to know, that his brothers were no longer cruel nor selfish, but one of them was willing to suffer, so that his brother might be spared. Joseph could not any longer keep his secret, for his heart longed after his brothers; and he was ready to weep again, with tears of love and joy. He sent all of his Egyptian servants out of the room, so that he might be alone with his brothers, and then he said:

"Come near to me; I wish to speak with you." They came near, wondering. Then Joseph said:

"I am Joseph; is my father really alive?"

How frightened his brothers were, as they heard these words spoken in their own language by the ruler of Egypt and for the first time knew that this stern man, who had their lives in his hand, was their own brother whom they had wronged! Then Joseph said again:

"I am Joseph, your brother, whom you sold into Egypt. But do not feel troubled because of what you did. For God sent me before you to save your lives. There have been already two years of need and famine, and there are to be five years more, when there shall neither be plowing of the fields nor harvest. It was not you who sent me here, but God; and he sent me to save your lives. God has made me like a father to Pharaoh and ruler over all the land of Egypt. Now I wish you to go home, and to bring down to me my father and all his family."

Then Joseph placed his arms around Benjamin's neck, kissed him, and wept upon him. Benjamin wept on Joseph's neck. Joseph kissed all his brothers, to show them that he had fully forgiven them; and after that his brothers began to lose their fear of Joseph and talked with him more freely.

Afterward Joseph sent his brothers home with good news, and rich gifts, and abundant food. He sent also wagons in which Jacob and his sons' wives and the little ones of their families might ride from Canaan down to Egypt. Joseph's brothers went home happier than they had been for many years.

The Story Of Moses, The Child Who Was Found In The River

The children of Israel stayed in the land of Egypt much longer than they had expected to stay. They were in that land about four hundred years. The going down to Egypt proved a great blessing to them. It saved their lives during the years of famine and need. After the years of need were over, they found the soil in the land of Goshen, that part of Egypt where they were living, very rich, so that they could gather three or four crops every year.

Then, too, the sons of Israel, before they came to Egypt, had begun to marry the women in the land of Canaan who worshipped idols, and not the Lord. If they had stayed there, their children would have grown up like the people around them and soon would have lost all knowledge of God.

But in Goshen they lived alone and apart from the people of Egypt. They worshipped the Lord God, and were kept away from the idols of Egypt. In that land, as the years went on, from being seventy people, they grew in number until they became a great multitude. Each of the twelve sons of Jacob was the father of a tribe, and Joseph was the father of two tribes, named after his two sons, Ephraim and Manasseh.

As long as Joseph lived, and for some time after, the people of Israel were treated kindly by the Egyptians, out of their love for Joseph, who had saved Egypt from suffering by famine. After a long time another king began to rule over Egypt, who cared nothing for Joseph or Joseph's people. He saw that the Israelites (as the children of Israel were called) were very many, and he feared that they would soon become greater in number and in power than the Egyptians.

He said to his people, "Let us rule these Israelites more strictly. They are growing too strong."

Then they set harsh rules over the Israelites, and laid heavy burdens on them. They made the Israelites work hard for the Egyptians, build cities for them, and give to the Egyptians a large part of the crops from their fields. They set them at work in making brick and in building storehouses. They were so afraid that the Israelites would grow in number that they gave orders to kill all the little boys that were born to the Israelites; though their little girls might be allowed to live.

In the face of all this hate, and wrong, and cruelty, the people of Israel were growing in number, and becoming greater and greater.

At this time, when the wrongs of the Israelites were the greatest, and when their little children were being killed, one little boy was born.

He was such a lovely child that his mother kept him hid, so that the enemies did not find him. When she could no longer hide him, she formed a plan to save his life; believing that God would help her and save her beautiful little boy.

Moses in the bulrushes

She made a little box like a boat and covered it with something that would not let the water into it. Such a boat as this covered over was called "an ark." She knew that at certain times the daughter of king Pharaoh—all the kings of Egypt were called Pharaoh, for Pharaoh means a king—would come down to the river for a bath. She placed her baby boy in the ark, and let it float down the river where the princess, Pharaoh's daughter, would see it. She sent her own daughter, a little girl named Miriam, twelve years old, to watch close at hand. How anxious the mother and the sister were as they saw the little ark floating away from them on the river!

Pharaoh's daughter, with her maids, came down to the river, and they saw the ark floating on the water, among the reeds. She sent one of her maids to bring it to her so that she might see what was in the curious box. They opened it, and there was a beautiful little baby, who began to cry to be taken up.

The princess felt kind toward the little one, and loved it at once. She said, "This is one of the Hebrews' children." You have heard how the children of Israel came to be called Hebrews. Pharaoh's daughter thought that it would be cruel to let such a lovely baby as this die out on the water. Just then a little girl came running up to her, as if by accident, and she looked at the baby also, and she said: "Shall I go and find some woman of the Hebrews to be a nurse to the child for you and take care of it?"

"Yes," said the princess. "Go and find a nurse for me."

The little girl—who was Miriam, the baby's sister—ran as quickly as she could and brought the baby's own mother to the princess. Miriam showed in this act that she was a wise and thoughtful little girl. The princess said to the little baby's mother, "Take this child to your home and nurse it for me, and I will pay you wages for it."

How glad the Hebrew mother was to take her child home! No one could harm her boy now, for he was protected by the princess of Egypt, the daughter of the king.

When the child was large enough to leave his mother Pharaoh's daughter took him into her own house in the palace. She named him "Moses," a word that means, "Drawn out," because he was drawn out of the water.

Moses, the Hebrew boy, lived in the palace among the nobles of the land, as the son of the princess. There he learned much more than he could have learned among his own people; for there were very wise teachers. Moses gained all the knowledge that the Egyptians had to give. There in the court of the cruel king who had made slaves of the Israelites, God's people, was growing up our Israelite boy who would at some time set his people free!

Although Moses grew up among the Egyptians, and gained their learning, he loved his own people. They were poor and were hated, and were slaves, but he loved them, because they were the people who served the Lord God, while the Egyptians worshipped idols and animals. Strange it was that so wise a people as these should bow down and pray to an ox, or to a cat, or to a snake, as did the Egyptians.

When Moses became a man, he went among his own people, leaving the riches and ease that he might have enjoyed among the Egyptians. He felt a call from God to lift up the Israelites and set them free. At that time he found that he could do nothing to help them. They would not let him lead them, and as the king of Egypt had now become his enemy, Moses went away from Egypt into a country in Arabia, called Midian.

He was sitting by a well, in that land, tired from his long journey, when he saw some young women come to draw water for their flocks of sheep. Some rough men came, and drove the women away, and took the water for their own flocks. Moses saw it, and helped the women and drew the water for them.

These young women were sisters, the daughters of a man named Jethro, who was a priest in the land of Midian. He asked Moses to live with him, and to help him in the care of his flocks. Moses stayed with Jethro and married one of his daughters. So from being a prince in the king's palace in Egypt, Moses became a shepherd in the wilderness of Midian.

Moses did not remain a shepherd. While he was tending his sheep God appeared to him in a burning bush and told him that he should return to Egypt and become the leader of his people. The Lord told him that the wicked Egyptians would be punished for the ill-treatment they were giving the Israelites. In your Bible, you will find in the book of Exodus how God wonderfully fulfilled his promise. The Egyptians were punished by many plagues, and finally allowed the Israelites to go. They crossed the Red Sea in a wonderful way, and traveled for a long time through a wilderness, where God fed them day by day with manna from heaven. God also gave them rules as a guide for their daily living; these rules we call the Ten Commandments; yet they forgot the Lord so far as to make images and worship them.

The Story of Gideon and His Three Hundred Soldiers

At last the people of Israel came into the promised land, but they did evil in the sight of the Lord in worshipping Baal; and the Lord left them to suffer for their sins. Once the Midianites, living near the desert on the east of Israel, came against the tribes. The two tribes that suffered the hardest fate were Ephraim, and the part of Manasseh on the west of Jordan. For seven years the Midianites swept over their land every year, just at the time of harvest, and carried away all the crops of grain, until the Israelites had no food for themselves, and none for their sheep and cattle. The Midianites brought also their own flocks and camels without number, which ate all the grass of the field.

The people of Israel were driven away from their villages and their farms, and were compelled to hide in the caves of the mountains. If any Israelite could raise any grain, he buried it in pits covered with earth, or in empty winepresses, where the Midianites could not find it.

One day, a man named Gideon was threshing out wheat in a hidden place, when he saw an angel sitting-under an oak-tree. The angel said to him, "You are a brave man, Gideon, and the Lord is with you. Go out boldly, and save your people from the power of the Midianites." Gideon answered the angel:

"O, Lord, how can I save Israel? Mine is a poor family in Manasseh, and I am the least in my father's house."

The Lord said to him: "Surely I will be With you, and I will help you drive out the Midianites."

Gideon felt that it was the Lord who was talking with him, in the form of an angel. He brought an offering, and laid it on a rock before the angel. Then the angel touched the offering with his staff. At once, a fire leaped up and burned the offering; and then the angel vanished from his sight. Gideon was afraid when he saw this; but the Lord said to him: "Peace be unto you, Gideon, do not fear, for I am with you."

On the spot where the Lord appeared to Gideon, under an oak tree, near the village of Ophrah, in the tribe-land of Manasseh, Gideon built an altar and called it by a name that means, "The Lord is peace." This altar was standing long afterward in that place.

Then the Lord told Gideon that before setting his people free from the Midianites, he must first set them free from the service of Baal and Asherah, the two idols most worshipped among them. Near the house of Gideon's own father stood an altar to Baal, and the image of Asherah.

On that night, Gideon went out with ten men, threw down the image of Baal, cut in pieces the wooden image of Asherah, and destroyed the altar before these idols. In its place he built an altar to the God of Israel; and on it laid the broken pieces of the idols for wood, and with them offered a young ox as a burnt-offering.

On the next morning, when the people of the village went out to worship their idols, they found them cut in pieces, the altar taken away; in its place an altar of the Lord, and on it the pieces of the Asherah were burning as wood under a sacrifice to the Lord. The people looked at the broken and burning idols; and they said, "Who has done this?"

Some one said: "Gideon, the son of Joash, did this last night."

Then they came to Joash, Gideon's father, and said:

"We are going to kill your son because he has destroyed the image of Baal, who is our god."

Joash, Gideon's father, said: "If Baal is a god, he can take care of himself, and punish the man who has destroyed his image. Why should you help Baal? Let Baal help himself."

When they saw that Baal could not harm the man who had broken down his altar and his image, the people turned from Baal, back to their own Lord God.

Gideon sent messengers through all Manasseh on the west of Jordan, and the tribes near on the north; and the men of the tribes gathered around him, with a few swords and spears, but very few, for the Israelites were not ready for war. They met beside a great spring on Mount Gilboa, called "the fountain of Harod." Mount Gilboa is one of the three mountains on the east of the Plain of Esdraelon, or the plain of Jezreel, where once there had been a great battle. On the plain, stretching up the side of another of these mountains, called "the Hill of Moreh," was the camp of a vast Midianite army. For as soon as the Midianites heard that Gideon had undertaken to set his people free, they came against him with a mighty host.

Gideon was a man of faith. He wished to be sure that God was leading him, and he prayed to God and said:

"O Lord God, give me some sign that thou wilt save Israel through me. Here is a fleece of wool on this threshing floor. If to-morrow morning the fleece is wet with dew, while the grass around it is dry, then I shall know that thou art with me; and that thou wilt give me victory over the Midianites."

Very early the next morning, Gideon came to look at the fleece. He found it wringing wet with dew, while all around the grass was dry. But Gideon was not yet satisfied. He said to the Lord:

"O Lord, be not angry with me; but give me just one more sign. To-morrow morning let the fleece be dry, and let the dew fall all around it, and then I will doubt no more."

The next morning, Gideon found the grass, and the bushes wet with dew, while the fleece of wool was dry. Gideon was now sure that God had called him, and that God would give him victory over the enemies of Israel.

The Lord said to Gideon: "Your army is too large. If Israel should win the victory, they would say, 'we won it by our own might.' Send home all those who are afraid to fight."

For many of the people were frightened, as they looked at the host of their enemies, and the Lord knew that these men would only hinder the rest in the battle. So Gideon sent word through the camp:

"Whoever is afraid of the enemy may go home." Twenty-two thousand people went away, leaving only ten thousand in Gideon's army. But the army was stronger though it was smaller, for the cowards had gone, and only the brave men were left.

The Lord said to Gideon: "The people are yet too many. You need only a few of the bravest and best men to fight in this battle. Bring the men down the mountain, past the water, and I will show you there how to find the men whom you need."

In the morning Gideon, by God's command called his ten thousand men out, and made them march down the hill, just as though they were going to attack the enemy. As they were beside the water, he noticed how they drank, and set them apart in two companies, according to their way of drinking.

When they came to the water, most of the men threw aside their shields and spears, and knelt down and scooped up a draft of the water with both hands together like a cup. These men Gideon commanded to stand in one company.

There were a few men who did not stop to take a large draft of water. Holding spear and shield in the right hand, to be ready for the enemy if one should suddenly appear, they merely caught up a handful of the water in passing and marched on, lapping up the water from one hand. God said to Gideon:

"Set by themselves these men who lapped up each a handful of water. These are the men whom I have chosen to set Israel free."

Gideon counted these men, and found that there were only three hundred of them, while all the rest bowed down on their faces to drink. The difference between them was that the three hundred were earnest men, of one purpose; not turning aside from their aim even to drink, as the others did. Then, too, they were watchful men, always ready to meet their enemies.

Gideon, at God's command, sent back to the camp on Mount Gilboa all the rest of his army, nearly ten thousand men, keeping with himself only his little band of three hundred.

Gideon's plan did not need a large army; but it needed a few careful, bold men, who should do exactly as their leader commanded them. He gave to each man a lamp, a pitcher, and a trumpet, and told the men just what was to be done with them. The lamp was lighted, but was placed inside the pitcher, so that it could not be seen. He divided his men into three companies, and very quietly led them down the mountain in the middle of the night, and arranged them all in order around the camp of the Midianites.

Then at one moment a great shout rang out in the darkness, "The sword of the Lord and of Gideon," and after it came a crash of breaking pitchers, and then a flash of light in every direction. The three hundred men had given the shout, and broken their pitchers, so that on every side lights were shining. The men blew their trumpets with a mighty noise; and the Midianites were roused from sleep, to see enemies all round them, lights beaming and swords flashing, while everywhere the sharp sound of the trumpets was heard.

They were filled with sudden terror, and thought only of escape, not of fighting. But wherever they turned, their enemies seemed to be standing with swords drawn. They trampled each other down to death, flying from the Israelites. Their own land was in the east, across the river Jordan, and they fled in that direction, down one of the valleys between the mountains.

The war against Gideon

Gideon had thought that the Midianites would turn toward their own land, if they should be beaten in the battle, and he had already planned to cut off their flight. The ten thousand men in the camp he had placed on the sides of the valley leading to the Jordan. There they slew very many of the Midianites as they fled down the steep pass toward the river. And Gideon had also sent to the men of the tribe of Ephraim, who had thus far taken no part in the war, to hold the only place at the river where men could wade through the water. Those of the Midianites who had escaped from Gideon's men on either side of the valley were now met by the Ephraimites at the river, and many more of them were slain. Among the slain were two of the princes of the Midianites, named Oreb and Zeeb.

A part of the Midianite army was able to get across the river and to continue its flight toward the desert; but Gideon and his brave three hundred men followed closely after them, fought another battle with them, destroyed them utterly, and took their two kings, Zebah and Zalmunna, whom he killed. After this great victory, the Israelites were freed forever from the Midianites. They never again ventured to leave their home in the desert to make war on the tribes of Israel.

After this, as long as Gideon lived, he ruled as Judge in Israel. The people wished him to make himself a king.

"Rule over us as king," they said, "and let your son be king after you, and his son king after him."

Gideon said:

"No, you have a king already; for the Lord God is the King of Israel. No one but God shall be king over these tribes."

Of all the fifteen men who ruled as Judges of Israel, Gideon, the fifth Judge, was the greatest, in courage, in wisdom, and in faith in God.

The Story of Samson, the Strong Man

Now we are to learn of three judges who ruled Israel in turn. Their names were Ibzan, Elon, and Abdon. None of these were men of war, and in their days the land was quiet.

But the people of Israel again began to worship idols; and as a punishment God allowed them once more to pass under the power of their enemies. The seventh oppression, which now fell upon Israel, was by far the hardest, the longest and the most widely spread of any, for it was over all the tribes. It came from the Philistines, a strong and warlike people who lived on the west of Israel upon the plain beside the Great Sea. They worshipped an idol called Dagon, which was made in the form of a fish's head on a man's body.

These people, the Philistines, sent their armies up from the plain beside the sea to the mountains of Israel and overran all the land. They took away from the Israelites all their swords and spears, so that they could not fight; and they robbed their land of all the crops, so that the people suffered for want of food. As before, the Israelites in their trouble, cried out to the Lord, and the Lord heard their prayer.

In the tribe-land of Dan, which was next to the country of the Philistines, there was living a man named Manoah. One day an angel came to his wife and said:

"You shall have a son, and when he grows up he will begin to save Israel from the hand of the Philistines. But your son must never drink any wine or strong drink as long as he lives. And his hair must be allowed to grow long and must never be cut, for he shall be a Nazarite under a vow to the Lord."

When a child was given especially to God, or when a man gave himself to some work for God, he was forbidden to drink wine, and as a sign, his hair was left to grow long while the vow or promise to God was upon him. Such a person as this was called a Nazarite, a word which means "one who has a vow"; and Manoah's child was to be a Nazarite, and under a vow, as long as he lived.

The child was born and was named Samson. He grew up to become the strongest man of whom the Bible tells. Samson was no general, like Gideon or Jephthah, to call out his people and lead them in war. He did much to set his people free; but all that he did was by his own strength.

When Samson became a young man he went down to Timnath, in the land of the Philistines. There he saw a young Philistine woman whom he loved, and wished to have as his wife. His father and mother were not pleased that he should marry among the enemies of his own people. They did not know that God would make this marriage the means of bringing harm upon the Philistines and of helping the Israelites.

As Samson was going down to Timnath to see this young woman, a hungry lion came out of the mountain, roaring against him. Samson seized the lion, tore him in pieces as easily as another man would have killed a little kid of the goats, and then went on his way. He made his visit and came home, but said nothing to any one about the lion.

After a time Samson went again to Timnath for his marriage with the Philistine woman. On his way he stopped to look at the dead lion; and in its body he found a swarm of bees, and honey which they had made. He took some of the honey and ate it as he walked, but told no one of it.

Samson slaying the lion

At the wedding-feast, which lasted a whole week, there were many Philistine young men, and they amused each other with questions and riddles.

"I will give you a riddle," said Samson. "If you answer it during the feast, I will give you thirty suits of clothing; and if you cannot answer it then you must give me the thirty suits of clothing." "Let us hear your riddle," they said. This was Samson's riddle:

"Out of the eater came forth meat, And out of the strong came forth sweetness."

They could not find the answer, though they tried to find it all that day and the two days that followed. At last they came to Samson's wife and said to her:

"Coax your husband to tell you the answer. If you do not find it out, we will set your house on fire, and burn you and all your people."

Samson's wife urged him to tell her the answer. She cried and pleaded with him and said:

"If you really loved me, you would not keep this a secret from me."

At last Samson yielded, and told his wife how he had killed the lion and afterward found the honey in its body. She told her people, and just before the end of the feast they came to Samson with the answer. They said:

"What is sweeter than honey? And what is stronger than a lion?" Samson said to them:

"If you had not plowed with my heifer,
You had not found out my riddle."

By his "heifer,"—which is a young cow,—of course Samson meant his wife. Then Samson was required to give them thirty suits of clothing. He went out among the Philistines, killed the first thirty men whom he found, took off their clothes, and gave them to the guests at the feast. All this made Samson very angry. He left his wife and went home to his father's house. Then the parents of his wife gave her to another man.

After a time Samson's anger passed away, and he went again to Timnath to see his wife. But her father said to him:

"You went away angry, and I supposed that you cared nothing for her. I gave her to another man, and now she is his wife. But here is her younger sister; you can have her for your wife, instead."

Samson would not take his wife's sister. He went out very angry; determined to do harm to the Philistines, because they had cheated him. He caught all the wild foxes that he could find, until he had three hundred of them. Then he tied them together in pairs, by their tails; and between each pair of foxes he tied to their tails a piece of dry wood which he set on fire. These foxes with firebrands on their tails he turned loose among the fields of the Philistines when the grain was ripe. They ran wildly over the fields, set the grain on fire, and burned it; and with the grain, the olive trees in the fields.

When the Philistines saw their harvests destroyed, they said, "Who has done this?"

The people said, "Samson did this, because his wife was given by her father to another man."

The Philistines looked on Samson's father-in-law as the cause of their loss; and they came and set his home on fire, and burned the man and his daughter whom Samson had married. Then Samson came down again, and alone fought a company of Philistines, and killed them all, as a punishment for burning his wife.

After this Samson went to live in a hollow place in a split rock, called the rock of Etam.

The Philistines came up in a great army, and overran the fields in the tribe-land of Judah.

"Why do you come against us?" asked the men of Judah, "what do you want from us?"

"We have come," they said, "to bind Samson, and to deal with him as he has dealt with us."

The men of Judah said to Samson:

"Do you not know that the Philistines are ruling over us? Why do you make them angry by killing their people? You see that we suffer through your pranks. Now we must bind you and give you to the Philistines, or they will ruin us all."

Samson said, "I will let you bind me, if you will promise not to kill me yourselves; but only to give me safely into the hands of the Philistines."

They made the promise; and Samson gave himself up to them, and allowed them to tie him up fast with new ropes. The Philistines shouted for joy as they saw their enemy brought to them, led in bonds by his own people. As soon as Samson came among them, he burst the bonds as though they had been light strings; and picked up from the ground the jawbone of an ass, and struck right and left with it as with a sword. He killed almost a thousand of the Philistines with this strange weapon. Afterward he sang a song about it, thus:

"With the jawbone of an ass,
heaps upon heaps,
With the jawbone of an ass,
I have slain a thousand men."

After this Samson went down to the chief city of the Philistines, which was named Gaza. It was a large city; and like all large cities, was surrounded with a high wall. When the men of Gaza found Samson in their city, they shut the gates, thinking that they could now hold him as a prisoner. But in the night Samson rose up, went to the gates, pulled their posts out of the ground, and put the gates with their posts upon his shoulder. He carried off the gates of the city and left them on the top of a hill not far from the city of Hebron.

After this Samson saw another woman among the Philistines, and he loved her. The name of this woman was Delilah. The rulers of the Philistines came to Delilah and said to her:

"Find out, if you can, what it is that makes Samson so strong, and tell us. If you help us to get control of him, so that we can have him in our power, we will give you a great sum of money."

Delilah coaxed and pleaded with Samson to tell her what it was that made him so strong. Samson said to her:

"If they will tie me with seven green twigs from a tree, then I shall not be strong any more."

They brought her seven green twigs, like those of a willow tree; and she bound Samson with them while he was asleep. Then she called out to him:

"Wake up, Samson; the Philistines are coming against you!"

Samson rose up and broke the twigs as easily as if they had been charred in the fire, and went away with ease.

Samson and Delilah

Delilah tried again to find his secret. She said:

"You are only making fun of me. Now tell me truly how you can be bound." Samson said:

Samson, to rejoice over him; and Samson was led into the court of the temple, before all the people, to amuse them. After a time, Samson said to the boy who was leading him:

"Take me up to the front of the temple, so that I may stand by one of the pillars, and lean against it."

While Samson stood between the two pillars, he prayed:

"O Lord God, remember me, I pray thee, and give me strength, only this once, O God: and help me, that I may obtain vengeance upon the Philistines for my two eyes!"

Then he placed one arm around the pillar on one side, and the other arm around the pillar on the other side; and he said, "Let me die with the Philistines."

He bowed forward with all his might, and pulled the pillars over with him, bringing down the roof and all upon it upon those that were under it. Samson himself was among the dead; but in his death he killed more of the Philistines than he had killed during his life.

Then in the terror which came upon the Philistines the men of Samson's tribe came down and found his dead body, and buried it in their own land. After that, it was years before the Philistines tried again to rule over the Israelites.

Samson did much to set his people free; but he might have done much more, if he had led his people, instead of trusting alone to his own strength; and if he had lived more earnestly, and not done his deeds as though he was playing pranks. There were deep faults in Samson, but at the end he sought God's help, and found it, and God used Samson to set his people free.

Bible Stories

The Death of Samson

The Story of Ruth, the Gleaner

In the time of the Judges in Israel, a man named Elimelech was living in the town of Bethlehem, in the tribe of Judah, about six miles south of Jerusalem. His wife's name was Naomi, and his two sons were Mahlon and Chilion. For some years the crops were poor, and food was scarce in Judah; and Elimelech with his family went to live in the land of Moab, which was on the east of the Dead Sea, as Judah was on the west.

There they stayed ten years, and in that time, Elimelech died. His two sons married women of the country of Moab, one named Orpah, the other named Ruth. The two young men also died in the land of Moab; so that Naomi and her two daughters-in-law were all left widows.

Naomi heard that God had again given good harvests and bread to the land of Judah, and she rose up to go from Moab back to her own land and her own town of Bethlehem. The two daughters-in-law loved her, and both would have gone with her, though the land of Judah was a strange land to them, for they were of the Moabite people.

Naomi said to them, "Go back, my daughters, to your own mothers' homes. May the Lord deal kindly with you, as you have been kind to your husbands and to me. May the Lord grant that each of you may yet find another husband and a happy home."

Then Naomi kissed them in farewell, and the three women all wept together. The two young widows said to her:

"You have been a good mother to us, and we will go with you, and live among your people."

"No, no," said Naomi. "You are young, and I am old. Go back and be happy among your own people."

Then Orpah kissed Naomi, and went back to her people; but Ruth would not leave her. She said:

Naomi and Her Daughters-In-Law

"Do not ask me to leave you, for I never will. Where you go, I will go; where you live, I will live; your people shall be my people; and your God shall be my God. Where you die, I will die, and be buried. Nothing but death itself shall part you and me."

When Naomi saw that Ruth was firm in her purpose, she ceased trying to persuade her, so the two women went on together. They walked around the Dead Sea, crossed the river Jordan, climbed the mountains of Judah, and came to Bethlehem.

Naomi had been absent from Bethlehem for ten years, but her friends were all glad to see her again. They said:

"Is this Naomi, whom we knew years ago?"

Now the name Naomi means "pleasant." Naomi said:

"Call me not Naomi; call me Mara, for the Lord has made my life bitter. I went out full, with my husband and two sons; now I come home empty, without them. Do not call me 'Pleasant,' call me 'Bitter.'"

The name "Mara," by which Naomi wished to be called means "bitter." Naomi learned later that "Pleasant" was the right name after all.

There was living in Bethlehem at that time a very rich man named Boaz. He owned large fields that were abundant in their harvests; and he was related to the family of Elimelech, Naomi's husband, who had died.

It was the custom in Israel when they reaped the grain not to gather all the stalks, but to leave some for the poor people, who followed the reapers with their sickles, and gathered what was left. When Naomi and Ruth came to Bethlehem, it was the time of the barley harvest; and Ruth went out into the fields to glean the grain that the reapers had left. It so happened that she was gleaning in the field that belonged to Boaz, this rich man.

Boaz came out from the town to see his men reaping, and he said to them, "The Lord be with you"; and they answered him, "The Lord bless you."

Ruth and Boaz

Boaz said to his master of the reapers: "Who is this young woman that I see gleaning in the field?"

The man answered: "It is the young woman from the land of Moab, who came with Naomi. She asked leave to glean after the reapers, and has been here gathering grain since yesterday."

Then Boaz said to Ruth, "Listen to me, my daughter. Do not go to any other field, but stay here with my young women. No one shall harm you; and when you are thirsty, go and drink at our vessels of water."

Then Ruth bowed to Boaz, and thanked him for his kindness, even more kind because she was a stranger in Israel. Boaz said, "I have heard how true you have been to your mother-in-law Naomi, in leaving your own land and coming with her to this land. May the Lord, under whose wings you have come, give you a reward!"

At noon, when they sat down to rest and to eat, Boaz gave her some of the food. And he said to the reapers:

"When you are reaping, leave some of the sheaves for her; and drop out some sheaves from the bundles, where she may gather them."

That evening, Ruth showed Naomi how much she had gleaned, and told her of the rich man Boaz, who had been so kind to her. Naomi said:

"This man is a near relation of ours. Stay in his fields, as long as the harvest lasts." So Ruth gleaned in the fields of Boaz until the harvest had been gathered.

At the end of the harvest, Boaz held a feast on the threshing-floor. After the feast, by the advice of Naomi, Ruth went to him, and said to him:

"You are a near relation of my husband and of his father, Elimelech. Now won't you do good to us for his sake?"

When Boaz saw Ruth, he loved her; and soon after this he took her as his wife. Naomi and Ruth went to live in his home; so that Naomi's life was no more bitter, but pleasant. And Boaz and Ruth had a son, whom they named Obed; and later Obed had a son named Jesse; and Jesse was the father of David, the shepherd boy who became king. So Ruth, the young woman of Moab, who chose the people and the God of Israel, became the mother of kings.

The Story of David, the Shepherd Boy

Living at Ramah, in the mountains of Ephraim, there was a man whose name was Elkanah. He had two wives, as did many men in that time. One of these wives had children, but the other wife, whose name was Hannah, had no child.

Every year Elkanah and his family went up to worship at the house of the Lord in Shiloh, which was about fifteen miles from his home. At one of these visits Hannah prayed to the Lord, saying:

"O Lord, if thou wilt look upon me, and give me a son, he shall be given to the Lord as long as he lives."

The Lord heard Hannah's prayer, and gave her a little boy, and she called his name Samuel, which means "Asked of God", because he had been given in answer to her prayer.

Samuel grew up to be a good man and a wise Judge, and he made his sons Judges in Israel, to help him in the care of the people. But Samuel's sons did not walk in his ways. They did not try always to do justly.

The elders of all the tribes of Israel came to Samuel at his home in Ramah; and they said to him, "You are growing old, and your sons do not rule as well as you ruled. All the lands around us have kings. Let us have a king also; and do you choose the king for us."

This was not pleasing to Samuel. He tried to make the people change their minds, and showed them what trouble a king would bring them.

They would not follow his advice. They said: "No; we will have a king to reign over us."

Samuel chose as their king a tall young man named Saul, who was a farmer's son of the tribe of Benjamin. When Saul was brought before the people he stood head and shoulders above them all. Samuel said:

"Look at the man whom the Lord has chosen! There is not another like him among all the people!"

All the people shouted, "God save the king! Long live the king!"

Then Samuel told the people what should be the laws for the king and for the people to obey. He wrote them down in a book, and placed the book before the Lord. Then Samuel sent the people home; and Saul went back to his own house at a place called Gibeah; and with Saul went a company of men to whose hearts God had given a love for the king.

After three hundred years under the fifteen Judges, Israel now had a king. But among the people there were some who were not pleased with the new king, because he was an unknown man from the farm. They said:

"Can such a man as this save us?"

They showed no respect to the king, and in their hearts looked down upon him. Saul said nothing, and showed his wisdom by appearing not to notice them. But in another thing he was not so wise. He forgot to heed the old prophet's advice and instructions about ruling wisely and doing as the Lord said. It was not long before Samuel told him that he had disobeyed God and would lose his kingdom.

When Samuel told Saul that the Lord would take away the kingdom from him, he did not mean that Saul should lose the kingdom at once. He was no longer God's king; and as soon as the right man in God's sight should be found, and should be trained for his duty as king, then God would take away Saul's power, and would give it to the man whom God had chosen. But it was years before this came to pass.

The Lord said to Samuel: "Do not weep and mourn any longer over Saul, for I have refused him as king. Fill the horn with oil, and go to Bethlehem in Judah. There find a man named Jesse, for I have chosen a king among his sons."

Samuel knew that Saul would be very angry, if he should learn that Samuel had named any other man as king. He said to the Lord:

"How can I go? If Saul hears of it, he will kill me."

The Lord said to Samuel: "Take a young cow with you; and tell the people that you have come to make an offering to the Lord. Call Jesse and his sons to the sacrifice. I will tell you what to do, and you shall anoint the one whom I name to you."

Samuel went over the mountains southward from Ramah to Bethlehem, about ten miles, leading a cow. The rulers of the town were alarmed at his coming, for they feared that he had come to judge the people for some evil-doing. Samuel said:

"I have come in peace to make an offering and to hold a feast to the Lord. Prepare yourselves and come to the sacrifice."

He invited Jesse and his sons to the service. When they came, he looked at the sons of Jesse very closely. The oldest was named Eliab, and he was so tall and noble looking that Samuel thought:

"Surely this young man must be the one whom God has chosen."

But the Lord said to Samuel:

"Do not look on his face, or on the height of his body, for I have not chosen him. Man judges by the outward looks, but God looks at the heart."

Then Jesse's second son, named Abinadab, passed by. The Lord said: "I have not chosen this one." Seven young men came and Samuel said:

"None of these is the man whom God has chosen. Are these all your children?"

"There is one more," said Jesse, "the youngest of all. He is a boy, in the field caring for the sheep."

Samuel said:

"Send for him; for we will not sit down until he comes." So after a time the youngest son was brought in. His name was David, a word that means "darling," and he was a beautiful boy, perhaps fifteen years old, with fresh cheeks and bright eyes.

As soon as the young David came, the Lord said to Samuel:

"Arise; anoint him, for this is the one whom I have chosen."

Then Samuel poured oil on David's head, in the presence of all his brothers. No one knew at that time the anointing to mean that David was to be the king. Perhaps they thought that David was chosen to be a prophet like Samuel.

From that time, the Spirit of God came upon David, and he began to show signs of coming greatness. He went back to his sheep on the hillsides around Bethlehem, but God was with him.

David grew up strong and brave, not afraid of the wild beasts that prowled around and tried to carry away his sheep. More than once he fought with lions, and bears, and killed them, when they seized the lambs of his flock. David, alone all day, practiced throwing stones in a sling, until he could strike exactly the place for which he aimed. When he swung his sling, he knew that the stone would go to the very spot at which he was throwing it.

Young as he was, David thought of God, and talked with God, and God talked with David, and showed to David His will.

After Saul had disobeyed the voice of the Lord, the Spirit of the Lord left Saul, and no longer spoke to him. Saul became very sad of heart. At times a madness would come upon him, and at all times he was very unhappy. The servants of Saul noticed that when some one played on the harp and sang, Saul's spirit was made more cheerful; and the sadness of soul left him. At one time Saul said: "Find some one who can play well, and bring him to me. Let me listen to music; for it drives away my sadness."

One of the young men said: "I have seen a young man, a son of Jesse in Bethlehem, who can play well. He is handsome in his looks, and agreeable in talking. I have also heard that he is a brave young man, who can fight as well as he can play, and the Lord is with him."

Then Saul sent a message to Jesse, David's father. He said: "Send me your son David, who is with the sheep. Let him come and play before me."

Then David came to Saul, bringing with him a present for the king from Jesse. When Saul saw him, he loved him, as did everybody who saw the young David. David played on the harp, and sang before Saul. And David's music cheered Saul's heart, and drove away his sad feelings.

Saul liked David so well that he made him his armor bearer; and David carried the shield and spear, and sword for Saul, when the king was before his army. But Saul did not know that David had been anointed by Samuel.

After a time, Saul seemed well; and David returned to Bethlehem and was once more among his sheep in the field. Perhaps it was at this time that David sang his shepherd song, or it may have been long afterward, when David looked back in thought to those days when he was leading his sheep. This is the song, which you have heard often:

"The Lord is my shepherd; I shall not want.

He maketh me to lie down in green pastures;
He leadeth me beside the still waters,
He restoreth my soul;
He leadeth me in the paths of righteousness for his name's sake.
Yea, though I walk through the valley of the shadow of death,
I will fear no evil; for thou art with me;
Thy rod and thy staff, they comfort me.
Thou preparest a table before me in the presence of mine enemies;
Thou anointest my head with oil; my cup runneth over.

Surely, goodness and mercy shall follow me all the days of my life:

And I will dwell in the house of the Lord forever."

The Story of the Fight with the Giant

All through the reign of Saul, there was constant war with the Philistines, who lived upon the lowlands west of Israel. At one time, when David was still with his sheep, a few years after he had been anointed by Samuel, the camps of the Philistines and the Israelites were set against each other on opposite sides of the valley of Elah. In the army of Israel were the three oldest brothers of David.

Every day a giant came out of the camp of the Philistines, and dared some one to come from the Israelites' camp and fight with him. The giant's name was Goliath. He was nine feet high; and he wore armor from head to foot, and carried a spear twice as long and as heavy as any other man could hold; and his shield bearer walked before him. He came every day and called out across the little valley:

"I am a Philistine, and you are servants of Saul. Now choose one of your men, and let him come out and fight with me. If I kill him; then you shall submit to us; and if he kills me, then we will give up to you. Come, now, send out your man!"

But no man in the army, not even King Saul, dared to go out and fight with the giant. Forty days the camps stood against each other, and the Philistine giant continued his call.

One day, old Jesse, the father of David, sent David from Bethlehem to visit his three brothers in the army. David came, and spoke to his brothers; and while he was talking with them, Goliath the giant came out as before in front of the camp calling for some one to fight with him.

They said one to another:

"If any man will go out and kill this Philistine, the king will give him a great reward and a high rank; and the king's daughter shall be his wife."

David said:

"Who is this man that speaks in this proud manner against the armies of the living God? Why does not some one go out and kill him?"

David's brother Eliab said to him:

"What are you doing here, leaving your sheep in the field? I know that you have come down just to see the battle."

David did not care for his brother's words. He thought he saw a way to kill this boasting giant; and he said:

"If no one else will go, I will go out and fight with this enemy of the Lord's people."

They brought David before King Saul. Some years had passed since Saul had met David, and he had grown from a boy to a man, so that Saul did not know him as the shepherd who had played on the harp before him in other days.

Saul said to David:

"You cannot fight with this great giant. You are very young; and he is a man of war, trained from his youth."

David answered King Saul:

"I am only a shepherd, but I have fought with lions and bears, when they have tried to steal my sheep. And I am not afraid to fight with this Philistine."

Then Saul put his own armor on David—a helmet on his head, and a coat of mail on his body, and a sword at his waist. However, Saul was almost a giant, and his armor was far too large for David. David said:

"I am not used to fighting with such weapons as these. Let me fight in my own way."

So David took off Saul's armor. While everybody in the army had been looking on the giant with fear, David had been thinking out the best way for fighting him; and God had given to David a plan. It was to throw the giant off his guard, by appearing weak and helpless; and while so far away that the giant could not reach him with sword or spear, to strike him down with a weapon that the giant would not expect and would not be prepared for.

David took his shepherd's staff in his hand, as though that were to be his weapon. But out of sight, in a bag under his mantle, he had five smooth stones carefully chosen, and a sling,—the weapon that he knew how to use. Then he came out to meet the Philistine.

The giant looked down on the youth and despised him, and laughed.

"Am I a dog?" he said, "that this boy comes to me with a staff? I will give his body to the birds of the air, and the beasts of the field."

The Philistine cursed David by the gods of his people. And David answered him:

"You come against me with a sword, and a spear, and a dart; but I come to you in the name of the Lord of hosts, the God of the armies of Israel. This day will the Lord give you into my hand. I will strike you down, and take off your head, and the host of the Philistines shall be dead bodies, to be eaten by the birds and the beasts; so that all may know that there is a God in Israel, and that He can save in other ways besides with sword and spear."

David ran toward the Philistine, as if to fight him with his shepherd's staff. But when he was just near enough for a good aim, he took out his sling, and hurled a stone aimed at the giant's forehead. David's aim was good; the stone struck the Philistine in his forehead. It stunned him, and he fell to the ground.

Israelites attacking the Philistines

While the two armies stood wondering, and scarcely knowing what had caused the giant to fall so suddenly, David ran forward, drew out the giant's own sword, and cut off his head. Then the Philistines knew that their great warrior in whom they trusted was dead. They turned to flee to their own land; and the Israelites followed them, and killed them by the hundred and the thousand, even to the gates of their own city of Gath.

So in that day David won a great victory and stood before all the land as the one who had saved his people from their enemies.

The Story of Solomon and His Temple

During the later years of David's reign, he laid up great treasure of gold and silver, and brass, and iron, for the building of a house to the Lord on Mount Moriah. This house was to be called "The Temple"; and it was to be made very beautiful, the most beautiful building, and the richest in all the land. David had greatly desired to build this house while he was king of Israel, but God said to him:

"You have been a man of war, and have fought many battles, and shed much blood. My house shall be built by a man of peace. When you die, your son Solomon shall reign, and he shall have peace, and shall build my house."

So David made ready great store of precious things for the temple; also stone and cedar to be used in the building. David said to Solomon, his son: "God has promised that there shall be rest and peace to the land while you are king; and the Lord will be with you, and you shall build a house, where God shall live among His people."

But David had other sons who were older than Solomon; and one of these sons, whose name was Adonijah, formed a plan to make himself king. David was now very old; and he was no longer able to go out of his palace, and to be seen among the people.

King David

Adonijah gathered his friends; and among them were Joab, the General of the Army, and Abiathar, one of the two high-priests. They met at a place outside the wall, and had a great feast, and were about to crown Adonijah as king, when word came to David in the palace. David, though old and feeble, was still wise. He said:

"Let us make Solomon king at once and thus put an end to the plans of these men."

At David's command they brought out the mule on which no one but the king was allowed to ride; and they placed Solomon upon it; and with the king's guards, and the nobles, and the great men, they brought the young Solomon down to the valley of Gihon, south of the city.

Zadok, the priest, took from the Tabernacle the horn filled with holy oil, that was used for anointing or pouring oil on the head of the priests when they were set apart for their work. He poured oil from this horn on the head of Solomon, and then the priests blew the trumpets, and all the people cried aloud, "God save King Solomon."

All this time Adonijah and Joab, and their friends were not far away, almost in the same valley, feasting and making merry, intending to make Adonijah king. They heard the sound of the trumpets, and the shouting of the people. Joab said: "What is the cause of all this noise and uproar?"

A moment later, Jonathan, the son of Abiathar, came running in. Jonathan said to the men who were feasting:

"Our lord King David has made Solomon king, and he has just been anointed in Gihon; and all the princes, and the heads of the army, are with him, and the people are shouting, 'God save King Solomon!' David has sent from his bed a message to Solomon, saying, 'May the Lord make your name greater than mine has been! Blessed be the Lord, who has given me a son to sit this day on my throne!'"

When Adonijah and his friends heard this, they were filled with fear. Every man went at once to his house, except Adonijah. He hastened to the altar of the Lord, knelt before it, and took hold of the horns that were on its corners in front. This was a holy place, and he hoped that there Solomon might have mercy on him. Solomon said:

"If Adonijah will do right, and be faithful to me as the king of Israel, no harm shall come to him; but if he does wrong, he shall die."

Then Adonijah came and bowed down before King Solomon, and promised to obey him, and Solomon said, "Go to your own house."

Not long after this David sent for Solomon, and from his bed he gave his last advice to Solomon. Soon after that David died, an old man, having reigned in all forty years, seven years over the tribe of Judah, at Hebron, and thirty-three years over all Israel, in Jerusalem. He was buried in great honor on Mount Zion, and his tomb remained standing for many years.

The great work of Solomon's reign was the building of the House of God. It was generally called the Temple. It was built on Mount Moriah, one of the hills of Jerusalem. King David had prepared for it by gathering great stores of silver, stone and cedar-wood. The walls were made of stone and the roof of cedar. Solomon had great ships that visited other lands and brought precious stones and fine woods for the building. Seven years were spent in building the Temple, and it was set apart to the worship of God with beautiful ceremonies in which Solomon, in his robes of state, took part.

Solomon was indeed a great king, and it was said that he was also the wisest man in the entire world. He wrote many of the wise sayings in the Book of Proverbs, and many more that have been lost.

Building the temple

The Story of Elijah, the Prophet

Bible Stories

One of the greatest of all the kings of the Ten Tribes was Jeroboam the second. Under him, the kingdom of Israel grew rich and strong. He conquered nearly all Syria, and made Samaria the greatest city of all those lands.

But though Syria went down, another nation was now rising to power—Assyria, on the eastern side of the river Tigris. Its capital was Nineveh, a great city, so vast that it would take three days for a man to walk around its walls. The Assyrians were beginning to conquer all the lands near them, and Israel was in danger of falling under their power.

One of the kings who ruled over Israel was named Ahab. He provoked the anger of the Lord. His wife, Jezebel, who was a worshiper of Baal, persuaded him to build an altar to the false god.

Elijah, a prophet of the Lord, was sent to him and proposed a test. Two altars were built; one to Jehovah and one to Baal. The priests of Baal called upon their god to send down fire; but there was no answer. Then Elijah called upon the Lord God of Abraham, Isaac and Israel, and fire came down and burnt up the offering.

The people turned upon the priests of Baal and killed them all. Later the wicked queen, Jezebel, coveted a vineyard for Ahab, and she caused Naboth, the owner of the vineyard, to be placed in front of the battle. When he was slain, Ahab took the vineyard.

Once more Elijah came and denounced Ahab and Jezebel, telling them that they had done wickedly, and that the Lord would punish them.

In a little while the prophet's words came true, for Ahab was slain in battle and Jezebel was put to death by order of King Jehu. Elijah was taken up to heaven in a chariot of fire.

Jezebel put to death

There was another prophet, a companion of Elijah, whose name was Elisha, a brave and courageous man who did not fail to deliver God's message.

Bible Stories

It happened that when Elisha was an old man there came to him King Joash, who had been made king when he was only seven years old. Joash was now a young man and was trying to do right in the sight of the Lord. But he felt the need of the prophet's aid, and he came to Elisha and said:

"My father, my father, you are more to Israel than its chariots and horsemen."

Elisha, though weak in body, was yet strong in soul. He told Joash to bring him a bow and arrows, and to open the window to the east, looking toward the land of Syria. Then Elisha caused the king to draw the bow; and he placed his hands on the king's hands. As the king shot an arrow, Elisha said:

"This is the arrow of victory; of victory over Syria; for you shall smite the Syrians in Aphek and shall destroy them."

It happened as Elisha had foretold and the Syrians were defeated and their cities taken.

The Story of the Fiery Furnace

There was in the land of Judah a wicked king named Jehoiakim, son of the good Josiah. While Jehoiakim was ruling over the land of Judah, Nebuchadnezzar, a great conqueror of the nations, came from Babylon with his army of Chaldean soldiers. He took the city of Jerusalem, and made Jehoiakim promise to submit to him as his master. When he went back to his own land he took with him all the gold and silver that he could find in the Temple; and he carried away as captives very many of the princes and nobles, the best people in the land of Judah.

When these Jews were brought to the land of Chaldea or Babylon, King Nebuchadnezzar gave orders to the prince, who had charge of his palace, to choose among these Jewish captives some young men who were of noble rank, and beautiful in their looks, and also quick and bright in their minds; young men who would be able to learn readily. These young men were to be placed under the care of wise men, who should teach them all that they knew, and fit them to stand before the king of Babylon, so that they might be his helpers to carry out his orders; and the king wished them to be wise, so that they might give him advice in ruling his people.

Among the young men thus chosen were four Jews, men who had been brought from Judah. By order of the king, the names of these men were changed. One of them, named Daniel, was to be called Belteshazzer; the other three young men were called Shadrach, Meshach and Abed-nego. They were taught in all the knowledge of the Chaldeans; and after three years of training they were taken into the king's palace.

King Nebuchadnezzar was pleased with them, more than with any others who stood before him. He found them wise and faithful in the work given to them, and able to rule over men under them. These four men came to the highest places in the kingdom of the Chaldeans.

At one time King Nebuchadnezzar caused a great image to be made, and to be covered with gold. This image he set up, as an idol to be worshipped, on the plain of Dura, near the city of Babylon. When it was finished, it stood upon its base or foundation almost a hundred feet high;

so that upon the plain it could be seen far away. Then the king sent out a command for all the princes, and rulers, and nobles in the land, to come to a great gathering, when the image was to be set apart for worship.

The great men of the kingdom came from far and near and stood around the image. Among them, by command of the king, were Daniel's three friends, the young Jews, Shadrach, Meshach, and Abed-nego. For some reason, Daniel himself was not there. He may have been busy with the work of the kingdom in some other place.

At one moment in the service before the image, all the trumpets sounded, the drums were beaten, and music was made upon musical instruments of all kinds, as a signal for all the people to kneel down and worship the great golden image. But while the people were kneeling, there were three men who stood up, and would not bow down. These were the three young Jews, Shadrach, Meshach, and Abed-nego. They knelt down before the Lord God only.

Many of the nobles had been jealous of these young men, because they had been lifted to high places in the rule of the kingdom; and these men who hated Daniel and his friends, were glad to find that these three men had not obeyed the command of King Nebuchadnezzar. The king had said that if any one did not worship the golden image he should be thrown into a furnace of fire. These men who hated the Jews came to the king and said:

"O king, may you live for ever! You gave orders that when the music sounded, every one should bow down and worship the golden image;

and that if any man did not worship, he should be thrown into a furnace of fire. There are some Jews, whom you have made rulers in the land, who have not done as you commanded. Their names are Shadrach, Meshach and Abed-nego. They do not serve your gods, nor worship the golden image that you have set up."

Then Nebuchadnezzar was filled with rage and fury at knowing that any one should dare to disobey his words. He sent for these three men and said to them:

"O Shadrach, Meshach, and Abed-nego, was it by purpose that you did not fall down and worship the image of gold? The music shall sound once more, and if you then will worship the image, it will be well. But if you will not, then you shall be thrown into the furnace of fire, to die."

These three young men were not afraid of the king. They said:

"O King Nebuchadnezzar, we are ready to answer you at once. The God whom we serve is able to save us from the fiery furnace, and we know that he will save us. But if it is God's will that we should die, even then you may understand, O king, that we will not serve your gods, nor worship the golden image."

This answer made the king more furious than before. He said to his servants:

"Make a fire in the furnace hotter than ever it has been before, as hot as fire can be made; and throw these three men into it."

Then the soldiers of the king's army seized the three young Jews, as they stood in their loose robes, with their turbans on their heads. They tied them with ropes, dragged them to the mouth of the furnace, and threw them into the fire. The flames rushed from the opened door with such fury that they burned even to death the soldiers who were holding these men; and the men themselves fell down bound into the middle of the fiery furnace.

The fiery furnace

But an angel befriended them and they were unhurt.

King Nebuchadnezzar stood in front of the furnace, and looked into the open door. As he looked, he was filled with wonder at what he saw; and he said to the nobles around him:

"Did we not throw three men bound into the fire? How is it then that I see four men loose walking in the furnace; and the fourth man looks as though he were a son of the gods?"

The nobles who stood by could scarcely speak, so great was their surprise.

"It is true, O king," at last they said to Nebuchadnezzar, "that we cast these men into the flames, expecting them to be burned up; and we cannot understand how it happens that they have not been destroyed."

The king came near to the door of the furnace, as the fire became lower; and he called out to the three men within it:

"Shadrach, Meshach, and Abed-nego, ye who serve the Most High God, come out of the fire, and come to me."

They came out and stood before the king, in the sight of all the princes, and nobles, and rulers; and every one could see that they were alive.

Their garments had not been scorched, nor their hair singed, nor was there even the smell of fire upon them.

Then King Nebuchadnezzar said before all his rulers:

"Blessed be the God of Shadrach, Meshach, and Abed-nego, who has sent his angel, and has saved the lives of these men who trusted in him. I make a law that no man in all my kingdoms shall say a word against their God, for there is no other god who can save in this manner those who worship him. And if any man speaks a word against their God, the Most High God, that man shall be cut in pieces, and his house shall be torn down."

After King Nebuchadnezzar died, his kingdom became weak, and the city of Babylon was taken by the Medes and Persians, under Cyrus, a great warrior.

The Story of Daniel in the Lions' Den

The lands that had been the Babylonian or Chaldean empire now became the empire of Persia; and over these Darius was the king. King Darius gave to Daniel, who was now a very old man, a high place in honor and in power. Among all the rulers over the land, Daniel stood first, for the king saw that he was wise and able to rule. This made the other princes and rulers very jealous, and they tried to find something evil in Daniel, so that they could speak to the king against him.

These men saw that three times every day Daniel went to his room and opened the window that was toward the city of Jerusalem, and looking toward Jerusalem, made his prayer to God. Jerusalem was at that time in ruins, and the Temple was no longer standing; but Daniel prayed three times each day with his face toward the place where the house of God had once stood, although it was many hundreds of miles away.

These nobles thought that in Daniel's prayers they could find a chance to do him harm, and perhaps cause him to be put to death. They came to King Darius, and said to him:

"All the rulers have agreed together to have a law made that for thirty days no one shall ask anything of any god or of any man, except from you, O king; and that if any one shall pray to any god, or shall ask anything from any man during the thirty days, except from you, O king, he shall be thrown into the den where the lions are kept. Now, O king, make the law, and sign the writing, so that it cannot be changed, for no law among the Medes and the Persians can be altered."

The king was not a wise man; and being foolish and vain, he was pleased with this law that would set him even above the gods. So without asking Daniel's advice, he signed the writing; and the law was made, and the word was sent out through the kingdom, that for thirty days no one should pray to any god.

Daniel knew that the law had been made, but every day he went to his room three times, and opened the window that looked toward Jerusalem, and offered his prayers to the Lord, just as he had prayed in other times. These rulers were watching near by, and they saw Daniel kneeling in prayer to God. Then they came to the king, and said:

"O King Darius, have you not made a law, that if any one in thirty days offers a prayer, he shall be thrown into the den of lions?"

"It is true," said the king. "The law has been made, and it must stand."

They said to the king: "There is one man who does not obey the law which you have made. It is that Daniel, one of the captive Jews.

Every day Daniel prays to his God three times, just as he did before you signed the writing of the law."

Daniel in the lion's den

Then the king was very sorry for what he had done, for he loved Daniel, and knew that no one could take his place in the kingdom. All day, until the sun went down, he tried in vain to find some way to save Daniel's life; but when evening came, these men again told him of the law that he had made, and said to him that it must be kept. Very unwillingly, the king sent for Daniel, and gave an order that he should be thrown into the den of lions. He said to Daniel: "Perhaps your God, whom you serve so faithfully, will save you from the lions."

They led Daniel to the mouth of the pit where the lions were kept, and they threw him in; and over the mouth they placed a stone; and the king sealed it with his own seal, and with the seals of his nobles; so that no one might take away the stone and let Daniel out of the den.

Then the king went again to his palace; but that night he was so sad that he could not eat, nor did he listen to music as he was used to listen. He could not sleep, for all through the night he was thinking of Daniel. Very early in the morning he rose up from his bed and went in haste to the den of lions. He broke the seal and took away the stone, and in a voice full of sorrow, he called out, scarcely hoping to have an answer:

"O Daniel, servant of the living God, has your God been able to save you from the lions?"

Out of the darkness in the den came the voice of Daniel, saying:

"O king, may you live forever! My God has sent his angel and has shut the mouths of the lions. They have not hurt me, because my God saw that I had done no wrong. And I have done no wrong toward you, O king!"

Then the king was glad. He gave to his servants orders to take Daniel out of the den. Daniel was brought out safe and without harm, because he had trusted fully in the Lord God. Then by the king's command, they brought those men who had spoken against Daniel, and with them their wives and their children, for the king was exceedingly angry with them. They were all thrown into the den, and the hungry lions leaped upon them, and tore them in pieces, as soon as they fell upon the floor of the den.

After this King Darius wrote to all the lands and the peoples in the many kingdoms under his rule:

"May peace be given to you all abundantly! I make a law that everywhere among my kingdoms men fear and worship the Lord God of Daniel; for he is the living God, above all other gods, who only can save men."

Daniel stood beside king Darius until the end of his reign, and afterward while Cyrus the Persian was king over all the lands.

The Story Of Jonah And The Whale

At this time another prophet, named Jonah, was giving the word of the Lord to the Israelites. To Jonah the Lord spoke, saying:

"Go to Nineveh, that great city, and preach to it; for its wickedness rises up before me."

But Jonah did not wish to preach to the people of Nineveh; for they were the enemies of his land, the land of Israel. He wished Nineveh to die in its sins, and not to turn to God and live. Jonah tried to go away from the city where God had sent him. He went down to Joppa and took a ship for Tarshish.

But the Lord saw Jonah on the ship; and the Lord sent a great storm upon the sea, so that the ship seemed as though it would go to pieces. The sailors threw overboard everything on the ship; and when they could do no more, every man prayed to his god to save the ship and themselves. Jonah was now lying fast asleep, and the ship's captain came to him, and said:

"What do you mean by sleeping in such a time as this? Awake, rise up, and call upon your God. Perhaps He will hear you and save our lives."

The storm continued to rage around the ship; and they said:

"There is some man on this ship who has brought upon us this trouble. Let us cast lots and find who it is."

Then they cast lots, and the lot fell on Jonah. They said to him, all at once:

"Tell us, who are you? From what country do you come? What is your business? To what people do you belong? Why have you brought all this trouble upon us?"

Then Jonah told them the whole story, how he came from the land of Israel, and that he had fled away from the presence of the Lord. They said to him:

"What shall we do to you, that the storm may cease?"

Then Jonah have:

"Take me up and throw me into the sea; then the storm will cease and the waters will be calm; for I know that for my sake this great tempest is upon you."

But the men were not willing to throw Jonah into the sea. They rowed hard to bring the ship to the land, but they could not. Then they cried unto the Lord, and said:

"We pray thee, O Lord, we pray thee, let us not die for this man's life; for thou, O Lord, hast done as it pleased thee."

At last, when they could do nothing else to save themselves, they threw Jonah into the sea.

At once, the storm ceased, and the waves became still. Then the men on the ship feared the Lord greatly. They offered a sacrifice to the Lord, and made promises to serve him.

The Lord caused a great fish to swallow up Jonah; and Jonah was alive within the fish for three days and three nights. In the fish Jonah cried to the Lord; and the Lord caused the great fish to throw up Jonah upon the dry land.

Notice all through this story that, although Jonah was God's servant, he was always thinking about himself. God protected Jonah and saved him, not because he was such a good man, but because he wanted to teach him a great lesson.

By this time Jonah had learned that some men who worshipped idols were kind in their hearts, and were dear to the Lord. This was the lesson that God meant Jonah to learn; and now the call of the Lord came to Jonah a second time:

"Arise, go to Nineveh, that great city, and preach to it what I command you." So Jonah went to the city of Nineveh; and as he entered into it, he called out to the people:

"Within forty days shall Nineveh be destroyed."

He walked through the city all day crying out only this:

"Within forty days shall Nineveh be destroyed."

Jonah preaching to Nineveh

The people of Nineveh believed the word of the Lord as spoken by Jonah. They turned away from their sins and fasted and sought the Lord, from the greatest of them even to the least. The king of Nineveh arose from his throne, and laid aside his royal robes, and covered himself with sackcloth and sat in ashes, as a sign of his sorrow. The king sent out a command to his people that they should fast, and seek the Lord, and turn from sin.

God saw that the people of Nineveh were sorry for their wickedness, and he forgave them, and did not destroy their city. But this made Jonah very angry. He did not wish to have Nineveh spared, because it was the enemy of his own land; and he feared that men would call him a false prophet when his word did not come to pass. Jonah said to the Lord:

"O Lord, I was sure that it would be thus, that thou would spare the city; and for that reason I tried to flee away; for I know that thou was a gracious God, full of pity, slow to anger, and rich in mercy. Now, O Lord, take away my life, for it is better for me to die than to live."

Jonah went out of the city, and built a little hut on the east side of it, and sat under its roof, to see whether God would keep the word that he had spoken. Then the Lord caused a plant with thick leaves to grow up, and to shade Jonah from the sun; and Jonah was glad, and sat under its shadow. But a worm destroyed the plant; and the next day a hot wind blew, and Jonah suffered from the heat; and again Jonah wished that he might die. The Lord said to Jonah:

"You were sorry to see the plant die, though you did not make it grow, and though it came up in a night and died in a night. And should not I have pity on Nineveh, that great city, where are more than a hundred thousand little children, and also many cattle,—all helpless and knowing nothing?"

Jonah learned that men, and women, and little children, are all precious in the sight of the Lord, even though they know not God.

The Story Of Jesus, The Babe Of Bethlehem

Soon after the time when John the Baptist was born, Joseph the carpenter of Nazareth had a dream. In his dream he saw an angel from the Lord standing beside him. The angel said to him:

"Joseph, sprung from the line of king David, I have come to tell you, that Mary, the young woman whom you are to marry, will have a son, sent by the Lord God. You shall call his name Jesus, which means 'salvation,' because he shall save his people from their sins."

God's people had had several kings. Some of them had been selfish and cruel, but Jesus was to be a new kind of king, one who would save, not destroy men.

Soon after Joseph and Mary were married in Nazareth, a command went forth from the emperor Augustus Cæsar through all the lands of the Roman empire, for all the people to go to the cities and towns from which their families had come, and there to have their names written down upon a list, for the emperor wished a list to be made of all the people under his rule. As both Joseph and Mary had come from the family of David the king, they went together from Nazareth to Bethlehem, there to have their names written upon the list. For you remember that Bethlehem in Judea, six miles south of Jerusalem, was the place where David was born, and where his father's family had lived for many years.

It was a long journey from Nazareth to Bethlehem; down the mountains to the river Jordan, then following the Jordan almost to its end, and then climbing the mountains of Judah to the town of Bethlehem. When Joseph and Mary came to Bethlehem, they found the city full of people who, like themselves, had come to have their names enrolled or written upon the list. The inn or hotel was full, and there was no room for them; for no one else knew that this young woman was soon to be the mother of the Lord of all the earth. The best that they could do was to go to a stable where the cattle were kept. There the little baby was born, and was laid in a manger, where the cattle were fed.

On that night, some shepherds were tending their sheep in a field near Bethlehem. Suddenly, a great light shone upon them, and they saw an angel of the Lord standing before them. They were filled with fear, as they saw how glorious the angel was. But the angel said to them:

"Be not afraid; for behold I bring you news of great joy, which shall be to all the people; for there is born to you this day in Bethlehem, the city of David, a Savior who is Christ the Lord, the anointed king. You may see him there; and you may know him by this sign: He is a newborn baby, lying in a manger, at the inn."

Then they saw that the air around and the sky above them were filled with angels, praising God and singing:

"Glory to God in the highest. And on earth peace among men in whom God is well pleased."

The Nativity

While they looked with wonder, and listened, the angels went out of sight as suddenly as they had come. Then the shepherds said one to another:

"Let us go at once to Bethlehem, and see this wonderful thing that has come to pass, and which the Lord has made known to us."

Then as quickly as they could go to Bethlehem, they went, and found Joseph, the carpenter of Nazareth, and his young wife Mary, and the little baby lying in the manger. They told Mary and Joseph, and others also, how they had seen the angels, and what they had heard about this baby. All who heard their story wondered at it; Mary, the mother of the child, said nothing. She thought over all these things, and silently kept them in her heart. After their visit, the shepherds went back to their flocks, praising God for the good news that he had sent to them.

When the little one was eight days old, they gave him a name; and the name given was "Jesus," a word that means "salvation," as the angel had told both Mary and Joseph that he should be named. So the very name of this child told what he should do for men; for he was to bring salvation to the world.

The Story of the Star and the Wise Men

For some time after Jesus was born, Joseph and Mary stayed with him in Bethlehem. The little baby was not kept long in the stable sleeping in a manger; for after a few days they found room in a house; and there another visit was made to Jesus by strange men from a land far away.

In a country east of Judea, and many miles distant, were living some very wise men who studied the stars. One night they saw a strange star shining in the sky, and in some way, they learned that the coming of this star meant that a king was soon to be born in the land of Judea. These men felt a call of God to go to Judea, far to the west of their own home, and there to see this newborn king. They took a long journey, with camels and horses, and at last they came to the land of Judea, just at the time when Jesus was born at Bethlehem. As soon as they were in Judea, they supposed that every one would know all about the king, and they said:

"Where is he that is born king of the Jews? In the east we have seen his star, and we have come to worship him."

But no one of whom they asked had ever seen this king, or had heard of him. The news of their coming was sent to Herod the king, who was now a very old man. He ruled the land of Judea, as you know, under the emperor at Rome, Augustus Cæsar. Herod was a very wicked man, and when he heard of some one born to be a king, he feared that he might lose his own kingdom. He made up his mind to kill this new king.

He sent for the priests and scribes, the men who studied and taught the books of the Old Testament, and asked them about this Christ for whom all the people were looking. He said: "Can you tell me where Christ, the king of Israel, is to be born?" They looked at the books of the prophets, and then they said: "He is to be born in Bethlehem of Judea; for thus it is written by the prophet, 'And thou Bethlehem in the land of Judah are not the least among the princes of Judah; for out of thee shall come forth one who shall rule my people Israel.'"

Then Herod sent for the wise men from the east, met them alone, and found from them at what time the star was first seen. Then he said to them:

"Go to Bethlehem; and there search carefully for the little child; and when you have found him, bring me word again, so that I also may come and worship him."

The star in the east

Then the wise men went on their way toward Bethlehem; and suddenly they saw the star again shining upon the road before them. At this, they were glad, and followed the star until it led them to the very house where the little child was. They came in, and there they saw the little one, with Mary, its mother. They knew at once that this was the king; and they fell down on their faces and worshipped him as the Lord. Then they brought out gifts of gold and precious perfumes, frankincense and myrrh, which were used in offering sacrifices; and they gave them as presents to the royal child.

The flight into Egypt

The massacre of the innocents

That night God sent a dream to the wise men, telling them not to go back to Herod, but to go home at once to their own land by another way. They obeyed the Lord, and found another road to their own country without passing through Jerusalem where Herod was living. So Herod could not learn from those men who the child was that was born to be a king.

Very soon after these wise men had gone away, the Lord sent another dream to Joseph, the husband of Mary. He saw an angel, who spoke to him, saying:

"Rise up quickly; take the little child and his mother, and go down to the land of Egypt, for Herod will try to find the child to kill him."

Then at once Joseph rose up in the night, without waiting even for the morning. He took his wife and her baby, and quietly and quickly went with them down to Egypt, which was on the southwest of Judea. There they all stayed in safety, as long as the wicked king Herod lived, which was not many months.

King Herod waited for the wise men to come back to him from their visit to Bethlehem; but he soon found that they had gone to their home without bringing to him any word. Then Herod was very angry. He sent out his soldiers to Bethlehem. They came, and by the cruel king's command they seized all the little children in Bethlehem who were three years old, or younger, and killed them all. What a cry went up to God from the mothers in Bethlehem, as their children were torn from their arms and slain!

But all this time, the child Jesus whom they were seeking was safe with his mother in the land of Egypt.

Soon after this king Herod died, a very old man, cruel to the last. Then the angel of the Lord came again and spoke to Joseph in a dream, saying: "You may now take the young child back to his own land, for the king who sought to kill him is dead."

Then Joseph took his wife and the little child Jesus, and started to go again to the land of Judea. Perhaps it was his thought to go again to Bethlehem, the city of David, and there bring up the child. But he heard that in that part of the land Archelaus, a son of Herod, was now ruling, and who was as wicked and cruel as his father was.

He feared to go under Archelaus' rule, and instead took his wife and the child to Nazareth, which had been his own home and that of Mary his wife before the child was born. Nazareth was in the part of the land called Galilee, which at that time was ruled by another son of King Herod, a king named Herod Antipas. He was not a good man, but was not as cruel or bloody as his wicked father had been.

So Joseph the carpenter and Mary his wife were again living in Nazareth. And there they stayed for many years while Jesus was growing up. Jesus was not the only child in their house, and he had many other playmates among the boys of Nazareth.

The Story of the Child in the Temple

Jesus was brought to Nazareth when he was a little child not more than three years old; there he grew up as a boy and a young man, and there he lived until he was thirty years of age. We should like to know many things about his boyhood, but the Bible tells us very little. As Joseph was a working man, it is likely that he lived in a house with only one room, with no floor except the earth, no window except a hole in the wall, no pictures upon the walls, and neither bedstead, nor chair, nor looking-glass. They sat upon the floor or upon cushions; they slept upon rolls of matting, and their meals were taken from a low table not much larger than a stool.

Jesus may have learned to read at the village school, which was generally held in the house used for worship, called the "synagogue." The lessons were from rolls on which were written parts of the Old Testament; but Jesus never had a Bible of his own. From a child he went with Joseph to the worship in the synagogue twice every week. There they sat on the floor and heard the Old Testament read and explained, while Mary and the younger sisters of Jesus listened from a gallery behind a lattice-screen. The Jewish boys of that time were taught to know almost the whole of the Old Testament by heart.

It was the custom of the Jews from all parts of the land to go up to Jerusalem to worship at least once every year, at the feast of the Passover, which was held in the spring. Some families also stayed to the feast of Pentecost, which was fifty days after Passover; and some went again in the fall to the feast of Tabernacles, when for a week all the families slept out of doors, under roofs made of green twigs and bushes.

When Jesus was a boy twelve years old, he was taken up to the feast of the Passover, and there for the first time he saw the holy city Jerusalem, and the Temple of the Lord on Mount Moriah. Young as he was, his soul was stirred, as he walked among the courts of the Temple and saw the altar with its smoking sacrifice, the priests in their white robes, and the Levites with their silver trumpets. Though a boy, Jesus began to feel that he was the Son of God, and that this was his Father's house.

Jesus with the Doctors of the Law

His heart was so filled with the worship of the Temple, with the words of the scribes or teachers whom he heard in the courts, and with his own thoughts, that when it was time to go home to Nazareth, he stayed behind, held fast by his love for the house of the Lord. The company of people who were traveling together was large, and at first, he was not missed. But when night came and the boy Jesus could not be found, his mother was alarmed. The next day Joseph and Mary left their company and hastened back to Jerusalem. They did not at first think to go to the Temple. They sought him among their friends and kindred who were living in the city, but could not find him.

On the third day, they went up to the Temple with heavy hearts, still looking for their boy. And there they found him sitting in a company of the doctors of the law, listening to their words and asking them questions. Everybody who stood near was surprised to find how deep the knowledge of this boy in the word of the Lord was.

His mother spoke to him a little sharply, for she felt that her son had not been thoughtful of his duty. She said: "Child, why have you treated us in this way? Do you not know that your father and I have been looking for you with troubled hearts?"

"Why did you seek for me," said Jesus. "Did you not know that I must be in my Father's house?"

They did not understand these words; but Mary thought often about them afterward; for she felt her son was no common child, and that his words had a deep meaning. Though Jesus was wise beyond his years, he obeyed Joseph and his mother in all things. He went with them to Nazareth, and lived contented with the plain life of their country home.

As the years went on, Jesus grew from a boy to a young man. He grew, too, in knowledge, in wisdom, and in the favor of God. He won the love of all who knew him, for there was something in his nature that drew all hearts, both young and old.

Jesus learned the trade of a carpenter with Joseph; and when Joseph died, while Jesus was still a young man, Jesus worked as a carpenter, and helped his mother take care of the family. And so in the carpenter shop, and the quiet life of a country village, and the worship of the synagogue, the years passed until Jesus was thirty years of age.

The Story of the Stranger at the Well

While Jesus was teaching in Jerusalem and in the country places near it, John the Baptist was still preaching and baptizing. But already the people were leaving John and going to hear Jesus. Some of the followers of John the Baptist were not pleased as they saw that fewer people came to their master, and that the crowds were seeking Jesus. But John said to them: "I told you that I am not the Christ, but that I am sent before him. Jesus is the Christ, the king. He must grow greater, while I must grow less; and I am glad that it is so."

Soon after this, Herod Antipas, the king of the province or land of Galilee, put John in prison. Herod had taken for his wife a woman named Herodias, who had left her husband to live with Herod, which was very wicked. John sent word to Herod, that it was not right for him to have this woman as his wife. These words of

John made Herodias very angry. She hated John, and tried to kill him. Herod himself did not hate John so greatly, for he knew that John had spoken the truth. But he was weak, and yielded to his wife Herodias. To please her, he sent John the Baptist to a lonely prison among the mountains east of the Dead Sea; for the land in that region, as well as Galilee, was under Herod's rule. There in prison Herod hoped to keep John safe from the hate of his wife Herodias.

Soon after John the Baptist was thrown into prison, Jesus left the country near Jerusalem with his disciples, and went toward Galilee, the province in the north. Between Judea in the south and Galilee in the north, lay the land of Samaria, where the Samaritans lived, who hated the Jews. They worshipped the Lord as the Jews worshipped him, but they had their own Temple and their own priests. And they had their own Bible, which was only the five books of Moses; for they would not read the other books of the old Testament. The Jews and the Samaritans would scarcely ever speak to each other, so great was the hate between them.

When Jews went from Galilee to Jerusalem, or from Jerusalem to Galilee, they would not pass through Samaria, but went down the mountains to the river Jordan, and walked beside the river, in order to go around Samaria. But Jesus, when he would go from Jerusalem to Galilee, walked over the mountains straight through Samaria. One morning while he was on his journey, he stopped to rest beside an old well at the foot of Mount Gerizim, not far from the city of Shechem, but nearer to a little village that was called Sychar. This well had been dug by Jacob, the great father or ancestor of the Israelites, many hundreds of years before. It was an old well then in the days of Jesus; and it is much older now; for the same well may be seen in that place still. Even now, travelers may have a drink from Jacob's well.

Jesus with the Samaritan woman

It was early in the morning, about sunrise, when Jesus was sitting by Jacob's well. He was very tired, for he had walked a long journey; he was hungry, and his disciples had gone to the village near at hand to buy food. He was thirsty, too; and as he looked into the well he could see the water a hundred feet below, but he had no rope with which to let down a cup or a jar to draw up some water to drink.

Just at this moment a Samaritan woman came to the well, with her water-jar upon her head, and her rope in her hand. Jesus looked at her, in one glance read her soul, and saw all her life.

He knew that Jews did not often speak to Samaritans, but he said to her:

"Please to give me a drink?"

The woman saw from his looks and his dress that he was a Jew, and she said to him:

"How is it that you, who are a Jew, ask drink of me, a Samaritan woman?"

Jesus answered her:

"If you knew what God's free gift is, and if you knew who it is that says to you, 'Give me a drink,' you would ask him to give you living water, and he would give it to you."

There was something in the words and the looks of Jesus that made the woman feel that he was not a common man. She said to him: "Sir, you have nothing to draw water with, and the well is deep. Where can you get that living water? Are you greater than our father Jacob, who drank from this well, and who gave it to us?"

"Whoever drinks of this water," said Jesus, "shall thirst again, but whoever drinks of the water that I shall give him, shall never thirst; but the water that I shall give him shall be in him a well of water springing up unto everlasting life."

"Sir," said the woman, "give me some of this water of yours, so that I will not thirst any more, nor come all the way to this well."

Jesus looked at the woman, and said to her, "Go home, and bring your husband, and come here."

"I have no husband," answered the woman.

"Yes," said Jesus, "you have spoken the truth. You have no husband. But you have had five husbands, and the man whom you now have is not your husband."

The woman was filled with wonder as she heard this. She saw that here was a man who knew what others could not know. She felt that God had spoken to him, and she said:

"Sir, I see that you are a prophet of God. Tell me whether our people or the Jews are right. Our fathers have worshipped on this mountain. The Jews say that Jerusalem is the place where men should go to worship. Now, which of these is the right place?"

"Woman, believe me," said Jesus, "there is coming a time when men shall worship God in other places besides on this mountain and in Jerusalem. The time is near; it has even now come, when the true worshippers everywhere shall pray to God in spirit and in truth; for God himself is a Spirit."

The woman said: "I know that the Anointed one is coming, the Christ. When he comes, he will teach us all things."

Jesus said to her:

"I that speak to you now am he, the Christ!"

Just at this time, the disciples of Jesus came back from the village. They wondered to see Jesus talking with this Samaritan woman, but they said nothing.

The woman had come to draw water, but in her interest in this wonderful stranger, she forgot her errand. Leaving her water-jar, she ran back to her village, and said to the people:

"Come; see a man who told me everything that I have done in all my life! Is not this man the Christ whom we are looking for?"

Soon the woman came back to the well with many of her people. They asked Jesus to come to their town, and to stay there and teach them. He went with them, and stayed there two days, teaching the people, who were Samaritans. And many of the people in that place believed in Jesus, and said:

"We have heard for ourselves; now we know that this is indeed the Savior of the world."

The Story of the Fishermen

When Jesus began to teach the people by the river Jordan, a few young men came to him as followers, or disciples. Some of these men were Andrew and John, Peter and Philip and Nathanael. While Jesus was teaching near Jerusalem and in Samaria, these men stayed with Jesus; but when he came to Galilee, they went to their homes and work, for most of them were fishermen from the Sea of Galilee.

One morning, soon after Jesus came to Capernaum, he went out of the city, by the sea, followed by a great throng of people, who had come together to see him and to hear him. On the shore were lying two fishing boats, one of which belonged to Simon and Andrew, the other to James and John and their father Zebedee. The men themselves were not in the boats, but were washing their nets near by.

Jesus stepped into the boat that belonged to Simon Peter and his brother Andrew, and asked them to push it out a little into the lake, so that he could talk to the people from it without being crowded too closely. They pushed it out, and then Jesus sat in the boat, and spoke to the people, as they stood upon the beach. After he had finished speaking to the people, and had sent them away, he said to Simon Peter:

"Put out into the deep water and let down your nets to catch some fish."

"Master," said Simon, "we have been fishing all night, and have caught nothing; but if it is your will, I will let down the net again."

They did as Jesus bade them; and now the net caught so many fishes that Simon and Andrew could not pull it up, and it was in danger of breaking. They made signs to the two brothers, James and John, who were in the other boat, for them to come and help them. They came, lifted the net, and poured out the fish. There were so many of them that both the boats were filled, and began to sink.

When Simon Peter saw this, he was struck with wonder, and felt that it was by the power of God. He fell down at the feet of Jesus, saying: "Oh Lord, I am full of sin, and am not worthy of all this! Leave me, O Lord."

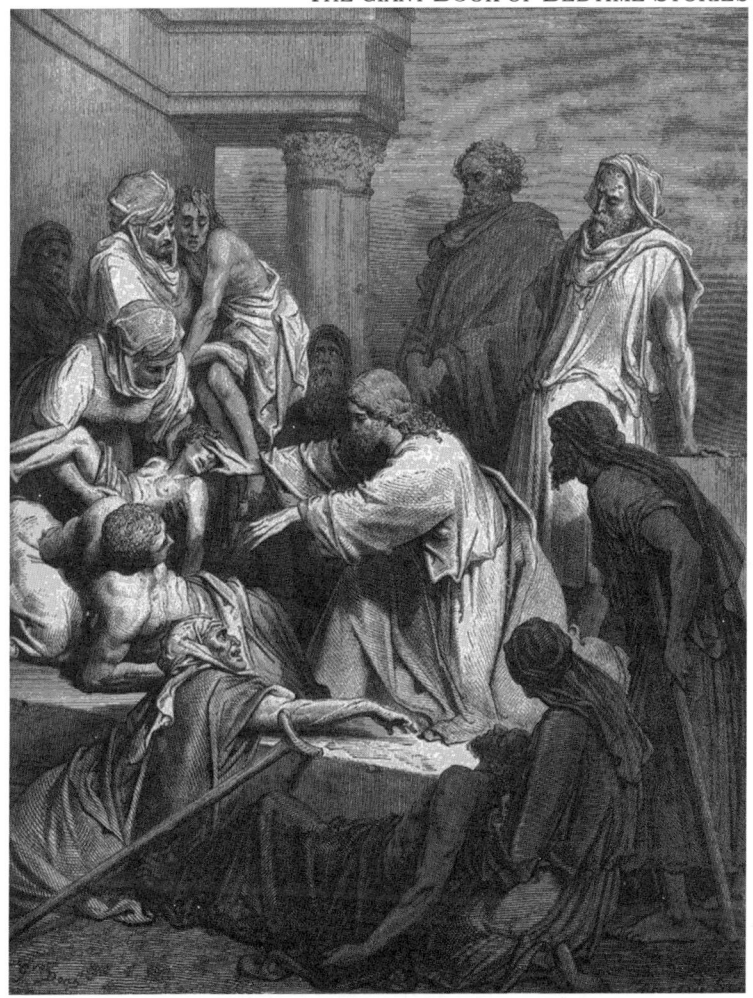

Jesus healing the sick

But Jesus said to Simon, and to the others, "Fear not; but follow me, and I will make you from this time fishers of men."

From that time these four men, Simon and Andrew, James and John, gave up their nets and their work, and became disciples of Jesus.

On the Sabbath, after this, Jesus and his disciples went together to the synagogue, and spoke to the people. They listened to him and were surprised at his teaching; for while the scribes always repeated what other scribes had said before, Jesus never spoke of what the men of old time had taught, but spoke in his own name, and by his own power, saying, "I say unto you," as one who had the right to speak. Men felt that Jesus was speaking to them as the voice of God.

On one Sabbath, while Jesus was preaching, a man came into the synagogue who had in him an evil spirit; for sometimes evil spirits came into men, and lived in them and spoke out from them. The evil spirit in this man cried out, saying:

"Let us alone, thou Jesus of Nazareth! What have we to do with thee? Hast thou come to destroy us? I know thee; and I know who thou art, the Holy one of God!"

Then Jesus spoke to the evil spirit in the man:

"Be still; and come out of this man!"

Then the evil spirit threw the man down, and seemed as if he would tear him apart; but he left the man lying on the ground, without harm.

Then wonder fell upon all the people. They were filled with fear, and said: "What mighty word is this? This man speaks even to the evil spirits, and they obey him!"

After the meeting in the synagogue, Jesus went into the house where Simon Peter lived. There he saw lying upon a bed the mother of Simon's wife, who was very ill with a burning fever. He stood over her, and touched her hand. At once, the fever left her; she rose up from her bed and waited upon them.

At sunset, the Sabbath day was over; and then they brought to Jesus from all parts of the city those that were sick, and some that had evil spirits in them. Jesus laid his hands upon the sick, and they became well; he drove out the evil spirits by a word, and would not allow them to speak.

Feeding the Multitudes

Jesus had chosen twelve out of the many who flocked about Him wishing to be His disciples, and these twelve were called apostles. He sent them forth to preach the gospel, giving them power to cast out evil spirits and to heal diseases; and when they were about to go forth upon their mission, He gave them instructions regarding what they were to do, and warned them of the persecutions which would be heaped upon them. He also bade them be strong and not fear those who had power to kill the body only, because the soul was far more precious. So the apostles went out into the cities and towns, preached the word of God, and carried blessing with them.

When they came back they told Jesus what they had done, and they went with Him across the Sea of Galilee to a quiet spot where they could rest and talk over their work.

But the people went around the sea, or lake, to join them on the other side; and when Jesus saw the crowds He was sorry for them, and taught and healed them again as He had done so many times.

Jesus teaching the multitudes

In the evening His disciples urged Him to send the people away that they might buy food for themselves in the village; but Jesus said, "Give ye them to eat."

The disciples thought this would be impossible. "We have here but five loaves and two fishes," they told Him; and when He said, "Bring them hither to Me," they obeyed Him with wonder.

Then Jesus commanded the people to sit down in groups upon the green grass; and He took the loaves and gave thanks to God for them, and broke them into pieces, handing them to His disciples to give to the people.

He divided the fishes also in the same way, the disciples went about among the groups giving each person a share, and everyone had enough to eat; for although there were about five thousand men there, besides women and children, the food was sufficient for all. Even more than this, when the multitude had eaten all that they wanted, the disciples gathered up twelve baskets full of the broken pieces.

When the people saw this wonderful miracle which Jesus had done, they wished to make Him king at once, for they thought He was the Promised One for whom they had been so long waiting, and they did not know that the kingdom of Christ was not to be an earthly kingdom.

But Jesus would not allow them to make Him king, and He left them and went up on the top of a mountain alone.

On another occasion when a great crowd had gathered to hear Him and had been for a long time without food, He called His disciples to Him and told them that He felt very sorry for the people because they had been fasting three days, and He could not send them away so weak and hungry for fear they would faint before they could reach home.

But His disciples said they did not know where they could get food for so many, as they were in the wilderness.

Bible Stories

Jesus asked them how many loaves of bread they had, and they told Him seven, and a few small fishes.

Then Jesus bade the people sit down on the ground around Him, and He took the seven loaves and the fishes and offered thanks to God; afterwards, He broke the loaves into pieces as He had done before and gave them, with the fishes, to His disciples, and the disciples distributed them among the people. As they gave out the food it continued to increase wonderfully, so that all the people were fed; and even after that there was food enough left so that they took up seven baskets full, although about four thousand men, with many women and children, had eaten.

These miracles show not only the power of our Lord, but His tenderness and thoughtfulness for those around Him in the everyday affairs of life. He not only cared for the souls of His people, but for their physical comfort as well; for His heart was ever open to the cry of human need.

One of the first acts by which He manifested His power to the men who afterwards became His disciples, was an act of helpfulness.

He saw two ships by the Lake of Gennesaret with the fishermen near by washing their nets, and going aboard one of the ships, which belonged to Simon Peter, He asked him to put out a little way from land; then, when His request had been complied with, He taught the people from the ship.

After He had finished His teaching, He said to Simon, "Launch out into the deep and let down your nets for a draught." Simon told Him that they had worked all night and had caught no fish, but that they would do as He bade them.

And when they had done so, the net was filled so that it broke, and they had to call to their partners in the other ship to come and help them; and both ships were filled. Then Peter, James, and John left all to follow Jesus.

Jesus Calms the Tempest

At one time when Jesus had entered a ship to cross the Sea of Galilee with His disciples, a great storm arose and the waves nearly covered the little vessel, so that they were apparently in great danger.

The disciples were frightened, but Jesus was asleep and the storm did not disturb Him. As it grew worse and worse and the disciples became more than ever afraid, they went back to where Jesus lay and wakened Him, crying out, "Master, dost Thou not care that we perish?"

When they said this, Jesus arose and spoke to the winds and the sea, saying, "Peace, be still!" Then at once the wind went down and the sea became calm, and the hearts of the men were filled with wonder and still greater faith and awe, while they said to one another, "What manner of man is this, that even the wind and the sea obey Him?" They had not yet learned that Jesus had power over all things whenever He chose to exercise it.

Jesus calms the tempest

At another time when the disciples had crossed the Sea of Galilee, expecting that Jesus would join them upon the other side, a storm came up, suddenly as before, and the waters were quickly piled up in great waves; for the lake was narrow and deep, and the storms usually burst in full fury with little warning, doing much harm before there was a chance to escape. At this time the disciples had hard work to row the boat against the wind, and it was tossed about here and there by the waves in the middle of the sea until, toward morning, Jesus went out toward it, walking upon the water.

Jesus walking on the water

When the disciples saw Him coming they thought it was a spirit and were frightened: but He spoke to them, saying, "Be of good cheer; it is I, be not afraid."

The Story of the Sermon on the Mount

Among the Jews there was one class of men hated and despised by the people more than any other. That was "the publicans." These were the men who took from the people the tax that the Roman rulers had laid upon the land. Many of these publicans were selfish, grasping, and cruel. They robbed the people, taking more than was right. Some of them were honest men, dealing fairly, and taking no more for the tax than was needful; but because so many were wicked, all the publicans were hated alike; and they were called "sinners" by the people.

One day, when Jesus was going out of Capernaum, to the seaside, followed by a great crowd of people, he passed a publican, or tax-gatherer, who was seated at his table taking money from the people who came to pay their taxes. This man was named Matthew, or Levi; for many Jews had two names. Jesus could look into the hearts of men, and he saw that Matthew was one who might help him as one of his disciples. He looked upon Matthew, and said:

"Follow me!"

At once, the publican rose up from his table, and left it to go with Jesus. All the people wondered, as they saw one of the hated publicans among the disciples, with Peter, and John, and the rest. But Jesus believed that there is good in all kinds of people. Most of the men who followed him were poor fishermen. None of them, as far as we know, was rich. And when he called Matthew he saw a man with a true and loving heart, whose rising up to follow Jesus just as soon as he was called showed what a brave and faithful friend he would be. The first of the four books about Jesus bears Matthew's name.

A little while after Jesus called him, Matthew made a great feast for Jesus at his house; and to the feast he invited many publicans, and others whom the Jews called sinners. The Pharisees saw Jesus sitting among these people, and they said with scorn to his disciples:

"Why does your Master sit at the table with publicans and sinners?"

Jesus heard of what these men had said, and he said:

"Those that are well do not need a doctor to cure them, but those that are sick do need one. I go to these people because they know that they are sinners and need to be saved. I came not to call those who think themselves to be good, but those who wish to be made better."

One evening Jesus went alone to a mountain not far from Capernaum. A crowd of people and his disciples followed him; but Jesus left them all, and went up to the top of the mountain, where he could be alone. There he stayed all night, praying to God, his Father and our Father. In the morning, out of all his followers, he chose twelve men who should walk with him and listen to his words, so that they might be able to teach others in turn. Some of the men he had called before; but now he called them again, and others with them. They were called "The Twelve," or "the disciples"; and after Jesus went to heaven, they were called "The Apostles," a word which means "those who were sent out," because Jesus sent them out to preach the gospel to the world.

The names of the twelve disciples, or apostles, were these: Simon Peter and his brother Andrew; James and John, the two sons of Zebedee; Philip of Bethsaida, and Nathanael, who was also called Bartholomew, a name which means "the son of Tholmai"; Thomas, who was also called Didymus, a name which means "a twin," and Matthew the publican, or tax-gatherer; another James, the son of Alpheus, who was called "James the Less," to keep his name apart from the first James, the brother of John; and Lebbeus, who was also called Thaddeus. Lebbeus was also called Judas, but he was a different man from another Judas, whose name is always given last. The eleventh name was another Simon, who was called "the Cananean" or "Simon Zelotes"; and the last name was Judas Iscariot, who was afterward the traitor. We know very little about most of these men, but some of them in later days did a great work. Simon Peter was a leader among them, but most of them were common sort of men of whom the best we know is that they loved Jesus and followed him to the end. Some died for him, and some served him in distant and dangerous places.

Before all the people who had come to hear him, Jesus called these twelve men to stand by his side. Then, on the mountain, he preached to these disciples and to the great company of people. The disciples stood beside him, and the great crowd of people stood in front, while Jesus spoke. What he said on that day is called "The Sermon on the Mount." Matthew wrote it down, and you can read it in his gospel, in the fifth, sixth, and seventh chapters. Jesus began with these words to his disciples:

"Blessed are the poor in spirit: for theirs is the kingdom of heaven.

"Blessed are they that mourn: for they shall be comforted.

"Blessed are the meek: for they shall inherit the earth.

"Blessed are they which do hunger and thirst after righteousness: for they shall be filled.

"Blessed are the merciful: for they shall obtain mercy.

"Blessed are the pure in heart: for they shall see God.

"Blessed are the peacemakers: for they shall be called the children of God.

"Blessed are they which are persecuted for righteousness' sake: for theirs is the kingdom of heaven.

"Blessed are ye when men shall revile you, and persecute you, and shall say all manner of evil against you falsely, for my sake.

"Rejoice, and be exceedingly glad: for great is your reward in heaven: for so persecuted they the prophets which were before you.

"Ye are the salt of the earth: but if the salt has lost his savor, wherewith shall it be salted? It is thenceforth good for nothing, but to be cast out, and to be trodden under foot of men.

"Ye are the light of the world. A city that is set on a hill cannot be hid. Neither do men light a candle, and put it under a bushel, but on a candlestick; and it gives light unto all that are in the house. Let your light so shine before men, that they may see your good works, and glorify your Father which is in heaven."

It was in this Sermon on the Mount that Jesus told the people how they should pray, and he gave them the prayer that we all know as the Lord's Prayer.

And this was the end of the Sermon:

"Therefore, whosoever hears these sayings of mine, and does them, I will liken him unto a wise man, which built his house upon a rock:

"And the rain descended, and the floods came, and the winds blew, and beat upon that house; and it fell not; for it was founded upon a rock.

"And every one that hears these sayings of mine, and doeth them not, shall be likened unto a foolish man, which built his house upon the sand:

"And the rain descended, and the floods came, and the winds blew, and beat upon that house; and it fell: and great was the fall of it."

The Story of the Miracle Worker

There was at Capernaum an officer of the Roman army, a man who had under him a company of a hundred men. They called him "a centurion," a word that means "commanding a hundred"; but we should call him "a captain." This man was not a Jew, but was what the Jews called "a Gentile," "a foreigner"; a name which the Jews gave to all people outside their own race. The entire world except the Jews themselves were Gentiles.

This Roman centurion was a good man, and he loved the Jews, because through them he had heard of God, and had learned how to worship God. Out of his love for the Jews, he had built for them with his own money a synagogue, which may have been the very synagogue in which Jesus taught on the Sabbath days.

The centurion had a young servant, a boy whom he loved greatly; and this boy was very sick with palsy, and near to death. The centurion had heard that Jesus could cure those who were sick; and he asked the chief men of the synagogue, who were called its "elders," to go to Jesus and ask him to come and cure his young servant.

The elders spoke to Jesus, just as he came again to Capernaum, after the Sermon on the Mount. They asked Jesus to go with them to the centurion's house; and they said:

"He is a worthy man, and it is fitting that you should help him, for, though a Gentile, he loves our people, and he has built for us our synagogue."

Then Jesus said, "I will go and heal him."

But while he was on his way—and with him were the elders, and his disciples, and a great crowd of people, who hoped to see the work of healing—the centurion sent some other friends to Jesus with this message:

"Lord, do not take the trouble to come to my house; for I am not worthy that one so high as you are should come under my roof; and I did not think that I was worthy to go and speak to you. But speak only a word where you are and my servant shall be made well. For I also am a man under rule, and I have soldiers under me; and I say to one 'Go,' and he goes; and to another, 'Come,' and he comes; and to my servant, 'Do this,' and he does it. You, too, have power to speak and to be obeyed. Speak the word, and my servant shall be cured."

When Jesus heard this, he wondered at this man's faith. He turned to the people following him, and said:

"In truth I say to you, I have not found such faith as this in all Israel!"

Then he spoke to the friends of the centurion who had brought the word from him:

"Go and say to this man, 'As you have believed in me, so shall it be done to you.'"

Then those who had been sent, went again to the centurion's house, and found that in that very hour his servant had been made perfectly well.

On the day after this, Jesus with his disciples and many people went out from Capernaum, turned southward, and came to a village called Nain. Just as Jesus and his disciples came near to the gate of the city, they were met by a company who were carrying out a dead man to be buried. He was a young man, and the only son of his mother, and she was a widow.

When the Lord Jesus saw the mother in her grief, he pitied her, and said, "Do not weep."

He drew near, and touched the frame on which they were carrying the body, wrapped round and round with long strips of linen. The bearers looked with wonder on this stranger, set down the frame with its body, and stood still. Standing beside the body, Jesus said:

"Young man, I say to you, Rise up!"

And in a moment, the young man sat up and began to speak. Jesus gave him to his mother, who now saw that her son, who had been dead, was alive again.

And Jesus went through all that part of Galilee, working miracles, preaching, and teaching in all the villages, telling the people everywhere the good news of the kingdom of God.

The children loved to gather around him, and when his disciples would have driven them away he said, "Suffer the little children to come unto me and forbid them not, for of such is the kingdom of heaven."

Jesus healing the blind man

One Sabbath day, as Jesus and his disciples were walking in Jerusalem, they met a blind man begging. This man in all his life had never seen; for he had been born blind. The disciples said to Jesus as they were passing him: "Master, whose fault was it that this man was born blind? Was it because he has sinned, or did his parents sin?"

For the Jews thought that when any evil came, it was caused by some one's sin. But Jesus said:

"This man was born blind, not because of his parents' sin, nor because of his own, but so that God might show his power in him. We must do God's work while it is day, for the night is coming when no man can work. As long as I am in the world, I am the light of the world."

When Jesus had said this, he spat on the ground, and mixed up the spittle with earth, making a little lump of clay. This clay Jesus spread on the eyes of the blind man; and then he said to him: "Go wash in the pool of Siloam." The pool of Siloam was a large cistern, or, reservoir, on the southeast of Jerusalem, outside the wall, where the valley of Gihon and the valley of Kedron come together. To go to this pool, the blind man, with two great blotches of mud on his face, must walk through the streets of the city, out of the gate, and into the valley. He went, and felt his way down the steps into the pool of Siloam. There he washed, and then at once his life-long blindness passed away, and he could see.

When the man came back to the part of the city where he lived, his neighbors could scarcely believe that he was the same man. They said: "Is not this the man who used to sit on the street begging?"

"This must be the same man," said some; but others said: "No, it is some one who looks like him."

But the man said, "I am the very same man who was blind!"

"Why, how did this come to pass?" they asked. "How were your eyes opened?"

"The man, named Jesus," he answered, "mixed clay, and put it on my eyes, and said to me, 'Go to the pool of Siloam and wash,' and I went and washed, and then I could see."

"Where is this man?" they asked him.

"I do not know," said the man.

Some of the Pharisees, the men who made a show of always obeying the law, asked the man how he had been made to see. He said to them, as he had said before:

"A man put clay on my eyes, and I washed, and my sight came to me."

Some of the Pharisees said:

"The man who did this is not a man of God, because he does not keep the Sabbath. He makes clay, and puts it on men's eyes, working on the Sabbath day. He is a sinner!"

Others said, "How can a man who is a sinner do such wonderful works?"

And thus, the people were divided in what they thought of Jesus. They asked the man who had been blind: "What do you think of this man who has opened your eyes?"

"He is a prophet of God," said the man.

But the leading Jews would not believe that this man had gained his sight, until they had sent for his father and his mother. The Jews asked them:

"Is this your son, who you say was born blind? How is it that he can now see?"

His parents were afraid to tell all they knew; for the Jews had agreed that if any man should say Jesus was the Christ, the Savior, he should be turned out of the synagogue, and not be allowed to worship any more with the people. So his parents said to the Jews:

"We know that this is our son, and we know that he was born blind. But how he was made to see, we do not know; or who has opened his eyes, we do not know. He is of age; ask him, and let him speak for himself."

Then again, the rulers of the Jews called the man who had been blind; and they said to him:

"Give God the praise for your sight. We know that this man who made clay on the Sabbath day is a sinner."

"Whether that man is a sinner, or not, I do not know," answered the man; "but one thing I do know, that once I was blind, and now I see. We know that God does not hear sinners; but God hears only those who worship him, and do his will. Never before has any one opened the eyes of a man born blind. If this man were not from God, he could not do such works as these!"

The rulers of the Jews, these Pharisees, then said to the man: "You were born in sin, and do you try to teach us?"

And they turned him out of the synagogue, and would not let anyone worship with him. Jesus heard of this; and when Jesus found him, he said to him:

"Do you believe on the Son of God?"

The man said:

"And who is he, Lord, that I may believe on him?"

"You have seen him," said Jesus, "and it is he who now talks with you!"

The man said, "Lord, I believe."

And he fell down before Jesus, and worshipped him.

The Good Shepherd and the Good Samaritan

Soon afterward Jesus gave to the people in Jerusalem the parable or story of "The Good Shepherd."

"Verily, verily (that is, 'in truth, in truth'), I say to you, if any one does not go into the sheepfold by the door, but climbs up some other way, it is a sign that he is a thief and a robber. But the one who comes in by the door is a shepherd of the sheep. The porter opens the door to him, and the sheep know him, and listen to his call, for he calls his own sheep by name and leads them out to the pasture-field. And when he has led out his sheep, he goes in front of them, and the sheep follow him, for they know his voice. The sheep will not follow a stranger, for they do not know the stranger's voice."

The people did not understand what all this meant, and as Jesus explained it to them, he said: "Verily, verily, I say unto you, I am the door that leads to the sheepfold. If any man comes to the sheep in any other way than through me and in my name, he is a thief and a robber; but those who are the true sheep will not hear such. I am the door; if any man goes into the fold through me, he shall be saved, shall go in and go out, and shall find pasture.

"The thief comes to the fold that he may steal and rob the sheep, and kill them; but I came to the fold that they may have life, and may have all that they need. I am the good shepherd; the good shepherd will give up his own life to save his sheep; and I will give up my life that my sheep may be saved.

"I am the good shepherd; and just as a true shepherd knows all the sheep in his fold, so I know my own, and my own know me, even as I know the Father, and the Father knows me; and I lay down my life for the sheep. And other sheep I have, which are not of this fold; them also I must lead; and they shall hear my voice; and there shall be one flock and one shepherd."

The Jews could not understand these words of Jesus; but they became very angry with him, because he spoke of God as his Father. They took up stones to throw them at him, and tried to seize him, intending to kill him. But Jesus escaped from their hands, and went away to the land beyond Jordan, at the place called "Bethabara," or "Bethany beyond Jordan," the same place where he had been baptized by John the Baptist more than two years before. From this place, Jesus wished to go out through the land in the east of the Jordan, a land that is called "Perea," a word that means "beyond." But before going out through this land, Jesus sent out seventy chosen men from among his followers to go to all the villages, and to make the people ready for his own coming afterward. He gave to these seventy the same commands that he had given to the twelve disciples when he sent them through Galilee, and sent them out in pairs, two men to travel and to preach together. He said:

"I send you forth as lambs among wolves. Carry no purse, no bag for food, no shoes except those that you are wearing. Do not stop to talk with people by the way; but go through the towns and villages, healing the sick, and preaching to the people, 'The kingdom of God is coming,' He that hears you, hears me; and he that refuses you, refuses me; and he that will not hear me, will not hear him that sent me."

The Good Samaritan

Bible Stories

And after a time the seventy men came again to Jesus, saying:

"Lord, even the evil spirits obey our words in thy name!"

And Jesus said to them:

"I saw Satan, the king of the evil spirits, falling down like lightning from heaven. I have given you power to tread upon serpents and scorpions, and nothing shall harm you. Still, do not rejoice because the evil spirits obey you; but rejoice that your names are written in heaven."

And at that time, one of the scribes—men who wrote copies of the books of the Old Testament, and studied them, and taught them—came to Jesus and asked him a question, to see what answer he would give. He said: "Master, what shall I do to have everlasting life?"

Jesus said to the scribe: "What is written in the law? You are a reader of God's law; tell me what it says."

Then the man gave this answer:

"Thou shalt love the Lord thy God with all thy heart, and with all thy soul, and with all thy strength, and with all thy mind; and thou shalt love thy neighbor as thyself."

Jesus said to the man: "You have answered right; do this, and you shall have everlasting life."

But the man was not satisfied. He asked another question: "And who is my neighbor?"

To answer this question, Jesus gave the parable or story of "The Good Samaritan." He said: "A certain man was going down the lonely road from Jerusalem to Jericho; and he fell among robbers, who stripped him of all that he had and beat him; and then went away, leaving

The Good Samaritan at the inn

him almost dead. It happened that a certain priest was going down that road; and when he saw the man lying there, he passed by on the other side. And a Levite, also, when he came to the place, and saw the man, he too went by on the other side. But a certain Samaritan, as he was going down, came where this man was; and

Bible Stories

as soon as he saw him, he felt a pity for him. He came to the man, and dressed his wounds, pouring oil and wine into them. Then he lifted him up, set him on his own beast of burden, and walked beside him to an inn. There he took care of him all night; and the next morning he took out from his purse two shillings, and gave them to the keeper of the inn, and said: 'Take care of him; and if you need to spend more than this, do so; and when I come again I will pay it to you.'"

"Which one of these three, do you think, showed himself a neighbor to the man who fell among the robbers?"

The scribe said: "The one who showed mercy on him."

Then Jesus said to him: "Go and do thou likewise."

By this parable, Jesus showed that "our neighbor" is the one who needs the help that we can give him, whoever he may be.

The Story of the Palm Branches

From Jericho, Jesus and his disciples went up the mountains, and came to Bethany, where his friends Martha and Mary lived, and where he had raised Lazarus to life. Many people in Jerusalem heard that Jesus was there, and they went out of the city to see him, for Bethany was only two miles from Jerusalem. Some came also to see Lazarus, whom Jesus had raised from the dead; but the rulers of the Jews said to each other:

"We must not only kill Jesus, but Lazarus, also; because on his account so many of the people are going after Jesus and believe on him."

The friends of Jesus in Bethany made a supper for Jesus, at the house of a man named Simon. He was called "Simon the leper"; and perhaps he was one whom Jesus had cured of leprosy. Jesus and his disciples, with Lazarus, leaned upon the couches around the table, as the guests; and Martha was one of those who waited upon them. While they were at the supper, Mary, the sister of Lazarus, came into the room, carrying a sealed jar of very precious perfume. She opened the jar, and poured some of the perfume upon the head of Jesus, and some upon his feet; and she wiped his feet with her long hair. And the whole house was filled with the fragrance of the perfume.

But one of the disciples of Jesus, Judas Iscariot, was not pleased at this. He said: "Why was such a waste of the perfume made? This might have been sold for more than forty-five dollars, and the money given to the poor!"

This he said, but not because he cared for the poor. Judas was the one who kept the bag of money for Jesus and the twelve; and he was a thief, and took away for his own use all the money that he could steal. But Jesus said:

"Let her alone; why do you find fault with the woman? She has done a good work upon me. You have the poor always with you, and whenever you wish, you can give to them. But you will have me with you only a little while. She has done what she could; for she has come to perfume my body for its burial. And truly I say to you, that wherever the gospel shall be preached throughout all the world, what this woman has done shall be told in memory of her."

Jesus riding into Jerusalem

Perhaps Mary knew what others did not believe, that Jesus was soon to die; and she showed her love for him, and her sorrow for his coming death, by this rich gift. But Judas, the disciple who carried the bag, was very angry with Jesus; and from that time, he was looking for a chance to betray Jesus, or to give him up to his enemies. He went to the chief priests, and said: "What will you give me, if I will put Jesus in your hands?"

They said, "We will give you thirty pieces of silver."

And for thirty pieces of silver Judas promised to help them take Jesus, and make him their prisoner.

On the morning after the supper at Bethany, Jesus called two of his disciples, and said to them:

"Go into the next village, and at a place where two roads cross; and there you will find an ass tied, and a colt with it. Loose them, and bring them to me. And if any one says to you, 'Why do you do this?' say, 'The Lord has need of them,' and they will let them go."

They went to the place and found the ass and the colt, and were loosing them, when the owner said:

"What are you doing, untying the ass?"

And they said, as Jesus had told them to say:

"The Lord has need of it."

Then the owner gave them the ass and the colt for the use of Jesus. They brought them to Jesus on the Mount of Olives; and they laid some of their own clothes on the colt for a cushion, and set Jesus upon it. Then all the disciples and a very great multitude threw their garments upon the ground for Jesus to ride upon. Others cut down branches from the trees and laid them on the ground. And as Jesus rode over the mountain toward Jerusalem, many walked before him waving branches of palm trees. And they all cried together:

"Hosanna to the son of David! Blessed is he that cometh in the name of the Lord! Blessed be the kingdom of our father David, that cometh in the name of the Lord! Hosanna in the highest!"

These things they said, because they believed that Jesus was the Christ, the Anointed King; and they hoped that he would now set up his throne in Jerusalem. Some of the Pharisees in the crowd, who did not believe in Jesus, said to him:

"Master, stop your disciples!"

But Jesus said:

"I tell you, that if these should be still, the very stones would cry out!"

And when he came into Jerusalem with all this multitude, all the city was filled with wonder. They said: "Who is this?"

And the multitude answered:

"This is Jesus, the prophet of Nazareth in Galilee!"

And Jesus went into the Temple, and looked around it; but he did not stay, because the hour was late. He went again to Bethany, and there stayed at night with his friends.

These things took place on Sunday, the first day of the week; and that Sunday in the year is called Palm Sunday, because of the palm branches that the people carried before Jesus.

Many people heard him gladly, but the great city was deaf to his pleadings. "O Jerusalem, Jerusalem," he cried, "thou that kills the prophets, how often would I have gathered thy children together, even as a hen gathers her chickens under her wings, and ye would not!"

The Story of the Betrayal

At the foot of the Mount of Olives, near the path

Jesus in the garden

over the hill toward Bethany, there was an orchard of olive trees, called "The Garden of Gethsemane." The word "Gethsemane" means "oil press." Jesus often went to this place with his disciples, because of its quiet shade. At this garden, he stopped, and outside he left eight of his disciples, saying to them, "Sit here while I go inside and pray."

The flesh is weak

He took with him the three chosen ones, Peter, James, and John, and went within the orchard. Jesus knew that in a little while Judas would be there with a band of men to seize him; that in a few hours he would be beaten, and stripped, and led out to die. The thought of what he was to suffer came upon him and filled his soul with grief. He said to Peter, James, and John:

"My soul is filled with sorrow, a sorrow that almost kills me. Stay here and watch while I am praying."

He went a little further among the trees, flung himself down upon the ground, and cried out:

"O my Father, if it be possible, let this cup pass away from me; nevertheless, not as I will, but as thou will!"

So earnest was his feeling and so great his suffering that there came out upon his face great drops of sweat like blood, falling upon the ground. After praying for a time, he rose up from the earth and went to his three disciples, and found them all asleep. He awaked them, and said to Peter: "What, could you not watch with me one hour? Watch and pray that you may not go into temptation. The spirit indeed is willing, but the flesh is weak."

He left them, went a second time into the woods, fell on his face, and prayed again, saying:

"O my Father, if this cup cannot pass away, and I must drink it, then thy will be done."

He came again to the three disciples, and found them sleeping; but this time he did not awake them. He went once more into the woods, and prayed, using the same words. And an angel from heaven came to him and gave him strength. He was now ready for the fate that was soon to come, and his heart was strong. Once more he went to the three disciples, and said to them: "You may as well sleep on now, and take your rest, for the hour is at hand; and already the Son of man is given by the traitor into the hands of sinners. But rise up and let us be going. See, the traitor is here!"

The betrayal

The disciples awoke; they heard the noise of a crowd, and saw the flashing of torches and the gleaming of swords and spears. In the throng they saw Judas standing, and they knew now that he was the traitor of whom Jesus had spoken the night before. Judas came rushing forward, and kissed Jesus, as though he were glad to see him. This was a signal that he had given beforehand to the band; for the men of the guard did not know Jesus, and Judas had said to them:

"The one that I shall kiss is the man that you are to take; seize him and hold him fast."\

Jesus said to Judas, "Judas, do you betray the Son of man with a kiss?"

Then he turned to the crowd, and said, "Whom do you seek?"

They answered, "Jesus of Nazareth."

Jesus said, "I am he."

When Jesus said this, a sudden fear came upon his enemies; they drew back and fell upon the ground.

They answered, "Jesus of Nazareth."

Jesus said, "I am he."

When Jesus said this, a sudden fear came upon his enemies; they drew back and fell upon the ground.

After a moment, Jesus said again, "Whom do you seek?"

And again they answered, "Jesus of Nazareth."

And Jesus said, pointing to his disciples, "I told you that I am he. If you are seeking me, let these disciples go their own way."

The Story of the Empty Tomb

After Jesus was taken before the high-priest where he was ridiculed and the people spat upon him, he was taken before the Roman Governor, Pontius Pilate, who ruled over Judea. He heard their complaints, but did not find any cause for putting him to death. But at last he yielded to their demands, although he declared Jesus was innocent of all wrong.

Jesus was beaten

And so Pontius Pilate, the Roman governor, gave command that Jesus should die by the cross. The Roman soldiers then took Jesus and beat him most cruelly; and then led him out of the city to the place of death. This was a place called "Golgotha" in the Jewish language, "Calvary" in that of the Romans; both words meaning "The Skull Place."

Jesus with the cross

With the soldiers, went out of the city a great crowd of people; some of them enemies of Jesus, glad to see him suffer; others of them friends of Jesus, and the women who had helped him, now weeping as they saw him, all covered with his blood and going out to die. But Jesus turned to them and said:

Jesus crucified

"Daughters of Jerusalem, do not weep for me, but weep for yourselves and for your children. For the days are coming when they shall count those happy who have no little ones to be slain; when they shall wish that the mountain might fall on them, and the hills might cover them, and hide them from their enemies!"

They had tried to make Jesus bear his own cross, but soon found that he was too weak from his sufferings, and could not carry it.

They seized on a man who was coming out of the country into the city, a man named Simon, and they made him carry the cross to its place at Calvary.

It was the custom among the Jews to give to men about to die by the cross some medicine to deaden their feelings, so that they would not suffer so greatly. They offered this to Jesus, but when he had tasted it and found what it was, he would not take it. He knew that he would die, but he wished to have his mind clear, and to understand what was done and what was said, even though his sufferings might be greater.

At the place Calvary, they laid the cross down, stretched Jesus upon it, and drove nails through his hands and feet to fasten him to the cross; and then they stood it upright with Jesus upon it. While the soldiers were doing this dreadful work, Jesus prayed for them to God, saying: "Father, forgive them; for they know not what they are doing."

The soldiers also took the clothes that Jesus had worn, giving to each one a garment. But when they came to his undergarment, they found that it was woven and had no seams; so they said, "Let us not tear it, but cast lots for it, to see who shall have it." So at the foot of the cross the soldiers threw lots for the garment of Christ.

Two men who had been robbers and had been sentenced to die by the cross, were led out to die at the same time with Jesus. One was placed on a cross at his right side, and the other at his left; and to make Jesus appear as the worst, his cross stood in the middle. Over the head of Jesus on his cross, they placed, by Pilate's order, a sign, on which was written:

"This is Jesus of Nazareth,
The King of the Jews."

This was written in three languages; in Hebrew, which was the language of the Jews; in Latin, the language of the Romans, and in Greek. Many of the people read this writing; but the chief priests were not pleased with it. They urged Pilate to have it changed from "The King of the Jews" to "He said, I am King of the Jews." But Pilate would not change it. He said:

"What I have written, I have written."

And the people who passed by on the road, as they looked at Jesus on the cross, mocked at him. Some called out to him:

"You that would destroy the Temple and build it in three days, save yourself. If you are the Son of God, come down from the cross!"

And the priests and scribes said:

"He saved others, but he cannot save himself. Come down from the cross, and we will believe in you!"

And one of the robbers, who was on his own cross beside that of Jesus, joined in the cry, and said: "If you are the Christ, save yourself and save us!"

Today you shall be with me in heaven

But the other robber said to him: "Have you no fear of God, to speak thus, while you are suffering the same fate with this man? And we deserve to die, but this man has done nothing wrong."

Then this man said to Jesus: "Lord, remember me when you come into your kingdom!"

And Jesus answered him, as they were both hanging on their crosses: "To-day you shall be with me in heaven."

Before the cross of Jesus his mother was standing, filled with sorrow for her son, and beside her was one of his disciples, John, the disciple whom he loved best. Other women besides his mother were there—his mother's sister, Mary the wife of Cleophas, and a woman named Mary Magdalene, out of whom a year before Jesus had sent an evil spirit. Jesus wished to give his mother, now that he was leaving her, into the care of John, and he said to her, as he looked from her to John: "Woman, see your son."

And then to John he said: "Son, see your mother."

And on that day John took the mother of Jesus home to his own house, and cared for her as his own mother.

At about noon, a sudden darkness came over the land, and lasted for three hours. In the middle of the afternoon, when Jesus had been on the cross six hours of terrible pain, he cried out aloud words which meant:

"My God, my God, why hast thou forsaken me!" words which are the beginning of the twenty-second psalm, a psalm which long before had spoken of many of Christ's sufferings.

After this he spoke again, saying, "I thirst!"

And some one dipped a sponge in a cup of vinegar, put it upon a reed, and gave him a drink of it. Then Jesus spoke his last words upon the cross:

"It is finished! Father, into thy hands I give my spirit!"

And then Jesus died. And at that moment, the veil in the Temple between the Holy Place and the Holy of Holies was torn apart by unseen hands from the top to the bottom. And when the Roman officer, who had charge of the soldiers around the cross, saw what had taken place, and how Jesus died, he said: "Surely this was a righteous man; he was the Son of God."

After Jesus was dead, one of the soldiers, to be sure that he was no longer living, ran his spear into the side of his dead body; and out of the wound came pouring both water and blood.

Even among the rulers of the Jews a few were friends of Jesus, though they did not dare to follow Jesus openly. One of these was Nicodemus, the ruler who came to see Jesus at night. Another was a rich man who came from the town of Arimathea, and was named Joseph. Joseph of Arimathea went boldly in to Pilate, and asked that the body of Jesus might be given to him. Pilate wondered that he had died so soon, for often men lived on the cross two or three days. But when he found that Jesus was really dead, he gave his body to Joseph.

Then Joseph and his friends took down the body of Jesus from the cross, and wrapped it in fine linen. And Nicodemus brought some precious spices, myrrh and aloes, which they wrapped up with the body. Then they placed the body in Joseph's own new tomb, which was a cave dug out of the rock, in a garden near the place of the cross. And before the opening of the cave they rolled a great stone.

And Mary Magdalene, and the other Mary, and some other women, saw the tomb, and watched while they laid the body of Jesus in it.

Bible Stories

On the next morning, some of the rulers of the Jews came to Pilate, and said:

The burial of Jesus

"Sir, we remember that that man Jesus of Nazareth, who deceived the people, said while he was yet alive, 'After three days I will rise again.'

The angel at the tomb

Give orders that the tomb shall be watched and made sure for three days, or else his disciples may steal his body, and then say, 'He is risen from the dead'; and thus even after his death he may do more harm than he did while he was alive."

Pilate said to them:

The ascension

"Set a watch, and make it as sure as you can."

Then they placed a seal upon the stone, so that no one might break it; and they set a watch of soldiers at the door.

And in the tomb, the body of Jesus lay from the evening of Friday, the day when he died on the cross, to the dawn of Sunday, the first day of the week, when he arose from the dead and appeared unto his disciples.

But the brightest day in all the world was this Sunday morning. For on that day the stone was rolled away from the tomb and Jesus came forth from the dead to gladden his disciples. This he had told them he would do. On this Sunday morning, Mary Magdalene and another Mary, called Salome, came to the tomb, found the stone rolled away and an angel standing by the open tomb. He told them that Jesus was not there, but had risen.

Afterward Jesus was with his disciples for forty days, after which he was taken up into heaven.

The Story of Stephen, the First Martyr

In the New Testament, in the book of Acts, you will learn how the members of the church in Jerusalem gave their money freely to help the poor. This free giving led to trouble, as the church grew so fast; for some of the widows who were poor were passed by, and their friends made complaints to the apostles. The twelve apostles called the whole church together, and said:

"It is not well that we should turn aside from preaching and teaching the word of God to sit at tables and give out money. But, brethren, choose from among yourselves seven good men; men who have the Spirit of God and are wise, and we will give this work to them; so that we can spend our time in prayer and in preaching the gospel."

This plan was pleasing to all the church and they chose seven men to take charge of the gifts of the people, and to see that they were sent to those who were in need. The first man chosen was Stephen, a man full of faith and of the Spirit of God; and with him were Philip and five other good men. These seven men they brought before the apostles; and the apostles laid their hands on their heads, setting them apart for their work of caring for the poor.

But Stephen did more than to look after the needy ones. He began to preach the gospel of Christ, and to preach with such power as made every one who heard him feel the truth. Stephen saw before any other man in the church saw, that the gospel of Christ was not for Jews only, but was for all men; that all men might be saved if they would believe in Jesus; and this great truth Stephen began to preach with all his power. Such preaching as this, that men who were not Jews might be saved by believing in Christ, made many of the Jews very angry. They called all the people who were not Jews "Gentiles," and they looked upon them with hate and scorn; but they could not answer the words that Stephen spoke. They roused up the people and the rulers, and set them against Stephen, and at last, they seized Stephen, and brought him before the great council of the rulers. They said to the rulers:

"This man is always speaking evil words against the Temple and against the law of Moses. We have heard him say that Jesus of Nazareth shall destroy this place, and shall change the laws that Moses gave to us!"

This was partly true and partly false; but no lie is as harmful as that which has a little truth with it. Then the high-priest said to Stephen:

The martyrdom of Stephen

"Are these things so?"

And as Stephen stood up to answer the high-priest, all fixed their eyes upon him; and they saw that his face was shining, as though it was the face of an angel. Then Stephen began to speak of the great things that God had done for his people Israel in the past; how he had called Abraham, their father, to go forth into a new land; how he had given them great men, as Joseph, and Moses, and the prophets. He showed them how the Israelites had not been faithful to God, who had given them such wonderful blessings.

Then Stephen said:

"You are a people with hard hearts and stiff necks, who will not obey the words of God and his Spirit. As your fathers did, so you do, also. Your fathers killed the prophets whom God sent to them; and you have slain Jesus, the Righteous One!"

As they heard these things, they became so angry against Stephen, that they gnashed on him with their teeth, like wild beasts. But Stephen, full of the Holy Spirit, looked up toward heaven with his shining face; and he saw the glory of God, and Jesus standing on God's right hand, and he said:

"I see the heavens opened, and the Son of man standing on the right hand of God!"

But they cried out with angry voices, rushed upon him, and dragged him out of the council-room, and outside the wall of the city. And there they threw stones upon him to kill him, while Stephen was kneeling down among the falling stones, and praying:

"Lord Jesus, receive my spirit! Lord, lay not this sin up against them!"

And when he had said this, he fell asleep in death, the first to be slain for the gospel of Christ.

The Apostle Paul

Before his conversion to the faith of Christ, Paul was called Saul, and he persecuted the Christians, believing that they were doing wickedly and that he ought to punish them for it.

The conversion of Saul

The persecution of Paul

But while he was in the midst of these persecutions, and as he was journeying toward Damascus one day, he saw suddenly at noontime, a light shining in the heavens which was greater than the light of the sun, and he and all that were with him fell to the earth in wonder and awe. Then Saul heard a voice speaking to him and saying, "Saul, Saul, why do you persecute Me?" And Saul said, "Who art Thou, Lord?"

And the voice answered, "I am Jesus, whom you persecute."

Then Saul was instructed as to what he was to do, and was told that he would become a minister of Christ. From that time, Paul preached and taught the Christian religion, and converted many people to it.

But he was persecuted in his new work as he had persecuted others, being finally taken prisoner and threatened with scourging; he declared himself a Roman citizen, however, and therefore safe from such treatment, and went on openly confessing his faith and telling of his conversion, and he appealed for protection to the Roman emperor.

He was then put on board a ship as a prisoner to be taken to Rome. While they were at sea a violent storm came up, and Paul warned the sailors that they were in great danger; but they would not listen to him. At last the ship was wrecked, all on board being cast ashore upon an island, whither they had been carried, clinging to boards and broken pieces of the ship.

The barbarous people of the island treated them kindly, building a fire that they might dry their clothing and get warm; for it was cold and they were, of course, drenched.

The men were very glad to be safe once more; but a strange thing happened after a little: Paul gathered up an armful of sticks to put upon the fire, and as he placed them upon the flames, a viper, which is a kind of poisonous snake, came out of the bundle and clung to his hand; he shook it off into the fire, however, without the slightest sign of fear.

The shipwreck of Paul

Those who were about him thought that the hand would swell and that Paul would die from the effects of the bite, and they watched him closely, believing that this trouble was sent to him as a punishment for his sins. But no evil results came from the wound, and then the barbarians thought he was a god and looked upon him with great respect.

Paul and the men who were with him remained upon the island for three months. At the end of that time they went away in a ship, finally reaching Rome, where the prisoners were given up to the authorities; but Paul was allowed to live by himself, with only a soldier to guard him, and after a while he called the chief men of the Jews together and told them why he was there and preached to them the Word of God. His preaching was received by some with faith, but others did not believe.